Praise for C. Hope Clark

For Palmetto Poison

"Carolina Slade is the real deal - Southern charm, a steely determination, and a vulnerability she'll never admit to. Slade is at her absolute best in C. Hope Clark's PALMETTO POISON so hold on for the ride!"
—*Lynn Chandler-Willis, bestselling author and winner of the 2013 Minotaur Books/PWA Best First Private Eye Novel Competition*

For C. Hope Clark's other Books

"With a story that moves so fast you are sure to get a case of literary whiplash, LOWCOUNTRY BRIBE is almost impossible to put down. Southernisms dot the landscape of the page like so much Spanish moss, as Carolina Slade carries us along for the ride through rough and righteous terrain. Written with grace and ferocity, Clark promises us more installments of the Carolina Slade Mystery series and I for one can hardly wait for a second helping of this unpredictably un-pretentious and hard-scrabble down-home gal."
—*Rachel Gladstone,* Dish Magazine

"Terrific. Smart, knowing, clever . . . and completely original. A taut, high-tension page-turner—in a unique and fascinating setting. An absolute winner!"
—*Hank Phillippi Ryan, Agatha, Anthony and Macavity winning author*

"In C. Hope Clark's novel, TIDEWATER MURDER, Carolina Slade establishes herself as a new genre superstar, taking her place beside Dave Robicheux and Harry Bosch. Well-written and informative about a little-known arm of law enforcement, Clark has written a story that carries the reader along as surely as the tides of the lowcountry. Don't miss this one!"
—*Carl T. Smith, Author of* A Season For Killing *and* Lowcountry Boil

"Riveting. A first-rate mystery and a real education. C. Hope Clark continues her series following Carolina Slade, an agriculture investigator, in Tidewater Murder. All I can say is if all government employees had Slade's get-the-job- done tenacity, I wouldn't mind paying taxes."
—*Donnell Ann Bell, Author of* The Past Came Hunting *and* Deadly Recall.

"High tension in the Lowcountry. Feds, farmers and foreigners collide in this coastal crime novel with as many twists and turns as a tidal estuary."
—*Janna McMahan, national bestselling author of* Anonymity *and* Calling Home

"I want Carolina Slade to be my new best friend. Smart, loyal, tough but compassionate, she's the kind of person I want on my side if I'm in trouble. In her second outing, a missing tomato crop, dead bodies, and Gullah voodoo lead Slade into the dark heart of the new south, where the 21st century collides with the past and the outcome can be deadly. As a native South Carolinian, I thoroughly enjoyed revisiting my home state in this engrossing and unusual mystery, and I look forward to seeing more of Hope Clark's refreshing heroine."
—*Sandra Parshall, award-winning author of the* Rachel Goddard mysteries
sandraparshall.com

"This story sweeps you up in an instant and carries you far, far away. Clark's intensely lush and conversational writing will keep you wanting more, turning the pages almost faster than you can read them."
—Rachel Gladstone, *Dish Magazine*

"Clark lives in South Carolina, has a degree in agriculture, has worked with the USDA for 25 years, and is married to a former federal agent. This information appears on the novel's back cover. By the time readers finish the novel and find out the worst that can possibly happen, they will have discovered that Clark also knows the territory of deftly plotted fiction, realistic dialogue and place settings, and how to tell a story that burns like a stiff drink with a touch of sugar."
—*Malcolm Campbell, Amazon, Amazon UK, Goodreads, Malcolm's Roundtable Blog*

C. Hope Clark's other titles from Bell Bridge Books

Tidewater Murder (Book Two: A Carolina Slade Mystery)

Lowcountry Bribe (Book One: A Carolina Slade Mystery)

Palmetto Poison

A Carolina Slade Mystery: Book 3

by

C. Hope Clark

Bell Bridge Books

This is a work of fiction. Names, characters, places and incidents are either the products of the author's imagination or are used fictitiously. Any resemblance to actual persons (living or dead), events or locations is entirely coincidental.

Bell Bridge Books
PO BOX 300921
Memphis, TN 38130
Print ISBN: 978-1-61194-405-1

Bell Bridge Books is an Imprint of BelleBooks, Inc.

We at BelleBooks enjoy hearing from readers.
Visit our websites – www.BelleBooks.com and www.BellBridgeBooks.com.

10 9 8 7 6 5 4 3 2 1

Cover design: Debra Dixon
Interior design: Hank Smith
Photo/Art credits:
Landscape (manipulated) © Charles Mccarthy | Dreamstime.com

:Lppl:01:

Dedication

To Kathy Spiliotopoulos for her friendship, her international broadcasts to three continents about the wonders of Carolina Slade, and her eagerness to throw yet another damn fine book release party.

Chapter 1

I THREW MYSELF in front of the speaker behind the microphone.

Margaret Dubose stumbled and fell across the stage, a plastic cup barely missing her head. The missile exploded against the fire station's back wall, its contents of yellow liquid spraying across my feet and legs.

A male voice shouted from the spectators, "You don't give a damn about us, and you know it."

The crowd hushed. Scowls formed on a hundred faces I didn't know and couldn't predict. Mumbling grew and traveled in a wave until it filled the room.

The mayor who'd introduced us helped Dubose to her feet, then stood impotent. As the guest, Dubose waited for someone else to settle down the room. This event would unravel quickly if someone didn't take charge. The microphone stood five feet away.

My J.C. Penney loafers squished as I took a step. Grumbling ripened into loud chatter as the audience grew emboldened. I gripped the mic. "If you've got a grievance with Agriculture, now is not the time nor place to air it."

Liquid, lemonade from the smell of it, puddled under my toes as I stood on the temporary plywood stage decorated with potted petunias. The packed double-bay of the firehouse stood with doors open to accommodate the overflow of bodies. Summer heat in all its ninety percent humidity smothered us, even with the air-conditioning running full blast.

A dark-headed teenager in a sun-bleached Atlanta Braves hat pumped his fist in the air. "You're Carolina Slade, the skunk-striped bitch who arrests farmers."

The audience exchanged looks and gasps. I may have gasped, too.

The white streak through my dark auburn hair defined me clearly as the bitch. "As I said, Ms. Dubose and I are here to represent the Department of Agriculture to celebrate this new facility after the horrible fire last year," I said. "Let's not ruin that."

"Do you know who my uncle is?" The young man pushed his way toward the front of the crowd and pointed at Dubose. "She sure as hell does."

"Shut up, boy," said a gray-haired man. He grasped the teen's elbow and escorted him outside, the kid snatching his arm loose as they reached the door.

I never expected to play bodyguard to my boss, especially not in this tiny crossroad town. Director Margaret Dubose and I were visiting the rural community of Pelion, South Carolina on a United States Department of Agriculture goodwill mission to inaugurate the town's new firehouse. Our agency financed or granted funds for a myriad of projects in rural areas, not just farming. The annual Pelion Peanut Fair seemed the optimum setting for this dedication.

Decked out in designer jeans, white blouse, and a diamond on each hand, Dubose stood to the side of the podium, arms crossed. Her attention flitted from the kid to me. She raised a brow in silent communication, a language I knew well. She returned to the mic as I lifted the camera from around my neck and handed it to Monroe Prevatte, the third member of our USDA entourage. Dubose needed to finish her business without distraction, to assuage the situation with her well-honed manner, which I'd pretty much proven I lacked.

Instead, I would analyze the threat factor. What idiotic thought processes drove a kid to such a demonstration at a simple ceremony? I would spill more than lemonade on him if his lame brained stunt also ruined my Nikon. People stared as I repeated *excuse me* through the crowd and made my way toward the door that the teen had just exited. As I left, I heard Dubose's charm redirect their attention in her suave political manner.

Outside, three men in their late fifties physically held the young man against the brick wall, giving him the devil. The six-foot teen stood two inches above his tallest interrogator, but grudgingly acquiesced to the joint scolding with a scowl on his flushed, pock-marked face.

One of the men turned toward me. "My apologies, ma'am."

I laid a hand on his suntanned arm in acknowledgment and then faced the kid. My daughter would turn thirteen this month. Time to test myself on how to deal with a feisty teenager. "What's your name?"

"CJ Wheeler," he said through clenched teeth. The men freed him, and he jerked his shirt back into place.

The only Wheeler I knew of was the governor, but the name was common. "Okay, CJ. My name's Carolina Slade. But you already know that." I pinched the legs of my khakis. "Seems you ruined my pants and a pair of shoes. Do you think you're calm enough to explain what has you so upset?"

He leaned forward, the muscles in his forearms bulging as his fists tightened again. "The feds almost locked up my daddy yesterday, and I hear they still intend to send him to jail. He's done a million things for Lexington County. Farming's his life." Tears welled. "He don't deserve this." He jabbed at finger at me. "I know what you're up to. It's the government trying to make us dependent." He wiped his face. "It's bullshit, that's what it is."

Whoa, Nellie. This child carried a load on his shoulders. My agitation drained away at the sight of tears. I held up my hands. "CJ, I honestly know nothing about your daddy. What's his name, and what is he accused of?"

The stoutest man spoke up. His belly bulged underneath a festival T-shirt sporting a gold peanut character wearing a straw hat. "Two federal agents arrested Lamar on Thursday for dealing in illegal prescriptions from the VA. He was released on bail late that evening, Ms. Slade. Scared this boy to death."

I thrust out my hand for a proper introduction.

He gripped it like a vise. "Name's Tucker Shealy. I own a few hundred acres near here."

I nodded, seeking an ally. "You affiliated with that marvelous barbecue place in Batesburg-Leesville?" The two small towns had grown together over time and become one municipality. Everyone within a fifty-mile radius knew of Shealy's Thursday specials, vinegar or mustard based barbecue worth skipping out on your grandmother's cooking.

"A second cousin," he replied fast as a bullet, as if he'd answered the question a dozen times too many. He hitched up his jeans, though I didn't see how he'd get the belt up any higher without herniating something. "You ain't heard about Lamar's arrest?"

"Unless the crime's agriculture-related, we wouldn't be involved," I said, accustomed to giving explanations about all feds not knowing each other's business. "The government's made up of many different departments."

CJ gave me a skeptical look. "Don't you read the papers?"

If only he knew how many unread newspapers sat on my kitchen bar, still in their plastic wrap. "Not lately," I said, tired of everyone thinking we knew the plight of every farmer in the state.

The older man waved toward the crowd milling around rides and exhibits on the other side of the street. "Hell, we almost didn't have the peanuts for this festival because they hauled him off. He donates 'em each year." Shealy tilted his head toward the fire station. "He also donated to the rebuilding of this place. Lock him up, and you handicap this town. Hell, you'll upset the entire state, if you get what I mean."

No, I didn't *get* what he meant, but I feigned an understanding nod, as if he spoke the gospel.

The edge returned to CJ's voice. "They imported you from the Lowcountry to arrest farmers. I heard about you."

Great. So I was the Elliot Ness of Agriculture now after only eight months as the special projects representative. "CJ," I said, "I'm sorry, but I don't know your dad."

"Hmmph," he grumbled.

Barely thirty days ago, I'd solved a crime in Beaufort involving tomato farmers. The case left a knife scar along my rib cage, a bullet graze across my neck, and nightmares of floating in a dark ocean. I didn't intend to make such extreme cases a habit. I also saw no need to make this current dilemma mine.

Dubose informed me more than a few times that I needed focus and less mayhem, a clearer understanding of the limits of my responsibility. I'd strayed a little far outside my purview in Beaufort, and my boss possessed a long memory with keen clarity. Now I behaved like a trooper, in lock step with Dubose's needs and orders.

Time to bid these folks good day and return to my responsibilities.

As I thanked CJ's keepers, applause erupted inside, and someone released a few *whoop-whoops* from the fire engine horn. I stepped back to the doorway to see Dubose nodding, having completed her speech. Dang, I missed how well she did.

Dubose accepted handshakes from grateful residents. She glided through the crowd, leaving smiles and a trace of her charisma on each person like a true politician. She could equally slice through an adversary. I maintained a healthy, arm's-length respect for the lady.

Unbeknownst to the average taxpayer, the federal head of Agriculture in each state was a political appointee, serving at the leisure of the president, just like the United States attorney in each judicial district. The job dated back to an era when agrarian economies meant clout. These days, most of Washington was so screwed up with healthcare, economic wildfires, and partisan backbiting, it usually forgot we existed.

Monroe touched my elbow. In his mid-forties, my co-worker stood tall enough for me to look up to from my five foot seven height. Lanky, with a runner's body, he wore a yellow polo shirt that accented his tan and thick, wavy white hair. He was practically married to the job with no amorous thoughts—except for me. A few weeks ago he'd pledged that interest. I told him to get over himself since I already dated Senior Special Agent Wayne Largo. Monroe said he'd wait. We hadn't spoken about it since.

Monroe nodded toward Dubose. "Let's retrieve her and go." He leaned toward me and sniffed, then busted out in a laugh. "Dang if you don't smell sweet."

"Yeah, I'm into eau-de-lemon and sugar these days." Dubose remained knee-deep in hospitality, laughing softly as she buttered the rural gentlemen. "She's still fraternizing, but I'm definitely with you on the idea. Give her a minute."

"That young guy still riled?"

Off from the crowd, Shealy continued to console a pouting CJ. My heart ached for the boy. He itched to place blame on somebody for his father's issue, and I happened to be his best target at the moment. Pants could be washed. A child embarrassed about his father wasn't as easy to clean up. I wondered if my daughter would ever go to bat for me that hard.

Dubose strolled over in Prada sunglasses. Her floppy straw hat flaunted a thin, pastel scarf that trailed a foot down her back, covering short-cropped salt and pepper hair. She stood out like a new Cadillac at a tractor pull. I repressed a grin, enjoying the fact she didn't care.

"Anything I need to worry about, Slade?" she asked, listing her chin toward CJ. "What did that distraught young man say?"

"Kid was mad about his daddy, something unrelated to us," I said. "He sure seems to know you, though, ma'am."

"Yes, he does," she said.

I waited for follow up.

She didn't give it. "Let's go see the fair," she said. "I haven't been to one in ages."

Cavorting around a summer fair in this heat, avoiding disgruntled kids or others like CJ, was not my favorite Saturday pastime.

Children's squeals crescendoed, fell, then swelled again. The noises on top of the aroma of diesel exhaust told me carnival rides slung, spun, and flipped youngsters nearby. Dubose shifted her woven cotton purse on her shoulder and headed toward the commotion with Monroe and me in tow.

"I didn't hear. What was with that kid?" Monroe asked, shoving a protective arm in front of me as a truckload of teens rolled by.

"He thought we helped in his daddy's arrest. Lamar Wheeler."

Monroe bent closer. "Did you say Lamar *Wheeler?*"

"Am I supposed to shiver or something?"

"Highly regarded around here," he said. "Most of his acreage is in peanuts."

"I figured that."

Dubose probably knew the man. I, however, wasn't yet acclimated to the midlands and identified the movers and shakers as I went along, or as Dubose taught me.

I caught sight of CJ as he stormed between two booths selling fried candy bars and boiled peanuts, Mr. Shealy on his heels, scolding. Apparently CJ still had a full head of steam. A woman followed them. And had I spotted a badge on her belt?

"That kid can't cool off," I said to Monroe, who snapped candid pictures of Dubose for the agency's newsletter.

"That kid's daddy is chair of the Lexington County Agriculture

Committee," he said, "and takes trips to South America on bird hunts with his brother."

The temperature continued to rise with the heat index, but the Pelionites came out in droves, most of them with a sweating drink in one hand and a greasy paper plate of carnival food in the other. I watched Dubose study handmade purses at a booth ten feet away.

"Don't freak out at what I'm about to tell you," Monroe said.

"Okay," I said, scanning the crowd.

"Wheeler's brother is the governor."

"The governor?" I blurted. "Are you kidding me?"

He frowned. "You're as subtle as a drunk in church, you know it?"

Monroe bought us each a cool soft drink. I sipped as I ran Governor Wheeler's pedigree through my head, pausing to swat away a small bee attracted to my sticky clothes.

The media favored Wheeler, a homegrown-son who'd won the election based on agricultural roots. He'd earned an MBA from the University of South Carolina and success as a business broker in Atlanta. I knew only the family faces who posed with him for the news.

I turned to see Dubose chatting with an eighty-something, five-foot-nothing lady also wearing a straw hat, leaning on a matching bamboo cane. CJ ran up to them, said something, then turned on his heel, the old woman shaking her head. She said something to Dubose as both watched the kid march off.

A divine smell diverted my attention. A local civic organization had boiled a hundred bushels of nuts for the celebration. I imagined popping open a shell, sucking on the briny pods to draw out the overcooked, tender contents before dropping the sodden hulls on the ground. I could eat my weight in the state's official snack. But I had no time to snack.

We caught up to Dubose, whose temples shone with perspiration in spite of the wide-brimmed hat. To my left, someone mentioned the fire station. Two middle-aged women in a church booth wore simple cotton shifts, hair collected on top of their heads with pins like my grandmother used.

The heftier lady in blue said, "That group gave money to the building. Ain't right."

The red-headed woman shrugged, her peach floral dress falling well below her knees. "Maybe so, but we got a new firehouse. That's a blessing."

"But it's sinful money, just sinful."

"There's one of 'em now," said the redhead, nodding in our direction, but I couldn't tell which person in the crowd she meant.

"Something's brewing," I said to Dubose, tapping her shoulder. "Let's leave."

Glancing over my shoulder as we hustled to the exit, the tall church lady instead scolded a balding gentleman dressed in shorts and sandals. A prim short woman in plaid slacks joined him. At her insistence, they disappeared into the crowd.

Monroe jogged over to me. "Moods are a might testy around here. Lamar's issue might have everyone a tad grumpy."

"I've had enough Americana," I said. "Let's find the car. It's hot, and my underwear's sticking to me."

"Like a second skin," Dubose said, tugging at her cotton shell. "At least you took one for the team, Slade. Mine is pure sweat."

I chuckled, liking my boss even more.

Monroe leaned over and whispered, "You think that's funny, remind me to tell you what set off the church ladies. You'll love it."

"Tell me."

"In the car," he said. "You laugh too loud."

We wandered around the IGA parking lot searching for our government issued Explorer. Having arrived before the lot filled, the vehicle hid in a maze of cars, tractors, and super-suspension, four-wheel-drive trucks parked all which-a-ways.

"Damn fool boy," yelled a man. "Somebody call his daddy."

"Get back here, son," hollered another.

An impassioned crowd gathered at the entrance, at the edge of the parking lot.

I turned in time to glimpse CJ chewing up asphalt in his Jeep, driving way too fast for these crowded streets. He hung a hard left on Main and squealed out of town leaving a hundred miles worth of rubber on the road.

Dubose continued watching, concerned. I nudged her to keep moving.

"Peanuts for sale," shouted a man.

A peanut seller walked up, a box hung around his neck like a 1930s cinema girl. His tan slacks rode high, an inch above his Keds. He carried the awkward bearing of an adolescent, but the slight graying hair of someone in his late forties. "Roasted peanuts," he said in a husky voice contrary to his garb.

Roasted at a boiled peanut festival? Leave it to some kitchen entrepreneur to capitalize on an event.

"No thanks," Monroe said, walking on.

"The car's over there," waved Dubose.

Monroe jogged to beat her to the Explorer since he had the keys.

A petite blonde close to my age darted into me and bounced off. The muscle tone in her arms and legs showed serious time in a gym and belonged to the woman who'd been following CJ.

"Well, excuse *me*," she said, barely making eye contact. She rifled through her keys. "Damn redneck."

"Kinda the prerequisite for being out here, Daisy Mae," I said, not letting her slap a label on me and everyone else out here having a good time. Nobody rolled over me like that. Maybe a little bit of redneck did run through my veins.

She spun at my remark, and the keys flew out of her hand, landing at my feet. I scooped them up. "Lose something?"

Her hand snatched them out of mine, the key fob scratching my middle finger. I so wanted to show the cut to her in proper fashion, but Mom taught me different.

Voices sounded to my right, raised and angry. Over this woman's shoulder, I noted Mr. Shealy speaking with animation on his cell phone. The old matron with the hat stood three feet away from him, staring maliciously. A few others spoke in hushed tones.

"Leave that boy alone," shouted one of the women in our direction. "He hasn't done anything."

"Neither has his daddy!" screamed a man.

For a moment I thought they fussed at me, but I hadn't done anything to CJ. Then I realized their animosity focused on my new caustic lady friend standing nearby.

I moved to put distance between us and bumped the side of a hot car. I jumped back.

"Get off my fuckin' car," Ms. Rambo said.

"Give it a rest," I replied. "This is a small country festival, not the Bronx."

Three seconds felt like minutes as our gazes locked.

She blinked first. "I don't have time for you." She beeped open the silver Malibu and scrambled into the driver's seat. I molded against a neighboring truck to keep out of her path. She spit gravel and left in the same direction as CJ.

Her car may have had standard Georgia plates, but the woman agent's denim vest didn't hide the federal badge on her belt. She had pissed off half the Pelion population.

"Slade!" hollered Dubose.

I trotted toward the Explorer, one eye held on all those fussy people.

A federal agent at this event intrigued me. I assumed she needed to speak to CJ about his father, but who *was* she?

Whatever she wanted the kid for, my gut told me I was on his side.

Chapter 2

MONROE EASED our SUV through the meandering crowd of Pelionites to finally reach the town limits. He drove the two-lane Edmund Highway toward Interstate 26. Dubose relaxed in the front seat beside him, browsing messages on her Blackberry. We weren't breaking any speed records, but I suspected we'd be home by four.

As the tires hummed on asphalt, I sat behind Monroe and replayed the amazing assortment of people I'd run into during my Saturday workday, enough variety to fill a yearbook.

I marveled at the petulant agent who'd collided with me. Rude—a woman with issues. Why she was there, however, was more my train of thought. She definitely had her sights on the farmer's kid, CJ.

What type of agent was she? I knew feds spent more time chasing shadows and shuffling paper than drawing down on culprits, unlike their TV counterparts, but this one was in the field with mission in her eyes.

In my position, I solved administrative situations that teetered on the criminal line, but when cases turned ugly, I called in the Office of Inspector General for a real gun-totin' cop sporting a gold shield—a USDA senior special agent.

Agent Wayne Largo and I'd been an item for a number of months, short enough to still surprise each other in bed.

I'd never met his ex-wife Pamela, but knew she was a DEA agent. Toned, tanned, tiny, and tough, according to Wayne. The more I thought about it, the more the woman in the parking lot fit her description. Sort of made me like her less.

"Slade," Monroe said.

My eyelids fluttered, my deep thinking having carried me into a sneaky catnap. "Um . . . what?"

He contemplated me in the rearview mirror. "You haven't asked me what I learned at the festival."

I sat up. "So what twisted the churchwoman's panties in a wad?"

"What does Pelion make you think of?" Monroe asked.

"Peanuts maybe?"

Dubose released a dignified snicker, hinting at an obvious connection that escaped me.

Monroe's eyes twinkled in the mirror. "Pelion has a nudist place outside of town on the edge of the Clay River. Their logo was on that guy's polo shirt."

"Eww, a nudist colony," I said, as visions of the assorted sizes and girths of Pelion Peanut Party attendees flashed through my mind *sans* overalls and jeans. "The church ladies mentioned kids. Maybe they had a problem with naked little'uns buffing around with naked big'uns."

"It's a way of life for some," Dubose said. "And it's a nudist *resort*, not a colony."

I couldn't grasp the concept. Now, if I was the only female in a sea of sweaty bodybuilders with long dark hair and blue eyes . . .

As we passed rural homes, farms, rusted trailers, and a couple of Confederate flags, I pondered the type who'd enjoy a nudist facility. *Au naturel* didn't seem at all natural. The good Lord gave us fig leaves for a reason.

Monroe passed my camera over the backseat. "Scan though the pictures I took while you were outside with the boy."

I accepted the Nikon, then flipped it over, analyzing it.

"No lemonade on it," he said, easing up on the gas as a rusty, late-model Ford pickup slowed to turn. "See if there're any good pictures for this month's report to the national office."

I punched the menu button. "The straw hat looks good, ma'am," I said to Dubose. "Who was that old lady wearing one like it?"

"Mrs. Lucille Haggerty," she said. "She's been to all thirty of these festivals."

I smiled. Dubose remembered names like they were ingredients to a prizewinning recipe.

Fast forwarding through shots of rides, shows, and booths, I found a couple nice ones of the boss at the podium shaking hands in the crowd. Monroe snapped a bunch of pics and had a good eye for it. Then I found mine, more tastefully posed, of course. There was a picture of the fire station marquee, a ribbon on it for the grand opening, and one of Dubose greeting the mayor. Shame I'd missed the flying cup. That would've been one for the scrapbook. The next photo showed my teenage daughter lying topless on the neighbor's patio.

"What the hell?"

Pictures flashed across the tiny screen in my scrutinizing frenzy. One showed an innocent view of two young teen girls sunbathing on chaise lounges, at a distance, with nothing valuable showing. The next showed my neighbor's child, Starr, rubbing lotion on my daughter Ivy's back. Both of them topless. More bare shoulders and backs, just short of my daughter's teeny, thirteen-year-old breasts. Starr's, however, stood out in all their fourteen-year-old glory.

"Slade?" Dubose said, turning. "Anything I need to worry about? Delete what you need to."

My face burned in spite of the air conditioning. "No, ma'am. Appears my son took some pictures I wasn't aware of."

"He's how old now . . . eight?"

I grimaced. "Yes."

"Such a fun age," she said, pocketing her Blackberry. "Enjoy them while they're young."

I'd enjoy him intensely as soon as I got home. So intense that his chances of living to see nine were slim to none.

Dubose's hand slapped the dashboard. "Monroe, slow down."

The car dipped forward as Monroe braked. I fumbled to keep the camera in my hands. The seatbelt bit into my shoulder, knocking wind out of my lungs.

Blue lights of a highway patrol car strobed about fifty yards ahead. A Jeep had left the road. From the tracks gouged in the grassy hill, it had reached the crest and then rolled back to the road's edge, flipping over once or twice. I unlatched my seatbelt and scooted forward. The irritating agent from the parking lot was on her knees attempting to reach the driver.

"Dear Jesus," Dubose said, "it's CJ's Jeep."

"What?" My hand rose to my chest. I'd spoken with the kid only two hours ago.

Dubose's face was skewed in pain. Obviously, she was very familiar with this boy. Her gaze remained cemented to the accident then her hand snatched at the door handle.

"Hold on." Monroe ran the front window down as he eased alongside the trooper. "Can we help?"

The patrolman waved us on in a casual motion. "Poor kid's beyond help, sir. Best you drive on." Two cars stopped on the road's edge, passersby jumping out to help, or at least see what happened.

Monroe pushed the gas. Highway stretched between us and the accident. Dubose strained to watch out the back window, panic in her eyes.

"Ma'am, are you okay?" I asked.

Tears welled. She turned toward the side window. It was time to keep my mouth shut.

DUBOSE ACTED composed by the time we reached the office parking garage. Monroe dropped her off at her car, but she abruptly turned before we could drive off.

"We need to talk, Slade," she said, then tried to walk away.

I got out of the car and approached her, sensing a private matter. "Are we involved in the Lamar Wheeler matter?"

"I don't know yet." She glanced at Monroe. "Not here." I swear her eyes almost teared again. "This will be a mess now."

Then she gave me her back and got in her car.

She left, and Monroe drove me up to my new F-150. I caught myself scanning for my old car. When I moved to the country, I'd traded in my Taurus that too much resembled a federal G-car and purchased a vehicle with more size and personality.

"How well does she know these people?" Monroe asked, nodding back toward where we'd left Dubose.

I grabbed my purse and stepped out. "I believe that kid is the governor's nephew. He said Dubose knew him. You saw her reaction at the overturned Jeep." The thought gave me a shiver.

"Monday ought to be interesting," he said. "Interested in dinner?"

I heaved a sigh, showing him how much his comment bothered me. "Like I said before—"

He grinned.

I waved him away. "Get out of here, you idiot."

"Open invitation," he shouted, driving off.

His humor alleviated some of the wet-blanket feel to the day, but my smile slid off as I thought about CJ and what his death had triggered in Dubose. It would have been different if I'd heard about the accident from my recliner via the news, but I *saw* the wreck. He was high school age. *Damn.*

I drove toward Catfish Lane, depressed over the accident and disappointed and annoyed at my kids, debating which mood to employ when I reached home. At least my children lived and breathed, thank God. Their father had died last October, in a situation he'd intended to be my demise. Ivy and Zack knew only that their father died thinking of them. They'd proven quite resilient and weathered the shock amazingly well, aside from a couple of attitude issues earlier on with Zack. We relocated to Columbia from South Carolina's Lowcountry for my promotion and to start over. Our newly constructed home sat on three acres on the banks of Lake Murray—heaven on earth.

This time, however, my children had screwed up.

With my thoughts in a grumpy, jumbled mess, I dropped my purse and keys on the kitchen counter with a meaningful clunk. "Zack? Where are you?"

Ivy bebopped in, ear buds hanging around her neck, Madge the cat in her arms. "He's in the bathroom. What's he done now?"

Her sassiness, while innocent enough, rubbed at my raw emotions today. I pointed at her. "You'll do instead. Sit." I touched my ears then ran a finger like a knife across my neck. "Turn it off."

Her wary eyes followed me as I came around the end of the sofa and settled in a recliner across the coffee table from her, camera in hand. The cat took off. Ivy's tiny yellow shorts and white-eyelet cotton top accented her tan—a tan I knew came without lines.

I pulled up the most embarrassing of the six pictures and handed the Nikon to her. "Explain."

Ivy clicked through the pictures. Her head jerked up as she stared at me and then thrust out the camera. "Who took these?" She fell on the sofa, hand across her face in Scarlett O'Hara style. "This is a disaster!"

"Not quite the words I had in mind, young lady." I grabbed the Nikon and waited for her Oscar-winning performance to play out.

She sprang up. "What's Starr going to say? She'll never have me over again." After intense seconds of theatrical exclamations, she paused, her sighs escalating.

Here it comes, I thought. The grand finale. Yep. Tears slid down her face.

Emotion tugged at my maternal genes. However, common sense told me to stand fast and serve up the lesson. Another side of me wanted to lock her in her room until she was thirty.

I'd lose my mind if she wound up like CJ.

The toilet flushed. Zack walked into the den. "Hey, Momma. What's for dinner?"

"Your butt on a platter," I said. "Sit."

Wide-eyed, Zack plopped on the opposite end of the sofa from his sister. He shrugged at her. She glared back, making him scowl and stick out his tongue.

"I'm going to get you in your sleep," Ivy said between gritted teeth.

The doorbell rang.

I walked to the entryway. "Neither of you move."

"What'd I do?" Zack hollered.

"You'll find out soon enough." I opened the door.

Allegra Jo dropped a fat suitcase and held out her hands. "Hey, Big Sister. Mom said for you to put me up for a couple weeks."

I swallowed my surprise and the urge to line her up with Zack and Ivy on the couch for a tongue-lashing. "She did, huh?" I hadn't seen my only sibling in six months, and here she was as if aliens had dropped her on my doorstep. I didn't even know she knew where I lived.

"Yeah," Ally said, glancing around. "I finally filed the papers to dump Craig. Been at Mom's for the last two weeks. He wants the divorce, but he has so many questions about how to divide the stuff and calls all the time. I mean, seriously, how does one split up a bedroom group? There's a reason it's called a set." She lugged the bag inside, talking like a telegraph key. "Cool place, Sis. Can I get a tour?"

I shut the door to keep from air-conditioning the front yard and studied my sister. The neon smile, the coy tilt of one shoulder as she spoke, and the whiff of strawberry were all there. No evidence of a crisis. Of course not. She was Typhoid Mary when it came to crises. Nerves prickled under my skin as I held back criticizing her manners . . . and Mom's.

"Phones quit working in Ridgeville?" I asked.

I may have even rolled my eyes, but she kept babbling as she waved impishly at the kids, as if I hadn't said a word. "Mom said Craig's calls were driving her nuts, so I had to come here," she said, turning back to me. "You know how she likes her life neat and tidy."

I peeked outside and saw her old Honda in the driveway. Didn't she understand I liked my life neat and tidy, too? "Craig won't be calling here night and day, will he?" I asked.

She shook her head and pushed curls out of her face, natural ones I fought a curling iron to imitate. "Thank God we didn't have kids."

I loved my sister, but we lived on entirely different planets, our orbits only crossing on holidays. Heck, we didn't even share the same sun. "Ally, it would have been nice if you or Mom had called."

Angry threats and one solid, connected slap erupted from the kids in the living room followed by an "Ow!" and "Mom, he said he put my pictures on the Internet!"

Ally ignored me and rushed toward Ivy and Zack, her dark brown eyes dancing at seeing them. "Hey, kids!" She pulled back. "Whoa, what's with the tears, Ivy-belle?" She spun around. "Did I interrupt something?"

"You think?" I lugged her suitcase into the room. "You can sit down, too. I'll deal with you once I've finished with them."

Ally planted herself between the kids, a hand on Ivy's shoulder.

"It's a free country," Zack said. "I didn't do anything wrong. Who says I even took the pictures?"

I held out the camera. "So I took them?"

He frowned at the ridiculous question. "No."

"Did Ally take them?" I asked.

"How could she do that?" he said.

Raising a brow, I cocked my head. "So tell me who else took the pictures, son?"

Ivy's tears continued to pour down her face. "He's ruined my life!"

"Let's talk about you, Miss Princess," I said, shifting toward her. "Who twisted your arm to bare your teenage buds for anyone on the cove with binoculars?" I held up the camera. "Or one of these?"

At the mention of teenage buds, Ivy held hands over her chest. Zack snickered until I gave him a look that transmitted a threat he recognized without much interpretation.

"Are these pictures online, young man? I'll find them if they are."

"No, ma'am," he said, sinking into the sofa. "I just said that to make her mad."

"You wait," Ivy grumbled.

I narrowed eyes at my daughter. "He was wrong, but you set yourself up, little girl. You were just as wrong as he was."

After a bit more back and forth, with some creative scolding from me thrown in, everyone's emotional energy ebbed to where logic finally took charge.

"I'm immensely embarrassed," Ivy mumbled. "Embarrassed to death."

No, you're not anything *to death*, I thought. You're not wrapped around a steering wheel in a ditch. I held up the camera. "Deleting them is easy . . . this time." I erased each one, confirming them gone in front of my daughter so she'd sleep easier.

"There's nothing wrong with the human body," Ally said. "Some people believe—"

Seriously? "Not now, Ally," I said. "Kids, to your rooms. I'll call you when dinner's on the table."

The kids scattered, and I fixated on Ally. Memories of our childhood flooded back as she painted on her innocent look. I recalled the night she'd slid out of her second-story bedroom window and broke into the country club pool to skinny-dip with four friends. At age sixteen, she called me to pick her up from a party. My car's upholstery stank of pot for days after.

My sister rolled with any situation. She stood by me through most parental fights in our teens. Nonjudgmental by nature, however, she fell into mistakes and dragged others into her vortex. Bad came with the good. I'm sure that Mom, in her most genteel Southern manner, had expelled my sister after a bellyful of the hoopla that came with Allegra Jo Slade-Smith.

"I'm hungry," she finally said.

After snorting a chuckle, I stood and dragged her to the kitchen.

As we slapped mayo on turkey and lettuce, Ally informed me she was dropping the *Smith*, returning to her colorful maiden self, and sending Craig back to the Pee Dee swamp from where he was spawned—the home of NASCAR, cotton, and Springer Spaniel bird dogs. Poor Craig, our family's comic relief during the holidays, had been in over his head since he'd said, "I do."

After dinner, as Ally dragged her suitcase toward the guestroom, stuffed with enough clothes for a European tour, I all but lunged for my cell phone, craving a dose of Wayne. All I got was voicemail. His weekend work must suck, too.

After sandwiches on the back porch, the kids evaporated like fresh rain off a sun-baked tarmac. When I asked Ally how she was holding up with her divorce, her chatterbox throttled up and took off. As evening fell and she prattled on, I fixed us bourbon and Coke. I nodded once in a while, but worried more about what it was like at the Wheeler farm tonight, and how it would impact my Monday morning in Dubose's office. I smelled a case coming on, with politics in the middle of it.

BY EIGHT O'CLOCK Monday, I waited patiently at the conference table in Dubose's dark-paneled, deep red carpeted office while she swapped papers about on her desk. As expected, the news hounds were abuzz, and at least two national networks had referenced the Wheeler family's recent pile of misfortunes. We expected more coverage today.

But in this muffled office, removed from the hubbub of a state headquarters, we sat in silence a few moments, a faint waft of Dubose's cologne in the air.

"I knew about Wheeler's arrest," Dubose said, matter-of-factly.

I sat up straight. "I figured you did."

She leaned back, played with the links of her bracelet, and stared at the wall for a moment.

Dubose had inherited the state director's position last year. The first female to hold the post. A noble accomplishment in a state full of good old Southern boys, especially in agriculture. Not that I didn't adore Carolina males. They liked to wear the pants, and women loved being feminine. But a woman who balanced wiles, wit, and wisdom was hard as granite and seductive as hell, making her a remarkable force of nature. I placed Dubose in that category.

"Lamar Wheeler's not a man who sells or uses drugs," she said, breaking her silence. "He's devastated about CJ."

Chances were Dubose had remained silent about the Wheelers' dilemma for days, if not a week or more. Dubose and Dick Wheeler were two politicos who traveled the same circles, honoring the wishes of a common party. Governor Wheeler solicited Dubose's DC Beltway resources. When Dubose implemented some new federal program within the state, the Governor offered his arm for her to take. Standard issue politics.

But this was about Lamar Wheeler, the farmer, and the problem was drugs, not anything agricultural. We had a farmer in trouble with a law enforcement agency of the federal government, which took the situation out of everyone's grasp. Federal drug agents didn't cater to governors or agricultural directors. In my opinion, it was time to tend to other tasks, but etiquette was etiquette.

"When's the funeral?" I asked.

"Tomorrow. I'd appreciate it if you'd accompany me."

My gut sank. My last funeral had been for my best friend's ex—blown away by a drug dealer. The funeral before that was *my* ex—blown away by a farmer's shotgun. Nobody knows how to act at the damn services, and I never knew what to say.

Young people's funerals were the worst. All that energy shut down and locked in a box. Could I have said something different to CJ and altered events? "Yes, ma'am. Be happy to go with you."

From her high-backed chair, from behind immaculate tight curls that never seemed to grow out of their cut, she stared toward but not directly at me. "I owe Dick Wheeler. Lamar, too, of course."

I heard vulnerability.

"Not in this situation," I said, worried about the depth of her involvement. "It's proper to make an appearance tomorrow, but you don't want to get wrapped up in Lamar's drug charge. I understand you care because of CJ—"

She stiffened. "An appearance. Really, Slade?" Her smile stretched thin. "How's your workload?"

Uh oh. I had nothing urgent on my desk, and she knew it.

She twirled a fountain pen in manicured fingers. "I made an appointment for you."

"Guess I should meet Lamar Wheeler," I conceded and laid my own pen down in surrender. "I should ask how he intends to run the farm if he goes to prison and get a feel for its financial standing, though I imagine the Governor . . ."

The pen stopped spinning. Her eyes narrowed. "I said I don't think he did it."

I hushed. Her loyalties to this family apparently stood hard and fast. "Yes, ma'am."

The pen moved again. "At one this afternoon, Governor Dick Wheeler's taking a long lunch . . . with you."

The Governor? Hot panic ran through me. "Why?"

"Because I asked you." She scrunched her nose slightly. "You'll do fine." She rose, gestured for me to rise, and escorted me to the door. "If I don't see you this afternoon, meet me here at noon tomorrow. The service is at one."

She shut her door, and I stood in the lobby, feeling like a decoy for something I did not understand.

Chapter 3

AT HALF PAST noon, I left the Strom Thurmond Federal Building on foot, on a mission directed by my boss, completely winging it with my stomach in my shoes. Halfway down Richland Street, in spite of the broiling heat and stifling humidity, I stopped and gathered my senses.

Only one block behind my office building, the Governor's Mansion posed like a grand dame on nine acres in the heart of Columbia. The most thought I'd ever given the place was how I envied the gardener and his ability to keep the grounds blooming every month of the year.

The three-building mini-estate, overlooked by General Sherman in his destructive march during *The War*, had housed over thirty governors since 1868. I voted for the current occupant, Richard C. Wheeler, because he appeared honest, an advocate of law enforcement and education. He delivered the right words with a genteel swagger, minus the arrogance. Plus, I didn't like the other guy.

At the wrought-iron gate, I wiped sweaty palms with a tissue. Politicians asking favors eventually spelled trouble. Here was my chance to measure how forthright he was.

A local television station's camera truck parked on the curb. If a camera guy jumped out and rammed a mic under my nose, I'd sprint home to the federal building. But my federal ID badge granted entrance through the gate without fanfare, thank goodness. The young guard showed me which path to follow, which door to enter, and which receptionist to see.

I should've pressed Dubose harder about this impromptu meeting. My hands tried to press my wrinkled blouse, and I swore I'd never buy linen again. Mom would die if I told her I met the Governor wearing flats.

The size four blonde secretary in a chic gray suit with a gored skirt showed me into a study larger than my double-car garage. My heart jumped as the Governor rose from behind his desk.

He waved to a tufted leather chair. "Ms. Slade. Please, sit down."

We shook hands. I sat and crossed my legs, wincing at the scuffs on the toes of my shoes.

The Governor's long-sleeved shirt was crisp and pressed. His hand ran over an already straight tie. He smiled, showing whitened teeth. I recalled more hair. "Thanks for meeting me on such short notice," he said.

Of course. Like I'd worked *him* in. Manners with cream on top. But where was lunch?

He strode to a cherry wood credenza and poured two lead crystal glasses of ice water. I fought not to gawk like a star-struck teenager at the framed autographs, photographs, and original watercolors on the walls. A camo-dressed CJ grinned from a snapshot in a carved wooden frame, gripping a gobbler by the feet. His country-boy grin opened up a hole in my heart. I couldn't imagine what his family was going through.

I cleared my throat. "My condolences on the loss of your nephew."

"Thank you." He placed a cold glass in my hand before returning to the armchair across from me. My mouth was dry enough to spit sand.

He walked easy and appeared fitter than in his photographs. White-haired, a widower with three grown sons, he could turn heads even in bad lighting from a poor angle. Two granddaughters, about six and eight, posed in pastel smocked dresses and Shirley Temple bows, encircled by a silver frame on the wall behind his desk.

"Margaret speaks highly of you, Ms. Slade."

"That would be mutual, sir." Glass cupped in both hands, I envisioned how Mom would expect me to sit. *Ankles crossed, Carolina.*

The lighting reminded me of a manor library, absorbed by dark paneling. A vague odor of furniture polish caught my nose. Wheeler set his glass on the corner of a quaint end table that probably belonged to John C. Calhoun or some other Civil War politician. A navy coaster bore the state's crescent moon and Palmetto tree emblem. "Do you have family, Ms. Slade?"

"Yes, sir."

He steepled fingers under his chin. "I hear you're proficient at solving difficult problems."

So I'd been *discussed*. Weird how sitting here both flattered and scared me.

I wanted no part of politics. All the hinting between the lines, the unsaid innuendos everyone is supposed to understand by telepathy or body movement. I wasn't fluent in the language. I shifted, crossed the other leg, and took a stab at what to say. "Governor Wheeler, why am I here? Do you want me to visit the farm? Speak to your brother?" Stunned at how blunt I sounded, I added a delayed, "Sir."

"The farm's fine." He continued to stare at me. "I've instructed the family to cooperate with you. The Pelion community loves Lamar. Feel free to talk to them."

His tone bordered on condescension, eerie in light of the recent tragedy. I tugged my jacket across my chest. He smoothed his tie again.

"Often," he continued, "we learn more from acquaintances than from the man himself. Social and civic activities say a lot about a person."

What did that mean? "Excuse me? Sir?"

His lips tightened ever so slightly before they resumed a charismatic pose, a practiced presence. "There's history between our family and one up the road, outside Lexington." He paused. "Lamar's a fine individual, Ms. Slade. I'm not accusing anyone in particular, but I'm sure a few people are jealous of his success."

And of yours. "Sir, what exactly are you asking me to do? We seem to be dancing around. Plain talk leaves less room for misunderstanding."

He dished up a wry grin. "Lamar's not guilty of the drug charges."

"Surely you didn't bring me here to discuss your brother's innocence. I'm not even part of the investigating agency."

"That's *precisely* why I asked you here," he said.

The receptionist peeked in. Wheeler gave a double nod, and she disappeared again. He turned toward me. "Time is crucial in my job, as I'm sure it is in yours."

Wheeler stood, walked over, and shut the door. I steeled myself.

"Our State Law Enforcement Division checked the details about Lamar's arrest," he said. "DEA claims to have evidence against him. SLED Chief Stackson said the case isn't as solid as DEA would have us believe, but I have no authority to use state resources to investigate."

"You could hire someone."

His gaze fell to the carpet. "I already spoke with the attorney general. A private investigator can't penetrate a federal case." He looked up at me without raising his head, an eerie angle. "Since you examine irregularities, you might be able to ascertain details . . . maybe even flaws . . ."

I stiffened in my seat. "You want me to follow up on DEA? What kind of training do you think I have?" My breath caught. I'd sassed the Governor.

Again, only the barest tightening of his facial muscles as he leaned back. "I was led to believe that you are top notch, Ms. Slade. An investigator with a knack for finding flaws."

"I scout out stolen livestock and fraudulent paperwork, Governor, not drugs."

"Your last case involved drugs."

Geez. Just how much had Dubose told Wheeler?

His tone flattened. "Margaret assured me you were a team player."

"Yes, sir." What the hell was I missing? Dubose and I definitely needed a come-to-Jesus moment.

The Governor stood, downed the remnants of his water, and returned to his desk. "Lamar's been set up. I need to know everything DEA has on him."

Oh good Lord. "I have no access to their files. I'm not even an agent."

"Are you declining to help?"

Technically I could. But Dubose had condoned this meeting. "No, I'm willing to assist, but I feel I should run this by my boss."

"She knows."

Yeah, that's what bothered me. I slid my butt further in the chair, trying to read this situation. While I sympathized for this family, I wasn't eager to dive into this quagmire. None of this was in my job description.

Dubose, however, would quiz me about how this meeting went. If I walked out now, how much damage would befall my career? And the biggest question: what did she expect from me? And what would happen if the whole ordeal went sideways?

"What are the facts?" I asked.

He seemed to trust me, which probably had more to do with his need than my prowess. I was the designated tool, in more ways than one.

After a five-minute story of who loved and hated Lamar and the Governor, to include competitive farmers and political adversaries, I asked where to start.

"The Fants, probably. But you're the agent."

No, I wasn't an agent. Had Dubose led him to believe that, or didn't he care? Regardless, the conversation waned. He was ready to move on and leave things in my lap.

"I can't promise anything," I said, hand rubbing their moisture down my slacks as I stood, "and I won't break any rules or laws." Hopefully I sounded respectful . . . and convincing. I felt neither.

"Of course," he said. "I'd appreciate if you would drop by next week. Same time? And please remain discreet. I won't remember our meeting if anyone asks."

Sure he wouldn't. Especially if I nosed around and stirred up some crap. This assignment stank, and Dubose's reputation dropped a notch.

Damn it all to hell.

I STROLLED ALONG Richland Avenue to the office, oblivious to Joe Public passing by. Replaying the conversation with Wheeler a dozen times, I cursed him pressuring me into this case, or whatever he called it. After a stop at the federal building's canteen to substitute a candy bar for lunch, I climbed the last two flights of stairs. Wheeler hadn't offered me as much as a cracker and cheese.

Finally on the tenth floor, I marched to Dubose's office.

She was out. Of course.

Stomping to my desk, I fell into my chair. The Governor wanted a clandestine investigation, and my boss had set me up with only a ten-minute warning. I snorted a soft, snarky laugh. Intelligent woman. She could be accused of nothing.

Nothing in writing, either. If anyone caught wind of this, somebody's reputation would suffer, and somehow I didn't see the Governor or Dubose getting political mud on their hands. Paranoia in place, I exchanged my Blackberry for my personal cell phone and hit speed dial.

Senior Special Agent Wayne Largo answered. "Hey, Babe. How's it going?"

A shiver ran up my spine. His deep south Alabama drawl always did a number on me, especially after an absence. He'd been in North Carolina for a week and returned late last night from investigating crop insurance fraud within the Risk Management Agency.

"Care to play catch up?" I asked.

"Your place or mine?" he said.

"Let's make it an early dinner. I need your expert advice."

My office had a window with almost as good a view as Dubose's, only an eighth the size. I stared ten floors down at the street and watched a homeless man drag his duffle bag into a swing under the maple trees in Finley Park.

"Work related?" Wayne asked.

"Yep," I replied, then in an afterthought added, "I did miss you."

"Same here," he said. "The Blue Marlin all right?"

"Make it at four, or we'll be stuck in a noisy bar crowd. Meet you out back at a quarter 'til."

I hung up and opened my email, making a mental note to ask Ally how long she'd be in town. Ivy and Zack started school in two weeks. After a five-minute call requesting her assistance as a babysitter, she'd shrewdly negotiated pizza on my American Express—after discussing weather, a torn hem in her jeans, and how to make veggie lasagna in one breath.

I shut down the computer and scurried to the elevator. No one would question my early departure due to the nature of my work. Most didn't dare ask my destination for fear my investigations involved them or someone they knew.

All but one.

Harden Harris, balding, overweight, and red-cheeked from years of alcohol, scanned me once over as I rounded the corner. Technically one of my peers in the state office, he managed Engineering and Appraisals, but most of his work was delegated to journeymen level specialists. He spent more effort avoiding work than if he caved and did his job. And he hated considering a woman his equal, much less a boss. Plus, I'd put a friend of Harden's in jail on my virgin case in Charleston.

His beady black eyes glared as if he could laser me into oblivion. "Skipping out early?" His words dribbled sarcasm, smoky gravel in his voice from two packs a day.

I punched the down button again. Working on the tenth floor made the wait for an elevator long, but a trek down the stairs was longer.

He hitched up slacks older than my daughter, as if hiding his gut empowered him.

The door opened to an empty car. I stepped in and hit the close button.

He wedged his foot between the shutting doors and stepped on. "You in a hurry, Ms. Slade?"

"What floor?" I asked.

He waited until the door closed. "Yours, bitch."

My insides clenched into an iron knot. I punched the basement button. "Straight to hell together, then."

This man could suck the meanness right out of me and into the open, and that nagged me worse than his unseemly behavior.

The car dropped to the eighth floor, the canteen level, but nobody got on since the eatery closed at two. An extra dose of adrenaline kicked in. "They should've locked you up after Charleston."

"Your mouth is gonna get you in trouble one day," he growled.

The car stopped on three, Social Security's floor. Two elderly ladies waited to get on.

"Watch yourself. I hear a storm's brewing," he said in my face, pepperoni breath stealing mine. Then he exited.

"Oh my," said one of the senior women. "I didn't bring an umbrella."

I patted her on the shoulder. "Don't listen to him. He always thinks it's raining."

Harden stayed on my bad side, and my long absences in the field gave him ample space to attempt to sabotage my career. I intended to stick close to the Columbia vicinity for a while and cramp his style. Dubose thought him relatively harmless, but kept him at a distance most of the time, thanks to reminders from me and a couple others. I hoped she never paid a price for giving him so much rein.

Exiting the basement level, I blinked up into the sun, hand shading my eyes. Wayne leaned on the railing overlooking the exit from the street, dapper in dark slacks and a button-down shirt, sleeves rolled up three-quarter length, always with the cowboy boots. His dark hair needed a trim, but I liked it long. The beard, however, was close-cropped and handsome despite the hints of gray. Peering up at him made him appear taller than six foot. He had six years on me, and I liked that, too.

As the Columbia resident agent of Agriculture's Office of Inspector

General, he occupied an office on the third floor, with the promise of a partner downstream once he established a substantial caseload. He stayed on the road more than I liked, chasing down criminal activity. He was the department's only agent in the Carolinas. Agriculture's OIG didn't have an FBI budget.

We rarely went to work or left together. People talked. Such scrutiny almost cost us our jobs in the past, so we played it low-key. No advertising the fact we played as hard by night as we worked by day. Dubose knew, as did a handful of others. Thus far we maintained a professional face, earning respect for keeping it that way.

As soon as we were out of sight of the building, he gave me a good scrunchy hug. "How was the peanut festival?"

I related CJ's accident. "Not a day I want to relive."

"Damn," he said. "That's a shame."

Once we reached the parking garage, he draped an arm around my shoulder. I slid mine around his waist.

"That's more like it," he said.

"You'll never guess what Pelion is known for."

"Um, what's a Pelion?"

I chuckled. "A small town not far from here. But they have a nudist colony. No, wait." I cleared my throat. "A nudist *resort*. Can you believe that? Here in South Carolina."

His mouth drew up in a quizzical smirk.

I laughed. "Yeah, kinda what I thought."

"In Pelion?"

"Well, not in town, but a few miles out."

He poked me in the side. "I'll have to check that out."

"Oh, please, spare me. Think about the people in the federal building," I said. "Now imagine them all naked."

"Oh," he said.

"Yeah, not exactly the Playboy Mansion, Cowboy."

We left in my pickup. I parked only two slots from the front door of the Blue Marlin. In a frustrated mixture of desire and anxious need for professional support, I planted a kiss on Wayne deep enough to curl both our toes.

He kissed harder. I sighed, satisfied with the tension release.

He lifted his head and gave me a lopsided grin. "You won't get information out of me that easily."

I kissed him once more before grabbing my purse. "Let's eat. I missed lunch for reasons that will intrigue you."

He threw me a mock frown. "A nooner with another guy?"

I raised my eyebrows. "Actually, a one-o'clocker."

He held the door open for me as we left ninety-five degree heat for the cold air of the restaurant. A tiny, black-skirted hostess, needing a few cheeseburgers on her bones, escorted us to a secluded booth at the rear, Wayne's bootheels going mute as they hit the carpet.

"A Chablis," I said to the girl, to take her ogling off Wayne. "He'll take a Wild Turkey neat."

"So, who's the guy?" Wayne asked after she left.

I recognized nobody seated nearby. "Don't say anything to anyone, you hear?"

"Hey, I took out an Alabama lieutenant governor before, remember? Nobody knew until they handed down the indictment."

"Well, this governor's mine," I said.

"Really?" He studied me. "How are you involved with the Governor on a case before I am?"

"It's not like I asked for it," I said. "It's not even Agriculture's deal. It's DEA's, if you can believe that." I let the idea sink in. Hell, it hadn't fully sunk in for me. "One of our farmers is accused of siphoning off expired prescription drugs from the Veterans Hospital. To make the situation more interesting, he just happens to be the Governor's brother. They arrested him last week, but he's out on bail. He hasn't done wrong by us."

Wayne cocked his head. "Why is this your business?"

I crooked a finger to bring him close, but the waitress appeared with our drinks and fried green tomatoes. She hovered over Wayne. I gave her a look that could brand cows. She left, and we bent forward again.

"Dubose, for reasons unbeknownst to me, believes I should investigate," I whispered. "She set up the meeting."

He looked skeptical. "What the hell for?"

"I don't know. She didn't tell me."

"And you didn't think to ask?"

Did he have to rub it in? "Anyway, the Governor said his brother isn't guilty."

"What a novel claim." Wayne popped a tomato slice in his mouth.

"He asked me to check it out and report again in a week. Guess I'll visit the farm and ask questions." I pinched a piece off another tomato. "Where would you start?"

"What's the real motive here, Slade? Your focus?"

"Try to find evidence, maybe mistakes that'll get his brother off. I think."

Wayne grimaced through his short, dark beard. "That's totally out of your realm. It's criminally related. I don't like it. Can you get Dubose to put something specific in writing?"

"Dubose doesn't give me written orders."

He sipped his whiskey. "*I* get authorization letters."

His agent's badge came complete with arrest and shoot-em-up authority. Mine allowed me to investigate but take no action. I called him or his kind to take over what I uncovered. Robin to his Batman.

"This isn't your case, and Dubose isn't your boss," I said. "Different circumstances."

"Maybe they didn't ask for me by name, but they did the next best thing, Butterbean."

I slumped in my seat as reality set in. Son of a bitch. "They figured I'd use you." Molars clenched, I threw my napkin on the table. "Damn. They can't ask you without issuing formal instructions through your Atlanta headquarters. You can tread where I can't. My investigation isn't official, so I don't have to prove where I acquired my information."

He tossed back the rest of his drink and flashed a slick smile. "And you fell for it. Imagine that."

Chapter 4

ONCE FIVE O'CLOCK hit, people began pouring into the Blue Marlin restaurant. Wayne finished the last of our appetizer as I only watched. My insides had fluttered all afternoon, sending warning signals to a brain one step behind, unable to discern the intentions of Dubose and the Governor. They'd suckered me into digging around in Lamar Wheeler's case, trying to find enough flaws to get him off, knowing I knew a real-life federal agent who could operate under the DEA radar. I'd been foolish to think for a second that they were in awe of my abilities.

I chugged the last of my wine and squeezed the glass, wanting to throw it against the wall. "Why couldn't they just ask straight out, Wayne? You're with Agriculture, too."

"Culpability," he said with a shrug that said I'd missed the obvious. "They need a scapegoat in case it backfires."

I set the glass down. "God, I hate politics."

The waitress arrived, again, smiling at Wayne as she placed his meal just so before him. Her flirtatious manner evaporated as she gave me mine. *He's twice your age, hon.*

Wayne's shrimp and grits looked appealing enough to grace the cover of *Southern Living Magazine*. My crab cakes fit my mood.

"You sure it's DEA?" he asked. "It could be the Office of Inspector General guys from the VA. They handle crimes against the Veterans Administration, like I do for Agriculture."

"I'm pretty sure, since I literally ran into a DEA agent on Saturday in Pelion. Well, she ran into me."

He lifted a forkful. "You ask her about your farmer?"

"Too busy getting out of her way before she plowed over me."

The fork hovered.

"Blonde, five-foot nothing, foul-mouthed."

He chewed slowly, thoughtfully.

"You gonna make me ask or what?" I said.

He raised his gaze to meet mine. "Ask what?"

I told myself I needed to know the identity of the DEA agent for professional reasons. But who was I fooling? Wayne dated a simple bureaucratic fed—namely me. My stubborn standoffs with Department of

Agriculture agents paled in comparison to his ex-wife's escapades with drug runners. Pamela dated pumped-up DEA guys.

"Was that your ex, or does DEA make a practice of hiring pint-sized female tornados?"

Wayne laid down his fork and held up his empty glass. The waitress spotted him over the heads of customers and nodded.

I bit a lump of crab, my blood pressure rising because I couldn't read his grey-blue eyes. "You need liquid reinforcement to answer?"

Once the waitress delivered the whiskey, I snared the drink, gulped once, and winced. It burned like wildfire going down. "Is Pamela in town?"

The biggest question in my mind was whether Wayne had known she was coming. No. The biggest question was whether she'd been in town, and he'd met up with her and not told me.

"Sounds like her," he said, meeting my stare. "She works the Southeast, Slade. She has cases, maybe including this Wheeler deal." He turned his attention back to his plate.

My eyes narrowed. "You—"

"Don't," he said, nailing me to the spot with a penetrating glare. "I divorced her. Not the other way around." He jabbed the air with his fork. "Don't pick a fight."

"I don't pick fights, Lawman. I'm asking you a question, and you sound like you're deflecting. Would you hook up with her if she was here?"

The corner of his mouth almost slid into a grin, but he caught himself. "Hook up?"

"You know what I mean. Maybe talk about old times and how they weren't so bad?"

"I'd consider speaking to her, if that's what you mean. Nothing is coincidental when it comes to Pamela. I would meet her to make sure she's only after your farmer."

"What does that mean?"

"Kay's in town," he said.

Wayne's sister had vanished in Atlanta a year ago. During my first case in Charleston, he'd struggled between finding my abducted children and hunting for his sister. She was an addict, or used to be. She was known to disappear only to reappear a few months later. Pamela had used Kay in a sting operation, lost her in the ensuing fracas, and continued to hunt her. Kay was Wayne's only family. She'd never been gone this long.

Sympathy for him clashed with my disdain for secrets. My dead ex had held secrets for years. Why hadn't Wayne told me about Kay being in Columbia?

"You're panting," he said.

"I'm pissed. Since when do you keep secrets from me?"

"I've known about Kay for a couple weeks, so don't get your dander up. We have spoken twice, and briefly at that. Pamela's called me three times." Concern etched his features. "She traced Kay here. It's delicate."

"You haven't seen your sister?"

He shook his head. "Kay won't come out in the open. I've put out feelers."

"Need my help?" I knew his sister's flighty behavior gnawed at him. My own sister wasn't exactly stable, but she was a nun compared to Kay.

"No," he said. "But I appreciate the offer."

"Does superhero Pam-e-la know about me?"

"No doubt. I'm sure she caught the rumors in Atlanta."

I waved a hand as if passing permission. "So call her since y'all are so chatty these days. Three calls from her, you said. Make it four and ask her about the Wheeler case. Hell, invite her to dinner."

He laughed. "Sure. Candlelight all right with you?"

"Suits me fine, because I'll be there. How about tomorrow night?"

"Are you serious?" he asked.

"Yep."

"My place or yours?"

"Pick a restaurant," I said. "I want to be able to get up and leave if she gets violent again."

"She gets that way on a case," he said. "A bit like someone else I know."

"Spare me the personal knowledge. I think I'm handling this well enough as it is." I flicked a crumb at him. "And I'm nothing like her."

He straightened and fished his cell phone from his pants pocket, then resettled in his seat. "Let's do it tonight. Care for dessert?" he asked, hitting one number. He placed the phone to his ear, watching for my answer.

He had the witch on speed dial?

"Sure," I said, tapping on the table. "Ally's babysitting. Wait until you hear the latest about *my* sister. She—"

He held up his palm. "Pamela? Wayne. No, I'm not checking up on you. Quit doing that a long time ago, Babe."

Babe?

"How about dinner? Yes, now. The Blue Marlin."

Shock rolled down to my toes, chilling me like an alpine avalanche. First, Dubose, and then the Governor. Now my boyfriend's ex on a second's notice. Right friggin' here and right friggin' now. A trifecta for a positively shitty day.

Warmth rose into my face. I'd already called the woman a bitch in Pelion. Or did I just think it? I know I called her a redneck. No, she called me that.

Wait a minute. This might not even be the same person.

"Good," Wayne said in the phone. "See you in twenty minutes." He slipped the phone back into his pocket. "There." He reached for his drink. "Take your best shot when she gets here."

I shut my gaping mouth and grabbed my purse to dig for my favorite lipstick. "If I had time, I'd be mad at you, Wayne. What's my strategy?" The compact mirror reflected aging lines of tension.

"Just ask the pertinent questions," he said. "Without knocking her nose out of joint."

My lipstick missed the mark in my anxiety. I snatched a napkin to wipe away the smudge and start over. "What are we asking her?" I mumbled, rolling my lips together. "Damn, I thought I'd at least have time to think. I ought to horsewhip you."

He laughed. "Your whip or mine?"

I grunted. "Be right back." I hurried to the bathroom to compose myself and rehearse a few questions in my head.

Was this a good sign that he wanted me to meet Pamela? Or did he react to the whiskey in his hand and two under his belt? Shit. Part of me had always wanted to meet her. Another part wanted her to remain past tense. I didn't want to see how sexy she smiled or sense what attracted Wayne to her in the first place . . . or what still might catch his eye. I reworked the edges of my mascara and corrected my lipstick. What if she maintained a nickname for him? Like lover? What if the small-breasted witch showed up braless in her tight-ass jeans?

My brush fell out of my hand into the sink. Damn my hair!

I returned to the table with ten minutes to spare . . . then jumped up and pushed in next to Wayne.

I spotted her first. At least five years younger than me, she wore low-riding jeans that fit like spray-on latex. The sleeveless, collared cotton top accented tanned arms and a toned physique buffed as if she learned to crawl in a gym. Hair bound tight behind her head in a long blonde ponytail, she scanned the room. I wanted to evaporate.

Once she told a waitress to order something and pointed to our table, she made her way over.

Wayne rose slightly as she reached the table. "You're looking good," he said.

"Likewise," she replied, seating herself. She held out her hand. "Pamela Largo. You must be Slade."

She had a man's grip. And she'd kept Wayne's name. For a moment I felt she owned more of him than I did. "Carolina Slade, but yes, you can call me Slade."

She squeezed; I squeezed. She studied; I maintained a stare. "Have we met?" she asked.

"Briefly," I said.

Her eyes lit up. The coin had dropped.

She ogled Wayne. "So tell me this, fella. I've been through this town three times before now and you never called, much less extended me a dinner offer. Could I be close to Kay?"

"Not why I asked you here," he said. "Are you still hunting her?"

She grinned at the obvious. "She knows facts about Barker we don't. She bolted. We need to pick her brain."

"Your people scared the crap out of her." He glanced around for listeners. "How do you know someone didn't chase her for cooperating with you? Like Barker?"

"We won't know until we talk to her, now will we?" She touched his forearm. "Tell her to come in. She'll listen to you. She always has."

Wayne withdrew his arm, his jaw tight. "Well, she's not listening to me now."

"So you *have* talked with her."

Pamela's soft pink smile graced the waitress who approached with what appeared to be a gin and tonic. Miss Muscle ordered a salad. I lacked a firm idea on how to dance this dance.

Wayne's foot nudged me under the table.

I nudged him back. "I understand you might be working the Wheeler case. As you know, I'm with USDA. He's one of our farmers. Can you give me a heads up about what's going on? He has a substantial debt with us, and we'd hate to see the place go under."

She stared at me through a mild grin. "I can't comment on an ongoing investigation."

Expected. I used the knowledge gained from the Governor. "So you can't comment that agents found empty bottles of expired prescription drugs from the VA in Lamar's apartment near the football stadium?"

She didn't blink. "Doesn't matter what you know, or think you know, I can't comment."

"Does it matter the guy's past is as clean as an operating room?"

"Same answer."

"Have you looked at anyone else?"

She brushed Wayne's arm, with sympathetic understanding on her face. "Your new lady has trouble with comprehension, doesn't she?"

I'm right here under your perky nose, bitch.

I was ready to kick Wayne, but then he rubbed my thigh and spoke up. "You guys didn't get froggy and jump too quick on this guy because he's the Governor's brother, did you?"

"Like I'm going to discuss details with her sitting here," Pamela replied. "He's good for it, Wayne. Trust me. Now, where's Kay?"

"I have no idea," he said, "and it worries me."

"Remember who you're talking to, Stud. She's not safe. Barker's a hard hitter, and she crossed him." Pamela speared lettuce then a cherry tomato on her fork. The woman even ate her salad with authority.

Wayne spoke with a hard edge. "Haven't seen her in a year. You forced her underground when you screwed up."

I might as well have been in the bathroom with her sarcasm and his contempt dominating the conversation. From my perspective, Wayne had lucked out escaping her marital clutches without serious scars.

"You here for Kay or Lamar?" I asked, squeezing back into the volley.

"Either, both," Miss Muscle said. With nary a wrinkle on that creamy complexion, she showed clear resolve, maintaining a steely-eyed connection with Wayne.

"Are they connected?" I asked.

Both of them gave me quizzical looks. Okay, so I hadn't thought through that question.

Pamela hadn't bested me yet. I'd sling questions until she got sick of them, even if it meant waiting until the doors closed and waitresses turned over chairs and vacuumed under my feet.

"Who informed on Wheeler?" I asked. "Some political malcontent?"

"Nope," she fired back.

"Somebody sucked you in because of the Governor, that's for sure," I said. "Anonymous hotline most likely."

"Nothing to do with the Governor." She grinned like a TV emcee. "Our own people found it."

I laughed. "Right. You have agents in every city, snooping through people's trash for drugs."

"Regulatory?" Wayne asked her.

"Maybe," she said.

I wasn't sure what that meant, but Wayne could enlighten me later.

As taught in my abbreviated training, I asked questions one way, then returned minutes later to ask from a different, disguised angle. She chuckled softly at my attempts.

We were the next to the last table to clear out, but before we did, I knew they'd not found the meds on Lamar, just in his place. Wayne asked if the VA's IG had been consulted and received a negative.

"It's late." Pamela slid to the end of her booth and stood. She checked her ponytail. "It's been fun, don't you think?"

"A blast," I replied. "We *must* do it again."

She leaned on the table, no longer cute. "Lady, this polite little interrogation probably told me more than it told you. The farm's your only concern. I have no time for law enforcement groupies." She touched Wayne's cheek. "Later, Stud."

She left. That's when I noticed she wore boots like he did.

"What's regulatory?" I asked him as we watched the curves of her ass sashay out the door.

"Investigators sort of like auditors. They monitor pharmaceutical outlets, anyone who has a DEA number authorized to administer controlled substances. You know . . . accountability."

I gathered my purse. Miss Pamela gave me not a lot to sink my teeth into. Nothing made me want to dig in and explore this situation more than causing a rift in her high-and-mighty, supposedly nothing-to-it case.

Wayne had asked her about jumping too quick to make an arrest. An arrest meant agents on the ground should be done with the grunt work. So why would Pamela hang tight in Columbia, unless her case wasn't so iron-clad?

Or, she hunted Kay.

My gut impression of her, however, was spot on. Ambitious witch.

Wayne and I left the restaurant at midnight. The wine long worn off, I drove. In the six short blocks back to the parking garage, Wayne remained quiet, possibly because of the late hour, probably because of Pamela.

The orange halogen lights guiding our way up Assembly Street gave the capital city a sepia, 1930s frozen-in-time flavor. We drove by a dark Oliver Gospel Mission. Even the homeless were tucked in for the night.

"What's wrong?" I asked, as I parked the car next to his.

"I can't help you with Wheeler, Slade."

"But I need to know what my next step should be. I don't know what I'm doing."

He rested his left arm across the back of my seat. "The Governor is out of line. No telling what you're getting dragged into. And you're following Dubose like a new puppy. She's using you."

The personal affront made me press my back against the door. I hoped he was wrong.

He didn't wag a finger or brag that he knew better. After a year, he'd memorized what phrases set me off.

When nothing was said for a few seconds, he kissed me on the cheek and opened his door. "Sleep on it. Then get yourself out of this before it turns messy. Nobody investigates blind."

Chapter 5

BY TWO FORTY in the morning, I'd decided to shed the Wheeler case. Pilfering through DEA's business seemed amateur and stupid in broad daylight, an untenable position professionally. I'd tactfully approach Dubose after the service. No telling how many Tums I'd chew before then, or how stiff a bourbon I'd have when I got home. I drifted back to sleep at five, once I convinced myself I could stick to my decision.

I woke cursing the alarm. Dressing in a stereotypical charcoal gray suit for a funeral further darkened my mood, especially once I opted for a white blouse instead of color. I excused myself quickly out the door when Ally danced a perky, bluebird-on-your-shoulder move around my kitchen in her cotton bathrobe, singing at the top of her lungs. I'd never understand her.

At the office, Dubose beckoned me from my duties around noon in time for CJ's service. We exchanged pleasantries on the way to the car, then fell silent, as if mentally preparing for the event.

The sun shone bright on the soft salmon-colored stucco exterior of historic Trinity Cathedral as we approached Sumter Street, a stone's throw from the capitol building. In a church mostly spared during the Civil War, a muffled organ played somber hymns as we opened the carved entry door to the mahogany pew two-thirds up the aisle and sat on red velveteen-covered cushions. Arches curved high overhead to the left and to the right, adding depth and a European flavor to the setting. Uniforms and dark-suited bodyguards with wires spiraling out of their ears manned the front and back exits.

South Carolina and federal power elite of both sexes quietly shook hands in pews behind and in front of them, uttering words like *shame, young,* and *loss.* Heads pivoted when Governor Wheeler entered. His sad eyes connected with each one, his charisma apparent even in the gloomy atmosphere. He made his way up front and sat in a pew reserved for dignitaries. A man I presumed was Lamar entered with a tiny lady in her eighties holding his arm and assumed his position next to the Governor.

"Is she the woman from the peanut fair?" I asked low to Dubose.

"Lucille Haggerty," she whispered. "The grandmother."

"What about the mother?"

"Shhh."

So Dubose knew three generations of the family.

Organ music swelled, playing Bach. Pressure rose in my chest. Losing a child had to rank among the worst tragedies in the universe. Lamar must be devastated. Dubose glanced over after my third sniffle, so I inhaled and squeezed my lids shut.

When I opened my eyes, Pamela winked at me from two rows up as she slid into a seat. Her simple black shift accented her curves, the pearl studded earrings a classy touch. Her blonde hair was down, held back from her face with a satin hairband. She resembled someone's high-class country club daughter instead of a kick-boxing federal agent.

How tacky was crashing a funeral?

The minister positioned himself behind the podium. Whispers ceased, replaced by an occasional soft sob. He introduced "O God, Our Help in Ages Past," a hymn that took me back to Vacation Bible School. As the minister read from *The Book of Common Prayer*, the Episcopal setting reminded me of when Mom made us attend like clockwork. She almost cut me from her will when I went to college, shed the Episcopalian formality, and loosely became Presbyterian. The last time I'd warmed a pew was five years ago. I almost felt God thump me on the back of my head.

The service was simple and the minister eloquent. He spoke of CJ in life, which underlined how short his was. I bowed my head at the end, while the guy in front of me spoke to his neighbor about an upcoming Senate bill.

Dubose wiped away a tear, so I allowed myself a sniffle.

Once the family exited, the congregation rose, no one in a hurry to leave except for those with bodyguards, which only made them easier to recognize. High school girls openly cried, their mothers consoling. High school boys clenched teeth, attempting to act grown. I'd have stayed seated, waiting for the congestion to thin, but Dubose waded into the horde. I followed, my nose running. Outside, she said we'd continue on, not returning to the office. Oh God, I hated this part . . . the cemetery.

The South Carolina Highway Patrol blocked roads and directed traffic for twenty miles as we meandered through Cayce, then South Congaree. The procession picked up speed beyond the airport. At the ditch where CJ had overturned his Jeep, we saw no rutted ground, severed fence posts, or mud. Flowers, balloons, and stuffed panthers, the Pelion High School mascot, smothered the hill.

We lost two-thirds of the mourners en route, but the remainder overwhelmed the area as troopers in stiff-arm semaphore directed drivers to park. This rural Pelion church and its 150-year-old cemetery weren't accustomed to so much company. Dubose and I eventually waited amongst a hundred souls around the grave site. The family awaited us under a dark blue canopy. The crowd contained fewer celebrities and more locals, to include working people from local farms. The diversified skin color said a lot for the community's respect for the Wheelers.

I'd brought an umbrella in case of rain. The weatherman, however, missed the mark. The sun shone bright and hot.

I felt twenty pounds heavier under the oppressive humidity. Dubose refused my offer of shade, having donned yet another wide-brimmed hat. I stood alone under my black fold-out travel umbrella, my only option having been an orange and white Clemson University golf monstrosity. With the Wheelers in the upper ranks of the University of South Carolina Gamecock Club, appearing with the arch rivals' colors seemed distasteful.

Unable to understand the minister, I observed people. From two thousand dollar suits and five hundred dollar handbags to work boots and jeans. Willingness to attend said more than wardrobe.

Unable to be patient, a pair of shifting sneakers caught my attention. Upon closer scrutiny, I recognized the challenged man who had tried to sell roasted peanuts at the boiled peanut celebration. A big woman in her seventies held one arm around his shoulders, more to control than to console. He behaved as a child, bored and antsy.

Once the minister ended his prayer of benediction, everyone shuffled in line to see the family, reaching to softly shake hands with a neighbor. Dubose made her way to Lamar.

"I'm so terribly sorry," she said, with a lightweight brush of a hug. "I want you to meet Carolina Slade from my office."

The big man moved sloth-like, weary and spent, dark circles under red-rimmed eyes. "Dick told me about you. Excuse me for not being myself."

"No worry at all. I'm so sorry about CJ."

He nodded and turned to shake another hand. Even with all this going on, the Governor had informed his brother I'd be coming. Either I was the last desperate chance for Lamar, or someone gave me more professional credit than I was due. Or the Governor was worried about more than I understood. No matter; I was declining this investigation.

Dubose spoke to Dick Wheeler, and I fell back, having sense enough to keep a distance in public from the man who vowed to deny our connection. I mingled, introducing myself to people who couldn't care less, mentally rehearsing my recusal speech to give Dubose.

Petite Mrs. Haggerty received hug after hug. But before I reached her, the matronly woman managing the peanut vendor engulfed the grandmother in an embrace, her sagging triceps swinging with the motion.

"Lucille, hon. How you holding up?" She had one of those boisterous country voices, loud enough to call hogs from the next county.

Lucille leaned into the big woman. "My baby's gone, Addie."

My heart broke watching the frail woman, and an errant tear fell. The grandmother saw it. "Do I know you?"

"I'm sorry, ma'am. Just wanted to speak." I wiped my face.

"Who are you to cry for my boy?" she asked, almost childlike.

"Carolina Slade, from the Department of Agriculture. We do business with your son Lamar."

Her facial lines deepened. "He ain't my son."

I'd stepped over some invisible line. "My mistake, ma'am."

The pixie of a woman came alive with fire in her eyes. "Lamar killed my boy. Might as well have crashed the car, the bastard."

I never heard such a timid voice say *bastard* and make it stick so well. No doubt CJ's aggravation about his daddy's arrest, fueled by teenage temper, contributed to the accident.

Addie smiled. "We appreciate your kindness, but Lucille needs to get home."

"Um, sure. Again, my condolences." I searched over heads as the mourners thinned. Thank goodness Dubose scouted for me, ready to leave.

We walked a hundred yards to the car. I was ready to peel off panty hose and wad them in my purse by the time we got there, but I thought it a tad uncouth to do in front of the boss.

Air-conditioning cranked on high, I opened the windows a few inches to allow the pent up heat to escape. "Thought you said Lucille Haggerty was Lamar's mother."

"No," Dubose said, carefully removing her hat. "I said she was CJ's grandmother. Lamar's wife died of cancer eight years ago. Lucille's her mother. She lives with Lamar."

"Under the same roof?"

Dubose arranged her hat on the seat. "Oh yes. She took care of the boy. Lamar and Lucille will kill each other without CJ around now. He bound that family together."

Enough. "Excuse me, ma'am, but it's obvious you know these people mighty well."

"Politics, Slade. Just politics."

Sure it was. Now was as good a time as any to deliver my speech. "I've given the Wheeler dilemma a lot of thought."

She smiled. "Glad to hear it."

Pig crap. I inhaled and tried again. "I mean, I have second thoughts about doing this."

"Doing what, your job?"

"I'm not sure I'm qualified to help Lamar Wheeler." Or the Governor.

She moved the air-conditioning vent away from her. "Lamar is our client. His future is our future." Dubose hesitated for effect, as if giving one of her speeches, her manicured hands stroking each other in preparation for gesturing. I knew the routine.

"I'm your superior," she said, "and I promised the chief executive of this state we'd look out for the agricultural interest of the Wheeler family. What part of what I just said isn't in your job description?" Each word was delivered a bit more caustic, yet so controlled. "That's why I named you special projects representative, to handle most anything. I have complete confidence in you."

I shifted in my seat, hands tight and clammy on the steering wheel.

"Let me reword it for you." From the corner of my eye I caught her staring, not knowing where to place my own gaze under such scrutiny. "Slade?"

"Ma'am?"

"What part of your job don't you like?"

Anxiety ran across my shoulders. "I like my job."

She smiled sweetly. "Yes, I know you do, Slade. What's the real problem?"

"Just feels outside my duties." I hesitated. "Too political."

There went those hands again. "But I'm a politician, and you work for me. It's simple."

"What about something in writing?"

She faced ahead. "Let's go home, Slade."

In the recesses of my exasperated brain, discretion told me to shut up. I couldn't acknowledge speaking to Wayne. They hadn't asked me to do so, but yet I knew they wanted me to.

Putting the car into drive, I saw no other option. In the name of my family, my career, and my future, I had to stumble on, see what I could do, and report as requested. I'd put on a show, find nothing, and say I did my best. How could they expect more?

Dubose spoke no direction, gave no specifics, and said nothing that would come back to haunt her.

How did politicians speak so much and say so little?

TWO DAYS AFTER the funeral, I parked the government's Taurus in Lamar Wheeler's circular driveway. I'd avoided Dubose since the funeral, and she allowed the distance. Wayne and I dodged the subject as well as any mention of Pamela, so he probably thought this case was history.

My plan was to have a couple of meetings with the family and friends, file a report to Dubose, and chalk it up to experience—a bump in the road of my newfound career. Soon everyone would realize I wasn't a substitute for a private investigator—or a full-fledged federal agent. I wasn't trained to poke holes in a DEA case.

The house's white siding gave the residence a cottage appearance at first glance. Once I took in the twelve-foot-high covered brick porch wrapping around three sides, architectural shingles, and plantation shutters accenting eight-foot windows, I sensed affluence masked in the simplicity. At least five thousand square feet, the house appeared four or more generations old.

White rockers adorned the porch, and a dozen fluffy ferns hung in style, matching the green paint of the shutters. Hostas overflowed in the shade of pines and maples as I made my way up the brick path. Under the railing, on both sides of the steps, deep forest-green cleyera bushes posed as backdrop to petunias, snapdragons, and miniature Shasta daisies. I suspected several thousand dollars' worth of mushroom compost fed all those gorgeous specimens. My place on Lake Murray harbored too many hungry deer to plant such an array of floral delicacies.

Lucille walked around the corner of the house as I put a foot on the step. A Hispanic gentleman had her arm, listening as she aimed with a white-handled, pastel floral cane at one bed, then another. A straw hat covered snow-white hair, large wrap-around sunglasses over half her face. She wore lemon yellow Bermuda pants, a white blouse with tiny flowers, and off-white orthopedic shoes. When she saw me, she motioned the man away and hobbled across the grass in my direction.

"What can I do for you, Ms. Slade?"

I shortened the distance between us and extended a hand. "I'm flattered you remembered me, Mrs. Haggerty. Your yard is gorgeous. How are you doing?"

She gave me a limp shake. "I'm living. About all I can say. When one loses her daughter, then her only grandson, what more is there than to wait for your last breath?"

While she painfully mourned, she still flashed a talent for the dramatic. Though tiny in stature, Lucille Haggerty was made of stern stuff.

"It must be hard on you," I said. "I can't imagine."

She faced me, but I couldn't see her eyes through the shades. "No, you can't."

Her head held a mild tremor, but she could hold a glare.

"I'm here to see Lamar," I said. "Our appointment was for ten."

She nodded toward the door. "Go on in. He's moping in the study instead of being a man. I expected to run this farm for him once they hauled his sorry ass to jail, but I guess I'll have to start sooner than planned."

I turned toward the porch then remembered my manners. "May I help you anywhere? To the porch? Inside?"

With a jerky hand, she removed her glasses. Droopy hazel eyes stared a hole in me. "Do I walk like a cripple?"

"No, ma'am. Pleasure to see you again."

She let loose a *humph* behind me as she returned her attention to her yard man, pointing her cane at a weed for him to pull. I mounted the steps and rang the doorbell. She shuffled to another bed, leaned on her cane, and pinched off a spent rose. Maybe this was how she dealt with grief—nursing plants and snipping off people's heads.

To my surprise, Lamar answered the door. Suffering coated his face, hung on him, and my throat tightened at the consideration that my intrusion painted me rude. My God, how did someone lose a child?

"Mr. Wheeler? Carolina Slade."

I smelled scotch. His eyes sank deep into red sockets. Sorrow weighed his shoulders. At one time he must have been a handsome man. While he resembled his brother across the eyes, he'd aged less gracefully.

"Come on in." He closed the door behind me and then led us to a room with a walnut desk and several overstuffed coffee-colored leather chairs. Maroon drapes covered the tall windows, dark gold braid on the valances. Sunlight flooded the room, thank heavens; the place otherwise resembled a funeral parlor.

A nine-inch brass peanut sat on the desk. Carolina Gamecock football prints bedecked one wall, Lamar's diploma from the school in the midst of them. Several large black and white photographs hung on the dark paneling, showing past farmers standing in their fields, baskets of peanuts at their feet. A painting hung over the fireplace of a slight woman, fortyish, with jet-black hair swooped up on her head. At least a dozen pictures stood on the mantel. The Governor posed with a woman, possibly his deceased wife. A younger version of him wrapped arms around Lamar and a girl their age wearing a graduation gown. Lamar's wedding picture showed him lean and handsome in front of a church altar. CJ grinned back from one with a baseball bat over his shoulder. He poised on the bow of a bass boat in another, shirtless and fearless.

Lamar was surrounded with shadows of people who'd loved him and lived with one who wished him dead. How alone he must feel.

He hunched at the window and sunk the remnants of his glass's contents. "God really shit on me this time," he said. "Sorry. Dick told me to answer your questions. What can I do for you?"

My voice almost failed me. "I'm here to help, Mr. Wheeler."

"Good luck with *that*." He walked unsteadily to a small bar in the corner.

I inhaled deep, reaching for courage. "Your brother mentioned people who might have a grudge against you, assuming . . ."

"Assuming I'm not a drug dealer?" He fumbled with the ice.

"I was going to say assuming DEA didn't screw up."

He slumped in an armchair that fit him well. "And who are you again?"

"I work with Agriculture, for Margaret Dubose. She's—"

"I know who she is." He downed half the glass. "She's wasting her goddamn time." He raised his glass. "Quote me."

Dubose again. She expected me to ferret out a solution for the Wheelers while they held secrets to their chest. I'd bet a week's pay there were enough skeletons in these closets to decorate a Transylvania castle. I'd bet a year's salary nobody wanted me to know.

Chapter 6

LAMAR WHEELER sank into his drink while I waited in a leather chair opposite him in his study. How was I to interview a man so depressed . . . and drunk? "Can you explain what happened with DEA?" I asked.

His hands hung so limp on the chair's arms, I feared he'd drop his glass. "This . . . shit . . . is nothing more than someone trying to smear Dick."

"But *you'd* go to jail, not the Governor." From the glaze in his eyes, his mind drifted. I sat forward to grab his attention. "Not that I'm accusing you."

He waved his glass. "This ain't Hollywood, it's South Carolina. Blood runs thicker in Dixie, sweetheart. From the sound of your accent you should know that."

I did. But why not set up the Governor instead of his brother? Unless they couldn't pin anything on the Governor, or someone hated them both and didn't care who caught the arrow in the chest. "Talk to me," I said. "I may not be DEA, but I've solved a few cases. I promised your brother I'd delve into this."

He laughed lazily. "They found bottles of expired prescription drugs in the trash at my condo. Dozens of people traipse in and out of my place: coaches, recruits, neighbors, business acquaintances, and—God forbid—friends. I find it hard to believe one of them dumped the crap."

I knew those condos, from reputation only. As a rival Clemson fan, I wouldn't receive an offer to party with too many Carolina Gamecocks. But drive anywhere near the stadium on a Friday before a football game, and you knew who was well-heeled and held the best pre-game celebrations.

Five condominium complexes bellied up to the Cockpit, the University of South Carolina's Williams Brice Stadium in downtown Columbia. All five complexes boasted the best location for Gamecock fans, and units sold for a premium. Lamar owned an address in the newest set of condos, and from his description, it held a decent view.

"Nobody lives there full-time, right?" I asked.

He grunted in affirmation. "Right. We just do get-togethers. Sometimes friends borrow the place. CJ was gonna stay there when he started school in the fall."

"DEA didn't ask for a list of people who'd used the condo?"

"Oh, they asked. Told them it was none of their business."

"Why? It might've helped your case."

He belched, letting air out through his nose. "So we nail one, and the rest hate me for implicating them in a crime? CJ's college and Dick's career would go down the toilet, not to mention my own. Chances are they'd never figure out who did it anyway, and I'd have dragged their names through the muck for nothing."

The guy made sense even drunk. Anyone visiting the condo could've baited the trap. Yet they pinned this so easily on Lamar. Maybe Wayne would connect those legal dots for me . . . once I admitted I still worked this case . . . and assuming he'd help me.

I retrieved my notepad and scribbled. "The pills came from the VA hospital. What's your connection there?"

"I'm a veteran. Tom's filled my prescriptions for years."

He had the means and knew a potential supplier. This kept getting worse. "The pharmacist?"

"Yeah." Lamar slid a piece of ice in his mouth and crunched it between his teeth. "He's been to the condo a time or two. Every vet around here knows Tom."

Bet that guy suffered several DEA visits. "Did DEA interview him?"

Lamar shrugged. "How the hell should I know? When they interrogated me, I called my lawyer. When he told me to clam up, they clammed up, too. Talk to them."

Since dating Wayne, I learned every agency relied upon an Office of Inspector General to investigate illegal matters relevant to their particular regulations. Other law enforcement arms like DEA, FBI, or ATF got involved when jurisdiction lines blurred or certain politics stepped in, plus they had their signature duties as well. OIG agents trained alongside most of these guys, but the world only knew of the main alphabet boys—the ones made famous in movies and television series. What made VA's OIG hand the case over to DEA?

I presumed the prestige of investigating the Governor's brother turned the tide more than anything, but I didn't want to assume. Not when I had to answer to South Carolina's chief executive tomorrow. Then I remembered the family feud the Governor mentioned in the mansion on Monday.

"Mr. Wheeler, would a local set you up? Is there a rivalry I need to check out?"

Lamar blinked as the questions swam their way to his brain. "I assume you mean the Fants. Yes, we fight over peanut sales, contracts, that kind of shit. I'd like to say I wouldn't put it past them, but don't see how. They ain't bright, and I damn sure didn't invite them into my place."

Lack of access did swing suspicion away from them. Unless they bribed somebody else to do it. "How far back does this feud go?" I asked.

Lucille strutted into the room, her cane animated. "That's enough, young lady. I won't have you stirring trouble at a time like this."

Lamar closed his eyes, grimaced, then gawked at the old woman. "Eavesdropping again, you old bitty?"

I winced at the harshness in his slurred voice.

She shook her cane at him. "And you're a nasty drunk. Go to bed. You're making a fool out of yourself."

He rose on wobbly feet and gripped the back of his chair. "I'm out of ice anyway, unless you want to fetch me some."

"Get," Lucille said. "Get on out of here."

Lamar hobbled to the doorway, stumbling as he maneuvered around Lucille, and left the room. The old woman followed him out.

I wrote hard and filled four pages in my small notepad, hustling to jot down details before they evaporated. I marked an asterisk above salient details to pursue, especially the pharmacist and those who visited the condo. I'd have another go at Lamar when he was sober, which I feared might be a while.

As I rose to leave, Lucille's cane taps and uneven gait warned of her approach. Funny how I didn't hear her come up on us before.

"You can go now," she said from the doorway.

"Yes, ma'am." The lady had a demanding yet confident way about her. "Mind if I ask you something before I go?"

She regarded the ceiling before answering. "My God, missy, haven't you asked enough questions?"

I slowly held out my hands in peace. "You seem to be the matriarch. I'd hoped to learn more about this feud situation to help Lamar."

She chuckled in condescension at me. "What do you think you are, a reporter? Don't use us as a plum for your career, girl." She moved toward the front door. "Lamar's past has caught up to him, and no amateur sleuth is going to change that."

I stepped outside and turned. "Do you mind if I ask—"

"Yes, I do," she said.

"But I'm here at the request of Governor Wheeler, to help your son-in-law. He said the family would cooperate."

"I'm not his kin," she said.

The door swung shut in my face, then locked. At least she didn't hit me with her cane.

I SCHEDULED A home-cooked dinner for Wayne, to drop the news to him I remained on the case. We'd moved the discussion out of the house to my back porch where ceiling fans hummed as a backdrop to our prickly conversation. Even in the dark I could sense his frustration.

I tucked a bare foot under my bottom and used the other to rock my chair. "Dubose all but gave me an ultimatum. I don't have a choice."

"This is out of your league and none of Dubose's business," he said.

"For the record, I agree, but my opinion has no bearing with these people." I hoped his feelings for me outweighed his concern about the situation. "Where do I go from here?"

He kicked his boots off and then removed his socks. After propping bare feet on the porch railing and unbuttoning his shirt, he slumped in his rocker and sighed. "I could refuse to help, but it'd only hurt you."

"Appreciate that observation, Cowboy."

He raked fingers through his dark hair. "Tell me the details again."

I covered the problem all the way back to CJ at the fair, knowing any little item might harbor a clue.

His after-dinner toothpick remained stationary against his bottom lip as he spoke. "Pamela was probably trying to find CJ or Lamar at the fair," he said. "When CJ bolted, she decided to follow him. That's how she conveniently happened upon the accident before you."

"Conveniently?"

"Have to ask her about that," he said. "Maybe she suspected CJ from the start and pinned it on the daddy in hopes the truth would come out. Maybe father and son had a business. Any of several possibilities."

I set my iced tea on the wrought iron table next to me and wiped a moist hand on my T-shirt. "How can they pin this on Lamar when so many people passed through his place that week? Anyone could've tossed those bottles in his trash. And why bottles with pills left in them? Like that was a bright idea."

"Agreed," he said. "But they don't have to prove it was anyone else. DEA met the standard for arresting Lamar for possession with intent to distribute. The pills were at his place, they weren't his legal prescription, and there were too many for personal use."

"But they can't prove he was in possession."

"Babe, they don't have to. He might be able to use such logic as part of his defense, but DEA has no obligation to run down other people. The evidence was in Lamar's house."

"Chicken spit," I mumbled, just as bothered by the situation as Wayne's use of the word *babe* for both Pamela and me.

I stood and leaned on the railing next to his propped feet. "Let's change the subject."

"Okay. To what?"

"Pamela."

He dropped his head back and exhaled. "I'd rather talk about the weather, the economy, anything but Pamela." He leaned toward me. "Pamela is his-tor-y. We are divorced."

"You call her *babe*."

He sat forward. "Really, Slade?"

"Really."

I wasn't comfortable in that woman's hot-bodied presence, and I was pissed she'd intimidated me. The result was a back step to childishness, and I wasn't proud of it. "Skip it."

"Thank you." He relaxed and turned his gaze to the moon's reflection on the lake down the hill.

The frogs raised their chorus, and the katydids tried to keep up. A muted splash meant a fish cut some creature's life short. I returned to my rocker, regretting the missed chance at a cuddle in Wayne's lap. Ivy cut loose a playful squeal inside, and I instinctively peeked in the window. She and Zack played cards with Ally at my kitchen table. Guess Ivy had won.

"I meet with Dick Wheeler on Monday for my first update," I said. "What do I say?"

"Tell him what you told me."

"He knows everything I know."

"Then tell him you're working on it. Don't embellish or make a promise. Frankly, the less said the better." Wayne reached down, swatted a mosquito, and scratched his ankle. "He might even drop something new on you if you keep quiet and give him the chance. Most people fill in silence with words."

Personally, I didn't mind silence. With two kids and a job crammed with boisterous bureaucrats, I craved quiet. What I didn't appreciate was the unspoken, and I sensed a lot of it bottled up in almost everyone these days, including Wayne.

I SPENT THE weekend pretending there was no such thing as a Wheeler.

But life pushed on, and I arrived at the Governor's mansion on Monday at two o'clock, as arranged. Following the token pleasantries, he offered me water. It was August, for goodness sake. What was wrong with iced tea? I ate beforehand this time, banking on the meeting being pure business *sans* lunch, like before.

Wheeler sat across from me, wearing another crisp white shirt. Smelling like the same cologne. The entire room's set up identical down to the placement of crystal glasses and coasters.

"So how goes it, Ms. Slade?"

"Your brother didn't offer much, sir," I said. "Mrs. Haggerty sure hates the man. I felt sorry for both of them."

Wheeler shook his head. "She turned bitter when Patsy died of cancer. It took my sister-in-law in a matter of months. Lamar came undone. Lucille stepped in for CJ. In my opinion, she threw herself into raising that child to weather the pain." He smoothed his tie. "Talk to the Fants yet?"

"No, sorry. Couldn't get to Lamar until Friday. But I'll . . ."

He waved a dispassionate hand. "You won't need to speak to the Fants now anyway."

What? "You told me they might be key players. Lamar and Mrs. Haggerty sure didn't want me to find them."

"Yes, I did steer you in that direction, but Lamar's making a statement today, poor man. It'll change everything."

I tensed, uncrossing my legs. Was the farmer about to confess? A sense of optimism swooped through me. Maybe this case was over, and I could get on with my normal job.

"So sorry, sir," I said. "I'm sure we can work something out about the farm when your brother leaves."

Wheeler's head remained eerily still, his gaze fixed unnervingly on me. "He's not going to jail quite yet."

"But you said . . ."

"I said Lamar will release a new statement. He'll admit to CJ's drug problem and that the pills belonged to his son."

Lamar was throwing his dead son to the wolves? "Is he sure he wants to do this?"

"Seems so."

That meant Lamar had either hushed CJ's crime and took the fall for him before the accident, or he planned to capitalize on his son's death after the accident, taking the opportunity to shift reasonable doubt. Not a bad defense. No friggin' wonder he drank. I bet Lucille Haggerty had used an accessorized cane to beat a couple of her oak trees to pulp over this turn of events.

"So I won't need you anymore, Ms. Slade."

"DEA won't be so quick to drop the charges, Governor."

For the first time he grinned. "Maybe not, but once we round up a few witnesses to CJ's extracurricular pastime, Lamar ought to be fine. At least according to our attorneys."

While Wheeler's plan wasn't all that palatable, relief washed over me. End of case. Done deal. Hallelujah.

Wheeler rose, hand outstretched. "Thanks for all you've done, and on such short notice."

I stood and took his hand. "I wasn't much help."

"Your loyalty impressed me most," he said, my hand now in both of his. "If you ever consider leaving federal service, give me a call. I'm sure I could find a place on my staff."

"Appreciate it," I said, backing away, eager to leave this man's presence. "I'll keep that in mind."

I strolled back to the office, an immense weight off my shoulders. Wayne would be pleased, and I'd dodged a situation that could have only thrown me in front of a train. As I reached the parking lot, however, my sense of relief evaporated. I wasn't buying the dead kid scapegoat routine.

My hand rested on the back door to the federal building as I pondered what was going on here. *Aw, damn.* Here was my chance to be rid of this case. A winning-lottery-ticket opportunity, for God's sake. Instead, a seething frustration built up in my chest.

I'd protected my ex's black reputation for the sake of my children. The scumbag had his own progeny kidnapped and planned my murder. Ivy and Zack had gone through hell, and thanks to careful attention to their behavior and needs, they'd adjusted. They'd have been basket cases if they knew the truth of their father's intentions.

Yet the Wheelers appeared more than willing to throw an innocent child's short life away to preserve their image. What had this poor boy endured for the sake of politics and family secrets?

I immediately desired to know where Dubose stood on this new situation.

As I stepped into my office, the intercom buzzed, Angela calling me up front. Dubose looked up as I entered. "Dick just called and said the case was dead."

"Lamar Wheeler is claiming his son owned those pills."

She frowned. "You sure?"

"The Governor told me." I leaned stiff-armed on a chair. "It doesn't feel right."

She dropped her pen on an open file, leaned back, and regarded me. "No, it doesn't."

"Don't ask me why, but I'd like to dig deeper. It's personal."

Dubose's brow raised. "What's personal about it?"

"My reason doesn't matter." I frowned, not wanting to air my history. "But who throws his own child under a bus?"

"Nobody worth a damn."

"Agreed."

Dubose grinned. "I knew I liked you. Keep investigating. Keep it discrete. And answer only to me."

Chapter 7

HAVING RELEASED my frustration about Wheeler's shift of blame from Lamar to CJ, I sat in a chair before Dubose's desk, wondering how Dubose remained one step ahead of me. "What's going on, Margaret?"

"Thought you wanted to dig deeper?" she replied

I blew out a breath. "I do."

She watched me slyly, waiting.

"You know more than you're saying," I said.

One brow raised, she continued waiting.

"Okay," I said, moving forward in the chair. "You drag me into this snooping gig at Wheeler's request and threaten my job if I don't comply. The Governor dismisses me from the task. You, however, want me to continue anyway. I naively jump at the chance." My radar pinged as if sighting an entire squadron of enemy planes. "Was I played?"

Dubose's brows eased. "No, Slade. Dick changed his mind. I haven't. Lamar's still our client. Agriculture is at risk if he goes to jail. And most importantly, you work for me, not Dick."

I sighed. Thirty minutes ago, I was home free from this mess with a job offer from the Governor. Had I waved my hand too quickly? "We aren't chasing stolen tractors. Plus, Dick Wheeler rescinded the invitation to question his family. How are we supposed to legally get involved?"

Impatience formed in the creases of her mouth. "You just flashed me backbone, Slade. Don't ruin it."

I recalled Wayne's advice to stay calm and cover my butt. "May I have this assignment in writing? I'd feel better if—"

Her expression hardened to steel. "No."

"I'm sorry," I said, studying her, "but I have to question your intentions."

We eyed each other, my heart pounding like a hummingbird. Silence reigned for what seemed like an age. I fought tug-of-war with myself not to stand down.

"It's not what it seems," she said with a firm quietness. "Yes, I have a personal interest, but that's all I'll say. Nothing compromises you." Her gaze faltered, then returned to meet mine, enough to plant doubt in my head. "Dick's hunting the easy way out to protect himself and the family."

"Do *you* know if Lamar's guilty?"

"I don't believe CJ did it," she said stone-cold.

My hands stretched under the table, and a knuckle cracked. I saw myself as the fall gal in an affair that would irritate a sea of federal badges. I was Dubose's lieutenant, the one who'd likely get shot in her stead.

"DEA swatted me out of their way already," I said, reaching for excuses.

She grinned. "I'm impressed you've already confronted them."

"Trust me, there was nothing impressive about it," I said, recalling Pamela's sass. "Ma'am, what's the goal here?"

"The truth."

"Do we have any idea what that is?" Using Wayne's words, I added, "An investigator doesn't go in blind."

She rested her chin in her hand. "If it appears Lamar will go to jail, we do damage control regarding his six figure loans."

"What if DEA drops the case?"

"We're not playing 'what if.'" Her phone buzzed. "I have to take this, Slade. Just do your job."

"This isn't really my job."

She glared hard. "Find out if Lamar is guilty and clear CJ's name, Slade. Two things. It's that simple." She picked up the phone and dismissed me with a nod toward the door.

I exited and stood in her lobby just like I had a few days ago. The Governor had played me. Dubose had as well. Not that she'd planned Wheeler's flip-flop. She'd have probably assigned this to me anyway, but I'd hopped in her lap and begged for it.

There was nothing simple about this at all.

I snatched open the main door, vowing to campaign for whoever ran against Dick Wheeler when he sought reelection. My respect for Margaret Dubose teetered on a razorblade.

Was I that gullible? I had been a year ago, before I'd crossed into investigations. Not that I'd mastered the new job, as proven by today's events.

Why *were* the Wheelers eager to smear a dead kid's name? Lamar could be a pill popper. Hell, so could the Governor and all their condo-partying, USC Gamecock-loving friends. But why was Dubose hell bent on stirring up trouble? Her stubbornness was just as pertinent in this mess as anything the Wheelers were doing.

As I entered my office, I remembered the Fants. If I investigated anew, I'd contact the clan in competition with the Wheelers. Even if they weren't involved, they'd know dirt. They might spill on the Wheelers . . . maybe even Dubose.

I allowed myself a half-grin and a personal second of satisfaction. A DEA female dynamo had told the world that Lamar Wheeler stole pills for distribution. The press release about CJ would change that.

Way to go, Pamela. Eat that crow.

I slumped in my desk chair and dialed.

Wayne picked up immediately. "How'd it go?"

I relayed the details, laced with the appropriate sighs and groans.

"Dubose is out of her mind, Slade," he said.

"Amen to that," I replied.

"And you're right on her heels, so don't act all innocent."

I chewed the inside of a cheek. "I don't need this right now, Wayne."

"I know you don't, but you let your emotions paint you into a corner, Butterbean."

I didn't know what to say.

"Listen," he said. "I've been mulling this over. Can you get away after lunch?"

"No problem," I scoffed. "Dubose labeled this high priority."

"Pick you up out back in an hour."

I hung up and searched through my notes for the Fants' phone number. They were peanut farmers, too, operating fifteen miles closer to Columbia than the Wheelers, outside Lexington.

Not finding the number noted anywhere, I logged into my computer. During the last few years, farmers had embraced the Internet, flaunting their commercial prowess and advertising products, vegetables, livestock, and cash crops. Certified SC Grown became a common logo in stores, markets, and tourist attractions. The local state level Ag Department maintained a website for its members, and the savviest farmers linked it to their own. That's how I found the Fants.

While the Wheelers ruled the state when it came to boiled peanuts, the Simeon Fant clan dominated the parched peanut market. They supplied all the events held in the Gamecock stadium, and, apparently, had done so for almost ten years. That by itself would create friction, having a rival peanut farmer in the Governor's mansion, especially one with a deep-pocket alumni connection to the school. The polar distinctions between the families, however, extended beyond their goober pea commerce. The Fants were big rival Clemson fans. With my agricultural economics degree from that upstate university, I understood their love for all things orange. The Fants were also members of opposite political parties. Could these families be any further divided?

I clicked on "About Us," and the screen flooded with family pictures at the state fair, ball games, even in the fields holding up freshly dug clumps of peanuts.

I did a double take on the fourth picture. There was Addie, Lucille Haggerty's bosom buddy from the funeral. Beside Addie stood the mentally challenged peanut vendor from the Pelion festival, the caption stating his name as Hugh. Various offspring filled other snapshots of the successful enterprise, but my interest returned to Addie. If the Wheelers and Fants hated each other so much, why did Addie and Lucille behave like doting sisters?

I dialed the farm's main number and asked for Simeon, the Fant patriarch, but the young receptionist said I'd have to leave a message. He was at Clemson, involved in football season preparations. The first home game was two weeks away, and serious scholarship donors often visited the campus where they were wined, dined, and enlightened about the new program. My token donation didn't warrant me a parking place within a half mile of Clemson's Death Valley, but I gladly supported my team. Such was the royal social strata of Southern college football. Give and ye shall receive. Give more and ye shall receive choice seats, premium parking, and a gold throne on the fifty-yard line.

I left a message for Simeon to call, telling the girl I had questions about Lamar Wheeler. She hesitated then gave me a polite, "yes, ma'am," which told me the Wheeler name had struck home.

Past time to meet Wayne, I grabbed my purse and ran out the door. Wayne had the car running, double-parked on Park Street behind the building.

"Where are we going?" I asked, clicking my seat belt.

"Garners Ferry Road," he said. "The VA. I know the IG agent. He's offered to bring us up to speed from his side of this case."

"He's willing to talk about a VA mistake?"

He nodded. "I believe he'll talk to me. It beats trying to squeeze it out of Pamela."

Amen to that. We'd get more out of the dead kid than Pamela. She'd probably steer us wrong.

Fifteen minutes later, Wayne turned onto the hospital property and drove around to a small lot containing a dozen cars. He parked and pulled out his phone. "I'm here."

A couple minutes later, an emergency exit door swung open. A tall, tightly groomed man in black-frame military style glasses blocked the door from closing with a brick before he walked over. The VA agent appeared more like a schoolteacher than a senior agent.

"Wayne! I've been meaning to come see you since you moved to town. There aren't too many IG types in Columbia. We ought to start a fraternity or something."

Wayne gripped his hand in a vigorous shake. "Great to see you, Steve. How's Debbie?"

"Still trying to sell real estate. Hasn't made a sale in six months, but she keeps at it." He chuckled and turned to me. "Who's this?"

Wayne laid a hand on my shoulder. "This is Carolina Slade from USDA. We'd like to talk with you about that Wheeler case you uncovered. The guy's one of Slade's farmers."

"Follow me." Steve led us back to the propped open door. "They gave you a partner? Took me six months to establish enough caseload to warrant one."

"She's not my partner. She's what they call—"

"I'm a special projects representative with Agriculture," I interrupted, showing him my credentials. I hated it when someone spoke as if I wasn't present.

Amusement flashed across Steve's face, but quickly disappeared. I sensed my status plummet to a degree above amateur.

We walked through an auditorium and up a double flight of stairs. The building appeared a century old with twenty-foot high ceilings, floral carpet, heavy brass hardware on the doors, and several lifetimes of enamel paint on the woodwork. He unlocked his office while I glanced at a triple row of theater chairs and what appeared to be an ancient projector stand.

"We don't advertise where we are," Steve said. "The VA only had this room over the auditorium to spare, but it suits me. Beats being in the federal building."

Steve beckoned to a gray foldout table and six metal chairs. "Have a seat. Now Slade, you're a special what?"

"Special projects representative."

He turned to Wayne. "What the hell is that?"

"Why're you asking him?" I said. "I do administrative investigations. Wayne takes over if they turn criminal."

Steve pursed his lips and squinted. "Okay. Didn't mean to step on your tootsies, sweetheart, but why should I speak to you?"

I cut a hard glance at Wayne as I gnawed on the word *sweetheart*. This was his connection, and I waited for him to make something of it before I diced up Steve with a personal dose of my special blend of feedback. There was networking, and then there was networking.

Wayne laid a restraining hand on my arm. "Steve and I went to Glynnco together years ago for federal training in Brunswick, Georgia." He nodded toward Steve. "Weren't you with NCIS then?"

Steve nodded slightly. "Yeah, but VA IG wanted to stick an agent in South Carolina. Since Debbie and I have family here, I jumped on it."

"Kind of like me and Agriculture," Wayne said.

I played with one of several paper clips scattered on the table and then slid it in my hair without a second thought, an old habit when my hair needed a cut. I picked up another and bent it again and again, weathering the man-chatter and insensible references to me.

"I appreciate you talking with us," Wayne said. "Slade has been instructed by her superior, a Schedule C political appointee, to delve into Lamar Wheeler. I offered to assist." He squinted a bit. "I thought illicit narcotics fell under your watchful eye. You screw it up, or they strong-arm it away?"

Steve raised cupped palms. "DEA thinks they carry big hairy balls." He glanced at me. "Excuse the language."

"Sure," I answered, deadpan, knowing the guy didn't give a damn what he said in front of me. His irritation with Pamela rang loud, though. She didn't carry those balls, but she acted like she did.

He then moaned about some irritating, jurisdictional squabble aftermath—whining, in my opinion.

"So who found what?" I asked. "Or have they sworn you to secrecy?"

Steve laughed bitter. "I'll speak to whomever I need to." He leaned back his chair. "Fact was, a pharmacy assistant came to me with his suspicions about expired pills that weren't being destroyed per the regs. They're logged out and incinerated so they don't walk off. I called DEA Regulatory who monitors that sort of thing, and then I spoke to a few employees. Regulatory interviewed Tom Holcomb, the pharmacist, and determined the missing inventory was no more than an administrative error."

"So how did they connect the dots?" I asked. "I mean, how did they find evidence in Wheeler's trash at his condo?"

"You got me on that one, but whoever did it had DEA swarming like ants to sugar." He scratched the side of his head. "They found the bottles and snared the biggest fish in the pond. Standard procedure. You know how that goes, Wayne. Throw a high-level Dick in the mix, and they go orgasmic."

So someone set up Lamar. Mentally I ticked off names, stacking up pros and cons for each name in the mix. CJ, the Governor, the Fants. "How well do you trust this pharmacist?" I asked. "He parties with the Wheelers."

Steve shrugged. "Tom? He's not the best bookkeeper, but he's cool with the vets. He wouldn't be near the top of my suspect list. I've known him for three years, ever since I moved here." He placed his feet on the floor and stood. "He ought to be in. Let me buy you guys a cup of coffee in the cafeteria on the way."

We wandered outside toward another red-bricked building. The hallway we entered was lined with black and white photographs, framed in dull dark wood as old as the 1920 settings in the images. Mules pulled sleds full of timbers and brick to equip thick-knotted workers with material to build the Dorn Veteran Administration Medical Center. History hung on these walls, watching over us as our heels clicked on polished linoleum tiles gleaning from fifty years of wax.

Having missed the lunch crowd, the three of us sat amid an ocean of empty tables. Leftover smells of hamburgers, fries, and something akin to spaghetti hovered in the air. A white-apron-clad server behind the counter recognized Steve, and at his beckon, brought us three coffees in white ceramic mugs.

"So is drugs most of what you do?" I asked. Why did these thick diner cups make coffee taste so good?

"I'm juggling twenty cases right now," he replied. "And no, they aren't all drugs. They're government contract fraud, real estate fraud, veteran abuse, benefits theft, and the occasional embezzlement scheme."

"Wow," I said.

Wayne grinned. "Who thinks agriculture investigates anything serious either, Slade?"

"It's just I've heard stories about the VA," I said.

Steve sighed. "The VA does a phenomenal job addressing veterans' needs. The people here are dedicated, as much or more so than any other hospital. These patients gave their all."

I sipped again and spoke from behind my cup. "The press doesn't spread that message."

"Tell me something I don't know."

"Sorry," I said, face warming. We were even now with our erroneous assumptions.

Steve grinned and stood. "The pharmacy is out that door, down the hall and to the left. Tom's the pharmacist; he's one of the ones I'm talking about."

We left the cafeteria for another hallway. Soon a black-lettered sign dangling from the ceiling tiles identified the pharmacy. I recognized the customer at the counter. His cigarette-style case was like the one we saw at the peanut fair, holding items stacked in rows, the neck strap puddled on the floor. A VA employee in a white coat leaned toward the man, attempting to explain something.

"That's Hugh Fant," I said to Wayne.

"You know him?" Steve asked. "Hey, Hugh. How's it going, fella?"

The visitor twisted toward us, his face softening in recognition of a friend. "Hey, Steve," he said, his voice much lower than his proclamation at the peanut festival.

The white-coated pharmacy employee straightened. "Let me get back to work, Hugh."

Hugh bent over and lifted his peanut package, adjusting it over his head and on each shoulder. He strutted with a mild limp away from us, toward a deeper part of the hospital.

"Is he a vet?" I asked.

"No," Steve said, watching Hugh depart. "He delivers free peanuts to the patients. The Fants send Hugh here one day a week. Occupies his time and makes him feel useful." He turned toward the employee on the other side of the counter. "By the way, this is Tom Holcomb who I told you about."

I held out my hand. As the pharmacist shook it, he dodged eye contact. The hair stood on my neck. Tom knew the Fants as well as the Wheelers? He inventoried the drugs? So why hadn't DEA swarmed all over this guy?

A creepy feeling crawled down my back, and I glanced over my shoulder. Where would Pamela hide a camera?

Chapter 8

I TURNED MY attention back to the Veteran's Hospital pharmacist, clad in a white lab coat that sported the name tag *Tom Holcomb*.

"I hear good comments about you," I said, aiming to win his confidence.

His grin appeared genuine, ear to ear. "We take care of veterans and do the best we can with what they give us. I like these guys . . . and gals."

I leaned on the counter. "I'll bet some of these vets can tell stories, huh?"

He chuckled. "Nobody can spin a tale like a vet, especially the older ones. I've heard stories that would keep you up at night. They're sad, funny, inspiring."

I glimpsed over his shoulder at the pills and bottles crowding the shelves behind a secured window. "Any of these funny, inspiring guys ask for free samples from your inventory here?"

He tensed. "On occasion."

"Would Lamar Wheeler be one of those occasions?"

Tom Holcomb's face clouded over. "He would not. And whether he asked or not, I've never dispensed pills without a prescription."

I set my plastic credentials on the counter. "Did DEA believe you?"

He studied the badge but didn't touch it. People didn't realize badges held varying levels of authority, or he'd have laughed at mine. I was winging it.

"I told them I didn't know anything," he said. "Then I contacted the VA's Regional Counsel, and they told me to forward all questions to them." Tom studied me, then Wayne and Steve, as if waiting for our counsel, too. "I thought about getting my own attorney. You never know when the feds want to pin something on you just to score."

Yes I did. All too well. I'd almost lost my job in Charleston thanks to overzealous feds who turned my whistleblowing against me.

"So how do you think Lamar Wheeler got his hands on those pill bottles?" I asked.

He shrugged. "Once a month we put the pills in a box, set them aside, then dispose of them in the incinerator."

He focused anywhere but on my eyes. I wasn't buying his too clean persona, not from a man responsible for letting narcotics spill into the public mainstream based upon the lot number on the discovered bottles. "So you always watch the meds burn every month?"

He gaped at Steve. "Am I supposed to answer her?"

Steve nodded. "She has the right to ask, Tom."

Tom grimaced. "Women investigators seem to be coming out of the woodwork."

"The incinerator?" I asked, wondering how my approach compared to Pamela's I'm-a-bitch-don't-mess-with-me method.

"DEA showed me the lot numbers on the bottles they found. I pulled the inventory, and that box was delivered on May 25 to Vernon, the guy who runs the incinerator."

"*Do you* watch the meds destroyed?"

"That day Vernon needed to run to his kid's game and went home early. Left me a note to put the box in a cabinet."

We should have found a private room to hold this conversation. "DEA talked to your guy Vernon to confirm this timeline?" I asked.

"Yes. Vernon returned the next day, and the box was gone."

"And they're happy with that?"

"Human Resources recommended I be disciplined for not witnessing the destruction. Guess that part made DEA happy." He glared. "I'm losing two weeks' pay. Vernon only got one. Sorry they didn't string me up by my male parts, ma'am, but that was all they found wrong."

This time I shrugged. "I'm doing my job, just like you."

He reached around and slammed a drawer shut. "The other bitch wanted me tarred and feathered, too."

"That'll do, Tom," Steve said.

"Anything you haven't told us?" I asked, standing tall to the pharmacist's challenge.

He leaned over the counter. "I have work to do."

"Hopefully protocol tightened since this happened," I said, unaffected.

Tom straightened. "Get the hell out of my pharmacy."

We left, because he had already turned his back and disappeared into the back room we didn't have access to.

Our steps echoed again on the linoleum tiles as we turned the corner that led us back past the cafeteria. The pharmacist took his licks and wasn't happy about it, like any worker caught screwing up. But how could the authorities trust his story? They accepted some of it for fact, or they wouldn't have doled out his discipline so fast. But those pills were not destroyed. So who delivered them to the Wheeler condo?

Steve whispered, "Hell of an interrogation technique there, Agent Ninety-nine."

I clenched my hands, not fond of the testing taking place between us. Steve seemed too fond of Tom, in my opinion.

Wayne cracked half a smile. "I'd watch myself, Steve."

"Tom is a bit smug," I said, wrestling for a stronger grip on the moment. I motioned to the ceiling. "There are surveillance cameras all over the place. Anyone check the recordings? And who else has a key to the incinerator? Better yet, are any master keys missing?"

Wayne bit his cheek, hiding his humor.

Steve stopped, however, with awe on his face. "We checked the tapes on the pharmacy camera and came up zilch. There isn't one for the incinerator. However, we haven't checked the master keys."

"What about the cameras between the pharmacy and the incinerator?" I tapped my head.

"I'm beginning to like her," Steve said, slapping Wayne's arm with the back of his hand.

I shoved open the exit door. "What's not to like?"

"Tell you what, Agent Ninety-nine," Steve said, holding the door. "I'll check the keys and recheck the cameras. Anything else I can do for you?"

I had a few suggestions, but nothing a lady would say in public.

WAYNE PROMISED to come to my place for dinner once he finished at the office. I fought traffic, eager to get home, change, and throw a salad together to go with my home fries and the burgers he'd grill on the patio. This case kept me local, nice for an evening at home with my family, especially with my sister around.

My year with Wayne had passed with more roller coaster moments than most couples experienced in a lifetime. While I couldn't imagine my world without him, I wasn't ready to make our union permanent. Our attraction especially escalated in cases we jointly pursued, but we butted heads over authority, jurisdiction, and whether or not I could handle myself in dangerous situations. I was no hero, but I didn't shirk responsibility, either. Wayne, however, went nuts when he couldn't control my safety. Sweet in concept; annoying in reality.

One day, I could see us married—the day he accepted me for who I was.

Six miles short of Chapin, I reached my house tucked back off Catfish Cove. My sister's Toyota was badly parked in my drive, and I had to squeeze mine past hers by allowing wheels to drop off into a bed of bushes.

For almost a week, Ally had filled the role of Best Aunt in the

Universe. She hadn't overstayed her welcome, and I could almost envision her living close by without too many calamities.

Ally tried anything the kids asked of her. She fished, not only digging up worms but also showing Zack how to create an earthworm farm in one of my flower beds. I could tolerate the thought these wriggly creatures abided in the ground, but a concentrated dose of them gave me the willies.

Ivy's chats with my sister, however, slid across the line of teenager to adult too easily and too often for me. The night before, Ivy was all ears when Ally explained how to entice a boy at school. When the topic morphed into why and how boys got hormonal, I interrupted and suggested we bake cookies.

Ivy could learn way too much from her aunt.

I set my purse on the counter. Wow, someone took time to polish the kitchen countertops, even mop the floor. When Wayne arrived, we could enjoy an all-American hamburger evening without much cleanup.

"Hey, Mom," Ivy said as she inched around me to reach the refrigerator.

I almost choked. "What the heck are you supposed to be?"

Ivy spun around, cookies in one hand, milk in another. The childhood treats clashed with the image defined by spandex bottoms and bikini top that tied in a knot between her almost nonexistent boobies, like Xena Warrior Princess meets Willy Wonka. With a flirtatious toss of her head, she closed her eyes, basking in herself. "Like it?"

"Not at all," I replied. "Where'd you find that?"

She cocked a hip, her head to the side. "I'm growing up, Momma. You really need to accept the fact I'm a teenager, which is practically an adult."

"So you're shocking me into submission?" I moved around to see how provocative her backside appeared. I recognized curves I hadn't noticed before. From behind she easily passed for three or four years older.

Ally pranced in, hair clipped on top of her head, stray curls accenting a face younger and smoother than mine. "Is she adorable or what?" she said, snatching one of Ivy's cookies.

"She looks like an adolescent hooker," I said.

Two sets of eyes rolled in sync.

I wasn't letting a whirlwind sister overpower my parental authority. "Are they returnable?"

Ivy laughed. "Like, really, Momma. I never pegged you for a prude."

Ally grinned at Ivy's exaggerated airs. "It's no big deal, Carolina. Chill. She's inside the house and clothed. Shouldn't that count for something?"

Déjà vu our life as kids. Ally danced, posed, and performed with a flamboyance I never cared to master, and our mother adored her cuteness. More level-headed, I was not the showcase Ally loved to be. Mother even used the full *Allegra Jo* in addressing my sister, adding extra spice to the simple mention of her name. Using Carolina for me, however, only served to nudge me into the lace and cotton eyelet environment I despised. It wasn't until I married a man whom I later abhorred did I muster the nerve to go by Slade and define a place for myself.

My mother hated it.

I carefully chose my words. "I appreciate that you took Ivy shopping, Ally, but I don't think the outfit is appropriate. She's barely thirteen."

"Which is more like when we were sixteen," Ally said. "Kids grow up faster today. They're more sophisticated, smarter."

Ivy hung on Ally's every word. At the moment, Aunt Ally ranked up there with any tousle-headed, slick-muscled, blue-eyed high school football player. No flaws whatsoever.

"The dress doesn't give them sixteen-year-old common sense," I replied, reestablishing my parental power. "Not that a sixteen-year-old has her act together either."

"Momma, you're ridiculous." Ivy forced a sigh for me to hear and eased half a step closer to Ally. "Don't let her make me take the clothes back, Aunt Ally."

My blood pressure rose as my stare warned my sister to select her next words carefully.

By her hesitation, Ally knew full well she stood in the middle of a battle. "Carolina—"

"Slade," I corrected.

"Just feels funny calling you by my last name," she said. "Anyway, let her keep the stuff. Maybe just let her wear it around her friend next door."

"Where's Zack?" I hadn't even checked on my second child, plus I needed a moment to find sure footing. "What's he wearing? Goth or Speedos?"

A kid's voice shouted, "Over here." He sat on the back of the sofa in the usual gym shorts and T-shirt, feet on the cushions, his handheld game player riveting his attention . . . most of it anyway. It appeared he enjoyed the drama from his smirk. "I ain't letting Aunt Ally buy me clothes."

"Butt on the seat; feet on the floor," I said.

He plopped down into place with a whump, throw pillow tumbling to the floor, his thumbs never missing a beat on the game.

Ivy stomped by me, heading toward the back porch. "You're unreal." Her dark temperament dissipated into a smile, however, as she opened the sliding doors to find Wayne about to knock. "Hey!" she said. "You doing the burgers? Cool."

He stepped in and leaned back, scanning her in that outfit. "Holy cow. What are you supposed to be?"

I hid the grin, pleased Wayne echoed my exact words.

"You like?" Ivy asked, beaming.

"Frankly, no," he said, a grimace on his face, considering me as if I'd made the wardrobe selection.

I held up my hands. Then I nodded toward Ally. "There's your culprit."

"I agree with your mother," Wayne said, walking toward me. "You're asking for trouble, little girl."

"Hmmph. Who are you to tell me what to wear?" she replied.

"Hey," he said, not flinching. "You asked me, remember?"

"You're not my father."

I moved between her and Wayne. "That's enough, young lady."

"Well, he's not. My father died thanks to you." She spun and stormed to her bedroom before I could order her to do so. She slammed the door, making Zack glance up only a second, ever humored when his sister lost her cool.

I exhaled hard at Ivy's vicious words. Alan Bridges died at the hands of his partner, a farmer he'd schemed with to end my life and collect the insurance money. The kids only heard their father died searching for them.

Thanks to that incident, I questioned myself . . . a lot. A farmer I knew for eight years and a husband for twelve installed a deep doubt in my psyche about my ability to judge character. I didn't want my children to know the depths of their father's flaws.

Few besides Wayne knew the entire story.

He stood at the sink, washing his hands. "Let it go, Slade."

"Let what go?" asked Ally.

"Nothing," I said, pretending to wipe mascara out of the corner of my eye.

She squinted. "What are you keeping from me?"

I turned on her. "What part of nothing did you miss?"

She shifted her weight to her left foot and adopted her famous cocked stance, her belligerence dripping all over my kitchen. "All I know is that our parents think you're a saint because of what happened in Charleston but won't tell me shit about it." She poked me. "And you shut down over a bad weather report."

"I'm no saint," I said, holding down my voice in spite of my anger. "Drop it."

Even with my husband dead, I remained embarrassed that he duped me for so long. My folks and I agreed for the kids' sake not to tell people the details. Ally's openness with Ivy only confirmed our decision. I'd tell the kids one day, but that day would be mine to choose.

"What were you thinking, Ally?" I asked, shifting from the past. "Just last week, Ivy sunbathed topless. Now you condone clothes like that? You're not her mother."

"And you're not mine, Sis."

I surveyed Ally Jo hard, and her eyes dared me to bring the argument. I wasn't her parent, but she had no damn problem putting me in the surrogate role now that Mother kicked her out.

"I'm Ivy's aunt, and what she seems to need these days is a buddy."

"Well, I'm her mother. My job is to keep her straight. I make sure she goes into the world equipped for whatever life dumps on her. There are enough victims out there."

Ally leaned on the counter. "She has to feel good about herself. You're too hung up on what people think."

I lobbed a rag toward Wayne to dry his hands, and then I pulled out the potatoes. They clunked into the sink as he stepped back. "There are rules, Ally," I said, jerking the knife drawer open. "Why can't you respect them, or at least ask my opinion before you attempt to experiment on my child?"

Wayne thrust a beer in Ally's hand. "Come outside and help me cook the burgers while Slade gets the fries ready."

Ally grabbed the barbecue utensils and marched out. Wayne turned at the patio door and mouthed, "It's okay."

Potatoes peeled in record time, skins stuck to both sides of the sink and up on the counter's edge. As the fryer heated, I poured a root beer over ice and tried to chill. By the time Wayne finished the burgers, I'd collect my wits.

I was right about holding Ivy to a standard, even if she hated me for a while. Ally had no children. The buddy part was easy. Mothering was the bitch.

Fries draining on a paper towel, I sprinkled Cajun seasoning on the wedges when I heard a muffled shout from outside. "Slade?" shouted Wayne again. Then he opened the door. "You better get out here."

I turned off the fryer and wiped my hands. "What?"

"The driveway. Hurry."

I ran outside and around the house to see Ally's car backing up. Ivy came out on the front porch.

"Ally!" I yelled. "What are you doing?"

"Finding a place where people aren't so judgmental," she hollered from her window. Her right front tire left a rut in my flower bed as she miscalculated the turn.

"Ally!" I hollered and ran, trying to keep up so she'd hear me. "Ally Jo. Listen!" She turned onto the road and ran the stop sign before heading east.

"I hate you," screamed Ivy at me from the sidewalk. "She's the best relative in the whole damn family, and you chased her off." She slammed the front door.

Panting from the run, I returned to the patio where Wayne still stood with his mouth agape. "What did you say to her?" I asked. Did Ivy just say *damn*?

He raised his hands in the air, a spatula in one. "Absolutely nothing. She wouldn't talk to me. I tried to make her lighten up, but she wasn't having it. The next instant she slid back in the house, returned with her keys and a bag, and started her car."

I pushed strands of hair tinged with sweat from the August humidity behind my ears. "Guess that's one less for dinner." She could be moody. She'd get over it.

Back in the house, I gathered paper plates and napkins with nervous hands. Ivy cried in her room. Zack returned to his perch on the back of the sofa, fixated on his game.

"Y'all fix your plates when you're ready to eat," I quietly told Zack. "The fries are here. There's no salad. Eat wherever you like." Then I poured more root beer and walked outside to the dock, a family picnic now the furthest thought from my mind.

A few moments later, Wayne sat beside me with a second plate of food. "Here, eat. Where do you think she went?" he asked, snagging one of my fries.

"Have no idea," I sighed. "She wouldn't go to her ex or our parents' place." Ally was between jobs, one of the casualties of her divorce, not that her job at the mall held a future. No telling how little money she had. We were light years different in personality and miles apart socially, but Ally Jo was my only sister.

"Give her a cooling period, at least until tomorrow," he said, rubbing my back.

"She doesn't want to hear from me." I threw a fry on the water. Two bream darted in, nabbing bites, bouncing the morsel like a fishing bobber.

Wayne threw another. "I'd kill to hear from my sister."

"Apples and oranges," I said, watching the fry float away. "Ally isn't a drug addict."

"We all have our demons, Slade."

Chapter 9

THE WEEKEND passed without any word from Ally. She didn't take my fourteen calls. I wasn't so much concerned about her anger as I was where she'd landed. Sunday night I threw myself upon the kindness of my neighbors, the Amicks, to keep an eye on Zack and Ivy during the upcoming work week. The surrogate grandparents eagerly accepted. They idolized my kids, a blessing since my parents lived over a hundred miles away in Charleston.

Ally's abrupt departure left a hole in the household. Her sunshiny disposition had elevated spirits this last week as she concocted new recipes, worked makeup magic on Ivy, and uncovered codes to save brave new worlds on Zack's electronic games. Now Ivy's lip stuck out like bad Botox. Zack found his sister highly amusing, which only escalated her pouty performance. All my fault, according to her. By now I felt uncomfortable enough to shoulder some of the blame. If Ally came home I'd tell her over a beer . . . maybe throw in a hug.

Alone in the midst of rush hour, I reached the conclusion Ally was more good than bad for Ivy. So how could I sell that to my daughter, bridge the gap between us, and save face?

At the office, Monroe Prevatte waylaid me as I exited the elevator, and we walked down the hall to my section. "What case you working on?" he asked.

I glanced furtively about the hall.

He grinned. "Covert stuff, huh?"

"Actually, yeah." I unlocked my door. "Come in for a minute."

He pushed the door closed behind us as I put my keys and purse away. "Me first," he said. "It's not my business unless you want it to be, but—"

"But what?" I asked.

"Harden Harris is snooping around," he said.

Monroe was a gentleman. Some days I felt rather derelict relying on such an intense affection when I had no plans to take it further. But I loved Monroe as a buddy and couldn't imagine work without him.

He always took up for me, or kept an eye out for who wasn't.

I stole a look out the tenth story window. What I wouldn't give to leave the building and spend the day gossiping with Monroe, eating lunch at that basement coffee shop on Main Street he liked so much, where we could solve the government's problems as if we held all the cards. Harden wasn't a new adversary; he always pried into my work but usually waited until I was out of town. Seemed he was growing bolder. "He's graduated from annoying to pursuing a vendetta because I cost his buddies their jobs in Charleston."

Monroe shrugged. "Thought you should know."

I spun my chair back toward him. "Thanks. I appreciate it."

He stood. "Well, I'm flying out to DC this afternoon, so I have three days' worth of phone calls and reports to do before I lift off. Wanted to give you fair warning about your nemesis." He paused. "Wayne helping on this one?"

"Yeah," I said. "Have fun on your trip. Don't do anything I wouldn't do."

"Somehow I don't think that's a problem," he said with a chuckle and left.

I scanned the city skyline, then studied folks below in Finley Park. In August, summer camps and daycares often brought children to play around the lake and fountain, tossing balls and Frisbees across the huge eighteen-acre span of grass. Couples lay on blankets. People frolicked in the sun, not realizing others spied from above through faceless windows. Nameless, silent, invisible.

Invisible indeed. Time to leave the office and drive toward Pelion. I knew someone who may have been silently watching Lamar Wheeler. Maybe not from ten flights up, but most certainly under his nose.

As I turned onto the black asphalt drive of the Wheeler farm shortly after ten a.m., I caught sight of a six-row Amadas digger turning peanuts behind a John Deere tractor. Usually fun to watch, the equipment dug down, lifted and overturned the plants, depositing underground peanuts on top of the soil. Why did people get so much satisfaction from watching machinery perform?

The rows were amazingly even, downright pretty. These days GPS systems synchronized those geometrically straight rows. Hungry birds danced and dived behind the digger, feeding on exposed bugs and peanuts.

In five or six days, once the peanuts dried, hired hands would put a combine in the field. An auger collected those pods off the ground and shot them into a container trailer as air blew through them. Cold storage then helped maintain a specific moisture level.

This impromptu visit on enemy territory was a hazardous chance on my part, and I sucked in ten deep breaths to clear my head and settle down. If I moved quickly enough, I could ask my questions and haul buggy without detection, like those blackbirds behind the digger. If Lamar was half the farmer his reputation purported, he'd be on the farm, not in the house.

I parked in the circular drive under the oaks, unannounced. Admiring the equally synchronized flower beds, I walked up the steps and rang the bell.

Lucille answered the door in tan cropped pants, a sea foam-green print button blouse, and tiny pearl earrings. She leaned on a softwood pine cane that sported a cream-colored handle. The woman collected canes like others hoarded shoes.

"Ms. Slade," she said, her chin firm and slightly raised. "Lamar isn't home. You should've called."

Holding down nerves, I stood tall. "Actually I was hoping to see you, ma'am."

"Is that so?" Her voice, stern and age-crackled, gave no doubt as to her displeasure. She held the door in check, open only a few inches.

I pointed toward the nearest flowers off the porch, ablaze with salmon, white, and hot pink blooms. "Your impatiens sure handle the heat well. I wish I had half your green thumb. Even a pinky's worth."

"It's all in the soil."

I nodded. "The dirt at my place is hard as rock. Heck, it *is* half rock."

The door eased open further, and my jitters backed off a notch. "Sounds like you have your work cut out for you." She stood still as a storefront Indian . . . measuring me.

"Ms. Haggerty, may I please come in?" I asked, now going for the direct approach. The smear campaign on CJ's name appeared on last night's evening news and this morning's edition of *The State* newspaper. "I don't agree with the media releases that those drugs were CJ's."

At the mention of her beloved grandson, her forehead softened, easing wrinkles. Any fool could see the effect that boy had on her, and my heart melted. She limped back and allowed me to enter. I reminded myself this covert intervention would give her peace as well.

She led me past Lamar's study toward a sitting room, and I nervously followed, feeling like such a trespasser. The ecru painted fireplace highlighted the room, showcased between two beige striped armchairs cradling powder blue pillows. Gardenias flavored the air from a bowl on the coffee table. Two *Lladro* porcelain figurines complemented the mantle. I never would have chosen dark tan paper for the walls, but the contrast worked well. The setting could master high tea and cucumber sandwiches as well as oatmeal cookies and a good book.

Once she took her seat, I settled into one of the armchairs, angled across from her. She propped her cane against the table, then entwined her thin, bony hands.

As if on cue, a short, middle-aged Hispanic woman entered the room. "You wish something to drink?"

Lucille nodded. "Two iced teas, Camellia."

The maid shuffled out. Ms. Haggerty released a well-controlled sigh. "Ask your questions, young lady."

"I know Lamar told his attorneys to release a statement saying the drugs found at the condo were CJ's."

Her brow furrowed. "Yes."

"I'd like to know your thoughts about what he's saying."

"Why?" she asked, boring holes in me. "What difference does it make? And what business is it of yours?"

I scratched my nose and repeated the line that got me in the door. "The people I work for don't believe CJ did it."

She grinned and contemplated her lap. "Bless Margaret's heart."

Margaret? "So you know Margaret Dubose?"

She observed me with her head slightly tilted, as if about to converse with a child. "She attended college with my daughter Patsy. They were friends for years before the cancer took my girl."

Camellia arrived with etched glasses of tea, a small pitcher, and shortbread cookies on a saucer. Once she served us, our drinks on strategically placed coasters, she left.

Ms. Haggerty readjusted to better reach the drink on her end table. She hardly dented the chair cushion. "Margaret knows this family, Ms. Slade. I have lunch or dinner with her once a month, to relive old times, to vent, to speak to someone who remembers when this family had *substance*."

I stopped with my glass halfway up. Her despondent tone touched me. How pitiful to live over seven decades only to see your family rise and then crumble, the youngest heir to predecease you.

"How long ago did your daughter pass away?" I asked.

She lifted a cookie with an unsteady hand. "Eight years last week."

Dang. The anniversary of her daughter's death and her grandson's funeral in the same week. No wonder Lamar drank so hard and was so devastated. I was surprised Lucille didn't appear more spent, then I deduced she might be stronger than all of them.

"Margaret is a dear," she said. "She and Patsy shared everything for twenty years. Even when Margaret's career climbed, she stayed in touch with us. It was so nice when she moved back to Columbia."

A whole new layer to my boss's world. She spoke little of her personal life other than to say her parents were dead and she had no other family.

"Margaret's like my own daughter." Lucille coughed, set her glass down with a clunk, the shake in her hand more prominent.

"You okay?" I asked, leaning forward.

She waved me back. "Just went down wrong." She cleared her throat once, then twice. "I'm old, Ms. Slade."

"Don't let me upset you."

"I'll tell you when you do."

Grinning for her benefit, I feared digging deeper for details. She acted tough, but age trumped stubborn, and I knew little of her health. I'd come this far, though, and now stood so close to learning more about this family's motives. "Well then, ma'am, with that in mind, do you think Lamar is telling the truth? I mean, about the drugs."

She snapped to attention. "No, I don't. CJ was a good boy. His mother raised him well. He was only ten when liver cancer took her."

"She was an alcoholic?" I asked.

"Absolutely not!"

"Sorry," I said, and lifted my tea in an attempt to regain the cooperating mood.

"Patsy parented CJ wisely and lovingly," she continued, "and she laid the groundwork for her son's standards. In spite of Lamar."

A shudder ran across my back. How easily I could have died in Charleston, leaving my ex to raise Ivy and Zack without me.

"He didn't know how to raise a child," Lucille said. "He only wanted to run this damn farm." She breathed heavier as the obviously worn topic seemed to weigh on her. "I was wishing he'd go to jail and lose the place. It already killed my daughter, so he says."

"I thought she died of cancer."

"She did," she said, staring at her plate. "From aflatoxin."

I flinched. Surely not. Anyone in agriculture knew the industry controlled moisture levels of peanuts to stay ahead of aflatoxin. Inspectors checked each peanut truck for the highly toxic mold before markets would accept the crop. To the best of my knowledge, nobody in the US had ever died of it.

I pondered whether to ask more, worried I'd already pushed too hard. But Lucille said she'd stop me if I did. "What makes you think that?"

"Does it matter?"

"No, ma'am. Guess it doesn't." I stood, almost ashamed, sort of scared of what she'd said. People didn't die from aflatoxin. The poor woman just needed to place blame somewhere. On that note, I figured it was time to leave. "Well, Margaret sent me to check on you." I touched her hand. "Anything else you feel a need to tell us?"

"Just say I appreciate her concern."

Her color seemed leached, her complexion paler than when I arrived. I wanted to feel her forehead. She reached for her cane but didn't stand. Instead, she gripped it with both hands in front of her, rubber tip digging into the beige and pastel oriental carpet.

"Mrs. Haggerty, you don't look well."

The sound of heavy footsteps approached from down the hall. I glanced at the doorway and then at Lucille, the chance to run slim. A slight trace of fear shone in her eyes, and I chose to sit and face the jury.

Dressed in work jeans and a button-up, short-sleeved denim shirt, Lamar did a double take when he appeared. "My brother told you to back off," he said, fists forming.

Oh, crap.

"Agriculture has an interest in this farm," I said, my voice shaking.

"And I'm the farmer, not her." He hit the doorframe with his palm. I jumped. "We're trying to get past this shit, don't you understand?" His voice rose to a crack on the end.

Lucille tried to stand, but wavered. I rushed to her side. "What's wrong, ma'am?"

She slumped to the floor. Quickly to my knees, I cradled her head. "Call an ambulance."

Lamar stared wide-eyed, hands locked in his hair.

I stretched over and snagged my purse, grabbed my cell, and dialed 9-1-1.

The farmer knelt beside Lucille. He gripped my wrist. "Go on, woman. I'll take care of my own family."

"Mr. Wheeler, let me—"

He snatched the phone from my hand, stood, and strutted across the room. He explained who he was and said he'd be the one handling Lucille's situation.

My mouth fell open. I tried for a second to put myself in his place, but Lucille seemed so alarmed when he walked in. I knelt back down next to her.

"Can you send a deputy as well?" he told the operator. "I have a trespasser who may have caused the medical emergency."

"What?" I exclaimed. Oh geez. Please let them not take him seriously.

He nodded as the person on the other end apparently told him what he wanted to hear.

Mrs. Haggerty's hand held mine in a tight grip. The clock ticked too fast. If this was indeed a stroke, she had sixty minutes to reach a hospital and receive the proper drugs to diminish long-term damage. Sparring with Lamar didn't help her, him, or me, so I continued watching Lucille, hoping he didn't shove me out the door. Instead, he paced the room like a caged animal.

EMS arrived along with a patrol car. I backed away as the paramedics rushed in and went to work on her. A middle-aged uniformed officer stepped in and nodded at Lamar. Then he closed his hand around my arm.

"Wait," I said, blood racing. "I was helping. We were having tea, for God's sake!"

"Make her leave, Bob," Lamar said. "She was interrogating my mother-in-law without an invitation. When I ordered her to leave, she refused. Then Lucille got upset and collapsed." He raised his arms, hands clenched, and yelled, "I can't deal with this right now. Would you please just get her out of here?"

The officer tilted his head toward the front door. "Come with me, ma'am."

For the sake of less chaos, I did as instructed, as if I could break loose. His fingers might be pudgy, but they worked just fine squeezing my arm.

He reached over and turned down the static on his radio before refocusing on me. "The paramedics will take care of her. My job is you. Come with me."

Chapter 10

THE DEPUTY manhandled me off the Wheeler's front porch and stopped in the circular drive, me on my tiptoes. Even twenty years my senior, the man's firm grip proved he still played the game well. "Mr. Wheeler says you're trespassing. Tell me why I shouldn't take you in."

"Mrs. Haggerty invited me in, Bob," I said, noting his name badge.

He studied me, one eye narrower than the other. "I saw the tray of cookies and extra glass for you, so don't get riled. Lucille ain't gonna entertain Lamar with crystal and china." He motioned his head toward the highway. "Just make me happy, drive away, and don't return. Deal?"

"I can do that."

Once I flopped into the front seat of my G-car, I enjoyed the sense of relief, letting the engine run, air conditioning on high. I was probably overreacting, but why did Lucille tense up when Lamar arrived? Maybe he didn't trust her to keep quiet about CJ's habit; maybe Lamar was the pill popper. Or maybe Lamar felt too damn culpable for what he'd done to his own son.

Grief and anxiety no doubt drove Lucille's words about her daughter's death. Aflatoxin. Silly. Farmers couldn't afford such rumors. A Salmonella scare several years ago all but paralyzed the peanut industry and cost the market and farmers millions of dollars. What fool would announce to the world that a government inspector traced a toxic mold to his crop? Nobody fell on their swords anymore.

Regardless, I was grateful Officer Bob didn't feel spunky enough to lock me up. I remembered Ally and dialed her again. No answer. "Call me," I said to voicemail.

I stopped for a chocolate chip milkshake at a drive-thru Dairy Queen to calm down. After dwelling on farm product contamination for the last couple hours, I decided to forego anything touching peanut oil. I'd sworn off barbecue for months after the hog case in Charleston. But it didn't take me long to crave a Little Pigs pork sandwich with mustard barbecue sauce and three dill pickles. If I shied away from every food product I knew a secret about, I'd be starving and fifty pounds lighter.

Back at the office, Lucille's condition ate into my peace. I rather liked the lady.

My phone buzzed. Dubose's secretary. "Slade? She wants to see you."

I threw on lipstick and checked my hair. Two minutes later I sat across the table from my boss.

"Why didn't you tell me about Lucille?" she asked, frustration evident in pink cheeks.

Her instant knowledge of my morning brought me up short. "I . . . I just got back." I glanced quickly to Dubose's desk as if some clue atop her files might enlighten me. "She fell ill right in front of me, but Lamar wouldn't let me stay and find out her status. Have you heard anything?"

Dubose left her seat and walked to the window where she sorted most issues. "She had a stroke, Slade. She can't speak. They're working on her." She returned to the table and leaned on the back of a chair. "What the hell happened? The police had to escort you out of the house?"

"It's not what it seems." Funny, I'd said that twice today. I replayed the event for her.

Dubose sighed, as if I'd caused the collapse of the American dollar, the stock market, and the entire housing industry. Then she rolled the chair from the table and eased into it. "Governor Wheeler's pissed."

Her use of a vulgar expression took me aback. What the hell did she expect? The Governor had said to leave his family alone. We . . . I didn't. "What did he say?"

"I was the third person he spoke with. After Lamar and Lamar's attorney. Dick asked why I hadn't dropped the issue after he instructed me to." Her brow knitted. "Good grief, Slade, I ordered you to be discreet."

I had to bite my tongue. "I didn't know she would collapse, and I wasn't expecting Lamar to waltz in."

"Meeting her at the house was plain stupid," she said. The executive chair rocked harder than usual.

I rested elbows on the table, not happy either. "I'm sorry events turned out the way they did, but I did as you *ordered.*"

She pondered my words. "Let me think about this. I'll touch base with you tomorrow." She shook her head, biting her bottom lip. "Right now I've got to see Lucille . . . if they'll let me."

I stood and left. Outside, I marveled at the day gone askew. For doing nothing wrong, why did I feel like I'd launched a nuclear missile?

DUBOSE DIDN'T come to work the next morning.

With Monroe gone on assignment and Wayne on a case in Chester County, I lunched alone. After nabbing a chicken salad on wheat from the canteen, I left the building and joined the ranks milling around Finley Park. However, I chose to relax on a swing under the maples, out of sight of those watching from neighboring office windows.

My feet tapped the cement walkway, keeping the chair in motion, as I nibbled my sandwich and worried, in spite of the nurturing greenery. Mockingbirds called, copying the finches, the noise coupled with slow motion traffic up Laurel Street and across Assembly.

I was almost ready to ask Wayne about how to run Ally down. Eventually Mom would call, asking for an update on how I tended to my sister, or to make sure we hadn't killed each other, and I had no idea what to say.

Feeling the need to do penance, I opted to walk up five flights of stairs. Then I took the elevator the next five floors, vowing to tackle all ten flights by October, like Monroe. Maybe I'd drop a few pounds by Christmas.

Dubose's secretary met me in the hall. "Mr. Harris wants to see you."

I scoffed playfully with her. "We can't always have what we want, Angela." I headed toward my office.

Six inches shorter than me, she almost jogged to keep up. "Slade, he's acting State Director."

I stopped. "Where's Dubose?"

"She went on leave. It all happened right after you left for lunch."

Six of us in the state office held the same rank, putting us on the level of cabinet members to the state director. To be fair, Dubose rotated the privilege of operating in her stead when she was on vacation or ill. To the best of my knowledge, she was neither.

Damn it. It must be Harris' week.

"Where's Dubose now?" I asked, my senses tingling.

Angela rested her hand on my forearm. "We don't know. She left me a message to put her on leave for at least two weeks. That's what she said, *at least*. That's not like her."

"No, it's not."

I walked toward the main office. I could handle Harden's ego, even endowed with temporary power. Angela coughed and spoke softly. "Crap hit the fan while you were at lunch, Slade. A guy from the US attorney's office met with Mr. Harris, then they asked me to find you ASAP."

Fear shot through me at Harden capitalizing on the change so soon, but I masked my concern. "Well, let's go see what he wants. It can't be too bad. Might be a case I need to testify for or some issue of another agency that spilled onto us. What makes you think anything hit the fan?" I asked.

She glanced nervously down the hall. "Because he had me call Washington," she whispered. "About you."

I left Angela staring at my back as I marched to Harden's makeshift kingdom, formerly Dubose's dignified inner sanctum. I knocked on the door and entered without permission.

Harden had already made himself at home behind Dubose's mahogany desk, the professional aura sucked from the room by the fat man's cheap-dressed presence.

"Are you looking for me?" I asked, then stutter-stepped, stunned Angela had omitted the fact the assistant US attorney hadn't left yet. The gray-suited man stood in respect. Harden didn't.

Amazing what can happen in an hour.

"We have an issue," Harden said, gnawing on an unlit Corona. Smoking wasn't allowed in the building, but Harden needed his pacifier.

"Have a seat," he said. "We've had a breaking situation that merits your attention."

My wings clipped by the visitor's presence, I sat in a chair opposite the suit. It didn't take a genius IQ to know nothing good would come from this meeting. "Angela said you needed me. Where's the state director?"

"So we're on the same page, I'm state director for the time being." His chest puffed like a bantam rooster, and if he'd been on his feet, he would've hitched up his pants. "Your incident at the Wheeler farm has everyone stirred."

"Okay." I knew better than to elaborate. With a sense of an incoming artillery barrage, my alert burst through orange to red, waiting for consequences to rain on my head. I wouldn't volunteer the coordinates.

The visitor spoke up. "Ms. Slade, I'm John Mason from the US attorney's office."

I remained respectfully silent.

He interrupted his own pause when I didn't reply. "Lamar Wheeler's attorney contacted DEA," Mason said, "who in turn contacted us."

"Wait a minute," I blurted, unable to keep a lid on my mouth. "The cops escorted me away from the Wheeler house due to a misunderstanding. I was visiting with Lucille Haggerty. We'd just had tea, for Christ's sake. Lamar burst in; Lucille collapsed."

Harden's smile tilted his corpulent face up on one side as he enjoyed the moment. "Either you were on government business, or you were socializing on the government's nickel. You can't have it both ways."

Wincing at Harden's crude Chicago mobster tactics, Mason continued. "DEA is accusing this agency of obstructing an official investigation."

I drew my shoulders back. "DEA concluded its investigation when they presented its findings to the grand jury and won an indictment. How could I obstruct a completed investigation having tea with a sweet old lady who was neither a witness nor defendant?"

Flaming frog fat, I'd feared this when Dubose ordered me to keep snooping. If she walked in the room now, I swear, I'd dump the whole damn mess in her lap. But I wouldn't have that luxury, and instead, floundered in deep water with no land in sight. "Besides, we have a right to visit the farm and protect the government's interest," I added.

Was that a smirk on Mason's face?

"Call it what you like, Ms. Slade, but Dubose has orders to take a leave of absence. Both of you will stay away from the Wheelers and their farm until DEA concludes its work."

Harden thrust forward, his chair groaning at the massive weight shift. "How the hell do you perform a risk analysis by speaking to Wheeler's mother-in-law anyway?"

Busted. If I said Dubose told me to investigate, I gave her up, when in actuality the visit was solely my idea. If I said I was snooping about CJ and drugs, then I incriminated myself of doing exactly what they suspected, interfering with somebody else's federal investigation. More than frog fat was about to burst into flame.

"She invited me in. And then Lamar showed up," I said.

"I'm just delivering the complaint," said Mason. "Are you guilty of obstruction? No. But your involvement and representation of the agency gives defense counsel an argument to weaken our prosecution. To a jury, the government is the government." He let that settle on me before adding, "We don't work for a governor."

No joke, but he didn't get hog-tied into this deal like I did.

"Regardless," Harden said triumphantly, "you're on paid leave for the week, until we decide whether or not to make it unpaid."

Heat rose in my face. "You haven't even warmed that chair yet, and you're disciplining me?"

Mason rose. "Sorry to meet under such circumstances, Mr. Harris." The men shook hands. The attorney turned to me. "Ms. Slade." With my hand gripped in his, he asked, "Don't you know Senior Special Agent Wayne Largo?"

"We're good friends."

He nodded and left, probably as anxious to go as I was to see him gone.

Wayne would hear about this underground before I had a chance to tell him. Fantastic.

I faced Harden. "Revenge is sweet?"

"You two skirts fucked up," he said, sucking hard on the wet cigar end. "Like I always knew you would."

Creep. "Have you spoken to the *head skirt*, by any chance?" I said. "Don't forget you have to answer to her when she returns."

"Dream on, sweet cheeks." He strutted around the desk and opened the door wide.

I scowled at him on the way out.

He laughed behind me. "That bitch ain't coming back."

Chapter 11

I TOOK MY LEAVE and exited the federal building as Harden ordered, heels punching the concrete on my way to the parking garage. I'd been banned from speaking to any of the Wheeler family, by the Governor and now the federal government. As much as I wanted to blame Harden, as much crap as he loved stirring for my benefit, most of this calamity fell on Dubose's shoulders. The only good thing about all this was that my assignment was more assuredly dead now. My foot abused the gas pedal as I headed home.

A flashing blue light lit up my rearview mirror at Malfunction Junction, where three interstates merged at the edge of Columbia. Shit. All I needed was a ticket to top off my day.

Moments after I pulled over, I met the gaze of a baby-faced state trooper through the window. He studied the backseat as I lowered the glass. "Ma'am, do you realize how fast you were going?" he asked in that dull monotone reserved for traffic violators.

Embarrassed and flustered, I couldn't decide on a yes or no answer. I handed him my license and registration and fought a pout.

"You were obviously in a hurry," he said.

I let my frustrations run. "My boss left, and they put an idiot in her place. The jerk's first act was to send me packing. My brain is cottage cheese right now." I slumped in my seat, heavy-hearted at the sound of the words. "Just write the ticket."

"One moment, please," He walked back to his vehicle and called somebody. Shortly, he returned. "Who in your family is a federal agent?"

I sat up. "My boyfriend. Why?"

"The sticker on your bumper says Federal Law Enforcement Training Center."

My cheeks reddened at the memory of Wayne tagging my car with the decal.

The trooper flashed a reserved grin. "Here," he said, handing me his business card. "No ticket. Just a warning to collect yourself before driving and a request for your boyfriend to call me. I'm trying to break into the federal sector."

"Thanks," I said, briefly wondering if he'd be willing to pull Harden over for me this evening as part of that deal. I smiled as if the trooper had fixed my day.

As the silver and blue cruiser eased around me back into traffic, I speed dialed Wayne.

"Hey, Babe," he said on the answer.

Hearing his voice made me painfully aware he was too far away to stroke my hair and instill a feeling of worth to my bruised ego. Anger rose as I recognized my weakness for validation.

"What's wrong?" Wayne asked. "You're thinking too hard on what to say."

"Before I forget, thanks for the bumper sticker on my truck."

He gave a short laugh. "Got pulled over, huh?"

"Yeah, and that was the *bright* spot of my day."

"So what else—"

"Dubose is gone. Harden's in her place. The moron placed me on admin leave for my participation in the Wheeler deal."

"Tried to warn you, Butterbean."

"You don't know the half of it. A deputy threw me out of Lamar's house this morning."

"You are kidding, right?"

My nails made creases along the steering wheel. "No, I'm serious as a pregnancy test."

He went silent. "Slade?"

"No, I'm not pregnant. Stick to what I'm saying." A MINI Cooper blew by my parked butt, and I imagined running over the damn thing with my F-150. "Assistant US Attorney Mason says hello. And please call Patrolman . . . whoever, his name's on his card . . . to make sure I don't get a ticket. I was doing eighty-five, and he was understanding about it."

"How many levels of law enforcement did you piss off?"

Chewing the inside of my cheek, I attempted to construct sensible sentences of explanation. I couldn't. "If you want to come to the house and be sweet, you're invited. If you plan to bring a lecture, don't bother."

His sigh blew heavy into the phone, and I could picture his expression. "Go home and have a glass of wine, Slade. Give me an hour to finish here, and I'll bring home some enchiladas."

"Fine," I said, too mad to be gracious. "If you're late, I'll be drunk."

"I won't be, and you better not be."

Knowing he was coming by later, however, slowed my chaotic mental replay of the day. I eased into traffic and headed southwest toward Catfish Cove, each mile reducing the kink in my back. Being home early, we could enjoy a family meal even if a restaurant fixed it. Sitting around a table with everyone seemed the best way to end the day.

Wine sounded delicious, too, and last weekend, the paper said Kroger featured hot chips on sale for a buck a bag. I swung into the grocery store lot at the Irmo exit, collected chips, a six-pack of Wayne's favorite beer also on sale, and a bottle of Chardonnay. Once I topped my gas tank, I took the two-lane home in lieu of the interstate. Thankful every day that I built on the lake, I looked forward to gym shorts and bathing suit top and taking my personal pity party to the dock.

My house emerged through the trees and across the water long before I rounded the cove and reached the drive. I glimpsed Zack stretched out on the grass in the backyard, with what could only be binoculars pressed to his face.

"Not again," I grumbled as the truck entered the asphalt drive. The kid was too young for serious hormones. However, the earlier episode of Ivy's friend semi-nude on her porch had roused the beast in him.

An Impala sat in the curve halfway down the five hundred-foot drive under the shade of maples, out of Zack's sight. The driver started the car and led me home. She parked where I usually did. I eased in beside it, every muscle taut.

Pamela got out in sunglasses, all cop-like.

Zack bolted into the house. I gathered my purse and groceries and walked past Pamela as if she stood invisible. At the end of the driveway, I stepped into the yard to where I could see the neighbor's porch. Ivy and Starr were scrambling their tanned behinds into shorts.

First things first. I turned toward Pamela and her smirk.

"Glad I don't have kids," she said.

I gripped the six-pack and fought the impulse to clock her upside the head with it. "What do you want?"

Leaning on the Impala, she crossed one boot over the other, like Wayne did. She fit her beige slacks like some damn Olympic gymnast. A black vest complemented a short-sleeved T-shirt. Her badge winked at me in the sun. "Came to see if we could reach an understanding."

"Was there a *mis*understanding?"

She glanced at her watch. "Since when do paper-pushers get home at two in the afternoon, or are you on some unique work schedule designed for . . . what is it . . . special project representatives?"

I glowered at her. "And how did you know to be here this time of day? Or do you enjoy watching adolescent asses face up in the sun?"

"Oh please," Pamela said, her head dipped sarcastically. "After talking to the US attorney, I called your boss . . . um, your new boss. What a guy. He'd tell me he was screwing a nun if I mentioned my badge. So cooperative."

"You can strut your ass right off my property." I headed toward the door off the garage, the shortcut to my kitchen. Crap, locked. The kids were using the sliding door to come and go. As I inserted my key, I heard her footsteps behind me.

Beer in the crook of my arm and bag in a loose grip, I spun around, clipping the door frame with the wine bottle. It fell through the bag, busting on the cement, atop my hot chips.

"Damn it!" I threw the ripped bag on the ground. "*You* had me sent home. What the hell is your problem? You know I did nothing to interfere with your case . . . premature and unfounded as it is."

She stooped and picked up several large pieces of glass. She salvaged the chips from under chunks of bottle and handed them to me dripping. "Where's Kay?"

The shift in subject left me speechless. Miss Thigh Master wanted Wayne's sister bad enough to cramp my reputation at work. She believed my pillow talk with Wayne included the whereabouts of his sister, when in fact, I wasn't pleased it didn't.

"I have no idea," I said, grabbing the bag.

Pam handed me a few large pieces of glass. "Don't play me."

"Says the lady who just played me."

"I'm better at it."

I scanned her perfect body for effect, which didn't take long with someone six inches shorter. "You don't know me well enough to say that."

She eyed me back. "Who's the one on leave?"

"Why did you feel threatened enough to complain to the US attorney?"

She raised her hands, as if trying to stop this runaway train we were on. "Slade, you don't understand what Kay is up against," she said, her voice no longer edgy. "I'm not trying to harm her."

The little con. "So why aren't you asking Wayne instead of me?"

"Okay, fine. Play it your way."

I noticed wine splattered over my shoes. Damn it! "Ask Wayne about his sister, not me. I have no idea where she is, which tells me Wayne doesn't know either." Then in a final shot to help me feel better, I added, "Not that I'd tell you if I knew."

I went into the garage, shutting the door between us. The dead bolt clicked loud enough to give me a small sense of satisfaction. A garage in August held enough heat to scald feathers off a chicken, so I didn't wait to hear the witch's car leave. Instead, I moved inside to the air-conditioning and set the chips in the sink. Rummaging through the refrigerator, I found no more wine, so I set the beer inside to chill and searched the cereal cabinet for the hard stuff. This day had spun into pure, unadulterated hell, warranting bourbon.

Zack hid and Ivy hadn't returned from next door, so I changed into shorts, a tank top, and flip-flops. "Zack?" I hollered. Family business needed tending.

"Ma'am?"

"Get out here."

My kid trotted out as if he'd been in his room for hours, barefoot and tousle-headed. "What you doing home so early?" he asked.

"A sixth sense told me you were up to something," I said. "What have you been doing?"

"Nothing," he said. "Ms. Amick ran to the grocery store, so I came in to get my game player. Mr. Amick's in his garden."

The kids ran back and forth amongst four houses in the cove, to include that of their daytime baby-sitters. When Ivy and Zack weren't fishing, swimming, or gardening with the Amicks, they were visiting the Baxter boys or Starr. I wouldn't be surprised if the binoculars belonged to Mr. Amick, lent to my son for bird watching.

"I saw you with the binoculars, my man. What did I tell you about stalking?"

His agitated body language told me everything. "I didn't take pictures this time, Momma."

"You still spied!"

"They shouldn't be naked," he said.

Oh, how right he was. "Get to your room," I ordered. He scurried out of sight. "And don't touch that game player," I added, reminding myself to take it away.

About the time the sound of Zack's footfalls disappeared into his bedroom, Ivy showed up at the sliding door.

She opened it awkwardly, hands full of suntan lotion, towels, phone, and assorted magazines. She slid the door shut, but before I could stomp a mud hole in her backside, she turned to face me.

"There's nothing wrong with nude sunbathing," she said. "Aunt Ally said so before you ran her off." With that, she strutted down the hall toward her bathroom.

I followed, mad she wasn't coming to stand before me. "So you've gone from topless to the whole shebang? You're not worried what idiot might drool over you and then take advantage when you least expect it? What if pictures of you made it to the Internet?"

She leaned over the bathroom sink, admiring her tan. "Aunt Ally says there's nothing wrong with full nudity in the proper setting."

"You're standing in the only proper setting," I said, my face burning.

She nudged me aside as she entered her bedroom. "There are nude beaches."

"Until you're on your own, young lady, you follow my rules, and that includes no public nudity. You have no idea what that can lead to."

She cocked a hip. "We ran around naked before."

"You were two . . . three at most! You weren't . . . sexually appealing."

Her face lit up. "You think I'm attractive?" She ran hands down her sides, as if feeling for curves, her eyes searching the mirror.

"No. I mean yes. I mean, not in the way you think." Aw, hell. I rubbed a hand over my face. "I'm going to strangle your aunt."

I recalled the times I let the phone ring, not wanting to listen to her latest soap opera. "Just wish she'd call," I mumbled.

"She did call."

I jerked my head around. "When?"

Ivy showed me her phone. "Here. This morning, see?"

The number had a 404 area code. "This isn't her."

"It was so her. She had to use somebody else's phone. Hers died, and she didn't have her charger."

I pictured my sister wandering the streets asking strangers if she could make a call. But I'd hoped she would've called me. What if this person befriended her in order to take advantage? I wrote the number down. "Don't erase that call," I said. "And you're grounded."

"Why?"

"For being outside unclothed," I said.

She huffed and puffed and sat on her bed. "That's unhealthy. Kids need Vitamin D."

I headed out of the bedroom then stopped. "I imagine you've absorbed enough Vitamin D to last you, say, about two weeks?"

"That's not fair," she shouted as I walked to the kitchen.

"Life's not fair," I shouted back. "If you want me, I'll be on the dock."

"Who would want you?" she said and slammed her door.

Her comments stuck like a knife in my heart. Indeed, not too many people wanted me these days. I opened the freezer, filled a large glass with ice, and poured a double shot of bourbon. A splash of Coke topped it off. After informing Zack he was likewise restricted to his room, I called the Amicks to relieve them of baby-sitter duties. I made my way to the dock, chips and drink in hand, flip-flops smacking the sidewalk.

A dogwood, a pine, and two maples shaded half the dock this time of day. I shed my shoes, eased my legs into the water, and chugged a third of the drink. Leaning back on one hand, I shoveled hot chips behind sips of Maker's Mark until my fingertips were red from cayenne pepper.

Wayne needed to explain this attitude his ex harbored for me. With my frustrations muted by sun, alcohol, and the gentle sway of tiny waves from the occasional boater up the cove, I let my mind drift into what Wayne and

I could be . . . and wound up thinking about Pamela.

I shifted attention to Dubose. She hadn't tried to call, which disappointed me. Did the agency actually order her to stay home? Or was it by choice? Everyone's reactions seemed exaggerated, and that both confused and intrigued me. Harden didn't count; he never knew what he was doing, and Pamela seemed hell-bent on Kay more than Wheeler. But the Wheeler family had closet secrets somehow involving Dubose. DEA jumped too quickly on Lamar's case and seemed too stubborn to admit to it, which made me wonder again, what was with the Wheelers?

I sensed the sun slide lower and the shade dissolve away. By now I was prostrate on the dock, the sun and the bourbon all but melting me through the planks into the water.

A shadow fell across me. I opened my eyes. Wayne peered down, his face about two feet from mine. "Thought I told you not to get drunk."

"I'm not," I said, sitting up.

"I smell bourbon."

"It's hot. I sweated out the alcohol."

He helped me up, and we moved to the covered part of the dock. "So fill me in," he said.

I elaborated on the way back to the house. My outdoor respite had done me good, and I relayed the details without sounding like Ivy.

Wayne brushed a leaf off my shorts. "Sounds like a helluva day, Butterbean. Might be time for me to give Pamela a call and tell her to cool her jets."

"I'd appreciate it," I said.

We walked up the hill, and upon reaching the back porch, Wayne opened the sliding glass door. The cool air drew us in. I headed toward the bedroom. A cold washcloth would bring me just enough to life to pour drinks and set the table for the Mexican food Wayne brought home.

He followed me. "Why's the place so quiet?" he asked. "Where're the kids?"

"Ivy sunbathed nude again. The whole enchilada this time," I said, then laughed at the reference to the food we were about to eat. "And Zack watched to make sure they did it right."

Wayne scowled, a slight lift to his mouth telling me he wasn't sure whether this was funny or serious business. "Are all teenage girls like this?" he said as we went back to the kitchen.

"Who knows? She's the only one I've ever had," I said. "I grounded both kids."

Ivy strutted out in shorts and a pastel shirt. Cute as a button, only I was afraid to give her the positive reinforcement.

"Aunt Ally called again," she said, showing her phone. "Same number."

I took the phone, studying the screen as if it would talk to me. "What'd she say?"

Hand on her backside, Ivy struck a pose. "I told her about the sunbathing and how you were unable to deal with it."

The familiar anger surged back. "I didn't ask what *you* said. Did she say where *she* was?"

Ivy tossed me a dramatic moan. "She said we were on the same wavelength, because she was grabbing rays just like me this afternoon . . . *sans* clothes, by the way."

"What?" I shouted. Then I wondered where my daughter learned the word *sans*. Where else? My illustrious sister.

Wayne took the phone and sorted through the history. "This it?"

Ivy leaned over and read. "Yes. She's using someone else's phone, she said."

Wayne looked up, amazed.

"What?" I asked.

"That's my sister's cell number."

Chapter 12

I HOVERED OVER Wayne's arm, trying to read the phone's face, as if that tiny screen would reveal the whereabouts of Ally Jo and Kay. "Where are they, Ivy?"

My daughter backed up at our sudden, intense interest in her phone conversations, eyes leery. "I don't know."

Wayne smiled warmly at Ivy. "Your mother is worried about your aunt. Stop and think. Did Ally say anything about where she was? Did she mention a nearby store? Go out to eat anywhere?"

"No, honest." Ivy's face threatened to crumble to tears. "I haven't done anything wrong."

"We know you haven't," Wayne and I said in unison, as I reached for her.

She jumped. The joint reply scared Ivy more. A long tear rolled down, and she hugged herself with one arm. "I said I don't know."

I drew her to me. "Okay, honey. Go get something to drink and settle down."

Once Ivy left the living room for the kitchen, Wayne's brow creased. "So Kay is still close. No wonder Pamela's sticking around. And no surprise she's making your life miserable on the Wheeler case to shake you up, and therefore me, in hopes we'll reveal info about Kay." He shook his head in wonder. "She'd definitely do something like that."

I slumped onto the sofa. Images of my sister hanging out with Wayne's crack-head sibling didn't sync in my brain. Did they spend the night in some moldy dive? Maybe Ally just happened upon Kay and asked to use her phone. I prayed it was the latter, but what were the odds of that?

Wayne sat beside me on the sofa. "I know what you're thinking. It's damn hard to believe they simply ran into each other."

"I'm thinking of my sister and yours in the same room," I said, then paused, careful to select my words. Ally Jo was a character. Her energy sucked others into her space, and her personality begged for attention. This time she may have been too magnetic for her own good.

Wayne stared, waiting for me to finish my thought.

I changed the subject. "Can't you call your sister?" Then I dropped the pretense. "Ally wouldn't know how to handle somebody like that."

"Kay won't rip her throat out, Slade."

I reached for a throw pillow, scrunching it in my lap. "I didn't mean that." Actually, I did.

"You aren't that hard to read."

Amazingly, my face didn't flush knowing he'd read my mind. I was worried, and concern was nothing to get embarrassed about.

"They aren't from the same world," I said, fighting my defensive urge. "Ally can be naïve."

He curled a long arm around me. "I'm not upset with you, Butterbean. I'm upset with my sister, your sister, and Pamela."

"Then answer me," I said. "Have you kept up with Kay? Does she still have her habit? You hold the connection. You gave her the phone, right?"

His arm fell off my shoulder. "I gave her the phone before Pamela took her on that asinine DEA sting. The account's in my name."

Before I could fuss about him holding this secret between us, he stopped me with a raised hand. "No, I haven't spoken to her. I just leave messages, like for her birthday last month. She never calls back. It was a way for me to keep a link in case of emergency . . . a way for her to get in touch when she's ready." He sifted through Ivy's phone history as he spoke. "In fact she knows not to use it much, or Pamela would eventually catch on and triangulate calls to locate her."

I leaned toward him to avoid being heard by Ivy and signaled he should keep his voice low. "Can't you get in trouble doing, what's it called, aiding and abetting?"

"No, Slade. It's called giving your sister a phone for safety. I never know where she is. Hell, I still don't."

In all our pillow talk and dockside conversations, Wayne rarely said Kay's name, much less discussed the more intricate details of why she was on the run. I'd respected that, knowing the simple mention of his sister flashed worry and pain across the bearded countenance of what usually was a laid-back, controlled hunk of a man. I'd left him alone. But now the need was obvious.

"What exactly did she do, Wayne?"

He raked his hand down over his chin. "It's what she didn't do."

In the kitchen, Ivy crackled a bag of chips. She was listening. I waited for Wayne to continue, deciding it was time for my daughter to grow up. "Go on," I said, louder, indicating with a glance toward Ivy's direction.

"Kay used drugs once upon a time," he said. "It's been almost eighteen months since I last knew she used. No dealing, ever. I'd have hauled her in myself if that were the case."

He glanced at me for reaction. I nodded.

"She thinks her dealer, a guy named Barker, shot one of his underlings."

"Thinks?" I asked.

"She was in the bathroom, heard a shot, came out, and saw Barker holding the gun over a body lying on the floor."

"Oh wow."

"Kay tried to find me," he said, "but I was out of town on another case and unavailable. She'd lost her phone service, couldn't pay the bill. So she ran down Pamela, scared shitless about what to do." He shook Ivy's phone in his hand. "That's why I gave her a phone and why I pay her bill. If I'd been there for her, the crap might not have played out this way."

While the sister subject never bothered me, I couldn't believe after a year together, we hadn't discussed her more. But with Pamela involved, maybe Wayne felt hesitant to explain. I'm not sure how I would have reacted. "Were you divorced by then?"

"Yeah, I told you how Pamela was. I played father more than husband. It was a good break, a smart decision on both our parts." He paused, as if recalling the past properly. "But Pamela wanted the collar. So she worked my sister until she agreed to help DEA catch the guy. At the last minute, Kay bolted. DEA hasn't been able to nail Barker, and Pamela thinks Kay might help her fix that problem."

"So it's all about Pamela." I'd hate to have the witch after me. "Is the shooter after Kay?"

"No one knows, but what would you think if you were Kay? One minute you damn near witness a murder, the next you skip a planned sting and disappear, with maybe both sides after you."

"No wonder she won't go back to Atlanta." I settled back on my cushion. "So how did our sisters find each other? The odds are friggin' unbelievable."

"Yeah, they are."

Ivy came in, unable to completely hide the awe in her eyes. I nodded for her to go to her room. She flashed relief, until Wayne spoke up. "Wait a minute, Ivy."

She halted, fear back on her face.

"Ivy needs to return the call," he said to me. "Ally'll be more inclined to talk to her."

Ivy's mouth tightened. "I'm not a snitch."

"This is important, honey" I said.

Wayne held out the phone. "Call her. When she answers, hand the phone to me. Later you can tell her we made you do it."

"You think?" Ivy said, slowly taking the phone. "I'm her only friend."

Another stab at me.

She hit redial. "Hello? Aunt Ally? It's me."

I tried not to appear anxious in front of my daughter, but my insides churned.

Ivy watched the floor, playing with a button on her shirt as Wayne and I watched her.

"Momma asked me to call you back and ask—"

I took the phone and rose off the sofa out of reach before Wayne could grab it. "Ally Jo Slade-Smith, where in holy hell are you?"

Wayne stood, touched my elbow, and mouthed *don't mention Kay*. I nodded.

Silence filled my ear as I prayed she didn't hang up. I kept talking. "Caller ID says you're someplace in Georgia."

"Who the hell would I know in Georgia?" Ally said, sass alive in her voice. "And don't get mad at Ivy talking to me, either."

"I haven't," I said, glad for the discourse. "If it makes you feel better, she's mad at me for calling you back."

"Good."

"So where are you?"

She sniggered. "A nudist resort."

"A what?"

She laughed. "Little Miss Ivy gave me the idea. I intended to head down to Florida, but after I left your place, I wound up at a restaurant in Lexington. A lady in the booth behind me talked about something called Nudestock coming up. I wasn't letting that comment get by me. She bitched about 'those perverts' so much I made her explain. And here I am." Her snicker sounded great. At least she was happy and not depressed like I imagined. That almost made me mad at her for putting me through all the worry.

"This place is in Georgia?" I asked, playing dumb. I suspected where she was, but wanted to hear it from her to be sure.

"Bet you never knew about Clay River Resort."

"Clay what?" I asked, knowing exactly where it was. "Where's your phone?"

"I'm staying with this cool girl about my age. Quiet, but she's nice. She left her phone here while she went out to the river beach. You can't carry anything that takes pictures . . . for privacy, you know. Wait a minute."

Hand across the mouthpiece, I whispered to Wayne, "I think I know where they are. It's not far."

Wayne's relief was palpable.

I returned the phone to my ear. "Ally?"

This time she whispered. "Gotta go. She's coming back."

"She doesn't know you used her phone?"

"No. Talk later. Bye." She hung up.

I handed the pink device to Ivy. "Thanks, hon. You can go back to your room."

She hesitated. "Everything okay?"

"Much better than we thought. It's cool."

She returned a soft grin and went to her bedroom.

My other case had died on the vine thanks to Dubose's dethronement, an assignment to shoot holes in Pamela's case against Lamar Wheeler in order to clear CJ. Now I had another case, to not only find Ally but also warn Kay. In a way, I had another shot at besting Pamela, somewhat of a consolation prize for not dismantling the DEA case. My silly sister had created opportunity without the first clue of how, her usual method of functioning through life.

After hugging Wayne and pulling him to his feet, I walked to the kitchen. "Care to take a drive?" I scanned the microwave for the time. "Five o'clock. Think a nudist colony would still be open?"

He already had his keys out, heading to the garage. "So Kay *did* listen to my advice."

"What'd you tell her?"

He waved me to hurry up. "Come on. I'll explain in the car."

I shook my keys. "I'll drive. Let's go, Cowboy. Time to wrangle up some sisters."

THE AMICKS WERE put on notice in case of emergency, the kids ordered to remain inside, house locked. I wouldn't be surprised if the Amicks retrieved them before the evening was over.

Happy to know Ally wasn't wandering dank alleys or picked up by a deranged truck driver, I drove relaxed with one hand on the wheel. Classic '70s rock played on the radio, and I reached over to turn up the Doobie Brothers.

This would be the first time Wayne had a chance to see his sister in a long time. He reclined his seat. I just hoped she was as relieved to see him.

"Good thing Ally took off in a snit after all, huh?" I said.

"Kind of seems that way." He relaxed with a smile beneath his beard. "I suggested in a voicemail that Kay go to a nudist place, or something that obscure. Just hated her always running."

"How did you . . ."

"You told me about it in the parking garage, right before I took you to dinner this week. Who'd think to search there?"

"Nobody," I said. "Good call."

"I'm glad she listened, which is a huge plus in itself. Now, maybe I can talk her home."

The August sun shined with a fluorescence that only enhanced our contented anticipation. Harden Harris couldn't ruin this moment. His disciplinary action enabled me to spend time making amends with my sister and finding Wayne's. This was excellent family stuff. One day soon we'd laugh and talk about the lemonade we made from all our lemons.

"She'd quit using last I saw her," Wayne said after a couple miles of quiet.

"That's what you said."

He was nervous, a bit excited. I tried to ease his mind. "Ally would've noticed if she was, I think. The fact she's staying with her is a good sign."

"Yeah," he replied, though we suspected Ally wouldn't recognize a drug addict if one approached her tripped out and bleary-eyed, offering her a hit. "Kay drove me nuts for three years, maybe four," he said. "When our folks died, Dad from pancreatic cancer and Mom from a heart attack six months later, Kay sank into that crap. She and Mom were close. Dad called her his baby girl."

My dad called me baby girl, too. I rested a hand on Wayne's thigh and patted once, happy to finally hear this history. But I knew the truth was Wayne had no idea what to expect when we came face to face with his sister.

We reached the midpoint across the Lake Murray Dam when I glanced again in the rearview mirror. "That car's familiar to me."

Wayne lowered the visor and studied the view behind us through the vanity mirror, then the passenger mirror. "Dammit."

"It's Pamela, isn't it?" I asked.

"Yep."

"So what do we do now?"

"Turn around."

I sighed. "Let me get to the other side of the dam first. You want to stop for pizza or chicken wings? I refuse to give your ex-witch the satisfaction of knowing she screwed up our plans."

WE PARKED, ENTERED the restaurant, and found a booth. The waitress set our appetizer on the table when I noticed the bitch at the entrance, scanning the crowd.

Pamela spotted us, sidled up to our table, and removed her sunglasses. She bumped her hip against Wayne who moved over in the booth.

"I'd offer you a bite, but you might take it, along with my arm off to the shoulder," I said, wishing my eyes were lasers.

She released one of those silent laughs of arrogance.

"What do you want, Pamela?" Wayne asked, his tone flat and cold as I'd ever heard.

She lifted a celery stick and dipped it in my ranch dressing. Her tongue licked a drip before she bit off a chunk. She aimed the piece in her hand at Wayne. "Earlier today, your girlfriend told me to talk to you about Kay, so here I am."

I wanted to slap her.

"No," Wayne said.

"No what?" Pamela asked. "She didn't tell you, or you won't say where Kay is?"

He lifted his tea glass. "I don't do games." He took a long sip, then another.

She rested her chin on the palm of one hand and waited for him to finish. "Seriously, she can help us run down Barker."

"Nail him on another charge. I'm sure there's an assortment to choose from."

She leaned in close. "But a murder charge is so much better."

"For who?" Wayne said, challenge in his tone. "Kay never saw the crime. Hang him on something else, Pamela, instead of having an orgasm about a murder stat for your record. And this isn't his only murder, I'm sure."

She eased against Wayne, her boobs mashing on the table. "I love it when you talk dirty."

"God, you're a piece of work," I said, unable to contain my venom. This woman brought out the worst in Wayne, and I wasn't enjoying the show.

"I'll be gone when you give me Kay." Pamela rubbed a hand on Wayne's arm. Then she sat back straight, all serious, her humor evaporated. "I'll take care of her, Wayne. Promise."

He moved his arm away. "You can't guarantee that." He shifted to face her, his bulk in the booth infringing into her space enough to make her back up to the edge of the seat. Her hand gripped the table's edge for balance.

"You'd sell your soul for a good collar," he said. "I haven't seen Kay in a year. She won't call me for fear you'll draw her back into that world. She's over it. Now *you* get over it."

"If you haven't seen her, how do you know she's *over it*, Stud?"

"Get the hell away from me," he said, lines creased deep around his eyes. "And stay away from Kay."

Pamela backed out of the booth, her dignity barely scratched. She reached into her snug back pocket and extracted a business card. "Here," she said, dropping it on the table before me. "Call me if you need anything.

You're in a bind about Wheeler. I can make some of that go away."

Then she walked out.

"Oh my God," I whispered. I'd never seen so much attitude in such a compact body.

Wayne exhaled hard, his brow knotted.

"How did you marry that?" I asked.

"How did you marry Alan?" he countered.

By the time the waitress brought the wings, handmade chips, and more tea, Wayne and I were each in our own world. He toyed with one wing. I drank tea. Our dinner got cold.

"Anything wrong?" asked the waitress during one of her rounds.

"Just had a bad day," I said. "Can we get a to-go-box?"

She signed our ticket and set it down. "Sure, hon. I know those days."

"You have no idea," Wayne said, too harsh for my mother's rules of etiquette.

Our waitress scurried away, soon back with the box, knowing better than to attempt small talk.

I reached for his hand. "Wayne."

"Let's go," he said, pulling out his credentials to retrieve some cash from behind the ID. "She might be gone by now."

I scraped wings and chips into the box, sauce slopping on the table. Then I slid out of the booth, licking my fingers and snatching up napkins on the way. In an afterthought, I grabbed Pamela's business card and jammed it in my jeans pocket. "You need a beer," I said to his back. "Maybe two."

"I need a couple hours with Pamela," he growled.

Outside, Pamela leaned on her car.

"Damn her," Wayne said as we got into his.

"Just head back home," I said.

As we peeled out of the parking lot, returning to my cove, a plan took shape. If he met with Pamela, maybe I could work their head-on collision to my advantage.

Chapter 13

THE NEXT DAY I slept in until ten, same as the kids. No calls from work and no obligations, thanks to my disciplinary leave. I stretched in bed, reveling in the freedom from office minutia, less disturbed about Harden's threats with so much sunlight coming through the windows. I'd weathered worse, not that Harden wasn't trying to give it his all against me.

Suddenly the remembrance of my sister slumbering at a nudist resort with Wayne's druggie sister shattered my tranquility. I bolted upright. Time to move.

After fixing a pancake breakfast under the wary eyes of my children, I showered and called Wayne. Timing was everything in what I hoped to do.

"So what's on your agenda today?" I asked.

"I want to find Kay, but Pamela's dogging my shadow," he said, in a mood only a shade better than last night. "She's outside my apartment as we speak."

"Seriously?"

"Yep, but I called her as if she wasn't there. Told her to meet me for lunch."

"You sure moved fast on that plan," I said. "What time?"

"One. So I won't see you until tonight."

I searched for a particular Pelion phone number online as we chatted. "Oh, so you don't want me there?" I asked, knowing better.

"No, I'll handle Pamela alone this time."

"I see. How long will lunch take?"

"Have no idea, Slade. Why?"

Ah, found the number. "Just curious. She's something else, Wayne."

"This is only about the Kay situation," he said, misreading that I worried about him lunching with his ex-wife. "That's all. I figure an hour. Two if she's difficult."

I banked on two hours. Pamela's middle name was *Difficult*. From the witch's persistence, I couldn't fathom what gift of persuasion Wayne could use to back her off, but he could try. And I hoped it took a long while.

With the phone number I found online saved in my cell, I returned to the kitchen to make a pitcher of sweet tea since Zack had swilled the last of it after breakfast.

"You've got no reason to worry," he said.

"I'm not worried." I filled a pot with tap water and placed it on the stove.

"What the heck are you doing?" he asked.

I stopped and sat at the bar. "It's called multitasking, a foreign concept for men. Now what was your question?"

"You asked me the question." He went silent a moment. "What are *you* doing this afternoon? Your agenda isn't exactly teeming with appointments."

This was another one of those moments that defined us. He disliked being in the dark, and I preferred he not know the intricacies of my investigative tactics. Just because he wielded authority didn't mean he could wind me up and aim me in the direction of his choosing. We played this back and forth, truth and half-truth, saying and not saying for so long now that we saw the other coming two states away.

"Go take care of business," I said. "Call me later. I want it blow by blow."

"Who says it'll come to blows?"

I released a sarcastic laugh. "Really? After watching you two yesterday? It'll be on the six o'clock news and half the Facebook pages on the Eastern seaboard if it goes longer than thirty minutes."

"Call ya later, Butterbean."

I disconnected.

The clock read eleven. Two more calls to make.

The first went to Providence Hospital. Through trial and error last night, I traced the hospital that admitted Lucille. I said yes to being a family member, but got caught when they asked for a name. Lamar gave the nurses a list, damn him.

My second call went to Clay River Resort.

"Hello? My name is Carolina Bridges." My first name and old married surname, both with little wear, seemed a safe bet for anonymity. "I'm a bit embarrassed to ask you this," I said in a hesitant voice. "Never mind. I'll call back another day."

"Ms. Bridges, you say?" said the pleasant lady on the other end of the line. Her voice ran almost breathless in an older Marilyn Monroe way. "Your nervousness is understandable. My name is Prissy Lever, the assistant manager here at Clay River Resort. Listen, sugar, most newcomers hesitate when they call us the first time. Slow down and take a moment. I'm here to answer any questions you have. We're a big step for some people."

She came across as a genuine sweetheart, with a natural magnetism to keep me on the phone. I wondered if she was naked.

I switched the phone to the other ear and moved to my bedroom, closing the door. "I heard about your colony, and I'm single, and it's something I've always thought about," I said, attempting to sound naïve yet curious, like a sixteen-year-old asking for birth control pills.

"It's not a colony, sugar," said Prissy. "We call it a resort. We're one of many sprinkled throughout the country under the American Association of Nudist Resorts. We have a website if you're interested. It might help you understand our way of life and"—she waited as if knowing I stood on the brink of a daring decision—"we'd love to have you visit."

I wrote down the website. "What are your hours?"

"We're open for visitors until six."

My brain shot jolts of excitement at what I was doing. "Okay," I said, exhaling for Prissy's benefit, maybe a little for my own. "Can I come by this afternoon? I'm off work this week."

"Certainly," she said. "I'll show you around. You do whatever makes you comfortable. Bring two towels, just in case."

"Just in case?"

Prissy giggled. "In case you fit right in the first day and need to use them. All guests are required to carry at least one. Can't wait to meet you. I'll leave your name at the gate. Carolina Bridges, right?"

"Yes, ma'am. See you at two." I still had no concept what the towels were for.

For an hour, I vacuumed floors and folded clothes out of the dryer. I fed Madge the cat and dusted the dining room twice.

I rehearsed how to react when I saw either of the sisters, not sure how to behave if they were nude. My only image of Kay came from a ten-year-old photo Wayne kept at his place, so recognition might be iffy. As unpredictable and flighty as Ally was, she would either hug me or flip me the bird.

Kay didn't know me, so how would she trust me to be who I said I was? There was a strong chance Ally told Kay about me and already sent her packing. The more I pondered it, the more that scenario disenchanted me. Ally never could keep her thoughts or personal business to herself.

At a minimum, however, I could apologize to my sister. Hadn't figured that part out yet. Ally felt ignored and untrusted about my past, not knowing what Mom, Daddy, and I harbored about the events that led to my children losing their father. I couldn't afford for the kids to hear the details. Just couldn't. Ally, however, interpreted all this as me not wanting her in my life. After the last week, that couldn't be further from the truth. She added so much to this house.

I ran to the hall linen closet. I owned one beach towel large enough to wrap around me with confidence. A regular towel would have to serve as backup. Didn't matter. There was no way on Hell, Earth, or Heaven I would shed my clothes in front of strangers. I slept in pajamas, for goodness sake. Tried sleeping nude a few times and wound up having convoluted dreams that involved tiptoeing naked through college classrooms during final exams.

Sunglasses on and kids at the Amicks, I headed toward Pelion, a forty-minute ride of nerves. With a half grin, I suspected Wayne and Pamela were duking it out about now. I couldn't wait to hear the details tonight. All the details. What restaurant. What they ate. Did she rub his arm again? Did he let her? Did he want to wring her neck or take her back to his place?

God, why did I think this was a good idea?

I punched the radio on to erase those visuals. Singing would keep me from thinking too hard.

On the outskirts of Lexington, my phone rang, caller unknown. "Hello?"

"Slade."

My foot hesitated off the gas, then I decided to pull over at the familiar voice. "Ms. Dubose?"

"Anything new on the Wheelers?"

My heart pulsed into my temples at her audacity. "Ma'am, do you realize I've been placed on admin leave due to *your* ordering me to investigate the Wheelers?"

"Yes, I do."

Exasperation swept through me like water through a New Orleans levee. "Well, I sure as hell don't appreciate your call for an update. You screwed with my career on some stupid personal whim of yours. I deserve answers."

"Yes, Slade, you do. Can you meet me in an hour? We'll have coffee, and I'll try to explain."

The clock ticked. I needed to get to Clay River during my window of opportunity, so I eased back on the highway. "Can't do it. I have an appointment." Wasn't sure I wanted to meet her. Even if she spilled her guts, what difference would it make? State Directors placed on leave never came back.

"Two hours, then," she said. "You're a fine lady, Slade. I'd like to call you a friend. At least hear me out."

"Meet me at Gervais & Vine," I said, my anger abated by her reply. "I might be a little late." Dubose liked that place. Few people in our office would find their way midday to a Mediterranean wine and tapas bar, usually more prone to burger joints.

She didn't respond.

"Ms. Dubose?"

"Call me Margaret."

"Okay, Margaret, does that restaurant suit you?"

"Yes, it's fine. I'll see you later this afternoon."

We hung up, Dubose clearly shaken and me mad.

The phone rang again. Caller ID said Dubose, the name I'd placed on the state office number, but obviously she wasn't there. I didn't want to answer this. Being on leave, I probably could get away with letting it go to voicemail.

The tone started its last repeat. I answered, the good angel on my shoulder winning the toss. "Carolina Slade."

"I need you to report back to work," Harden said gruffly.

Harden *Almighty* Harris. I pulled over again.

I wasn't surprised he needed me. He couldn't find his butt in the dark with both hands and a flashlight. "When?"

"This afternoon."

"I'm on leave, Harden."

"Not anymore," he said.

I had predicted he would sink up to his eyeballs in alligators as acting director but not this soon. It hadn't been forty-eight hours.

"You sounded miffed at me, so I scheduled some personal appointments," I said. "This is Wednesday. How about Friday?"

"How about *now?*" he said, barking the last word as if it would crawl through the phone and fetch me.

I coughed. "Sorry, but I'm not feeling well."

"Bullshit."

"What's so all-fired important, *sir?*"

"The Governor called. He needs you in Rock Hill tomorrow. The Catawba Tribe wishes to discuss a loan for a school."

"You know I don't do loans. I do administrative investigations, internal affairs, misconduct, congressional queries."

"Well, Dick Wheeler wants you to do this, as a favor to him."

"You heard the US attorney like I did. We're feds. Wheeler's not our boss. Anyway, the last favor I did for him backfired."

"You screwed that up."

"No, I didn't. Mrs. Haggerty suffered a friggin' stroke."

"See you in the morning," he said, at what I could assume was his lame attempt at compromise.

Enough was enough. Harden took every opportunity to rake my reputation over hot coals while temporarily in charge. Or else this was his attempt at earning the Governor's favor for some future use. More than likely both. If I caved, he'd destroy me. If I fought him, he'd eventually destroy me, unless the agency put Dubose back in charge. Maybe Dubose had insight on that possibility.

"Am I being reprimanded or not? Which is it, Harden? You trust me or you don't." Then a thought came to me. "I need to run this by my attorney."

He grumbled. "Oh shit and be damned. We're dealing with attorneys now, are we?"

I shrugged, wishing he could see me do so. "You started this mess by listening to the US attorney. I'll call you tomorrow, assuming I can get some guidance this quick."

"The Governor—"

"Sorry, have to speak to counsel first."

"I could label you insubordinate."

"Not on my *own* time, *sir.*"

He hung up. I had no intention of hiring an attorney. Harden was up to something. All I could do now was stall, and hope.

My highest priority, however, was to find Ally. I started the car and pulled just shy of Clay River's gated entrance. The guy glancing out the window from the small building at the gate wore a Grateful Dead T-shirt. He smiled and then turned his attention to something back down on his desk as if giving me time. How many other people like me had hesitated in this very spot . . . at the last minute?

Was that guy wearing anything below the T-shirt?

What did a genuine nudist act like? Surely these people recognized the perverts from the naturalists, the eerie inquisitive lots from the hippies I assumed occupied this place. What if all these people were legit hippies? That meant a lot of fifty-and sixty-year-old bodies strutting, flopping, sagging around. A commune came to mind, minus the tie-dyed shirts, sandals, and ragged jeans. Well, maybe with the sandals.

Did I want to do this? The reflection in my dresser mirror each morning showed someone not too far out of shape, but definitely not toned. My hand rubbed across my belly, feeling the scar from Zack's birth, the knife wound from my last case.

Now was the time to do this, while Wayne occupied Pamela's attention.

I closed my eyes. Wayne would owe me.

Chapter 14

MY HEART THUMPED double-time as I drove up Clay River's meandering asphalt drive lined with thick evergreens and oaks. RVs, from Airstreams to tin cans, and about fifteen cars lined up five hundred yards down to the right, behind a small copse of long-needle pines. No societal favorites here. I searched intently among people scattered over a huge grassy field for Ally's shock of unkempt hair, trying to ignore all the nakedness.

Feeling foolish, my thoughts chose to make fun of me and recall Ivy in her natural state on Starr's back porch. After comments of *ick* or *gross*, would she call me a hypocrite or think me bold and cool? Young, tight bodies could speak naively about natural living and shedding the status-consciousness of clothing while the rest of us dodged mirrors to avoid seeing the sag.

What if Ally told Ivy I refused to embrace nudity? I'd argue I entered Clay River against my standards, to save my sister. If I shed clothes, which wasn't going to happen, I might send the wrong message to Ivy.

Screw it. Ivy would pass judgment no matter what. She'd reached the age where I was flawed. Period.

My front tire dropped off the road, and I hastily returned my attention to driving.

I glimpsed a sixty-something man in a Carolina Gamecock ball cap grilling outside his trailer in the shade, with nothing on but an apron and sandals, his backside slightly lighter than the rest of him. Another guy of similar age sat nearby on a folding lounge chair, beer in hand, legs sprawled wide.

They really did go Adam and Eve out here. I shoved my movie-star-sized sunglasses back up on my nose.

The road ended at the office, three-quarters of a mile from the highway. I parked and let the engine idle, the air-conditioning aiding my composure. Then in a mental do-or-dare challenge, I switched off the engine, gathered my two towels, and exited.

The simple but efficient prefab metal building resembled those erected on farms and church properties. A sign by the entrance listed allowed and disallowed items, under a banner that exclaimed, "Sixty acres of natural bliss!" Coolers, towels, picnic blankets, and tote bags accepted in the pool area. Phones, cameras, and camcorders forbidden anywhere, except with management's prior authorization. No access to the pool area with clothes. Guests must sign in at the front desk and be accompanied by members.

August and September events included High Stakes Bingo, Pig Pickin' at the Pit, Dancin' with the DJ, a volleyball tournament, and the infamous Nudestock, the concert Ally mentioned. I did a double take at a Grandparents' Day celebration and the suggestion members bring their non-nudist grandchildren and grandparents for a cook-out. Labor Day weekend boasted a 5K run to benefit a children's park in Pelion. That raised an image. Each weekend marked an occasion when they raised money for charitable causes.

A covered yet open barbecue area housed at least twenty picnic tables, with a brick cooking pit at one end. I saw the edge of a pool behind the main building, along with bare shoulders and fannies, snatching my attention away when full-frontal visions of seniors assaulted me.

Lifting my purse higher on my shoulder, I scrunched the towels against me. The resort would almost pass for a standard vacation campground. I didn't see a den of iniquity, but neither did I yearn to join in and sing Kum Ba Yah unclothed around a campfire with everything on display. Sparks, ants, mosquitoes . . .

The glass front door to the office flew open, and a woman in the buff, ten years older than me, stepped out, with lots of dark, tanned skin making her blonde hair almost platinum. "You must be Carolina!"

I held out a hand and had to lock my gaze onto hers. "Yes'm, happy to meet you. You must be Prissy." Her name slayed me.

She waved at a lanky man traipsing across the parking lot wearing only a bandanna on his head. "Hey, Francis!" He lazily returned the greeting. She returned her attention to me. "Come on in, sugar," she said. "Before I show you around, we have some paperwork to fill out."

I jerked back. "I'm not signing up yet. I . . . I haven't seen the place."

She laid a hand on my arm and purred. "It's okay. I'll explain all the details to you."

She led me into a paneled room one would never envision inside a metal building. Plush sea foam colored carpet, greenery accented with exotic floral arrangements, and delicious top treatments on the windows gave the interior class. About to sit in a stuffed leather chair, I caught myself. No telling whose bottom had graced this very spot.

Prissy spread a towel across her tweed-upholstered chair before taking a seat.

"Oh," I said, realizing the purpose of my towels. I eased my bottom on the edge of the chair and set my purse on the floor.

"So," she said. "You're interested in our resort?"

"Um, yes. My sister thought it would do me good."

She chuckled. "Gotta love sisters. Mine wouldn't be caught dead in here. I offered her a free membership, but oh no." Her eyes rolled as she leaned on her desk, loose boobs resting on her forearms. "Your sister seems to care about you, Carolina. That's sweet. You're lucky."

Her words weighed heavier than she knew. "So, how does this work?"

Those soft blue eyes squinted. "Have we met before?"

She looked familiar, but seeing all her extra folds of skin didn't help my recall. I studied the walls for clues. A couple of certificates showed Clay River met the local health code and belonged to the national organization. Then I spotted the framed Pelion Peanut Party poster.

Miss Plaid Pants! The lady who'd dragged her guy away from the nasty church women as I struggled to rush Dubose to the car. My opinion of her rose a notch. But, no way in Hades did I want her remembering me as the USDA lady, affiliating me with Dubose or anyone else.

"You do ring a bell," I said. "Doesn't that drive you crazy?"

"Amen." She clicked her pen a couple times. "Never mind. It'll come to me or it won't."

Ice cubes of fear cracked and served, I settled into investigation mode and the character I chose to play. Her request for a driver's license forced me to reveal my correct mailing address. She seemed okay with the fact that my name change was the result of divorce. My sleuthing felt rather disjointed, and I kicked myself for not drawing up questions, or a cover, in advance. What else did I forget?

"Who sees this information?" I asked, pen hovering over the blanks. "If anyone at work found out—"

"Sugar, this is as close to Fort Knox as you can get when it comes to identity protection. Applications remain in a safe. Call everyone by whatever first name they give you permission to use. We don't compare social stature or disclose secrets. We have teachers here. Doctors, lawyers, business owners, you name it, they're members. Your information remains discreet, because others understand."

"So you introduce me as—"

"Whatever you choose." She stood, and I got another eyeful. "Let's take the golf cart. I'll show you the pool first and then drive you to the river beach. The trail leads us back alongside the cabins and RVs and ends at the pavilion. Please leave your phone in my office."

Thank God for that phone policy. No one could catch me in a snapshot. And I sure didn't want such pics on my phone. Zack would love that!

"There's a ladies' restroom across the hall," she said.

I smiled. "Thanks, I'm good."

"In case you're ready to test the waters."

"Oh." I could feel my parts tightening, rebelling. "Um, again, I'm good."

"Your call."

"No, seriously, I have to leave in an hour, so I don't have time to mingle."

She patted my shoulder. "You're fine. Let's go."

We left the cool interior for the blistering summer heat. We slid into Prissy's golf cart chariot. She popped a mild wheelie leaving the parking lot as my hands reached for nonexistent handles, and wound up gripping the edge of the roof instead.

We circled behind the building past the outdoor pool. According to my naked NASCAR driver, a smaller indoor pool kept members returning in winter months. Apparently more people my age showed up on the weekends.

So far no sign of Ally.

We passed another older gentleman. I couldn't hold back asking *the* question, even if I wasn't interested in joining. "What about guys getting . . . I mean, what if a man sees a girl and . . ."

She flashed me a crooked grin. "What if a man gets an erection?"

I feigned picking something off my shirt. "Yes."

She stopped the cart and patted her towel. "That's what this is for, to cover up until the urge fades, but sugar, it doesn't happen often. With everyone in the buff, the erotic aspect disappears. Before long, everyone looks the same. We relax. The first-time guys are too nervous anyway." She started moving again, taking a hard left. "On the outside chance it does happen, he can always jump in the pool."

"I see," I said, acting as if she'd just told me how to add herbs to a casserole. This investigation bordered on, as Ivy would say, far too much information. We entered a wooded trail. I flicked a mosquito away. Bet they sold bug spray by the gallon. Prissy eased the cart to the side of a dock that led to the beach. "Splendid day to take a tour. Weekdays are slow," she said.

Nobody was there. Great. I could take a break from seeing people's privates. Still no Ally, though.

Clay River earned its name. The hauled-in sand couldn't keep the red clay from escaping along the bank's edges. Seclusion beckoned, though. Cute painted signs stood on either side of the river, warning boaters and fishermen where they were. "Nudists on guard!" said one. "Drive safe, nudists ahead." Fencing jutted into the water a little ways up one side, and as I studied the other end, I noted similar protection a hundred yards in another direction.

"Don't you get gawkers?" I asked.

"Not as often as you'd think," she said. "They get more embarrassed than we do. Some members throw their towels over themselves. Most don't care." She pointed north. "Besides, the water gets mighty shallow up that a ways, so not all boats can get through here. We've never had a problem."

Fully mature skyscraper trees on both sides muffled all but the laps of water. I could see myself with Wayne, splayed on my beach towel, eyes closed, sun kissing parts of me that never saw daylight.

"Sweet, huh?" she asked.

"Immensely," I said.

"The river works wonderful magic on guests."

Birds chattered to each other, sounding petite and fairy tale-ish. A bullfrog released an early croak. "Get me out of here, or I'll never leave," I said.

She giggled and turned back through the woods to a clearing lined with two dozen cabins. "One bedroom units with sleeper sofas," she said. "Six have lofts. We don't get much need for family reunions."

"You rent these?" I scanned the small, rustic buildings, seeking anything familiar. "Are they all spoken for?"

"They're all full. One gentleman has been with us for almost a year."

We cruised past. I tried not to appear interested in more than a future vacation plan when I spotted a familiar target. Ally's red Toyota parked between a Lexus and another Toyota, blue. "These cabins are cute as they can be," I said, noting the number twenty-four on the door. Of course it would be the address on the end, where Kay would be farthest away from the common area entrance, maybe a mile.

"What if I wanted to share? I mean, if I rented a place, and a girlfriend asked to visit. I have a buddy in Beaufort who'd go gaga over these."

"There's an abbreviated form, so we know who's here. We copy her driver's license. She signs in and out and agrees to follow the rules."

So Ally and Kay both registered.

Prissy seemed eager to alleviate any concerns. "We're thorough, Ms. Bridges. Folks lose their membership if they bring in ill sorts. We screen everyone. New people like you visit four or five times before joining so they learn the life, but also so we get a feel for how they'd fit in. A background check, annual dues, and a contract serve us well. We're rather self-policing. The minute anybody feels uncomfortable with, say, someone flirting or crossing a line, management steps in. We love this place and don't want to jeopardize its future existence."

Right. With all these dictates and mandates, how had Kay wormed her way in and not been considered shady enough to turn away? Unless she had a fake driver's license, maybe. She wouldn't use her real name.

We headed up a trail toward the RVs. Few people sat outside midafternoon in August. Nude or not, the weather was hot and humid. The pavilion came back into sight, and Prissy explained about dances, parties, and award presentations.

"You'll see more people around the pool in an hour or two," she said as she rounded a turn leading us back to the office. We jolted to a halt where we started, and she twisted in her seat. "So, what do you think?"

"It's awesome," I said, glancing around as if admiring the view.

We returned inside. The clock on her wall read three thirty. Dubose expected me at four, forty miles away. I'd be late.

But Ally was here. She was either in cabin twenty-four or by the indoor pool where I hadn't looked yet.

"Care to join me at the pool?" Prissy asked.

"I have to be in downtown Columbia around four," I said.

She frowned. "Oh, sugar, you'll never make that."

I faked disgust. "I know. I so want to spend more time here. Can I glance at the indoor pool before I run off? We missed that."

Happy to oblige, she stepped toward the door. "It's closed, but sure, come on."

Crap. No chance Ally was there. However, Prissy's fanny already jiggled as she fast-walked down the hall, her floral body splash wafting, clashing with some sort of sweet mild disinfectant they used elsewhere.

I hustled to catch up. At the other end of the building, she opened a metal door with a window and flicked on the light switch to reveal a pool. The acidic bite of chlorine hit my nose. "Y'all have this planned well," I said. "Who wouldn't want to join?"

She nudged me with an elbow. "I think we might have a new member," she said in a singsong voice.

Windows lined the other side of the room, showing the outside pool area, the level strategically blocking waist-down views of those in the sun. A girl stood up, her attention obviously on her deck chair as she tried to reposition it.

"There's someone your age," Prissy said. "She's a guest. Rather quiet, but sweet."

I'd have known the girl as Wayne's sister from a hundred yards away. Kay resembled her brother: dark hair, tall, and introspective. I'd expect her feet to sport cowboy boots if we weren't at a place that flaunted bare tootsies. Cute girl, but she avoided eye contact, and tension controlled her movements. Like watching a bird on a porch railing, I imagined her darting away if I moved.

Ally Jo stood, reached behind her head, and retied hair off her neck. Suddenly I sought a place to hide. Of course the room stood bare of furniture and wide open. My heart rate calmed when I realized the windows were lightly tinted, and she probably didn't see me. As panic passed, relief flooded in. I knew where Ally was, and she was fine.

Prissy ran around the pool toward the window. "Oh, there's another guest," she said. "Now that one is crazy fun." She corrected herself. "In a good way, sugar, in a good way. She keeps us in stitches. Never meets a stranger." Prissy knocked rapidly on the window three times. "Hellooo!"

Both girls looked up at the repetitive taps, as did a half dozen other people. All waved.

Prissy laughed loud for their benefit. She waved toward me. "New visitor," she shouted.

She turned and clapped her hands together. "You're already missing your appointment. Why not meet the girls? Remember, it's nude-only at the pool, but what a perfect situation to warm-up to us."

Kay grinned shyly and sat back down. Ally's eyeballs seem to grow larger than her head.

Busted.

"Carolina?" she said, muffled through the glass.

Prissy turned to me. "You know her?"

I braced myself for the possible disrobing of my pretense. "My sister."

When Prissy squealed, I almost came out of my shoes. "That's the sister you spoke about? I knew there was something I liked about you. Here I've been rattling on about Clay River, and you practically had your mind made up when you walked in. Her name is Ally, right?"

"Allegra Jo," I said, before realizing the breach on protected personal information. "But yes, Ally."

She turned back to the window. "Oh, she's gone." She giggled again. "I bet she's coming around to greet you. Let's go back up front."

By the time we scurried to the office, Ally waited in the very spot on the sofa where I'd sat before, her pink towel under her. Prissy squealed again and hugged Ally who then faced me. I never realized she shaved . . . *down there*. A butterfly tattoo graced her right boob, only a sneeze above her nipple. Artsy, maybe even cute. A ring pierced her navel. Mom would have a cow.

"Hey, Sis," Ally said. "Didn't expect you to come around so soon to our lifestyle."

"Yeah, well . . ." How could I say I came to snatch her ass back home without insulting the hostess? My cheeks warmed in spite of my efforts to play it casual. With the lines between my character and reality smudged to smithereens, words vanished. I hadn't imagined this scenario.

Prissy hooked her arm in mine. "I was telling Carolina that now was the perfect time to venture out since she has you to show her the ropes."

"I think that's a marvelous idea," Ally said with the raise of a devious brow. "We've talked about nude sunbathing at the house several times. Haven't we, Sis? I'm tickled silly you finally want to give it a go."

Chapter 15

MY NAKED SISTER picked my purse off the floor and led me out of Prissy's office, across the hall, and into the ladies' room. "You made that woman believe I couldn't wait to strip and become one of her nudists," I said, throwing my towels in a chair. "That wasn't fair, Ally."

She tossed her hair back and eyed me with daggers. "Aren't *you* the pot calling the kettle black? What the hell are you doing here anyway, Miss High Horse?"

"Damn it, I came to talk to you." *And save your butt.* She likely knew nothing about Kay's drug-ridden past, and the low lifes who accompanied it. She didn't need to know. My goal was to get her home and inform Wayne that Kay seemed well hidden at Clay River.

Ally assumed a flaunting pose, one arm in the air, enjoying her buffness. "Well, here I am, Sis. Say what you came to say, and it better be good."

"I'm sorry you felt you needed to run off."

"That's it?"

"Come on home," I said. "Ivy hardly looks at me since you left."

"Don't blame Ivy," she said. "She's doing what comes natural."

"She's thirteen, Ally. I can't have her strutting around nude."

Ally swung her hip to the other side. "Nudity isn't an age thing. Didn't you pay attention to Prissy's spiel?"

"Ivy is my responsibility."

"All I did was tell her how a natural lifestyle works."

I exhaled the mother of all sighs. Here I stood in a nudist colony . . . um, resort . . . trying to make amends and remove my sister from a potentially volatile situation, and all she wanted to tell me was how to raise my child—naked at that. My pulse spiked. We had no time for this.

"Just come home, Ally," I said in a flatline, impatient tone.

She laughed. "No wonder Ivy bucks your authority."

I hit my chest once with a fist. "She's *my* daughter, not yours," I said. "I decide when it's okay for her to strip down in front of people."

Ally fixated on me for a second. "You haven't spoken to her about this, have you?"

I opened my mouth, then closed it. "Not yet."

"Figures," she said. "Good that I explained the etiquette of baring all since you won't."

Someone tapped on the door. "Everything okay in there, ladies?"

"Fine, Prissy," Ally said in a loud voice. "Be out in a minute." She turned to me and let words fly. "I told her to limit her nudity to the proper setting, like here or her bedroom. We spoke about the dangers and the impressions she gives people. Still think old aunty can't dole out advice?"

She'd done what I should have—probably better than I would since she owned Ivy's adoration. Didn't give her the authority, though.

"You know I'm right," she said, counting my silence as a concession. "Don't get all pompous on me, little sister. You're no saint."

"You're not either, but you try to play one around me," she said.

"Get over yourself. Geez. This is about Ivy."

"No, it's not," she said. "It's about you not handling situations well. It's about you not trusting other people."

Okay, that was a bit exaggerated. "Once you have a couple of kids I'll listen to your sage advice. Until then, it's none of your business."

She crossed her arms, her heel bobbing up and down in double-time.

My sibling and I never won or lost a squabble with each other. We slung comments until we tired of the effort. The silence hung heavy as we fidgeted.

"I've had enough," Ally said and turned to leave.

A skinny, gray-headed nudist came in, glanced at Ally, then me, and went into a stall. I turned water on in the sink so I wasn't listening to her activity.

"Wait a minute," I said to Ally, teeth gritted.

Once the lady came out, she washed her hands as I pretended to dry mine. She smiled. I smiled. She darted away.

In that two minutes, the tension eased between my sister and me.

Ally stepped forward and undid a button on my shirt. Then another. "So, do I undress you, or do you remember how to do it yourself?"

"Don't be stupid." I held my shirt shut. "Let's just go home . . ."

She shook her head. "You don't get it. You don't come here and fetch me. Tell Ivy I love her." This time she was halfway out the door, knowing the mention of Ivy would hook me.

"Stop!" I said, not sure whether to tell her about Kay's past. "You don't understand."

"It's not like I haven't seen everything you've got," she said.

We were getting nowhere, her on one planet, me on another. We needed conversation, but she wasn't giving me the time. I looked down at my undone buttons.

Ally grinned as if reading my mind. She flicked her wrist. "Off with it."

In spite of my reservations to rub, um elbows, with nudists, this was probably my lone chance to warm up to Ally, maybe speak to Kay and get a read on how desperate she was. I'd maybe win my sister back if I disrobed. Public nudity, however, flew in the face of everything Mom beat into us in her passive aggressive, hoity-toity manner.

Wait. That meant refusing Ally was listening to my mother over my sister.

"All right," I said and hastily removed my shirt.

My belongings in a locker, two towels draped over my arm, and sunglasses on my face, I followed my sister out. Prissy waved from her desk, busy on the phone. As sunlight hit parts of me that hadn't seen daylight since my wading pool days, I instinctively moved a hand over strategic areas.

"Let it go, Sis," Ally said. "Your hand isn't big enough to cover it all."

"You calling me fat?"

"Nope, just naked," she said. "Flaunt it."

A seventyish lady left the pool as we entered, thanking us as we held the gate open for her, no different than at the mall. I felt almost invisible, and admittedly, the sensation wasn't so bad. Memories popped into my head of delicious relaxation in my bedroom under the ceiling fan, nude and stretched across cool sheets after a long hot commute from work, always wishing Wayne were there.

Four members lounged on the opposite side of the pool, in the shade. Understandably since their advanced ages gave them a higher chance of skin cancer. A sixtyish couple waded up to their necks in the pool, talking to another couple seated on the edge. I tried not to study my own skin, feeling young in contrast yet pondering which parts of me would sag first as time trudged on.

Ally dragged another lounge chair next to hers and motioned for me to sit. Kay smiled as I tried to nonchalantly drape a towel across my belly, the other already under me per the rules. Ally waved toward me. "Nancy, this is my sister, Carolina. Wait." She threw me a weird look. "You want to be called Slade or Carolina?"

Kay's smile faded. "Slade?"

Of course Kay used an alias. However, I almost croaked at my sister's ignorance of mine. I had Prissy call me Carolina for a reason. "Either name is good," I said.

"Don't know why she won't use the name my parents put on her birth certificate," Ally said, leaning back in her chair, eyes closed. "She can call herself Gecko for all I care. She's stark naked, and I made her do it. Ha!"

The sun beat down like a sauna. I lay back and pretended Ally hadn't botched my name. Kay, however, remained upright on her chair, unable to melt like everyone else.

"My brother's seeing someone named Slade."

I remained reclined, eyes open behind the shades. "Yes, he is."

Anger tightened her face. "How the hell did you find me?"

Ally rose to her elbows. "I thought you came here to apologize to me." She dipped her sunglasses. "You're here for Wayne?"

No more repose. "I can do two things at once, Ally. Three actually, since I don't want you caught up in Kay's issues."

Ally twisted toward Kay. "What issues? And who's Kay?"

"How did you find me?" Kay repeated quietly. Her stiff manner spoke volumes—words she was unwilling to say in front of Ally.

"Does it matter?" I asked. "Your brother's worried sick. You're less than an hour away. Can't you give him a few moments? Maybe he can help."

"Damn," Kay said, snatching off her glasses. "Hasn't he told you anything?"

"Yes, he has," I said. "He's meeting with Pamela as we speak, getting her off your back."

Kay jumped up. "That bitch is here?"

Oh crap. I stood and held her arm. "No. Don't leave. Promise me you won't leave. Wayne will be devastated."

"Then tell me how the hell you found me, because if you can, that bitch definitely can."

No way I could tell her about Ally's call. Kay'd toss the phone, and Wayne would lose the only connection he held with her. "Doesn't matter. Come home and see your brother."

Ally's expression remained one of openmouthed astonishment. Kay snatched up her towel. "I like you, Ally, but you've got to be the leak to Slade."

If the topic hadn't been so sober, I'd have laughed at a spat amongst three unclad women, like some inane chick flick. Ally remained tangled in thoughts of what was happening, but Kay was about to go underground.

"Kay," I said. "My sister didn't know I'd come here. In fact, she had no idea we're looking for you. Please. Let Wayne help. He's a federal agent, for goodness sake."

She scowled at me. "So's Pamela. So are those DEA assholes. Wayne can't do anything. Tell him that. I'll call him. Tell him that, too." She stuffed her belongings in her bag.

"Your name is Kay?" Ally asked, a mental step behind.

"Thanks for being a friend," Kay said, touching Ally's shoulder. "Haven't experienced one of those in a long time." Then, tote bag in hand, she pulled away from my grasp.

"Can't you think of somebody other than yourself?" I said. "He's all the family you have."

She whirled on me. I staggered back, raking my big toe on the cement in my stumble. "Butt out," she said, then left, letting the gate bang behind her.

I slowly turned to make eye contact with my sister.

She shook her head. "You can fuck shit up without even trying, you know that?" She gathered her towels and sun lotion. "Why didn't you come to me first and let me talk to Nancy . . . um, Kay?"

"You don't understand. It wasn't a you-or-her move."

"You are unfriggin-believable, Carolina."

"Quit sounding like Mom," I replied, monotone.

She got in my face. "Well, maybe you need a dose of Mom. Girl, you need a critical reality check on how to tread in other people's lives." She started to leave, then pivoted back on her heel. "Thanks for using me."

I reached for her. "Ally."

"Don't, Carolina. Just don't."

"Are you coming home?"

She poked her head back around the corner, glaring over the gate. "What do you think?" Then she disappeared.

I sat down and studied the ground, lost as to my next move, bruised from the blow of Ally's words. This mess wasn't over, either. This screw-up measured miniscule on the chart compared to what it would be when I got home and confessed to Wayne.

Only one accomplishment, and I thanked God for it. Kay no longer trusted being around Ally, removing my sister from Kay's danger zone.

I could have planned this better, but had no clue how.

"Crap!" Dubose's plea to meet me flashed to mind. No phone to check the time. I ran inside, then to the restroom. My phone read four fifteen. I called Dubose twice and got voicemail, leaving her a message to hang tight at Gervais & Vine. I'd be there as soon as I could.

Prissy walked in. "Well, how did our first day go?"

I tripped stepping into my slacks and then couldn't get my bra straps untwisted. "Um, fine. It's just that appointment . . ."

"You coming back to see us? You didn't get to meet Calvin. He's our manager, and the cutest husband anyone could have," she said, giggling. "Mine, of course."

I fumbled with shirt buttons. "I'll be back to meet him, I'm sure."

"You better," she said and glanced around. "Where's your sister?"

"She and her friend had plans. I kind of surprised them." I dug for keys in my purse.

"Yeah, but it was a good surprise."

"A humdinger," I said as I left the bathroom and the Matriarch of Nudity behind me and got in my truck.

I drove past the guardhouse. Dubose didn't answer her phone. The drive to downtown Columbia dragged like the proverbial molasses in January. Once at the restaurant curb, I threw keys to a valet to park my pickup and dashed inside, praying something would go right today.

"Whoa," said the hostess. "Can I help you?"

Breathless, I described Dubose as I craned my neck to scout the place. "I'm late. She was supposed to wait."

"Ma'am, I just came on at five, and as you can see, there's no one here fitting her description. Let me ask the bartender." She hustled to the bar, then soon returned. "He said the woman came, drank a glass of wine, and departed—maybe around four thirty."

"Thanks. That's friggin' great."

"Pardon?"

I held up a hand. "Sorry. Thanks."

The valet spent more time retrieving my vehicle than I spent in the restaurant. Of course rush hour choked the streets, and my truck crawled down Huger Street, seeking outlet to the interstate.

A black SUV changed lanes behind me, as if emulating my moves. I slowed to entice him to veer around. My cell phone rang.

I didn't want to pick it up. If it was the kids, they'd see me in ten minutes. Anybody else would only chew me out, so I didn't answer.

Whatever Dubose wanted to say could wait. She'd thrown me to the dogs anyway.

What would I say to Wayne? He'd suffered sleepless nights last year when he graciously put a hold on searching for Kay to help me rescue my kidnapped kids. Before we became an item. Back when I hadn't trusted him.

Now look what I'd done with his trust.

I stayed in the slow lane on the four-lane interstate, in no hurry to get home. Some run-down piece of junk circa 1980 remained behind me. Behind him, another black SUV almost tried to pass then hung back. Or was it the same one?

My attention darted between the start-stop traffic and my rearview mirror. Was that a tail?

Shag music came on the radio, and I jammed the button to cut it off. Not in the mood. Glancing up, I slammed brakes as traffic backed up at a clogged exit ramp. The SUV pulled into another lane and passed, losing itself in commuters anxious to get home. Guess nerves made me paranoid.

All too soon I pulled into my drive and parked. I sat for a moment to collect my wits.

My heart lurched into my throat when Wayne tapped on the window. "Hey, Butterbean." He reached for the door handle. "Where you been?"

I grabbed my bag and slid out, brushing off my shirt, unable to face him directly. "How'd your lunch go with Pamela?"

"We argued for over two hours."

"Told you," I said, forcing a grin.

"She professes to be protecting Kay, but I know better. I'll call someone higher up tomorrow. Pamela's too fanatical about losing her collar."

Delay of the inevitable was eating me up. "They were close?" I asked, stalling.

"Knew each other for three years. All the more reason for Pamela to cut her some slack."

"Sorry," I said, meaning it way more than he could fathom. My hands jittered. I gripped my purse. "Had an exhausting day."

"Babe." He drew me to his chest. "I'm the one who's sorry. Too much talk about me. You're fighting for your job, for goodness sake."

His tenderness pushed me over the cliff as my face buried in his shirt. "I saw Kay today." He gripped my arms and pushed back. "You what?"

"I spoke with Kay. She was at Clay River Resort with Ally. I tried to coax them back here."

He had a right to look shocked. "Why'd you go alone?"

"To help you find your sister. To retrieve mine. I pretended to be a potential member. Since you had Pamela occupied, I figured I wouldn't be followed."

He squeezed my arms harder. "She realized who you were?" he asked.

I tried to back away, but he held tight.

"Apparently you'd mentioned in a voicemail about your girlfriend named Slade." I shrugged under his grip. "How was I supposed to know?"

He held me closer, face hard. "What'd she say, Slade?"

"She said she had to leave, that you couldn't help her."

"Hell, you could've called me."

"While you were sitting across from Pamela?"

He turned away and leaned against the truck. "You just can't leave stuff alone, can you?"

"I was thinking about Ally, Wayne. About her being out there all by herself."

"And not about Kay."

"No, I thought about her, too. I asked her to come with me . . . begged her to call you. Told her you were worried."

His posture remained stiff, adversarial. "Did she say where she was going?"

"No."

"You didn't even ask, did you?" he said.

He had no intention of listening to my reason or see what I'd tried to do for him, for our sisters. "I'm sorry, Wayne, but look at it from my side. I don't feel right with my sister hanging around yours, not when she's got DEA on her butt for some sordid murder, for drugs. My sister doesn't need that kind of confusion in her life right now."

His eyes widened, then narrowed.

My phone rang.

Wayne glared at the bushes. I was afraid to interrupt his thoughts for fear of him giving me a knee-jerk response I didn't want to hear.

"Hello?" I said.

"Just checking to see if you're home," Ms. Amick said. "Ready for your babies back?"

Instinctively, I glanced toward the Amicks' house across the cove. My eye caught sight of a black Expedition.

"Dolly, did you buy a new car?"

"No, Slade, why? Oh, who's that backing out of my driveway?"

"Somebody lost," I said and turned back toward my dark, brooding man.

Ms. Amick snickered. "Well, the kids are on their way over. Have a good evening."

I wish.

The SUV drove away without slowing, headed toward Pebble Branch Drive. I didn't know anyone with that type of vehicle out here.

"Wayne, I keep seeing that car."

He didn't hear me as he studied his boots, his jaw working.

Phone in hand, I scrolled through the call history, waiting for Wayne to speak, expecting the missed calls to be his.

There were three missed calls from Kay.

Chapter 16

WAYNE LEANED against my truck in the driveway, his flat mouth telling me I'd erred big time. I held my phone toward him like an olive branch. "Kay tried to call."

He launched himself off the side of the vehicle and snatched the phone. "When?" he asked, scrolling.

"Probably on my way home."

He hit a button. "So why didn't you take her call?"

I didn't reply right away so he could call her back. Plus I didn't have a justified response. On the way home, I'd let my calls go to voicemail. She'd made it clear at Clay River that she disliked me finding her, so why would I expect her to call? Guilt stuck to me like syrup on pancakes.

Wayne snapped the phone shut and shoved it at me. "No messages, and she won't pick up."

Feeling sorry for not taking her call was one thing. Scaring her away at Clay River represented another sin altogether.

"Wayne, I'm—"

"Don't bother."

My stomach churned. My soul screamed remorse. "I understand how you . . ."

He twisted around and glared. "Slade, I'm leaving before I say too much."

I hushed, biting my lip.

He left slowly, deliberately . . . painfully to me. His taillights had a permanent look to them.

The kids ran up the driveway, Zack behind Ivy, his foot trying to trip her with every other step. She took swings at him, missing each time.

"Hey, Mom. What's for dinner?" Zack asked, dancing around me as Ivy struggled to connect a slap.

"Pancakes," I mumbled.

"Bacon?" he asked.

"Sure," I replied, pocketing my phone.

"Blueberries?" he asked again.

"Yeah."

Ivy tilted her head. "Steak, pizza, and doughnuts? With sprinkles and cotton candy?"

"You got it," I said, opening the kitchen door.

Zack elbowed his sister. She pushed him away. "She's ignoring us, stupid."

Ivy's ire brought me back to the moment, and I caught on. But I didn't give a damn. I'd cook up the entire pantry to avoid conversation. I'd said enough for one day.

AROUND TEN P.M., I licked red cayenne pepper off my fingers. Some women ate tubs of ice cream. I devoured hot spicy potato chips, specifically Golden Flake, until my mouth burned. A beer quenched the heat. A calorie combination unsuitable to my hips but superb in taking my mind off my crumbling conscience.

I walked into the kitchen, washed and dried my hands on a dish towel. My cell rang.

"Slade."

"I was about to go to bed," I said gruffly, recognizing her voice.

"Please. Listen to me. I hoped to do this in person."

"I showed up this afternoon, and you weren't there."

"I'm sorry," Dubose said. "Figured you weren't coming."

"When and where this time?" I asked.

"Eight a.m. tomorrow at Lizard's Thicket in Irmo."

My brain failed to function before ten. Hers fired on all cylinders at dawn. "Why so early?"

"Because you need to know the details before someone terminates me and drags you back to work."

"They won't fire you," I said. "Why would they? And Harden'll just ship me somewhere, assuming he wants me back at all."

"Slade." Dubose spoke in a motherly fashion, laced with her subtle commanding presence I used to respect. "They need you. You're too good."

She had no idea how much her words eased at least one of my emotional wounds.

"I'm dispensable," she said. "Appointed politicians are a dime a dozen, good for no longer than a president's term." She gave a weak chuckle. "And at the rate this one's going, I'll be out in a year anyway."

Her stab at humor rubbed me wrong. None of this could be construed as jovial. "Listen, Margaret, this Wheeler situation is moot now, and excuse me for saying so, but why should I bother? We stirred up a lot of trouble."

"You pissed off the Governor," she said.

"*We* pissed off the Governor."

"Regardless, I'd like to arm you sufficiently to keep him at bay. Believe me, I can."

After hanging up, I crawled into bed with a Lisa Gardner mystery. Usually two chapters relaxed me enough to bookmark my page and cut off the light. Six chapters into the book and I remained awake, unable to forget the day. I threw the book on the bed. In four hours it would be light.

Was Wayne sleeping easy or lying awake thinking of me?

DRUGGY FEELING, I parked in the Lizard's Thicket parking lot and placed my calls again. Dialed Wayne . . . voicemail. Dialed Kay . . . same deal. Ally hadn't contacted me either. All were pissed. I got that.

Dubose, however, waited for me bright and lively, waving for the waitress to fill my cup before I even sat down.

"You look tired," she said.

I set my purse on the chair beside me. "Well, I've had a lot on my shoulders lately."

She studied me, then apparently decided to let my comment go. I silently sipped coffee as I fought to come alert.

Dubose ordered grapefruit and wheat toast. Such lightweight fare was like ordering grilled cheese and Tater Tots at a Victorian tearoom. I, on the other hand, gave the fine family restaurant its due respect ordering eggs, grits, bacon, and biscuits. Dubose asked that we finish breakfast before broaching the subject at hand. Something about digestive juices. The second cup of coffee brought me more alive. Once I could think clearly, however, I found it hard to eat. I dropped my fork and pushed the plate away.

"So, what's all the secrecy about our governor?" I asked.

"Cover your back." Dubose retrieved the napkin from her lap. "Dick Wheeler's not as forthright as he leads people to believe."

I grumbled from behind my cup. "Duh! Anyway, comes with the job, doesn't it?"

"Comes with the man." She dabbed her mouth. "I've known him for thirty years."

I did the math. Mid-twenties for her. Thirty for him. Both A-type personalities with sights set on serious career advancement. No shock that they might've hooked up. Actually explained why she offered to do the favor for Wheeler to begin with.

Dick Wheeler wanted me to help clear his brother, until a better offer presented the perfect defense—when CJ died. The commander-in-chief no longer needed us then, and our continued interest could sabotage his plan to use CJ. Then Lucille stroked out, and all Wheeler's loose ends were covered. I'm sure the old woman would cut the collective Wheeler throats if she were able.

"I dated Patsy, by the way."

My cup clinked on its saucer, and I quickly closed my mouth. "Um, what?"

"Patsy Wheeler. Only Patsy Haggerty back then."

The mention of Lamar's deceased wife stunned me. Never saw that coming.

She gave me a half grin. "Yes, Slade."

"Good Lord," escaped before I could stop it.

My thoughts raced backward, searching recent history. Dubose never flaunted a woman at her side at events. Of course not. Not in agriculture. Movers and shakers in the agriculture world had barely accepted females until the last decade, much less gays. Her biggest protest for her lifestyle meant never sporting a man at her side.

"But," I stammered, "Patsy married Lamar and mothered CJ."

Dubose nodded. "She said she experimented with me, but I never believed her. We remained fast friends, and if it hadn't been for CJ, we'd have made another go at it, I believe." She dropped her head back, eyes closed. "Imagine Dick's fear of *that* happening." Her short laughter made me laugh as well. The fleeting, giddy moment gave us both delight.

"Lucille and I stayed close, too." Her crow's feet crinkled. "Lucille preferred me to Lamar, if you can believe that."

My respect for her had returned. I pitied her, yet admired the hell out of her gumption.

She showed not the least hint of reservation. "But Dick doesn't want our past relationship known, for fear it'll tarnish his image."

"*This* is the leverage you're giving me?" Homosexuality held no shock factor. Ancient history about a deceased sister-in-law would barely leave a scratch on the Wheeler name. "Who would care?"

The cloud across her face caught me off guard. "I care, Slade. Patsy went through the typical torment about where she stood sexually, then about protecting the almighty Wheeler name." She picked up a spoon and stirred her coffee. "Do you know she had to agree to inherit nothing but a life estate to live on the farm until she died? Dick's idea. The family set up everything to go to offspring, eventually CJ, not that she minded that, but her sexual past cost her an inheritance. Her death was oh-so-convenient for Dick."

Was her hand trembling? The spoon went back on the table, and Dubose gripped her cup.

"Lamar let that happen?" I asked. "What kind of man does that?"

"Exactly."

"But would Dick Wheeler care after so long?"

"Yes, he would," she said tersely. "He runs on family values. Re-election is around the corner. Plenty of voters in this state oppose that type of relationship."

"Margaret, that's not very potent."

Her face hardened, a side of her I'd witnessed when she prepared to take a stand in meetings and nail it home. "He's a homophobe, Slade. When Lamar proposed to Patsy, Dick pitched a fit. He thought Lamar's blind love would ruin the farm's business and scare away votes for his run at the state Senate. Dick prepared the prenup to buy her silence."

"What a jerk. And Lamar's a piece of crap."

She sighed. "But I have more ammo than that. It isn't like he carried on an affair or embezzled money, and it happened years ago, but it'll rattle his cage if you ever bring it up. I found out through Patsy, who overheard Dick and Lamar arguing in their farm office. Lucille knows, too."

"Well, she can't talk about anything now," I said, regretting the old woman's stroke.

Dubose grimaced. "Yes, I know. I'm going to see her when I leave here. Promised Patsy on her deathbed I'd protect her mother, a major reason I came back to Columbia when this position came open with Agriculture." Her slight daze told me she relived the moment, and I gave her a second.

I cleared my throat. "So what's the ammo?"

She blinked. "Dick tried to bribe inspectors to accept Wheeler peanut loads in 2000. They had high mold levels."

I squinted, never considering inspectors that vulnerable. "How would you prove that? Peanuts are checked and graded. You think some licensed inspector will step up and admit he passed on mold? From that long ago? With Wheeler now the governor?"

She sat back in her chair as the waitress refilled our coffees. My appetite crept back, and I nibbled on a piece of bacon until the lady left.

Dubose rested her arms on the table. "USDA has a peanut standards board comprised of members of the industry. The salmonella scare a couple years ago happened at a facility owned by a board member. After that, the public isn't so trusting. It doesn't matter if someone confesses or not."

"I doubt proof exists, which means Wheeler has no worries."

She pulled at a curl behind her ear. "Slade, a politician fears the appearance of wrongdoing as much as the reality. Some people drool over such a juicy rumor, ambitious to erode Dick's career. Regardless of proof, voters believe such news items." She almost looked mischievous. "Add that to a suggestion that he threw CJ under the bus, along with the fact you and

I were booted for getting close, you actually pose a valid threat."

"Right." I remained skeptical. Dubose's behavior seemed almost too zealous from carrying a torch for Patsy and holding a vendetta against both the Wheeler men.

She winked. "Just the hint of the scandal would spawn wonderful front page news. Next year's his possible reelection. The timing's perfect."

I laid hands on one of hers. "Why are you doing this?"

She gave a slight smile at my gesture. "I care about you, Slade. Just like I care about Lucille. Like I care about CJ's and Patsy's names."

Now I was just confused. "I'm flattered, Margaret, but why did you try to help the Governor from the outset? I mean, if you hate him so much."

She drew away. "Keep your friends close, your enemies closer. You might apply that to Harden sometime. That and I needed to know the truth."

I'd almost forgotten about Harden. Shame she brought him up. "Speaking of Harden," I said, "what do I do about him? He's ready to do backflips for the Governor and drag me down in the process."

She set her napkin on the table and scooted her chair back to rise. "I'm not your fairy godmother, Slade. No doubt you can handle Harden. He's not nearly your equal as an adversary."

But she'd hovered over my shoulder more than a couple of times, waving her wand when I confronted legal, administrative, and inner-office adversity. I'd grown accustomed to having her as a mentor. "What about your position?"

"I'll be fine," she said. "Being released for convenience is common in my realm. New opportunities pop up, often thanks to attention from the termination. Right now it's all about Lucille, and I'll spend my free time with her."

"I'd hate to be you right now." It was hard enough being me.

She smiled, calmer than I'd be in her shoes. "Who knows? If nothing comes around, maybe I'll try something new—like your job."

I froze.

"Kidding, Slade." She grinned. "You need a stronger sense of humor."

I didn't need jokes. I needed . . . hell, who knew what I needed. All my moves had backfired lately. If I won the damn lottery tonight, I'd lose the ticket by morning.

No *Have a good life, Slade,* or *I'm sorry I dragged you into this, Slade.* She'd used me. And she meant to. She might even do it again, but next time I'd feel her cause was just.

Her valiant commitment to Patsy and Lucille told me she wasn't down and out. She still served a mission, one I understood more clearly now. As long as Dubose was around, and I was still with USDA, we'd continue investigating the Wheelers. I had a better feel for why she needed to clear CJ's name. She owed it to two women she loved.

I waved for the waitress to bring me another bowl of grits.

However, I was no fool. She'd lost her position of authority. I hadn't. While I could empathize, I remained her chess piece. She might care for me, but her need for revenge probably drove her to meet me for breakfast . . . to make sure I continued to play the game. I'd have to find a balance somewhere in that relationship.

TRAFFIC MOVED seamlessly, as if choreographed for some Department of Transportation public relations commercial. I'd semi-agreed with Harden to report today, Friday, after seeking legal counsel I never intended to hire. Ordering me to return for some random task not in my job description seemed lame. If he or the Governor wanted me out from under their feet, he could keep me on leave. My threats of an attorney held them at bay for the time being, but when I didn't follow through, they'd be on my back again.

I slipped into my office with a wink, the eyes of my assistant wide as I skulked by. Whitney did my timekeeping, so she knew Harden had kicked my butt out the door for a few days. I wanted to check messages and collect myself before he caught wind of my presence. I preferred to address Harden at my own speed.

A sweet tea from the canteen and half hour of contemplation would prepare me for facing the obnoxiousness that constituted Harden Harris. Like the lingering stench of a skunk, he left residual nasty on every person in his path. Backstabbing was his *modus operandi.*

As I mentally cursed Harden in assorted phrases, wishing I knew other languages to do it in, I checked voicemail. Ten callers, including Monroe and my best friend Savvy in Beaufort, left messages coded in whispers asking what the hell Dubose and I did to warrant disciplinary leave. No telling what Harden had told people in my absence.

I sat up and grabbed a pen at the next caller.

"Ms. Slade, this is Simeon Fant. You called while I was out of town. I'll only be here a few days, so if you'd like to talk, give me a call. My flight leaves Sunday right after church."

Seemed like months since I'd called the Fants seeking info about Lamar and his drug affiliation. I almost didn't care anymore except for being Dubose's eyes and ears.

Dick Wheeler had stomped on Dubose's and my careers without checking his shoes for the damage. With Harden playing puppy dog to the Governor, my duties could wind up in places like Union, Kingstree, and

McCormick, distant places in South Carolina to keep me out of Columbia. They'd harass me until I quit pestering them, or quit altogether. I had to tread carefully.

Why hadn't Dubose used the info on the Governor for her own salvation? Not wanting her sexual orientation aired in public while in office, most likely. Unemployed, she probably no longer cared, but she'd eventually seek another position, most likely political in nature. The fraudulent peanut inspections hanging over Wheeler's head could pack more power.

I decided to call Mr. Fant, who offered to meet with me in three hours, once he finished checking his peanut fields. The man surely knew his rival long enough and well enough to cough up some dirt. Dubose made taking on the Governor sound deceptively easy. Tell him what I know, get him off Agriculture's back, and retrieve my job. Assuming Pamela didn't slam me from her DEA vantage and connections with the US attorney's office.

I sighed. Wayne had said don't investigate blind.

I locked my office door, whispered to Whitney to forget I came in, and ran down the stairs to exit the building. Then in a fast walk, I made my way to the Governor's Mansion two blocks over. Time to test the water on Dubose's suspicion about Wheeler and judge his reaction. I'd either get him off my back or escalate my career's demise. It beat waiting for someone else to make a move.

A different guard manned the gate. I told him I worked at the Governor's request and needed to report on the assignment. He checked his clipboard.

"Ma'am, your name's not on the list. Sorry."

"How's he supposed to receive my update?"

He rubbed his chin in an exaggerated fashion. "I don't know. Maybe telephone, email, overnight express?"

I flashed my administrative credentials. "This is a serious case, sir."

He studied my badge and then wrote something down. "Sorry, ma'am," he said, focused on his paper.

Crap. He jotted down my identity. I had nothing to lose now. "Call Wheeler and tell him I'm here to discuss Patsy and the peanut inspectors."

His mouth turned into a half grin just as I realized my words sounded like a kids' movie. "No, ma'am, I won't. Please, be on your way."

"He's not even here, is he?"

"You know I can't say," he said with a sneer that confirmed my suspicion.

I spun and stomped off. Even at nine in the morning, the slight breeze brushed hot on my face, moved only by traffic as I pounded cement toward the State House. Columbia held a reputation as the most sweltering city in the state thanks to the asphalt, concrete, and landlocked location a hundred and thirty miles from the coast, but I walked anyway. Easier than retrieving my car from one parking garage and spending a half hour seeking another to reach a destination only six blocks from where I stood.

Besides, the time would organize the words I prepared to deliver to Dick Wheeler.

Chapter 17

IF I WERE THE Governor's guard, I might have called the State House and let someone know a crazy woman with a badge left in a huff after being declined access to the mansion. If he'd known where I marched, he would have had me followed.

Two blocks later, I stood on the corner of Assembly and Laurel Streets, waiting for the light to change. A few cars veered right on Laurel, passing in front of me. A black Expedition waited in line with them. Vehicles hung tight to each other, trying to catch the green light. In the crunch.

The light changed, and I trotted across the street toward the bankruptcy courthouse. Thoughts of Lamar, Lucille, Patsy, and Dubose rehashed in my head. Lucille mentioned aflatoxin the day of her stroke. Patsy died of cancer. The Wheelers dealt in bad peanuts. Dubose seemed downright crusading about it all.

This hadn't been my fight. But I'd become entangled in all this mess, becoming known to the Governor who now probably worried I knew too much, especially connected to Dubose.

I wasn't one to wait for the hammer to fall. My job hinged on regaining my footing somehow, and Dubose was trying to give me traction to come out on top. Besides, the more I learned from Dubose about the Wheeler mess, the more I got mad at how many times they rolled over people to get their way. I was now one of those people.

My steps turned into a march as adrenaline empowered me toward the state's political offices. I'd be a lot harder to fire than Dubose.

Weary of being on the wrong end of puppet strings, I decided it was time for proactive measures.

The muggy summer air radiated from the hot pavement and concrete. Business types mopped brows, stuffed restraining ties in their pockets, and shed suit coats in resignation. By the time I reached the State House steps, my underclothes were damp, and I was cranky and loaded for bear.

The Governor's Mansion sat small with a floor plan easy to maneuver, but the State House where Wheeler performed his elected duties stood tall and dignified, covering an entire city block. Dubose knew this place. I didn't. I walked around three sides of the block before finding the appropriate entrance. Perspiration glued strands of hair to my neck and forehead; sweat rolled down my back. Ordinarily, I preened and patted hair in place before a meeting. Screw that. Screw him. I straightened my blouse and strode inside, tucking damp strands behind my ears while taking two seconds to tilt my head and sniff for body odor.

"How do you do, young lady?" asked the metal detector guard, displaying a nicer demeanor than anyone who had crossed my path for two days. I grinned back. After my ID earned his approving nod, I continued, reminding myself my mission was not something worth grinning about.

After three wrong turns down polished tiled hallways, I resisted pounding on doors for directions. In the middle of yet another wrong hall, I stood to the side, frustrated the signs weren't worth a crap. Finally, I reached a young woman behind a desk who appeared to have nothing to do but answer a phone and stop whoever entered her space.

She lifted her gaze, neat in her crisp, cool, cotton top, her foundation and powder dry and smooth. She didn't miss a beat with her greeting, as if she couldn't see my melted, angry mess of an appearance. "May I help you?" Her smile could light up a runway.

"The Governor isn't expecting me," I said. "But he *will* see me."

"I'm afraid . . ."

I pulled out my credentials.

She took the badge from me and read the details. "I'm sorry, but—"

"Listen. He instructed me to research a sensitive matter. He missed an earlier appointment, and it's critical he receive my findings." It would serve him right if I dumped Dubose's knowledge right here in this girl's lap and see where it spread, but I needed to channel his energies to me and use him strategically.

I spoke in code, saying nothing but saying it firmly, sounding important without revealing facts. She politely waited for me to finish. Bet her momma was proud of her.

She tilted her perfectly coifed head. "Ms. Slade, Governor Wheeler isn't in and left no word about you. I can take your name and number and have someone on his staff call."

I recited my contact information. "Add this," I said, and dictated a brief message. When she asked me to repeat it, I grabbed the notepad, borrowed a pen from her too clean desk, and scribbled: *Uncovered an old issue of family significance. Suggest you get in touch. Carolina Slade.*

I slid the pad to her. She turned it around to read and asked, "Is that it?"

"Believe me, it's enough to make his day," I said and left.

Outside, the summer air smothered me going back more than it did coming. I'd be hard-pressed to keep my appointment at the Fants' farm.

My eager march of confrontation waned. If my message reached Wheeler's desk, which I considered a big if, he wouldn't call. I slung my purse on the other shoulder, resisting the urge to hit a tree with it.

At the sidewalk, I waited for the pedestrian light to change. Cars shot past, their occupants intent on business. I jumped back as a black SUV scraped its tire against the curb in front of me.

"Hey," I hollered.

The vehicle stopped.

I retreated two steps, expecting some legislator to jump out. The window lowered. A slicked up, dark-headed thirty-year-old in shirt, tie, and sunglasses studied me. "Are you Carolina Slade?"

The shock of the car braking dead in thick traffic and this man knowing my name evaporated as their identities hit me. "Who wants to know?" I asked. These gentlemen were no doubt the ones who tailed me not just today but yesterday and the day before. I hadn't been paranoid after all.

The passenger door clicked and began to open, and I envisioned movie scenes of suits grabbing victims from the curb and disappearing. I shoved the door closed, the man yanking his hand away just in time.

These clowns were SLED agents, or I was an astronaut. State Law Enforcement Division, the state's FBI and Secret Service combined. After a year of dating a federal agent, I recognized the genes.

The driver peered over, a cookie-cutter version of the first man, except for his close-cropped red hair. "We represent Governor Wheeler, ma'am."

"Really?" As if I couldn't tell?

"We'd rather not do this here," said the first.

My hackles raised, I brought my hands down hard on the door and leaned in. "Do what?" I said loudly. "What exactly would you do here in the middle of downtown? Arrest me? Put me in cuffs and haul me away?" I located my phone. "I'm calling the *feds*, boys. You're harassing a *federal* employee."

A car skirted around the SUV with a heavy hand on the horn. A couple of tourists hung back about twenty feet, curious. An assortment of bureaucrats walked by carrying briefcases, heads turning. Good, witnesses.

"No need for dramatics," the driver said. "Just delivering this message from Governor Wheeler: Back off."

The cliché rolled easily off my tongue. "Or what?"

He laughed and glanced back at his companion to share the joke. "We're aides, not Secret Service."

"We both know who you really are."

"And what should we tell the Governor is your response?"

I stepped away from the car and raised a hand in the air as if my answer ought to be obvious. "I'm too much of a lady to tell you here."

"Whatever, ma'am."

He powered up his window.

I stepped off the curb again and planted a lipstick kiss on the glass. "Enjoyed chatting with you, boys."

The SUV slid into traffic.

My muscles twitched; a giggle escaped. As I crossed the street and followed the sidewalk leading to my parking garage six blocks away, I couldn't get the smile off my face. That lipstick message probably left a better impression than the one I left with Miss South Carolina back in the State House. I marveled that Wheeler put SLED on my butt, using hard-earned tax dollars to stalk me. Amazing.

The revelation made me stop.

He felt threatened. With all that money, power, and family name to his credit, little old me niggled his pea-brain at night. I wasn't sure whether to smile or wet my pants, but it meant I had leverage.

My pace quickened, even headed uphill toward the federal building. A sense of satisfaction rolled through me as my proactive endorphins kicked in. Finally a sense of purpose. I would head out to the Fants' place anyway, calling en route. He'd be done checking his fields, so he'd be home anyway.

The walk left me panting by the time I reached the garage and entered my truck. I cranked the air-conditioner and angled two vents on my face. My brain churned through recent events and played out potential conversations with Fant. Then an idea about Kay stuck into the mix. I knew better than to backdoor Wayne again about his sister, so I picked up my phone to bounce thoughts off my resident expert.

"US Department of Agriculture, Office of Inspector General. Senior Special Agent Wayne Largo speaking."

"Your caller ID not working, lawman?"

"Habit," he said. "What do you need?"

Wow. Still pissed. I hoped a good night's sleep would soften his temper. "Come on, Wayne."

"What do you need, Slade? I'm slammed here. There's a chance I'll be called to Atlanta tomorrow."

My heart always jumped into my mouth when he mentioned Atlanta. That's where his headquarter hierarchy resided, and it represented the force that once fought to fire us both. "You in trouble?" I asked low.

He sighed. "No, there may be a case with some sensitivity to it. My dozen other cases get shoved to the back shelf if they need me, so I'm running full throttle." I heard papers shuffle.

"Heard from Kay?" I asked, hoping to expand the conversation.

"Why would I? You've talked to her more in one afternoon than I have in months. I ought to be asking you."

Ouch. Maybe it was best he *went* to Atlanta for a few days.

"Slade, why did you call?"

No *Butterbean* or Babe. Now wasn't the time to tell him my fledgling plan to call Kay and beg her to put us in touch with Ally—tell either or both we had a family emergency or something—in hopes they would come in.

I'd wanted to update him about Dubose and what she told me about Wheeler, but with Wayne's current attitude, I changed my mind.

"I thought we could have dinner," I blurted out.

"Not feeling it, Slade."

A jolt of trepidation shot through my chest.

"We'll talk later," he said and hung up.

I threw the phone on the seat. What could I have done differently with Kay? How could he overlook my concern for his sister?

Then I sank into the seat. My main preoccupation had been for *my* sister, not his. And he could tell. Still . . . Pamela would've followed me; she already proved that. But the harder I argued with myself, the more my methods appeared insane.

I should've just told him my plan.

But he'd have told me not to do it.

Crap. Fighting to regain a stronger sense of self, I pinched my nose between steepled hands. This wasn't as bad as the Beaufort case, was it? When we clashed over telling the truth to each other? Or Charleston, when we withheld information from each other?

I sucked in air, staving off tears. Would we break up over this?

I smacked the steering wheel. Wayne hadn't been able to control her, so how the hell was I supposed to? Kay was a grown woman, in a grown-up pile of shit. Anyone could see all I did was try to help.

On top of everything else, I'd sabotaged my relationship with my sister . . . for the sake of his!

I scrubbed my palms harshly across my eyes. Fine. Wayne could be that way if he wanted.

I lowered the air-conditioning a notch and put the truck in drive. As I exited the garage, I glanced instinctively toward the ten-foot wrought-iron fence surrounding the Governor's Mansion across the street. The son of a bitch probably sat a hundred yards from me at this very moment.

These political types hungered to be big, bad, and in charge. The tenuous balance of image, ethics, and desire to succeed bordered masochism. Wheeler thought himself impervious to career flaws. I'd sensed him too polished that first day in his office. My spider sense had proven right.

As I turned onto Huger Street, I caught an SUV in my rearview mirror pulling out of a side street, then following three cars behind.

I threw the truck in park in the middle of the road, got out, and stomped past the two other dumbfounded drivers to the SUV.

The red-headed dude didn't roll down his window this time.

"Listen," I said, tired of the cat and mouse. "If you knew anything about my life, you would've stopped me for fear of my nail file gutting either of you. You're stupid. Wheeler is stupid. Get this through your head, and pass the message on to him. He . . . Isn't . . . My . . . Boss."

I spun on my heel and returned to my truck. Time to head to the Fants' farm, doing just what I'd been warned not to do, even with the Hardy Boys on my tail. Their persistence made me want to dig even harder. Let them report that I'd ignored their warning.

Wheeler wouldn't like it, but he could get over it. I broke no rules. Besides, his pair of stalkers couldn't keep up with all my movements. Not unless they'd bugged my truck or something.

Wait. Had they bugged my truck? Surely not my house. Amateur sleuths bought bugs online all the time, but SLED guys only needed to check them out from an inventory of cop toys.

My gaze darted around the inside of my truck, wondering where anyone could hide an electronic device. Did people really do that sort of thing?

Traffic stopped again, and I almost didn't. I glanced in all my mirrors. No sign of the SLED boys. Cars finally crept forward, then dared to accelerate. I veered right into thicker traffic on its way to the interstate, knowing a second's delay would pen me up amongst those too scared to make a move.

A small grey sedan crossed from nowhere just as I picked up speed. I smashed the brake, but the sedan fought for control, dipping forward as the car in front of it stopped cold. No way I would miss the sedan's bumper.

I snatched the steering wheel right. My foot jammed the brake pedal to the floor as I missed the car, left the highway, and hit dirt and grass. I turned into the slide with Daddy's voice next to me, teaching me how to handle ice.

A brick wall surrounding a hotel parking lot loomed, and I covered my face. The truck's passenger side rammed the wall, and the window imploded. The seatbelt snatched me. My head snapped right, then left, smacking the glass on my side. Glass spewed across the cab in a fascinating tinkling chorus of thousands of tiny pieces.

Then everything paused.

Eyes closed, I tried to gather my wits in the strange silence, taking mental tally of my body parts. My head ached, and for some reason, I thought of the egg sandwich I ate for breakfast, and how I'd forgotten to add pepper. I opened my eyes and slowly shook my head to re-grip the present. Chaos roared in from all four sides.

"Ma'am? Are you all right?"

"Don't move her."

"I already called 9-1-1."

"Somebody get her ID."

I unbuckled my seatbelt. Where was my purse? I needed identification. Reaching under my seat, I suddenly saw the cubes of glass from the passenger window and gasped, amazed the front windshield remained intact. No blood, or was there? That's when I took intense notice of my extremities, testing for pain, sharp pangs of broken bone, or wet, sticky signs of cuts. Like after a bad head cold, my thoughts didn't want to stick.

"Ma'am? Can you hear me?"

"I'm fine," I said, wishing it so. "What did I hit?"

A small crowd gaped at me, faces etched with concern. Again I reached for my phone on the seat. Where the hell was my purse?

"You hit a brick wall," said a man in Army fatigues—most likely from the Army base. I liked him being there, all official and strong. "You need us to call anyone?"

"Are you from Fort Jackson?" I asked.

He laid a hand on my shoulder. "No need to move until EMS gets here anyway." He turned to someone behind him. "Can you tell people to back off? They're just confusing her."

Call? Who did I want him to call? Not Wayne. Monroe? No, he was in Washington. Ally was who-knows-where. What time was it? Daddy? Too far. He'd wreck trying to get to me.

Then one person came to mind. "Can someone find my phone, please?" I asked.

Men opened the two doors that worked. My phone fell on the ground. The Army sergeant handed it to me. "Need help to dial?"

I shook my head. My neck already stiffened, yet at the same time small shakes vibrated through me. Even finding Dubose's number in my call list, I screwed up dialing her the first time. With concentration, I managed on the second try.

"Slade?"

"Margaret." My voice choked. "I've been in an accident. Any chance you can come get me? I'm on Huger, at the Hampton Hotel. I think I ran into it."

"Be there in ten minutes."

I laid my head back on the seat. Finally. Somebody who gave a damn.

Chapter 18

OFFICERS ARRIVED on the crash scene. EMS pulled up, red lights flashing. I was off the road, but rubber-neckers slowed traffic. All I could offer onlookers was a dinged-up truck and a two-inch cut on the left side of my forehead. But creeping cars smothered the highway, which meant Dubose had gotten caught in the clog.

I sat further back in the EMS truck, facing away from the road to avoid recognition.

As my world came back into mental focus, I sighed.

"You okay, ma'am?" asked the medic.

The Fants. "I missed an appointment."

He shook his head, probably having heard that before.

A half hour later, Dubose's BMW crawled on the sidewalk to get around cars. In Bermuda shorts, sandals, and a soft green silk collared shirt, she hustled out, slammed her door, and trotted to the first uniform in her path, her mannerisms demanding answers. He directed her to me now seated in the backseat of a squad car, door open, since I'd declined going to the hospital.

"Slade, are you all right?" Like a mother, she stroked my hair, a soft touch on my bandage. I couldn't believe how such a simple caring gesture warmed me through.

"This is three times larger than it needs to be," I said, touching the gauze pad. "I'm fine. I'm sorry you had to come out here."

"Oh hon, I'm more than happy to do this. Can you go yet?"

"They're almost done writing the report. It shouldn't be long."

She took my elbow, prompting me to stand. "You ought to let them check you out at the hospital."

"Nothing's broken," I said, noting my shoulder and neck muscles tightening up.

"You're too stubborn," she replied and led me toward her car. "At least wait in a comfortable seat."

I laid back the BMW seat. A headache threatened to take me down, but nothing I couldn't handle after four aspirin. I held a ticket in my hand for failure to maintain control of a motor vehicle. Big surprise. What *had* I been able to control lately?

Dubose spoke to the cop, got an okay to leave, and sat in the driver's seat. "Weren't you hurt in a car accident in your Beaufort case?"

"Yeah," I said. "Charleston, too."

"I'd hate to see your insurance bill," she said.

"They don't count Beaufort. I was parked, and it wasn't my car." Wayne had saved my life that night, throwing himself over me, down on the seat as a bullet grazed my neck, right below my ear. The event scared the life out of him, and Monroe almost fainted at the sight of my blood.

I remembered the Governor's tag team boys and sat up, scanning the road even knowing they were long gone. "Have you noticed a black SUV hanging around here? Like they were watching us?"

She glanced around. "No, why?"

"Do you know your damn governor had two guys tailing me?"

Her head snapped around. "Are you saying the wreck was no accident?"

I hadn't meant to say that, but now that Dubose did, I wondered. "I don't know. But I was warned off. You know Wheeler. What do you think?"

She started the car and eased into traffic. "Does he know I talked to you about his past?"

"Are you saying there's a chance he ordered a hit?" I asked. "Really?"

She frowned. "That's not what I said."

"No, he doesn't know you and I spoke," I said. "But you know how he got when I questioned Lucille before her stroke. And he wouldn't like what I missed on my agenda this afternoon."

"What's that?" she asked, changing to the middle lane.

"Interviewing Simeon Fant about peanuts and drugs."

Her glance touched on me for a second as she checked traffic in her passenger sideview mirror. "Did he agree to see you?"

The knot on my head felt like Mt. Everest. "Sure did. Guess that's not happening."

"Don't see why not," she said. "Sit back. I'll get you there."

My truck now rested on the back of some towing contraption. My insurance agent said he'd have it inspected tomorrow and would set aside a rental for me in West Columbia this evening. Dubose didn't seem to mind chauffeuring, so why not keep the appointment, albeit late.

I counted my blessings she didn't inquire about Wayne's whereabouts. My tongue would've stumbled all over an explanation, and I didn't feel like the effort.

Dubose knew the way to the Fants. Big surprise. We passed the town of Lexington, and five miles later we turned into an asphalt drive that snaked through a crop of pecan trees toward a two-story, red-brick home.

A four-car garage reached out from the left side, and a covered walkway led into the building. To the right, one floor branched off to what appeared to be a self-contained apartment. I thought of Hugh Fant, the peanut vendor from the Pelion festival. Maybe he lived there, being dependent, yet independent.

Hollies, yaupons, and nandinas filled the beds under windows across the front, with nary a rose, impatiens, or vinca. A hint of melancholy rolled through me as I recalled the thick clusters of blooms in Lucille's flower beds. The Wheeler house was sweet and Southern. The Fant residence spoke of something more practical.

We parked and stepped up to the porch. I knocked on the door.

Addie Fant's large buxom frame, wrapped in a denim shift and feet shod with sneakers, filled the entry. "Well hey, Margaret. Haven't seen you in a coon's age," she said, then turned to me. "I'm Addie, Ms. Slade. I'm afraid you've missed Simeon." She took in my bandage. "Gracious, what happened to you?"

I shook my head, the abrupt thudding reminding me not to move so fast. "My apologies. My truck and I made friends with a brick wall on Huger Street a couple hours ago."

"Mercy, you all right?" She touched my elbow. "Why don't you two come sit. I'll get us something to drink. Y'all had lunch? I've got chicken salad in the fridge and fresh tomatoes from my son's garden."

We followed deeper inside the house. My stomach growled. "Your chicken salad sounds fantastic. In all the confusion, I forgot lunch."

"Sure thing," Addie beamed. "How about you, Margaret?"

"Works for me, too, Addie."

I sat slowly at the kitchen table overlooking the step-down den, a massive stone fireplace dominating the view. A ten-point whitetail buck mount stared at us from over the mantel. Antique flintlock pistols hung in shadow boxes on the wall. The dark yellow of the pine paneling dated the house back to the fifties or later. Early American décor claimed the rooms, making the huge place feel like a homestead. Nothing lavish, but far from cheap. Country affluence.

Dubose looked poised even in Bermudas, her jade earrings matching her top. Her casual equaled my best day in a suit. "Let me help, Addie," she asked, moving into the kitchen, opening a cabinet door like she lived there.

I leaned on the quilted placemat, admiring her collection of rooster items around the kitchen. Salt and pepper shakers, figurines, baskets. Her canisters appeared to be hand-painted crockery. A print of a Rhode Island Red and his hen hung over a heavy walnut buffet. "I hope your husband wasn't too upset when I failed to show," I said.

Addie scrunched her nose and waved a dismissive hand. "He figured something came up."

"Funny, I'm surrounded by chickens here, yet you guys are Clemson fans," I said. "Looks more like a University of South Carolina Gamecock setup to me, Ms. Fant."

A warm smile smoothed her facial lines. "My daddy said chickens come with living in the country. Can't help that USC picked one for a mascot. Some of these roosters sitting around here are my mother's. Kinda feels good having them here, like she might come in from feeding them in the yard."

Addie whipped through the kitchen like a seasoned chef and placed lunch on the table in minutes. She took a chair across from me. Dubose set our glasses down and took her place at the end of a table built for eight.

"Maybe I can answer some of your questions," Addie said. "I assume it has to be something about farming."

Stomach churning for food, I took a bite first. A perfect balance of celery and egg, without too much salt. The right mayonnaise brand. Mayo made chicken salad. "This is so good."

"I'm sorry. Enjoy your sandwich. Business in a minute." Our hostess faced Margaret. "I visited Lucille yesterday."

Dubose adjusted the napkin in her lap. "I saw her, too. Recovery doesn't look good."

Addie shook her head, adding an "unh, unh, unh" in agreement. "She never got over Patsy and never had a chance to get over CJ. With him gone, her little body collapsed."

I washed down another bite. "She didn't believe the story about CJ and the drugs," I said, in an attempt to introduce our purpose for this meeting. "I was there when she had her stroke."

Addie appeared to be holding back. "So I heard."

Dubose wiped her mouth. "Slade didn't cause the stroke, Addie."

"Of course not. The thought never entered my mind." Her chair squeaked under her as she shifted, belying her words.

"We were having a pleasant chat," I explained. "Tea and cookies. Then Lamar stormed in—"

She held up a hand. "Anything could've triggered her stroke, Slade."

She stopped, as if she remembered too much, then stared at the tablecloth, face sullen. Dubose reached over and laid a hand on her forearm. I felt wrong eating in the middle of such a serious topic and tried to chew discretely.

"We're here about Lamar," Dubose said.

"And Dick," I added. Dubose perused me with her reprimand face.

Addie wiped her eyes and then stared with a new soberness. "What about the Wheelers?" she said, her soft jowls firmer, like the tone in her voice.

"Lucille's paid a heavy price living under that family's roof. CJ did, too," Dubose said. "And you know good and well they made Patsy keep quiet. Lamar is about to get away with besmirching CJ's poor name."

For some reason, Addie stared at me. I stayed quiet. So she turned to Dubose. "Margaret, politics is bad enough in this state without this mess about Lamar. Look what it's done so far . . . to Lucille. To CJ."

Dubose put her napkin on her plate, expression stoic. "Dick asked me to learn more about the investigation, then turned on me, landing me a suspension. I'm not exactly tickled with that. I only offered to help because of my connection with Lucille."

Addie glanced from Dubose to me. "Simeon wouldn't tell you anything about this, so good thing he isn't here. And Lucille doesn't need any more bad news."

"I'd think she'd be relieved to see Lamar and Dick get their comeuppance," I said low, then pushed the plate and half-eaten sandwich aside. We were no longer having a lunch chat. Now I knew why Dubose had offered to drive. This family would've stonewalled me in a heartbeat.

Our hostess' sour expression showed an internal conflict about how much she should say.

Dubose leaned forward and in her charismatic voice pleaded. "Addie, please."

Addie slid sideways in her chair, in my direction, her posture representing a stalemate. So I just asked what needed asking. "Did Dick or Lamar ever pay inspectors to accept a bad peanut load?"

Her eyes flashed ever so much, enough for me to see she knew something. Strong, proper, well-raised women didn't gossip, at least not to new acquaintances. I sensed she might fall back on her upbringing—that and her deep respect for Lucille.

"Lucille and I go back to high school, you know," she said.

I wouldn't have guessed this woman to be almost eighty. She just looked rustic, wholesome, a little worn but cozy, like somebody's rowdy, body-squeezing grandmother. She wasn't slow on the draw, either. There was a truth in her eye telling me she knew more.

"Don't you think the public would like the truth about the Wheelers?" I said.

"I don't know who the Wheelers may have paid off," she said. "But Simeon thinks they did one time back. My husband knows the guys at the market better than I do. If someone got bought off today, they could identify the individual farm. They keep better records than before."

"Each farm?" I had little experience with peanuts. My grandfather grew cotton. In our Lowcountry region, farmers managed vegetables and fruits, with soybeans planted where there was enough flat acreage, when property taxes didn't make them too expensive to grow.

"Oh yes," she said. "All domestic and imported peanuts go through inspection after they've been cleaned or shelled and separated into graded lots, all identified with the original farm."

"What about in 2001?" Dubose asked.

Addie shrugged. "Not sure. September eleventh changed everything. Life was looser then."

"They still inspected for aflatoxin, right?" I asked.

She gave me a doleful grin. "You *have* talked to Lucille."

"I'm not sure how much truth there is in Lucille's suspicions," Dubose said. "She had just enough knowledge to over-rationalize and be dangerous. Cancer and peanuts are pretty far-fetched."

I played with the condensation trickling down my tea glass and onto the placemat. "Patsy knew Lamar paid off peanut inspectors. So why wouldn't Lucille know? Overlooking a high moisture load could mean they overlooked a fungus. Aflatoxin is produced by a fungus, right?"

Of course I didn't believe aflatoxin existed in the United States, but I needed to pry Addie loose.

Dubose reached across the long table, as if trying to touch me. "We can't prove any of this, Slade. Nobody can."

"Well, ladies, you're dealing with the Wheelers. It's how they operate." Addie tapped the table with her hand. "I do know this, though. In 2001 we suffered a big drought. None of us made our contracts. Some couldn't sell for mold issues. Many of us got stuck with loads. Yet the Wheelers sold every peanut. Simeon thinks Dick sold directly to some candy maker or private commercial user. Maybe a feed company. Simeon yanked Dick aside one evening at a county council meeting and told him if he did anything like that again, Simeon would personally take it to the FDA."

"How do we prove Wheeler did that?"

Dubose shook her head. "We can't." Addie appeared to agree.

"Wait, what about that company that went down a few years ago?" I said. "That was a company that bought bad peanuts."

Dubose scowled slightly. "They went under, Slade. Investigated, filed bankruptcy, and went out of business. People continue suing them and continue getting nothing."

I'd hoped the Fants had more intel than this. My thoughts fought for purchase on how to nail Dick. He seemed the only happy person in the Wheeler clan, and that rubbed me wrong, too. "But he—"

"Slade, move on," Dubose said. "I knew most of this and thought you needed to hear it, as well as meet the Fants. They're good people."

A too quiet Ms. Fant watched as if curious what I'd do next.

"Sorry," I said to her, all too aware now we were guests in her house, and no further into our investigating than before.

"No problem, sweetheart," Addie said. "Any other questions on your mind? You still have a sandwich on your plate."

An open door. Might as well ask about the other issue. "Okay, what's your take on Lamar blaming CJ for those prescription drugs found at the condo? You understand the family dynamics."

"Oooohh, child, don't get me started with that," Addie said, face drawn up in a knot. "That boy was just like Patsy, through and through. Dick Wheeler is just covering his ass, distancing Lamar and the farm from his glorious office." She gave a hard nod of her head. "Dick's peanut affiliation is purely a touch of Americana for his political career. If Lamar goes down, the farm has no overseer. Maybe someone looks at farm records; someone talks about instances like the one you mentioned." She gazed at me, as if waiting for me to get it.

"Oh, yeah," I said, fully understanding. "Everyone believes a story about a kid dealing drugs. With CJ dead, it's a win-win for Lamar, the Governor, the farm. Nobody snoops very hard. And nobody gets hurt."

Addie added, "Except Lucille."

"And sadly, again no proof," said Dubose. She clasped her handbag, as if tired of this useless back and forth. "Addie, it's been a pleasure. Sorry it took so long for us to meet again. We'll have to do this more informally sometime."

Addie rose, bumping her chair with her ample hip. She came around the table and enveloped Dubose in a whopper of a hug. "Any time, Margaret. Lucille would like us doing that."

I stood, reminded of the morning's incident. Sitting so long had calcified my joints. Thank goodness I didn't get Addie's extra-large squeeze, but she gripped my hand strong enough saying goodbye.

We headed toward the door. I spoke over my shoulder. "Do you think the Governor—"

Hugh Fant came up in his high-water khakis and Keds, just like he'd been dressed at the fair, at the VA pharmacy. He tucked his head and shyly returned our hellos with a wave.

"He seems so sweet," I said.

"He's my baby," Addie said, watching him head to the kitchen. "People underestimate that boy. Just because he's quiet and a bit slow doesn't mean he's not taking everything in."

"Listening more than talking," I said. "We should all do more of that."

Addie smiled at what must be a rare compliment of her son. "What were you asking about the Governor?" she asked.

Dubose reached behind me and yanked on my shirt. "Look at the time, Slade," Dubose interrupted. "We need to get your rental before they close. Thanks for the hospitality, Addie."

We left with a few more thanks, got in the BMW, and turned onto the highway back toward Columbia.

"She was talking, Margaret. What was the problem?" I asked.

"Hugh. He listens," she said. "Everyone accepts him as disabled, and nobody thinks he hears."

"Oh." I felt royally stupid, not heeding my own words to Addie about her son.

"So," I said, "I have just enough information about the Governor to be dangerous, like Lucille and her aflatoxin." I reclined the seat a notch. My headache, once reduced to a distant throb with the aspirin, returned with a vengeance. "Does that help me or make me more vulnerable?"

"Well, Dick knows I knew anything Patsy or Lucille did, and by now have shared it with you. I'd say you're good for now from his side. One day he'll no longer be in office, and all this will be moot anyway. You still have Harden to deal with, though."

"That's not very consoling." Then I thought of something, asking from under closed eyelids. "Why haven't you reported this to someone like Wayne to investigate?"

"The statute of limitation's probably expired."

"Not when you first knew about it," I said, glancing over.

She continued staring at the road. "If the inspector was bribed, and if the peanuts were bad, we saw no wave of illness or death as a result of it. You sure you want to lay your career on the line for such a slim case? Against someone with such clout? I'd like to keep peace with these people. I gave the info to you for leverage with Dick alone, not to create a federal case out of it. That's why I came with you, so this didn't get blown out of proportion."

Or maybe monitor what I was up to. After all, Dubose had a political career.

The BMW veered around a curve, and the sun shone hard in my eyes. The headache bit into my brain. I shut my lids and thought of poor Lucille. At the end of her days, she lay locked inside herself at that hospital with little to think about other than her offspring predeceasing her. Salmonella in peanuts killed and sickened folks. Who would believe an old woman trying to claim peanut mold killed her child?

The rental car was ready when we arrived. I thanked Dubose and settled into the Sebring. Sportiest wheels I ever drove. I chewed three more aspirin, then headed home.

I thought I caught sight of SLED's tail once or twice, but didn't care.

My brief, abrasive chat with Wayne returned to mind as did the plan about finding our sisters. My morning anger a distant history, I needed him to talk to me. After the discussion at the Fants about Patsy and CJ dying unexpectedly, I viewed our sisters important enough to get past our fussing. We'd regret missing opportunity to redeem our two families.

I picked up pizza for the kids. Hopefully they'd hug me for this, a welcome change from their recent behaviors. Pepperoni for Zack and a cheese combo for Ivy, to respect her experimental no-meat phase.

At home, I walked in to Zack's comment of "Pizza. Awesome!" which brought Ivy out of her room. "Probably pepperoni," she said. "What happened to your head?"

I peeled the bandage off. "It's nothing. Look in the pizza box."

She peaked in and grinned. As she set the table, Zack fixed drinks, one slice already in his hand. I brought up the results of a music reality show to make light conversation, when someone pounded on the front door. I jumped, shooting pain through tight muscles. I grabbed the back of my neck en route.

Zack ran in front of me.

"I'm home!" shouted Ally Jo, dropping her suitcase on the floor in the same spot she did two weeks ago.

"It's Aunt Ally," Zack shouted back to Ivy.

Ivy busted out of the kitchen and bear-hugged my sister. "So glad you're back."

"Me too, kiddo," she said. "Whose car is that in the drive?"

I managed to squeeze in after Ivy and hugged Ally, patted her back, then stepped aside for her to come in. "Didn't expect to see you."

She smirked. "What the heck happened to your head?"

"She hit it at work," Zack yelled, already back at the pizza.

Ivy dragged her aunt to the table.

So much for my cobbled, quasi-plan Wayne hadn't allowed me to explain. I'd intended to use each sister against the other in some way to make them come home.

It was a relief to have her back. But her arrival probably meant Kay had disappeared from Clay River. Not good.

I wondered if this was Fate's way of telling me, *here's your sister, now butt out.*

Chapter 19

ZACK RELUCTANTLY let Ally rub his hair as she followed the kids to the kitchen table. I stood glued to the floor, emotionally drained after a day of fights, wrecks, and SLED shadows; my throat tightened. My sister came home, just as I'd asked.

"Pizza, Aunt Ally," hollered Zack. "You can have some of mine."

"Throw two pieces on a plate for me," Ally said.

"I know which one you want," Ivy said. "No meat. Like we talked about."

Ally laughed. "Oh my gracious, this smells extraordinary. Kay eats health food, and I'd kill for cheese and grease." As I joined them, she studied my face, then eyed me up and down. She leaned in and whispered, "You look a mess. You want to tell me later?"

"Later," I said, grateful.

Ivy clung to my sister as if welcoming a mother returned from the dead.

Ally reached over and yanked my shirt as a reminder of our sunbathing moment. "Seems last time I saw you, you offered to do anything to get me out of Clay River. Here I am, and you act like someone dumped a baby on your doorstep."

"Of course I'm glad you're here," I said, then busted out in tears.

Ivy stood motionless, a slice of pizza in each hand. Zack's eyes grew to the size of two harvest moons.

Although three inches shorter, Ally enfolded me in her arms, letting my head drop and hide in her hair so I could sob. "Sis," she said. "Give it up, what's going on?"

"I worried so much about you being around Kay," I mumbled in to her shoulder. "Someone's following me. I wrecked the truck. They disciplined me at work for doing absolutely nothing wrong." I stopped to take in hitched breaths. In that pause, I realized what touched me most, and my tears flowed as if from a garden hose. "I'm just so happy you're safe, and home . . . and I think Wayne and I broke up!"

The tears wouldn't stop coming.

Ally stroked my hair. "Shhh, it's okay. I bet it's nothing we can't talk out and fix." I felt her weight shift as she motioned to the kids. "Your mom has had a hell of a week. Bet you had no idea, did you?"

They shook their heads in unison, unable to take their gazes off me. I started to pull away from Ally so I could move toward them, to console their worries, but Ally gripped me to remain fast.

"Tell you what, Zack," Ally said, her hug tighter, one hand rubbing my back now. "You and Ivy take your dinner to the porch, or better yet, out to the dock. Give us a moment or two, okay? Sometimes parents have days that suck just like you do. Understand?"

"Yes, ma'am," Zack said.

"Come on." Ivy threw their slices on plates. "Get the drinks, Zack."

My little man did as his big sister told him, and they scurried out the sliding glass door.

I felt like such a child.

Ally set me down at the table and poured me a glass of root beer. We always kept root beer in the house, the kids' favorite, and it seemed to suit the moment. I wiped my eyes with a napkin.

"Now," Ally said, sitting in the next chair, "let's talk." She slapped a piece of pizza on my plate, picked one up for herself, and took a huge bite. "Sorry," she mumbled. "Had to do that. I was going ape-shit with nothing junky to eat at Clay River." She swallowed a bite and rolled her eyes. "Hea—ven," she sang.

I grinned. My sister never failed to entertain.

Ally owned people skills I never mastered. Yet she couldn't stay focused on one job if her life depended on it. I had better hair; she strutted bigger boobs. Combined, we would've made the perfect girl. As levelheaded as I usually was, however, Ally Jo controlled the present moment.

"So," she said, "the accident explains the rental in the driveway. Let's move on to who's tailing you."

I sniffled and pinched my brow. "Thought you'd have brought up Wayne first."

"That's fixable," she said, glib. "Are you in danger? Who's following you?"

"The Governor, I think." I blew my nose in a napkin.

A surprised expression flashed across her face. "The Governor?" She laughed. "Well aren't you something special?"

Only my sister would laugh at being stalked. "Can you keep a secret?" I asked, desperately wanting to spill the last week of my life to someone who wouldn't chastise my judgment or report me to my boss.

"What are you talking about, Sis? I hid from you. What do you call that if not a secret?"

I snorted. "But I found you."

Her finger waggled. "No, Ivy found me, and only because I let her. And only because I knew she'd let you know I was okay."

My baby sister displayed more wiles than I gave her credit for.

She sipped her drink, washing down a bite of crust. "I just didn't expect you to have the gumption to set foot at a nudist camp. Kind of threw me off my game."

"You never skipped a beat, Ally. You made me strip."

"I didn't make you do anything. You almost walked out, then *you* decided to stick around to try and talk me and Kay into coming home." Her impish sneer made me laugh again. "You went nude for me, so I came back. Impressive. So I coaxed Kay into sticking around, at least give your words some consideration."

I sat up straight and set down my root beer. "She's not on the lam again?"

"*On the lam,*" Ally said in a James Cagney imitation.

"I'm serious. She's still at Clay River?" A ray of hope peeked through my days of gloom and doom.

"Last I checked, which was"—she checked her invisible watch—"two hours ago."

I almost teared up again. "I love you, Allegra Jo Slade." I reached across the table and dragged her to me in a hug, both our shirts raking across tomato sauce and cheese. I did make a difference, and I did convince Kay not to run. My plan worked!

"Don't move," Ally said in my grasp.

"What?" I whispered.

"Spies are watching."

The sliding door squealed open, and Ivy poked her head in. "Momma?"

We turned. "Yes?" I answered.

"You aren't gonna make Aunt Ally mad and chase her off again, are you?" A pout blossomed on my daughter's mouth, and her brows and skinny shoulders slumped, verbalizing her teenage distrust of a parent. "Please don't screw things up again, Momma."

Ally's hand covered her smile as she watched how the drama would play out.

"She's not going anywhere," I said, then turned to Ally. "You aren't, are you?"

She shook her head. "Nope."

"Satisfied? Now let us alone for a while," I said.

Relieved, Ivy smiled and went to her room.

Once the door latched, I sighed, blowing root beer breath across the table. "If one more person says I eff'd up his life . . . I think I need a real drink." I rose and went to the pantry where I kept the cereal. The bottles and boxes happened to fit on the same shelf. Guests hunting for Cheerios slid Jack Daniel's aside to reach it. I kept the sugar cereal in front, so the kids didn't have to. I'd have to rethink my bar setup when the kids got older. "You want one?" I asked Ally. "Rum, right?"

"And diet cola," she said. "Got any cherries?"

"In the frig, top shelf near the back," I said, setting the booze on the counter then splashing water on my face in the kitchen sink. I dried off with a paper towel as Ally opened bottles.

Her drink held four cherries, one impaled on a straw. I poured myself a bourbon and ginger, half speed.

I sat back down. "Now then, want to hear the rest of my issues?"

She snagged a cherry and ate it. "Sure, but first tell me why Kay would be *on the lam*. I gathered she's Wayne's sister from y'alls' coded discussion, and I kinda see the resemblance, but I don't get all the secrecy." She stood, went back to the kitchen, and poured extra liquor in her glass. "Consoling her delayed me from getting here sooner, but she's as tight as a snapping turtle on a fishing worm. What did you do . . ." she stumbled. "Um, why was she upset?"

I noted appreciably her detour from blaming me and took another swig from my bourbon. "Kay did drugs, Ally. Still might, I don't know, but she knew people who sold drugs. DEA used her to try and set up a dealer. Kay bailed on them, and she's been running for a year. Wayne's worried sick about who's after her." I squeezed Ally's arm. "See why I was so worried about you? On top of everything else, Wayne's ex-wife is the DEA agent searching for Kay." I leaned back. "There. Now you know. I went to Clay River to get you away from all that."

"I see," she said. No melodrama, as if I'd just told her about a forty percent chance of rain for tomorrow.

"You knew," I said, wondering how.

She shook her head. "Nope. Just doesn't bother me. She's a cool girl. No wonder her RPMs ran a little high. She never could chill. Smart place to hide, though. Who'd think to look for her at a nudist resort?"

The most predictable trait about Allegra Jo was unpredictability.

"She tried to reach me three times about an hour after I left there. Why won't she return my calls?"

Ally shrugged. "She's a little odd."

"I wonder if Wayne was able to contact her after he left here mad . . ."

Ally raised a brow. "That's why you two fought? What did you say to make him . . . never mind."

His anger when I returned from Clay River rushed back, then his annoyance when I called today. "I didn't involve him in my decision to go find you. He's one among many who think I tend to screw up lives."

Ally walked over, eased behind my chair, reached her arms around, and squeezed me, her cheek on my head. "Sorry, Sis. I feel kind of responsible."

I patted her arm. "Yeah, maybe I should've told him beforehand. Maybe you needed to know my intentions, too. I could've dodged the whole nude sunbathing bit."

"Who sunbathed nude?" Ivy had reappeared in the room. "Momma?" Both hands covered her mouth. "Oh. My. God."

"What did you hear?" I tried to replay the conversation in my head.

"That you went nude!" she said. "Isn't that enough? That'll traumatize me for life!"

Cornered. And it appeared she heard nothing about Kay. "I followed your aunt's advice and visited a nudist resort, with lots of other people. At a pool."

She spun toward her bedroom. "Oh my gosh. I can't believe my mother went naked in front of people. That's so totally disgusting." She shut her door. "That's just gross," she yelled.

Ally and I burst out laughing.

"Don't look now," Ally said low, "but I think you just eff'd up someone else's life again. Way to go, Momma."

She held up a palm, and I high-fived her. I knocked back the remains of my drink.

"I'll make the next round," Ally said, already doubling the liquor in her glass.

"Gotta pass." I checked the microwave clock. "Heading out. And I need you to slip into Clay River tonight."

"Why?"

"Kay likes you. You might be able to talk her in."

"I already checked out," she said. "Can't check in until morning since I'm not a member."

"Okay," I said, remembering the rules. "That'll work. Early tomorrow, then, before she leaves. But I need to let Wayne know."

She shrugged, not seeing the dilemma. "So call him."

"No," I said, retrieving my purse from the kitchen counter. "He turned me down once already today. Face to face, he'll listen."

"Oh no, no, no, you don't!"

I froze, panicked that I'd overlooked something erroneous in my logic. I'd done that a lot lately.

"We have to clean you up first, look." She walked me to the hall mirror and held me before it. "Would you kiss that?"

A couple of bruises decorated my temple and cheek. Shadow and mascara smeared from brow to nose. My eyes were red, the lids puffy. "Oh my God." I dashed out of her grip to the bedroom, stripping en route to the bath.

Thirty minutes later, I emerged primped, groomed, spritzed, and wearing my best jeans and a silk, short-sleeve blouse. Keys in hand, I darted toward the garage door and then stopped. "Ally, do you think Kay'll be there tomorrow?"

"Calvin and Prissy run more than a nudist resort, big sister. They collect lost souls. I told them to keep an eye on Kay."

"Meaning?"

"They're pretty incredible people who seem to gravitate to people in need." She walked over and shoved me. "Scoot, scoot. We can talk tomorrow. Go take care of your boyfriend. I'll cover the kids." She winked. "Take as long as you need."

I scooped three mints from the dish on the coffee table. "Thanks, and I'll take you up on that. Love you."

"Back at you, Sis."

As I started my rental, Ally ran out, a small Igloo cooler in hand. "You might need this," she said, handing it to me through the window. She stepped back and stood in the garage doorway with her hands framing her mouth. "Try not to screw it up." Then she grinned and shouted, "Just kidding!"

TRAFFIC PROVED light as I drove into town. Wayne probably worked late, however, preparing for his trip to Atlanta tomorrow. No problem. I had a key.

In hindsight, I probably overreacted to our disagreement being a break up. Hormones, stress, whatever, gone. Spruced up and motivated, I drove excited to Wayne's apartment seeking his input into how to draw Kay in. With Ally at our disposal, Wayne could tell us what to say to Kay, and how and when to say it.

I couldn't wait to see the look on his face when I told him about his sister.

Our spat, now that I thought about it, was no worse than others. Frankly, we'd endured worse and each time came out better and stronger for it. He would instantly see that my trip to Clay River accomplished its intent. He might not admit it, but that was okay. All that mattered was we were on the mend.

Praying he hadn't eaten yet, I stopped at his favorite burger joint in Five Points and ordered dinner for two. The co-ed behind the counter glanced at me oddly while ringing up the food. I glimpsed behind me to find the reason for her observation, then remembered my truck accident bruises. God, I bet I'd be all shades of blue tomorrow.

In the car, I set the sandwiches and fries beside the cooler Ally gave me, after I glanced inside to see a chilled bottle of Chablis she'd seen in my fridge. Yay Ally. My phone clock read seven thirty. If he wasn't there, dinner would be waiting when he arrived, along with another one of my apologies, a plea for his help, and maybe make-up sex for dessert.

Without fail, we clashed over cases, always over our views of how to pursue the truth. This time was no different. We had shared three cases in a year, each one pushing us to the edge then sling-shooting us back into each other's arms as soon as the situations closed. That edginess heightened my senses, making me a sharper investigator the same way adrenaline drove some people to lift cars off bodies.

I pulled my rental into the parking lot at Wayne's apartment complex and shut off the headlights. Some young woman ten years my junior scuffed past in flip-flops and entered the building opposite Wayne's. This apartment complex buzzed with tempting singles, all searching for the next level in their social lives.

I grabbed my purse, the sacks of food, and the cooler. Hands full, I stretched shoulder and neck muscles. A medicinal dose of wine would help those soon enough.

Wayne's government car sat in its assigned slot. At the apartment door, cooler and bags on the welcome mat, I changed my mind about ringing the bell and sorted through my keys. I lifted my goods and shoved the unlocked door open with my foot.

The apartment was a simple two-bedroom, one thousand square-foot model. Commercial grade carpet and eggshell paint. Nothing fancy. I glanced past the kitchen on the left, the master bedroom door on the right, and into the living room.

Pamela sat on the sofa, her legs tucked under her too-toned ass, her breasts snug in a white T-shirt, and a glass of something amber in her hand I already guessed was Wild Turkey.

She glanced to her right at me, glass resting on her blue jean-clad thigh. Her brow raised, she turned away, nodding her head in my direction. "You have a visitor, Stud."

Wayne stepped into my line of vision. "Slade?"

He stood in bare feet, wearing jeans and a black Lynyrd Skynyrd T-shirt, a similar glass of whiskey in his hand.

I kicked the door shut and went to the kitchen.

No tears, no tears. My heart beat like a hammer as my mind exploded with confusion.

I couldn't tell him about Kay, not with Pamela here.

Without a word, I unpacked the wine and set it in the refrigerator, then slammed the door. Head down, I set out plates and then the sandwiches, viciously cramming empty sacks in the garbage under the sink. I saw Wayne's bare feet appear beside me. I heard Pamela disappear into the bathroom.

"Slade," Wayne said low. "What are you doing here?"

"Thought you were in a hurry to get to Atlanta," I said, reopening the refrigerator for ketchup, afraid to stop being busy.

"They cancelled," he said.

"How fortunate for you two."

He blocked me, which wasn't difficult in his small kitchen. "She came by to talk about Kay." He frowned. "What happened to your face?"

"I hit a brick wall." I dropped the ketchup bottle loudly in the sink. "Please tell me you didn't tell her where your sister is . . . was."

"We're negotiating . . . is?" he asked.

I stared at him. "Who says Kay's still there? Ally came home. What does that tell you?"

"What?" He fell into a cross-armed stance, again judging, doubting.

One hand on hip, I leaned forward, eyes narrowed. "I came here to ask for your help because you said I shouldn't dive headfirst into . . . everything. I come with a peace offering in hand, and I find you with your ex."

"She's an agent, Slade."

"Don't patronize me." I shoved him off balance to get by. "When's the last time you entertained an agent in your living room, all barefoot and casual? Maybe I should've waited another half hour. I could've found the entertainment in the bedroom, or is over the back of the sofa more her style?"

The bathroom door opened. Pamela peered around Wayne. "Don't lose your sanity, sweetheart. I prefer the kitchen table, and he doesn't have one." She paused, wearing a crooked smile.

That evil bitch! I waited for Wayne to interrupt, but he only stared at the floor.

Pamela caught my glance toward him. "He won't get in the middle of this. Not against me."

Wayne raised his hands in exasperation. "Stop it, Pamela."

I sifted through my key ring and found Wayne's key. It wouldn't slide to come free, making my hands begin to tremble as Wayne and Pamela studied my effort. "Damn it," I muttered.

"What are you doing?" Wayne asked.

I ignored him and yanked open his kitchen junk drawer, through blurry vision found the pliers, and bent the ring until the key slid off.

I slapped the key on the counter with the pliers and left.

Just twenty minutes later, my knuckles ached from gripping the steering wheel as I drove home, imagining Wayne and Pamela, together again, the feature movie of the week.

The left side of my brain urged me to slow down. Maybe they simply talked shop as he insinuated. The right side told me I was a fool to give Pamela so much conservative credit. My heart felt embarrassed that I'd built myself up for such a letdown.

I didn't know what or who was right anymore, or what I was supposed to do about it.

Wayne always seemed to flop between sad and disgusted when he spoke of Pamela. She played guys, no doubt. Wayne kicked her butt to the curb for doing so with DEA agents while married to him. *He* divorced *her*. I repeated those three words over and over yet wondered if he'd regretted his actions once she resurfaced all taut, fetching, and in-your-face cute.

Who had drinks with their ex . . . and didn't tell their present number?

My speedometer read eighty, in a fifty zone. I slowed, giving my mirror a strong study for a squad car hiding behind a truck.

Ally would be stunned. She was on my side now, probably willing to jump on board with me on a plan to lure Kay back, but to hell with the plan now. Wayne knew where she was. He could go get her.

Pamela suspected I'd seen, even communicated with Kay. Let her keep suspecting. Pamela could tail me from here to Kansas, and all she'd ever see was my rear end, because I no longer held the notion to ever see Kay again.

Chapter 20

MORNING SUN MEANS nothing to kids with the freedom to sleep in. "Look after your aunt today," I said, stooping over Ivy in her bed. I kissed her temple. "I'll be home on time tonight."

How true. I no longer had a reason to *not* be home on time.

Ivy rolled over and sniffled, stirring until she found the perfect position, and then returned to sleep.

My daughter no longer snarled at me, thanks to her cool aunt in the house. I knew a phase when I saw one, but I craved my sweet innocent baby who used to run to me for any and all advice, from how to do a French braid to why boys were stupid. I lifted hair off her face and raked it back, taking the moment to stroke those beautiful dark tresses that mirrored mine, minus the white streak. A streak that seemed to grow in relation to the stress.

Ally maintained a shrewd grip on my kids using a combination of diplomatic oversight and belly-laughing fun. I'd hear all about their adventures when I got home, and cherish the fact they lived with such a doting relative. To come home to a clean kitchen—or better, dinner in the oven—was nirvana.

Once school started in another week, I suspected Ally's itch to find her own place might take hold. That wouldn't hurt my feelings, but if she found an apartment nearby I'd be happy. I made a mental note to plant that seed in her head tonight after dinner.

Wearing a nightshirt smattered with hearts, Ally lazed at the kitchen table with coffee, her eyes blinking away sleep. "You don't mind if I go back to bed after you leave, do you? We sort of stayed up late talking." She yawned. "How you doing, by the way?"

"Let's not go into it again, at least not this early in the morning. Nothing against you," I said, pouring coffee in a two-cup thermos. "Why'd you even get up? Go on back to bed." I nodded down the hall. "Your two alarm clocks will get you up soon enough."

She yawned again. "I figured that. Just checking on my big sister."

"I appreciate it, too." After unplugging the cell from the charger, I dropped it in my purse and lifted car keys from the counter. "Call if you need me." I scribbled my direct office number on the magnetic pad stuck on the refrigerator. "There you go. In case they escape their leashes."

She walked me to the door. "I'm sorry about Wayne," she said. "Did he call?"

"No," I said, checking voicemail on my cell phone . . . again.

"I thought you two were the real deal," she said. "But hey, look at me. I'm a divorce in process, so what do I know?" She hugged me. "Enjoy your first day back at work."

"Yeah." I shut the kitchen door behind me.

Just what I needed to forget breaking up with my boyfriend . . . a boss with a grudge.

Commuter activity zoned me out. I rolled off the entrance ramp into interstate traffic, my bumper hugging the car in front like the car behind hugged mine.

A year ago, I thought I'd landed the most amazing job on the planet, combining my agriculture and finance background with investigations. I was well paid for being nosy, with ample authority to do it. Dubose assumed the State Director's job, and we'd hit it off. She accepted Wayne professionally and understood I enjoyed him socially. Everything had been so damn sweet. Now I dreaded setting foot in the place.

I smacked the dash with my fist, angry at the manipulation, being used, getting screwed.

Traffic stopped for the thousandth time, and I braked too hard for the five hundredth, not used to the rental. My heart rebooted, fighting deja vu from the recent accident.

Inside the federal building, hordes of employees filled elevators, like water into buckets.

On the tenth floor, the door of the elevator opened at the same time as the one opposite. Three USDA employees exited and did a double take.

"Oh, hey Slade," one of them said. "Great to have you back. Sorry about the accident."

"Thanks," I said. "Had my share of bad luck lately."

"So I heard," he said and disappeared around the left corner as I turned right.

No telling what he heard with Harden in authority, free to mouth off to anybody with nobody over his head to contain him.

Whitney brightened as I entered, her fair, twenty-five-year-old complexion fresh, her disposition sunny. Six-inch earrings dangling a string of tiny seashells hung from under her short, blonde curls. She handed me a couple of messages. "So glad you're back, Ms. Slade." Her brow furrowed. "Wow, look at those bruises."

I touched the side of my forehead, wishing my hair covered it more. "I expect I'll have a few more before the day's out."

"Pardon?"

"Joke, hon. Speaking of jokes, has Mr. Harris asked for me?"

She snickered. "As a matter of fact, he did. You're to report to him ASAP."

I exhaled and dropped my chin to my chest. "Sorry, Whitney. I shouldn't have said that about him."

Her smile was a mainstay, and she gave me one of her best, as if reading my need. "I understand, Ms. Slade. We've missed you."

Everyone in our outfit snickered behind Harden's back, the token joke. Washington had made him a temporary substitute for Dubose. Either they didn't understand or didn't care that he had no skills whatsoever to pull off the role.

I headed to the State Director's office. The secretary motioned me straight in. Harden sat behind Dubose's beautiful mahogany desk, reading the day's edition of *The State*.

He folded the newspaper and tossed it on the desk. "So good of you to grace us with your presence, Slade."

"Good morning, Harden."

"How about Mr. Harris?" he said.

"Then it's Ms. Slade," I replied.

His eyes narrowed.

"Well, look at us," I said, holding up a hand with false astonishment. "We're already building a rapport." I sat and laid a pad on the table, just as I'd always done with Dubose. "What's on the agenda?"

"Nothing," he said.

"You're telling me all's right with the world and everybody's getting along?"

"Right," he said. "Guess I need to find something for you to do."

I drew in my fangs a bit. South Carolina wasn't huge as far as states went, but a three-hour drive wasn't uncommon to reach the furthest counties, all within a state director's purview to transfer any employee of his or her choosing. I sensed I teetered on the brink of something vindictive.

"It won't take long for something to go awry and need investigating," I said. "What do you need from me?"

He grinned. "To fill the loan manager role in McCormick County."

Wonderful. Eighty miles away on a two-lane road. Two hours one-way, easy. "For how long?"

"Until we hire someone to fill the job. Mark Cranston retired last month."

There was a reason the position sat empty. McCormick was mostly national forest. The county struggled to keep the remaining ten thousand people as inhabitants, as it had lost forty percent of its population in the last century. One day the squirrels would take over County Council.

"Dubose planned to close the office when Cranston left," I said.

"We're delaying that decision," Harden replied. "I'll give you the week to make arrangements."

Damn, already rearranging the furniture, the offices, policy. I squared my jaw and leaned on the table. "I'm not moving to McCormick, Harden. I just built a house near Chapin."

"Right. With all that money from your dead husband." His crow's feet deepened, accenting his smirk. "Must be nice."

"My family business is none of your concern."

"But your job is," he said.

This was getting nowhere. "You're director in a temporary capacity, Harden."

"That's Mr. Harris to—"

"Temporary," I said, my voice rising. "Dubose hasn't been relieved, and you haven't taken her place. I've been *acting director* before as well. I know your parameters."

He leaned back, and the chair groaned in protest, accustomed more to a long, lean female than this fat blob of a man.

"Dubose no longer works for USDA."

My gaze stuck on the Mont Blanc pen in its holder. Dubose used to twirl it between manicured fingers as we pondered one decision or another. She would've taken it with her.

My observation wandered to her plaques, a photo with the President, and several pictures on a credenza across the room. My eye stopped on one picture; I finally recognized the woman in lavender posed with Dubose. Patsy Wheeler.

"All her stuff will be gone by tomorrow," he said, noting my scan. He scrunched his mouth in pretense and shook his head. "Such a shame." Then he ogled me and grinned.

"Regardless of what you think, I have unfinished business on my desk," I said and rose.

His slick grin spread like spilled molasses. "McCormick, in one week." He raised a hand. "You may leave."

"My pleasure."

As I left, the pity in the secretary's eyes told me she already knew. When I reached Whitney, I exhaled.

"More bruises?" she asked.

"Black and blue," I said.

"Hold your calls?"

"If you don't mind."

I went into my office, closed the door, and spun the chair around to face Finley Park below.

McCormick? When I made loans in Charleston, back in my old position, I sported a sizeable portfolio of clients, keeping the district on the map in dollars loaned and payments collected. McCormick, however, couldn't break even. The last manager in that county ran a real estate business on the side, right out of our agriculture office because there wasn't enough need to keep the doors open otherwise. They let him retire rather than fire him for the indiscretion.

But how could I fight this? I didn't want to file a grievance. I swear I didn't. Complaints that floated to Washington usually stunted a person's career. But how could I leave the kids in Columbia every day, so far away?

I picked up the phone and dialed, praying Dubose was home. Maybe she could help, explain, make a call on my behalf. Perhaps Harden exaggerated about Dubose losing her job. God, let it be a stupid lie on his part to bait me.

My old boss answered, and my words rushed out. "Margaret, please tell me you're still with the agency."

She groaned. "Guess a governor trumped me this time, Slade. Washington called yesterday morning and cut me loose. They don't even have to give me two weeks' notice."

Scratch my plan. Who was I to ask for favors when her world fell apart? Regardless, one question begged asking. "Margaret, did I cause this by pushing too hard with Lucille, with Lamar, maybe even Wheeler?"

"I drew you into this, Slade," she said. "Damn Dick. I never thought the nasty son of a bitch would go this far."

I turned back from the window. "You know secrets about Wheeler and his Godforsaken family. Can't you use them?"

"Not on the phone," she said. "I have to come in this afternoon anyway. Meet me in the parking garage around three. I'll give you the sordid details." She sighed. "Maybe you'll give me the strength I need to go inside and clean out my desk. You seem to handle calamity so well, Slade. You've always amazed me."

I rubbed along the edge of my desk, embarrassed at her praise. "Of course I'll meet you. It's the least I can do."

"Thanks, Slade."

I disconnected, dropped the phone in my lap, and covered my face, elbows on the desk. How had a dumb-ass personal request by the Governor gotten so far off base? This man was paranoid to the cusp of insanity. God only knew how many times he'd abused his official capacity to hide an embarrassment, stick it to someone he didn't like.

Dubose didn't have to say it, but I knew. My investigative methods had crossed a line. Something as simple as questioning Lucille, talking to the pharmacist, maybe having cross words with Lamar, had roused the vile side of Dick Wheeler. He took out Margaret with a brief word in someone's ear.

My door creaked open, but expecting Whitney, I didn't look up.

"You all right?" asked a familiar voice.

I rushed around the desk and wrapped my arms around Monroe's neck. "You weren't here to watch my back, Monroe." My hug tightened, the first real sense of relief I'd felt in days.

He squeezed back. "Now *that's* a hug." After a long moment, he released me. His eyes widened. "What happened to your face?"

"Quick accident, long story."

"Nobody stabbed you this time, did they?"

I shook my head and smiled at his reference to the Beaufort case, drawing him into my office. "What have you heard? Wait, come sit down." I pulled him toward the two chairs in front of my desk. "When did you get back?"

"Yesterday. Word is you picked a fight with the Governor and got Dubose fired. That about it?"

I inhaled an irregular breath and held it, staring past Monroe to fight for emotional control I hadn't realized had escaped my grasp. "That's what they really think?"

He rubbed my arm and shoulder. "Afraid so. Where's Wayne in all this? I assumed he'd wade in broad and tall."

"He's been too busy," I said.

Monroe leaned in front of me and made me consider him. "Doesn't sound like him, Slade."

"Maybe I didn't know him as well as I thought," I said, breaking our gaze.

"I'd invite you to dinner, but I'd be taking advantage if you two just broke up." He slid forward in the chair. "What can I do to help?"

I told him about Harden sentencing me to McCormick, the accident, then about meeting Dubose at three. No way did I mention Pamela.

He smiled easily, as if we discussed a budget issue. "Tell you what. Since Harden's on your case, I'll occupy his attention when you go see Dubose. Otherwise, he might get mad enough to detail you to North Dakota."

We rose. I hugged him quickly before opening the door. "Like I said, always watching my back." I reached over, squeezed his hand, and stepped back.

He turned to leave.

"Monroe?"

He stopped. "Hmm?"

"I'm so glad you're here."

TRYING AS HARD as I could to focus and work, I closed the paper on a case in Rock Hill, where a recently divorced clerk used a government credit card to buy groceries. Then I replied to several Freedom of Information requests from journalists on what loans my agency made, who we'd foreclosed, and how many ribbon-cuttings we'd done in one part of the state compared to another. Monroe was overwhelmed with work, so I ate a paltry lunch of diet cola and chips in the park alone. At ten to three, I left via the stairs instead of the elevator, making my exit clean and unnoticed.

I entered the secondary entrance to the garage and walked to the third level. Dubose sat in her BMW, facing the wall in Harden's spot, his car no doubt in the State Director's slot on the first level, near the front.

The garage was empty of people, thank goodness. Several slots remained bare due to summer vacations. I walked toward her. She rolled down the window.

"How you feeling, Margaret?" I said from about ten feet away. Her first name came more easily now. "Surely we can put our heads together and—"

"Slade! Move!" she yelled.

I twisted in time to see a black SUV racing toward me.

I jumped up and slid across the hood like something out of the movies. Coming down off-balance on one leg, I collapsed on the cement floor. The sickening sound of metal on metal sent a lightning bolt of fear through me as the SUV shifted the BMW almost a foot in my direction. I crab-walked back until I pressed hard against another car. Then I waited, afraid to breathe.

Dubose's car shook as the SUV disconnected from it and reversed in a screech of rubber.

Afraid to stand, afraid to speak, scared shitless I'd make a noise, I imagined the Governor's agents putting silencers on Glocks, slipping covertly from their vehicle to end whatever the hell they thought they started. I forced my eyes to remain open, on guard, when I really wanted to scrunch them shut, ball up, and hide.

Body shaking, I searched, frantic for cover. Panic choked me as the SUV revved its engine. I pushed back harder against a car, wishing I could crawl up into its wheel well. There simply was no cover.

Chapter 21

THE SUV REVVED its engine as I hid behind Dubose's wrecked BMW, my backside against another silver sedan, my heart climbing into my esophagus. A door opened.

I heard footsteps from another direction. People hurrying down from the garage exit. I willed every cell in my body frozen, hopeful their presence meant help.

The SUV roared away, its tires burning rubber to concrete. I glimpsed it as it passed . . . damn it! The narrow angle prevented me from catching the tag, but I tried to memorize all I could about it. Tinted windows. Silver hubcaps with a crisscross, beveled design. Black. So much black. Then it was gone.

Two females arrived gasping.

"Oh my Lord, what happened?" said the short-haired blonde.

I stood, hand over hand on the side of a car, my trembling knees warning me it might not be a good idea. Then my stomach collapsed when six feet away I saw Dubose slumped unconscious in the front seat, head on the steering wheel. The handle slipped out of my hand as I yanked at the passenger side, but it was locked.

I ran around to the driver's side. "Margaret, are you okay?"

"Jesus, look at that woman in the car," exclaimed the blonde.

The driver's window had imploded on contact. Glass chips coated Margaret, the dash, hell, the entire interior. Her side airbag deployed, the spent fabric now hanging wrinkled and impotent next to her. I clawed, trying to grip a handle mashed useless into the metal. "Call 9-1-1!" I shouted, reaching inside in an attempt to find my way in.

The brunette woman punched buttons on her cell phone. The blonde tried to approach me. "You should sit down, sweetheart."

"Go to the front of the garage and direct them to the third level!" I yelled.

They stood blinking, gripping each other's arm.

"Go, damn it! Hurry!"

They jerked into each other at my voice and bolted, their heels clopping, echoing off the low concrete ceiling.

I shouted after them, "And tell the cops what you saw!"

Margaret opened her eyes. Thank God. "Stay awake for me," I pleaded. "Don't move. An ambulance is on its way." I shook the door trying to get to her, slicing my palms on the bent metal. So I kicked it. Nothing. I tried the inside handle, then the lock button again. Once, twice . . . The other three locks popped up.

I raced to the passenger side, snatched it open, kneeled on the cement and leaned in. My elbow rested on the floor so I could face her.

"Hey," I said. "How're you doing?"

"Don't know, Slade." She spoke slow, eyes dazed, forehead furrowed. "Are you hurt?"

"Not this time," I said, forcing a grin. "I'm experienced with accidents, remember?"

She smiled. Unsure whether she feared moving or couldn't, my heart lurched at the eerie way she remained still with only her eyes shifting. I stroked her right hand, the only part of her I dared touch. "Take it easy. Don't move."

Could she feel her legs, her arms? She might cause irreparable damage if she tried, so I didn't ask. The busted seatbelt told me she'd been strapped in, which meant she absorbed the brunt of the impact. Parts of mangled interior wrapped around her left leg. I couldn't imagine her foot lying in that direction without a bone broken somewhere. *Please*, I prayed, *let her spine be okay.*

Sirens filled the air in the distance.

"I haven't told you everything, Slade," she said. "It matters."

I stroked her face. It felt damp and too cool. The garage was shaded, the cement keeping most of the heat out, but it was almost ninety degrees in here. "Did you see the driver?" I finally asked.

"No," she said. "But the car . . ." She paused, squinting, as if replaying the incident.

"The SUV," I added.

"Yes. Didn't see." She licked her lips and took a shallow breath. "Don't forget Lucille. She . . . hurts so badly. She doesn't understand . . ."

My vision blurred hearing her slurred words. "I'll visit Lucille today. Why don't I deliver flowers from her garden, dig them up and place them in a pot near the window. Hell, I'll buy a grow light." I couldn't stop rambling, as if my voice might keep her awake.

A siren sounded at the garage entrance, the cacophony bouncing off the low ceilings, deafening, then only a motor noise as it reached our level.

"They're here, Margaret. They're here."

Margaret grinned. "Wish I could have made her feel better. I should have . . ." Her eyes drooped, then shut.

"Margaret?"

A hand touched my shoulder, and I glanced up at a police officer. "Ma'am? The ambulance is here. Let them deal with this, okay?"

The ambulance stopped, and two medics jumped out, equipment in hand. I backed away to watch, to hear, to learn how badly she was.

"Don't smell any gas," said the cop.

The medics moved in, and in seconds spouted respiration figures and blood pressure. I barely dared to breathe. "How is she?" I asked, my mouth quivering.

"Just let them work," the officer said, pulling me further away.

I fished my phone from my purse on the ground and then walked off a few yards until the call went through. "Monroe? There's been a wreck in the parking garage. EMTs are working on Dubose. I'm fine. Can you get over here?" I shut my phone, returned closer to the BMW, and slumped against another car.

A medic approached.

I waved toward the BMW, tremors running down my arms. "I'm okay. Tend to her."

He motioned to my hands, then my face. "Then what's the blood about?"

I opened my palms and flinched at the red.

Blood oozed. Using gauze to soak it up, the EMT analyzed the cuts. A fast wipe told him my hands merely transferred red to my face. "Nothing major, so I'll have to get to you later." He applied a huge stack of gauze on each hand, wrapped them with tape, and pointed to the rear of the ambulance. "Take a seat inside. One of us will have a closer look when we get a minute." He scurried back to Dubose.

Wasn't three minutes before Monroe jogged up, a half dozen employees behind him stampeding like a herd of bison. Harden huffed, bringing up the rear. A police officer walked over with pad in hand and peppered me with questions. I answered in short sentences. Black SUV. Didn't see the tag. Didn't see the occupants. I felt stupid having hid as Dubose took the blow.

I glanced at Monroe for moral support. He was on the phone standing against the half wall in a patch of sunlight. Harden held a phone to his ear, too. The crew gathered like a collection of reporters, each calling in a story lined up against the same side of the garage for better reception. My knees shook, and I noticed an ache in my shoulder.

The officer asked another question. "Is there any reason someone would try to hurt you or Ms. Dubose?"

"A black SUV has been following me lately." I mashed the tape across the gauze on my hand as red bled through, worried whether I should keep quiet about it.

The Governor had it in for us. How could I tell a uniform that and him believe it? The repeating movie loop in my head couldn't assure me who the driver aimed at, Dubose or me. I could argue either one.

The officer squinted. "Are you sure? What is it you do for a living?"

"I investigate internal issues for USDA. Employee misconduct and client fraud. The injured woman is my boss."

"Any names in particular come to mind?" the officer asked.

How could Wheeler go this far? He'd have to kill Dubose *and* me to avoid suspicion, and this attempt was too sloppy for that. He'd jeopardize his career, his so-called name.

"Ma'am?" the officer repeated. "Can you think of anyone who'd do this? A detective might be in touch, but I need you to relay what you saw, what you think, while it's fresh."

Maybe this was a scare tactic gone bad. I did thumb my nose at the SLED boys. This could be their way of warning me, and the driver simply miscalculated. The note I delivered at the capitol building could have prompted Wheeler to step up his game, and he grossly overstepped.

Damn, who the hell knew?

When I wouldn't give specifics, the officer quit taking me seriously. We completed the report. Possible hit and run, he called it. The driver driving too fast in a tight, confined area, taking the turn too quickly. He would put out a BOLO on the vehicle, with the damage to its front end hopefully a giveaway.

Monroe appeared at my side. "I called Wayne."

My heart skipped at the expectation of the Lawman. I was still angry, but needing him all the same, which only made me angrier. "Where's Harden?" I said, changing subjects.

"Over there," Monroe said, nodding. "He's fighting phone reception."

I rose from the ambulance and marched toward the opposite wall.

Harden pinched a burning cigarette, a glowering expression on his face as he read his phone. As I reached him, he shoved the device in his pocket and heeled out the cigarette. "Glad to see you're okay. What were you doing—"

"Shut up. Listen good, you son of a bitch."

His face reddened, a bitter frown deepening. "I know you're upset, but watch your mouth, Slade."

Monroe took a step in our direction.

I moved closer to Harden, wary of nearby ears. I'd have touched toes with the bastard, but his gut was in the way. "Call the Governor."

"You do not tell me what to do."

"Call him. Tell him a black SUV just put Dubose in the hospital. One of *his* SUVs."

Harden backed up. "That's a serious allegation," he said. "You better be prepared to substantiate it."

"Get me my damn appointment."

"I'll have your ass transferred, Slade."

I inched in, smelling tobacco and coffee. "Bring it on."

I turned in time to see attendants lift Dubose into the ambulance, and I broke into a run. "How is she?"

"She's stable enough to transport, but unconscious. Good thing with the bones she's broken."

As the EMT tried to shut himself in, I hit the side of the vehicle. "Wait, can I go with you?"

"Sorry, ma'am." They tightened the gurney. "We're taking her to Baptist. You can meet us there, but I warn you, they'll be working on her a while." He studied my hands. "You need to come on over, too, and have someone suture those lacerations." He closed up. The driver whooped the siren a few times to clear their path.

Harden waded into the crowd. "Back to work, everybody. We'll let you know when we hear something." He paused in front of me, and I stared him down.

Monroe trotted over. "Do we continue our meeting, Harden, or do you want to reschedule?"

"Make it tomorrow," he said, his gaze on me. "Check with Angela for an appointment."

"Call," I said, teeth clenched.

Harden turned and retreated out the back of the garage.

I studied his back, debating how long to give him to make my date with Wheeler. The Governor had gone too far. Maybe I'd made a mistake thinking someone as politically heavy-handed as Dick Wheeler wouldn't care about me nosing into his business. And maybe I'd underestimated his retaliation for doing so.

Shivers rolled through me, and my palms stung. My stomach was queasy.

This situation had grown more than messy. I'd given up the Wheeler drug case, yet the Wheeler mansion continued to hold the case against me. Bile rose in my throat, and a shake returned to my knees, my hands, as I feared for Margaret . . . for me . . . oh God, maybe everyone around me. I wasn't sure how to tackle someone so politically powerful, willing to hire someone to take people out.

"Damn it!" I yelled, forgetting the wounds, shoving both hands through my hair, scratching my scalp in hopes some sense would peel loose.

"Slade?" The familiar voice became familiar arms that enfolded me from behind. Wayne whispered words in my hair. "What the hell happened, Babe?"

I moved away, short-circuited. "Don't." My voice cracked, my head about to explode from arguments, plans, threats.

Wayne let me move an arm's length away, retaining a gentle grip on my wrist. "Come on," he said, drawing me toward him. "Get in my car. Let's get you to the hospital." He tried to lead me toward his car. "Monroe, hop in. Y'all can tell me what happened on the way."

Monroe moved closer, relief on his face as Wayne took charge.

But a flood of visuals returned. Pamela on the sofa. Wayne barefoot. The possible lie about going to Atlanta. The way Wayne percolated at the sight of his ex-wife. The crash again, and again. Margaret unable to move. I held out my hands. Blood.

Monroe approached me from my other wide. "Wayne's right, Slade. Go to the hospital. You've had a heck of a shock."

I awkwardly dug in my purse with huge wrapped hands, seeking my keys, just wanting to escape this whole scene. "Leave me alone."

I walked toward my car, rummaging, my head so befuddled. "I'm going to see Dubose then I'm heading home," I said, wanting my sister more than anyone else.

Wayne caught up to me. "Monroe? Stand here with her." He stole my purse and lifted my key ring.

"What are you doing?" I said, fuming.

Wayne slid the keys in his pocket. "I'm speaking to the officer in charge, then *I'm* driving you to the hospital. You're in no shape to get behind a wheel."

"Maybe I don't want you to take me."

Monroe took my elbow. "Quit, Slade."

I glanced at both men. "Maybe I would prefer Monroe escort me then."

Wayne reached in his pocket and handed the keys to my colleague. "Then take her. I'll be there in a few minutes."

"Why do you think you can get involved here?" I asked, unable to come down off the still-cresting emotional wave. Somebody needed to feel my wrath.

"You're traumatized, Slade." Wayne handed my purse back to me. "And I'm involved because someone tried to kill two federal employees. And since one of those employees is you, I'm especially involved." Then he marched over to the patrol car.

Monroe put me in the passenger seat of the vehicle and walked around to the driver's side.

"You're not on the rental agreement to drive this car," I said with an overdose of rancor as he sat behind the wheel. "It's rented in my name."

He gave me a sarcastic glance and started the engine. "Buckle your seatbelt."

I bungled with the belt until Monroe reached over and clicked me in. "Did you tell Harden we weren't coming back to work?" I asked.

He snorted once. "I doubt he'll care."

Six blocks away, we parked at Baptist Hospital and walked in the second level crosswalk over Taylor Street, without speaking. Monroe seemed wary about asking me questions. But my nerves still pinged, and I continued to fight minor quakes in my arms and legs.

"I'm worried about you," Monroe said as we turned at a marquis.

I restrained a retort, seeing the concern on his face.

A nurse walked through a set of double doors, letting through a whiff of alcohol and disinfectant. She halted at the sight of my blood-soaked bandages, then decided to escort us through the hospital maze to the ER.

She dropped us off at the desk, and I begged for news about Margaret as I juggled my purse and groped clumsily with a pen to fill out my papers. The nurse paused as an intercom blared for a doctor to contact an extension, but then said all they could reveal was that Margaret had just come in. When they realized I was the only person available who knew her, they asked me to fill out her papers, too. Monroe took the clipboard from me, requested my wallet, and took over, stopping here and there to ask me for details.

He handed the forms to the nurse for both Margaret and me and escorted my butt to a chair.

"Sorry," I mumbled.

"Of course you are," he said, staring past me to the hallway where patients entered for treatment.

"What does that mean?" I asked, studying a guy ten feet away with ice on his ankle.

Monroe gnawed the inside of his lip, blatantly displeased. "Stay here," he said. "I'll be back in a second." He returned with dampened paper towels. With gentle deliberation, he wiped my face, and I gasped when I saw the removed signs of blood. If I didn't get something in my stomach, I was going to hurl.

"Listen," he said, watching his task instead of me. "Let people care. What has the world done to force you into this sealed place where nobody can touch you?"

"What?" I uttered, taken aback. Where was the lecture about taking on too much responsibility or carrying torches? I flushed, unprepared at what I sensed Monroe called rude behavior. "I . . . can only handle so much at one time," I said, searching for the proper response.

"Do you care about me?" he asked, pushing my hair back.

His words pierced to the depth of my soul. "Of course I do," I answered, remaining still for him. "You and Savvy are my best friends." How could he think differently?

He picked up a second towel. "What about Wayne?"

"Him, too," I said, eager to be right, before recalling his evening with Pamela.

"Your family?"

I frowned and pulled back. "What kind of a question is that?"

His brow knotted, and he held my shoulder, bringing me back closer but also making me wince. His hand released as he scowled with regret, then touched my hair, letting it slide through his hands.

His cologne came back to me, a scent so familiar. Even in the car I hadn't noticed. Now I did and wanted to fall against his chest and be hugged, taking it in even more. Instead I stared like a shy child receiving her scolding.

His voice took on a softer tone, as if starting over with words he'd rehearsed. "Alan treated you horribly," he said. "Some of us get that. I bet your children don't even know. You commit wholeheartedly to people, Slade, sometimes at an overkill level, but it's always one-way with you. It's like you don't want us sometimes. I'm not talking about just me, either. I'm talking about everyone." A sigh escaped. "Especially Wayne."

I tried to force down a huge lump as emotion cut off my air. My eyes welled. Was I that hard? Wayne saw what I went through with Alan. He understood why I acted like I did, at least he said he did.

Seated in the middle of the room, bright fluorescents reflecting off the white tiles and soft blue walls, I felt exposed, almost spotlighted. What Monroe referenced was my protective mechanism. I thought I hid it well. After my introduction to the deceitful nature of people in the Charleston case, when everyone I knew held ulterior motives, I'd held myself together purely by operating solo. It was safer there. I was in control there. I shared only when it was safe.

I wasn't sure I knew how to behave any differently.

"Carolina Slade?" called a nurse.

I stood slowly, the shoulder aching, my hands stiff, my feelings cut to the bone.

Monroe waited in the lobby as they took me back to examine my hands. I held no desire to chat, not after Monroe's speech. The young doctor gave up with the jokes and soon passed me off to a nurse after putting in a few stitches in my right palm. The left wasn't deep enough to warrant more than a serious band aid, but she wrapped it in an excessive amount of gauze and tape. As she worked on me, Wayne walked in.

The nurse stopped. "Are you family?"

He flashed the badge. "Close enough."

She accepted his answer and slapped on a last piece of tape. "Make her rest. Don't think she knows yet how shocky she was." Then she disappeared.

Wayne moved close but didn't deliver the hug I expected. His expression was business, but I caught the pain in his expression. Had I done this to him, made him second guess whether he could care for me . . . like Monroe said?

I hung my head as if studying my huge hands, blinking hard, trying to decipher this quandary. I wasn't sure I truly understood.

"Feeling better?" he asked.

I shrugged, then changed my mind and nodded, still staring down.

He just stood there.

Gazing slowly up, I searched for signs of confusion, anger, or plain patience. My guess was he waited for my reaction to judge his own.

My attitude had quelled his natural charm, that million-dollar-smile that had snared me to begin with, his strong desire to see my needs fulfilled.

Had I chased him back to Pamela?

I whispered, "I'm sorry, Wayne."

But he didn't melt as I hoped. Instead he assisted me up and watched me hard, probably to check my steadiness.

"Can you use that badge and find out more about Margaret?" I asked tentatively.

"Already did. She's in surgery, fighting hard, they say, but the damage is extensive. Nothing else to know yet."

The nurse walked back in, handed me my documents, and directed me to the exit to the lobby. Wayne led me out of the exam room, touching my back as if to guide me, or catch me if I fell. Those boots clomping on the linoleum, we almost made it to the lobby entrance. "Slade, hold up," he said.

I turned. "Can we not do this here?"

"Who cares where we are?" he said. "Please call me next time." He raised fists, floundering for what to say, then released, rubbing palms on his jeans. "Oh hell, I don't want there to be a next time, but you know what I'm trying to say. Let me be there."

I didn't know what to say with my reputation for personal absorption so new and branded in my head.

"There is nothing with Pamela," he added like a period.

My nod had to suffice, and he seemed to take it as intended with a nod of his own. He reached around and pushed open the exit door before I could use my good shoulder.

Monroe waited, coffee cup in hand, and two more on the table beside him. He rose when he caught a load of my bandages.

"Looks worse than it is," I said, praying he'd returned to my old office buddy. "Any news?"

He shook his head. "We might as well leave. I expect it'll be a while."

"I'm staying," I said. "Wayne can drive you back to your car. I'll get myself home."

Both men sat down across from me.

"I said you can go."

They stayed silent. Monroe lifted a magazine. Wayne checked his phone.

So I tried listening to Monroe, letting two people who cared stand vigil for me. But I stood and walked to the window conflicted and exhausted, not accustomed to being babysat, not wanting to remain close enough for them to start questioning me. Because that's when the wall would come down, and I wasn't sure how fractured I'd be when it did.

AT EIGHT I called home again. No sooner had I put the phone in my purse, it rang. ID said unknown caller. I almost didn't answer.

"Who is this?" I asked, instinctively turning toward Wayne and Monroe.

A male voice I readily recognized spoke with reserve. "Be at the Governor's Mansion tomorrow at nine a.m. They'll have your name at the gate and let you through." He hung up.

I halted and stared at the phone amazed. Harden had made his call.

Wayne walked over. "Who was it?"

"The Governor. He wants to meet."

Those gray-blue eyes turned smoky dark. "How deep is this mess, Slade? What have you gotten involved in?"

"Have no clue, but I suspect I'll learn more tomorrow."

"I'm going with you," he said.

"No, you're not," I replied, surprised at my calm when I'd ordinarily argue, often nastily, against his effort to run my show. "For once, your credentials will do more harm than good." Then I caught myself and rested a hand on his chest. "Please. I appreciate the offer, but this is only talk. I'll be fine."

Monroe worried, Wayne almost frantic, but this was not their fight. Besides, if my meeting with the Governor went sideways, at least they wouldn't be involved.

Chapter 22

JUST PAST NINE at night, Wayne carried me home from the hospital and dropped me off, finding it difficult not to keep a hand on me in some fashion. He touched my elbow, my shoulder, the small of my back as we walked to the house from the car. Without explanation he gave me the space I claimed I needed by kissing me lightly, then telling Ally a bit too seriously to lock the doors behind me before he left. Noble and so concerned. Struggling to behave in a manner I'd approve.

He paused long enough to watch the melee of gasps and questions from Ally and the kids at the sight of my monster-sized bandaged hands before he finally stepped off the porch, moving to leave.

"Wayne?" I called, Zack standing guard on one side of me, Ivy hugging my waist, Ally ready to tend my needs.

He turned, his eyes taking in my support team. The glow of the porch light cast him in soft tones, and as he laid his gaze on me, the moment stole my heart.

I wished he could stay the night more than I'd ever wanted anything in my life. But leaving my family for a night's embrace would seem selfish. We also needed a chance to talk long, slow, and civilized. "I'll call you tomorrow after my meeting."

"I know," he said. "Go to bed and get some sleep. It'll help."

He walked away, moving slower than normal, and I went inside. I asked Ally to take the kids to the kitchen and pour me a root beer. Then before joining them, through the dining room window I watched Wayne's taillights disappear, wishing he'd fought more for the right to stay.

I pushed off the window sill, rolled a sore shoulder, and turned to the kitchen. Where were we going wrong? My chest tightened hard at the slightest chance of losing the man. I shoved him away harder than I fought to keep him. Monroe's poignant words of advice tonight brought that home to me. What did I fear? And why?

Ally and I relaxed on the porch after she served me dinner, cutting the noodles in front of me to Zack's delight. If my sister kept this up, she was destined for a more permanent role of housekeeper and nanny. Afterwards, the kids quickly found other interests once Ally and I announced we'd be outside, wine in hand. "Boring," Zack said, punching Ivy as she closed the sliding glass doors behind me.

I clicked on the ceiling fans and relaxed in my rocker, sipping a second glass of wine coincidentally like Wayne had suggested what seemed days ago. My back tried to sag, form to the rocker, but stove-up muscles refused to cooperate.

I closed my eyes and saw Margaret's pale complexion. Ally dropped her phone on the floor and I jumped, remembering falling off the BMW, hearing metal crush. All that glass popping. Margaret wrapped in metal.

Margaret. All alone in the hospital, like Lucille. Two strong women who didn't deserve what fate handed them. Common sense told me these events unfolded out of my control. However, remorse crept through all the dark places of my mind, hinting that I'd been present at both moments. The linchpin.

I doubted my own reasoning ability. What didn't I see? What had I done to cause such commotion? The back of my bandage rubbed hair out of my face. All my daring and brazen demands of the day almost faded into foolishness now that the night slowed my thoughts.

But if I stopped and failed to pursue the facts, I'd be left floating in a current of Harden's direction, the idiot guided by the Governor. What was I supposed to do with the few facts Margaret had given me, that she thought offered protection?

At times like this, my best friend Savannah served as confidante and cheerleader, making the darkest problem doable. I rationed her long-distance trips from Beaufort for the most serious dilemmas, but she was in Las Vegas, on vacation. No point in ruining her trip or risking her rushing to me, which she would, when there was nothing she could do.

Besides, Ally deserved my attention. Monroe's lecture reverberated in my ears about caring for those who cared for me.

"I'm scared to leave here," Ally said. "Your home feels like the best place on earth right now."

I smiled. "Glad to hear it, little sister."

Ally owned many of Savvy's personality traits, only with more of a loosey-goosey way of life that would drive me over a cliff, yet send her into bouts of laughter. I was the sensible daughter; she, the fun one. Our opposite styles aggravated each other on most occasions. She'd arrived at the house an irritating bimbo but had transformed into my support, even a friend. Was I in that much need of a sympathetic soul, or did I seriously miss my sister?

I whirled the wine around my glass, careful not to slosh any on my bandages. "Stay as long as you like, Ally. I could enjoy coming home to this."

"You can't afford me," she said, holding her glass up by the stem.

"I'm affording you now. Think about it. No rent. No utilities."

"No medical or retirement benefits," she said.

I laughed. "You've never had either. It makes Mom crazy the way you live."

"Maybe I need them now. My gosh, I'm thirty-five." She turned to me and clicked her tongue. "That makes you thirty-what . . . eight?"

"I quit counting once I had kids. They ruined my figure and my swagger. Savvy said I was a quintessential soccer mom."

For a while we listened to the chirp and treble of crickets and cicadas.

"I like your kids, Carolina."

"Borrow them whenever you like. They'll change your mind and steal your sanity in the process." I took a sip. "They cause wrinkles and gray hair."

Ally couldn't have children. Severe endometriosis at twenty-one damaged one ovary and impaired the other. Shame. She was better with kids in general than I was. She should've been a teacher, but college meant structure and that meant only attending two semesters before she quit. Even Mom ceased arguing about it. Daddy called her his wild child.

Ally went inside, retrieved the wine bottle, and returned to set it between us with a tube of crackers. She shut off the porch light and lit a mosquito candle. By eleven, the tree frogs had gone to bed, and the lake cove fell asleep. By eleven thirty, the bottle was empty, and a morose bit of melancholy settled around me.

"Don't give up on Wayne," Ally said, having heard many details of the day, except Monroe's advice.

"Not now, Ally." I finished the last drops in my glass then used my big toe on the wood floor planks to regain the chair's rhythm.

"He balances you."

I bit a reply along the line of how would she know. "You've never met Monroe," I said in the half-light, glad she couldn't see me.

She stopped rocking. "He's a loner. I can tell from the way you describe him. Wayne's a lot deeper pool of water. He wants a life with you."

"He's never said that."

"Damn, you can read it all over him. Are you blind?"

I pumped the rocker faster. She might be right, but I could hardly trust my judgment right now. My old sense of imbalance had resurged, the same feelings I once harbored around Alan. My ex poked at my self-esteem until it recoiled at the sight of him. I thought when he died such feelings would disappear, but even after wine and a rocker's embrace, the old instability nagged.

"Can't get Margaret out of my mind,' I said, "and I have no idea what to say when I confront the Governor in the morning. Give Wayne a rest for now."

"Suit yourself, Miss Scarlett, but one day you'll meet yourself coming in on the way out, and you won't like what you see."

I stood. "Let's go to bed."

She rose and slid open the patio door. "Shame you're only saying that to your sister, isn't it?"

EARLY THE NEXT morning, alone in my office, I lifted a paper tablet from my top desk drawer and drew two crooked columns, the best I could do with sore, wrapped hands. The PRO side meant give it up and move on. CON listed reasons to keep turning stones. For twenty minutes I jotted key items for each. The bottom line for both equaled self-preservation.

If I gave up this quest and cancelled my meeting with the Governor, would the driver come at me again? Could I live with the fact someone had aimed a vehicle at me and, so far, gotten away with it?

If I kept my appointment and continued snooping, would the culprit grow mad enough to succeed? History recalled my children kidnapped, caught in a whiplash from a past investigation. I'd have to implement some of those same precautions again—alter my routes, juggle my routine, order the school to follow specific instructions when they started next week. Ally helped me pick the kids up from school before, when we fought to change every routine we could think of.

She was bright enough to recognize the drill this time, though. We'd discussed locking doors and keeping the kids inside for now, calling me if anyone drove onto my property. I had taken a different route to work, up Broad River, the back way to Interstate 126. Tomorrow I'd note another way and go in early. Until this SUV's owner was found, my life had to be more irregular than it already was, which was saying a lot.

Blowing out a long sigh, I faced the fact that Ally would want details, not only about this case, but the one before when the kids were snatched and nobody fully explained why to her.

A big fat *why* for current events evaded all logic, though. Why would anyone come at me, unless I was too close to some truth? And how the hell did I word this face-to-face with Governor Wheeler without angering him more?

I gathered my scribbles and wound my way toward Monroe's division. Unless one of us was out of town, a day didn't go by without an hour in his office or mine, sometimes gravitating into a working lunch. I saw situations as black and white, while he could marvelously interpret shades of gray. Together we sorted personnel, loan, political, and PR issues, girding and arming each other before tackling demons. Maybe his logic would help me make sense of my options.

"Knock, knock," I said at his door.

He smiled and came around his desk. "Hey, come on in." He positioned one of his visitor's chairs for me. "Have a seat. You talk to the detective yet? You watching your back? Making yourself hard to follow?"

"Yes to all three," I said. "The detective by phone."

"Good."

As he sat across from me, I launched into my apology. "Sorry I mouthed off yesterday in the garage. I just—"

"Needed space," he finished, angling his chair in front of mine, only a foot apart at the knees. "Nobody likes feeling vulnerable, and someone almost killed you. Being babied escalated that vulnerability. I get it."

My mouth dropped open. "Wow. That's it. That's it exactly."

He tapped his temple. "Black belt mind reader. What can I say? How're your hands?"

They instinctively tried to curl. "They hurt, but they'll heal. Listen—"

"How's the rest of you holding up?"

I fought the blush, recalling his lecture in the hospital waiting room.

"Sleep helped," I said, uncomfortable with his ease at throwing me off track.

His unassuming voice, the smooth body language and musk cologne, even the carefully ironed creases in his khaki slacks gave me comfort, like hiding in a childhood tree house in your old backyard. "Enough about me. I need your advice. A lot went down while you were in Washington."

"Why am I not surprised?"

I rehashed the last few days. He nodded, sometimes scratching his neck, other times shaking his head. Then I whipped out my impressive chart. "So, what do you think?"

He studied my notes. "What's Wayne's take on this?"

I groaned. "Damn it, Monroe. I'm asking *you*. Wayne always thinks I've overstepped my bounds, or that I run around half-assed."

He held up the paper. "And would he be wrong? He's not up to speed on the details, I assume."

"No, he's not . . . up to speed, I mean. He's . . . a little disgruntled at me, I think. I don't know. It's awkward."

Last night I tried to tell myself that our caustic run-in at his apartment remained an issue, even as I struggled with Monroe's ER suggestion to let people care more. But Wayne had looked so worried as he left. He adored me, even if he returned to his ex for a brief moment of whatever it was. As Ally prattled on last night about the man, my deepest fear manifested itself in the open, rising to gobsmack me in my rocking chair. It kept me awake even after I went to bed.

Wayne loved me. An only-one-for-me kind of love.

And it scared me to where I ran to the bathroom at two a.m., turned on the noise of the faucet, and threw up.

There was something seriously wrong with tackling politics and deception while overlooking the love of a good man.

Monroe was shaking his head.

"What?" I asked.

"You left me for moment there. So what do you need?"

"There's another situation," I said, dying to spill everything, sick of juggling pieces of stories and bits of secrets. "You remember me mentioning that woman with the poor manners who rammed into me at the peanut festival?"

He thought a second. "Yeah, vaguely."

I filled him in on Pamela, DEA, Kay, and Clay River.

He laughed from his gut.

"This is miles from being funny, Monroe."

He wiped his eye. "I'm not laughing at you, Slade. I despise, yet admire, how Wayne snared two dynamic women. Most men would kill for one."

Yeah, one was plenty all right. That's why I was in Monroe's office, instead of several floors down in Wayne's, afraid to open up to him.

My nails tapped the chart. "Advice?"

"If you can find out about the bad peanut sales, I guess you should do so," he said, wary. "Important ammunition to have, but don't get yourself in trouble doing so."

"Really?" I said, surprised at his proactive reply.

"I'm not advocating you get passionate about it or anything," he replied. "While it never hurts to have a trump card in your pocket, just don't broadcast what you're doing." He pointed at me. "And don't dig to China for it. If the info is buried too deep, let it go. No heroics. Not sure I'd ask Wheeler about it this morning, though. Not until you do some homework."

"And the driver of the SUV?"

His hands collapsed into his lap. "Can you postpone this meeting? Give Wayne a chance to trace that car." A hint of worry showed in the lines around his mouth. "And he can protect you."

I didn't know what to say at Monroe's magnanimous gesture on Wayne's behalf, except it made him damn appealing.

"He's the best asset you have right now," he continued. "He'd move the mountains to the beach for you, my friend. I watched him wrestle hard with himself in the emergency room. He recognized the fact you needed alone time, his entire being wanting to lock you away and keep you safe."

Contrition rose in me yet again about Wayne, then about Monroe's loyalty. "You're something, Monroe."

"Yes, I am. So tell me about your sister."

I snickered. "She's nothing like me. She's like nobody I've ever met. Ally is Ally. A royal pain one day, a stand-up comic the next."

Monroe watched me, smiling, and I recognized his motive. A weight lifted a little from my shoulders. Now I could compartmentalize my fears, tuck them away, and do what he recommended. Check out the peanuts. Maybe handle Wayne.

And most definitely address the Governor. Because, giving up felt like giving up on Margaret, too. She'd risked her career to salvage hope in the names of Patsy and Lucille. Now I was her remaining lieutenant, entrusted to continue the campaign.

AN HOUR LATER, after a flash of my ID, the guard waved me through the gate at the Governor's Mansion. I hadn't told Harden where I was going this morning. He'd figure it out.

The hospital had stonewalled me again, the doctor's orders standing for Margaret not to be disturbed due to heavy sedation. My gut sank when they still listed her condition as critical. She fought to recover, maybe to live, as did Lucille, both women the fallout of one man's lust for the mansion.

Clearly Margaret knew more about the Governor than she'd said, and for some reason she'd felt the need to spoon-feed me information. This scum wasn't worth one of her breaths. If I gained nothing else out of this confrontation today, it would be to regain Margaret's job and get this man out of our business. Therein rested my goal. At least for today.

Scenarios on how to converse with Wheeler started and abruptly stopped in my head as I fretted over my strategy. My steps slowed until I realized I'd stopped on the front doorstep, frozen in what to say and how to say it. I seized the doorknob, ruing the action as pain shot through my hand.

The same Barbie doll secretary greeted me and showed me down the same hall, to the same upholstered chair in Wheeler's private office. "Coffee? Tea?" she asked, moving toward the credenza that displayed a delicate, plain white china coffee service.

"No," I said, with little patience for the formal airs.

She smiled with textbook comportment. "The Governor will be with you in a few moments. Our apologies for the delay." She eased the door shut behind her.

The pictures sprinkled around the room held new meaning. I'd never met the deceased Mrs. Wheeler or the twinkle-eyed granddaughters in cotton candy garb, but a sixth sense suggested they concealed as many secrets as the rest of the brood. They had to, especially belonging to a man who went to such lengths *against* his family to secure his image. Wish I knew how Mrs. Wheeler died.

Wheeler'd probably lie to me even today. However, what he said wasn't as important as what he did once I left. Another chill ran through me. I told Monroe I'd let him know when I returned to my office. I'd seen no black SUV this morning.

The door made no noise, and I jumped at the sound of Wheeler's voice, standing before I could make myself disrespect him by remaining seated.

"Ms. Slade." He eased in, fresh-faced, ironed, and crisp. "Thank God you're safe. I spoke with the hospital this morning. They've kept my people updated on Margaret."

He held out a hand and then withdrew when he saw the wrappings on mine. "Nobody told me you were hurt."

"She's critical, you know."

Wheeler sat, worry creasing his brow. "Yes, I heard. She's practically family, but I assume you know that."

"No, I didn't. How so?" I wanted to hear how he explained Margaret's connection to the family. And how he sounded doing it.

He shook his head. "Doesn't matter."

"So who were your men after? Margaret or me?"

None of my planned openings had started like this. Throwing out the question so crudely surprised me more than it probably did him. He stared quizzically. "You're distraught."

"Don't, Governor." I sat toward the front of the chair, sweeping a glance around the room. "Nobody else can hear. There's no podium, no hidden microphones or cameras."

A brow raised as his window dressing slipped. "I called you here out of sympathy and concern, Ms. Slade." He stood. "Instead, you accost me with accusations and sully the very office into which you've been invited." His hand curled around the phone receiver.

Nerves tingling and fear building at his shallow aplomb, I stood as well. "Go ahead. Make a call. Police reports are public information, and every police department has at least one minimum wage opportunist who'd sell a story to a gossip rag."

"So, you're blackmailing me," he said in a tone loud enough to make me wonder about a recorder.

"No," I replied. "In the event you are recording this conversation, I'll make myself clear. This isn't blackmail. It's about you trying to silence people through threats, intimidation, and attempted murder." Before he could interrupt, I held up a fat, white hand. "It's how you operate. You forced your sister-in-law to sign a prenup because she had a lesbian affair.

You use your brother Lamar as a lackey to maintain your American farmer image. You smear CJ's reputation because he's conveniently dead. You dismantle your family for political gain. Yes, I'm damn good at what I do, Governor, and you made a mistake calling on me to dig. Well, I dug."

His face reddened ever so much. "You are grievously out of line, Ms. Slade."

Adrenaline pumping, I knew I'd probably said too much. I pushed down the terror. The wounds on my hands stung from gripping the chair. I opened them, the pain a reminder to settle down.

He eased into his chair and corralled his behavior. "What do you really want?"

I held up two awkward fingers. "One, return Margaret's job. Two, get off my case."

"I didn't take her job."

"You made it happen." My anger festered as I recognized he'd regained his footing. "And I can identify your thugs."

An incredulous expression spread across his face. "My God, you actually think I ordered a hit on you."

What the hell else had we been talking about? "You asked me to check *out* your family, for God's sake. Then when I turn a couple of rocks, you turn on me."

He went around his desk and picked up the phone. "Get me SLED."

Fear zinged through me again. Would he call my display of emotion a threat of bodily harm? He could paint me as a stalker, especially after Lamar called the sheriff's office on me and insinuated such to them.

I fought the instinct to flee. A guard would only nab me before I left the building. Like that wouldn't scream criminal.

Authority filled Wheeler's voice. "Thomas? Dick here. I want car assignments for the last two days and someone who can talk specifics. Any car damages, too. Within the hour. We've had a complaint." He listened. "Sounds great, Thomas. Thanks." He hung up.

"Please," he said, a fresh, personal tone in his voice. "I told no one to harass you. I told someone to speak to you on one occasion. No stalking, no accidents, no intimidation tactics whatsoever. I'd be insane to go down that road. Nobody reaches this level of politics and behaves so foolishly."

I wasn't surprised at his words; I just didn't trust them. We'd see, however, when he decided whether to take some sort of action against me, a niggling pest of a nobody.

"If someone got out of line on my watch," he continued, "he'll answer to me and be charged. I want no renegades in my house."

I held up my bandaged hands. "Who else would try to do this?"

His demeanor turned sympathetic. "Margaret said you performed your job well. Surely you can name enemies other than me?" He hesitated, letting his words hit home. "Ms. Slade, I'll handle any situation on my turf, but you'll have to deal with those of your own making."

Had he feigned concern when he made his phone call about the car, or was he really apprehensive? Or simply covering his ass? In a position of power, murder was just another tool. A stretch interpretation on my part, but power begat arrogance, and once acquired was hard to relinquish.

Had I thrown sand or gasoline on this fire?

He apologized with all the right words about my misunderstanding, doling out condolences. I walked out in a surreal fog, but stamped this mission as accomplished. Wheeler'd either show his hand or leave me alone. I knew one thing, though. He had the need to find out what I knew, or he wouldn't have invited me to his office in the first place.

Chapter 23

I WALKED BACK to the federal building from the Governor's Mansion, not sure how to read Wheeler's intentions.

Monroe said it couldn't hurt to scavenge information on Wheeler's rumored past with the peanut inspections, so I was anxious to return to the office to research the industry. A computer search identified the Peanut Board, the state's master resource for the peanut industry. Then I noted the markets within reasonable proximity to the Wheeler farm.

The Governor felt he held the upper hand. In actuality, he did, but he possessed no clue I knew of about his supposed flim flam incident with the peanut inspector. I craved to put a viable threat together that would tone him down and make him leave Margaret and me alone for once and for all.

Armed for an exposé, I hit phone buttons to start calling peanut authorities, my energy piqued.

Then I hung up.

Case interviews mandated prepared questions and most of the expected, or suspected, answers. I flipped a page on my pad and wrote the number one. After six attempts at preparing interview questions, I dropped the pen in disgust. How does one tactfully ask about a ten-year-old sale via an unknown inspector who *might* have taken a bribe? And worse, about the current governor? They'd label me a fanatical moron with a trumped-up political ax to grind against a man with a clean record, beloved by two-thirds of the state.

I rested my chin in my hands, rubbing my nose. Maybe there was another angle. I typed aflatoxin and peanuts into Wikipedia. Found a press release about nine deaths and 691 sick people in forty-six states due to a candy manufacturer purchasing bad peanuts. Agency acronyms scrolled past like CDC, FDA, FBI, and FEMA. Lawsuits, bankruptcy, investigations.

Politicians spouted right and left, from both parties, united in ridicule for people who jeopardized one of the public's favorite food products. Washington passed a 2002 Public Health Security and Bioterrorism Preparedness Response Act labeling such contamination as potential terrorism. I remembered some of this, but never read the details.

The aflatoxin mold, not yet a recorded occurrence in the United States, was a proven carcinogen twenty times more toxic than DDT and linked with liver cancer. What were the chances that Patsy's cancer death was related to peanuts? She lived around them—daily. I was afraid to think it a possibility, though, without being compared to Lucille and her overzealous beliefs.

Margaret told me to let things be about the inspection, saying too much time had lapsed since the supposedly nasty deed. No proof. No recent reoccurrences that we knew of. Then thinking of Margaret triggered a notion.

I phoned the Fant residence, stunned when Simeon Fant picked up. Bingo.

"Mr. Fant, this is Carolina Slade. Sorry I missed our appointment the other day, but I enjoyed a lovely lunch with your wife."

He coughed, his voice rough as a crushed rock driveway. "What can I do for you?"

"Margaret Dubose is in the hospital. She was in a car accident yesterday."

"Oh my God," he said, his words dropping to a bass tone. "How is she? Addie'll be horribly upset."

"Margaret is a dear friend of mine, too, sir. She's in critical condition at Baptist Hospital. Room 366." Urgency tugged at me to check on her again since it had been over four hours since I'd called and been told yet again Margaret was critical and unable to speak.

Fant sighed. "Thanks for calling to let us know, Ms. Slade. That was kind of you."

I inhaled. "May I ask you a couple of questions, Mr. Fant? About marketing peanuts?"

"Hmph. I guess so."

He seemed gentlemanly enough. "I assume you spoke to Mrs. Fant?" I asked.

"I did."

I wrote the question as I asked it. "Do you recall any improprieties in 2000? When Mr. Wheeler may have . . . when y'all had the drought?"

"Can't recall."

"Do you know of anyone else who may know?"

"No, ma'am."

Too quick a reply, so I reworded. "Did people have trouble selling their crop back then?"

"Ms. Slade," he said, clearing his throat. "What are you trying to prove?"

"Isn't it obvious, sir?"

"I'm not a vindictive man, ma'am. And I have no reason to believe Dick repeated that error with the peanut inspector, assuming he made a mistake in the first place, which there is no proof of."

I let my pen wander on my notepad. "But you chastised him for selling bad peanuts. Did he unload them under the table?"

"Ms. Slade, do you remember the salmonella scare in '09?"

The wiki article still showed on my screen. "Of course I do. When they recalled so many products off the shelves."

"There was nothing wrong with the peanut butter, but it undermined the public's trust of the food industry in this country," he said. "And that was just salmonella. People in this part of the world don't understand aflatoxin. It makes salmonella seem like a stomach ache. The industry can't afford another incident because of something that *may have* happened ages ago. Walk away, ma'am."

So Simeon Fant felt the industry took priority over one man's indiscretions. Frankly, he made sense in an overall, umbrella kind of way. But that didn't clear Wheeler.

"You can't tell me anything, Mr. Fant?"

"What for?" he asked, escalating. "What the hell will you do with such information but create a damn panic? If it happened, it's ancient history. Forget it."

What would Margaret say to coax this man? I cleared my throat. "But—"

"I gave away peanuts for two years after that mess, at ballgames, fairs, car races in Darlington. That's how Hugh started his weekly trips to the VA, giving away roasted peanuts because they were considered safer than boiled or raw. But public perception can destroy a person, a business, an entire industry. Think about it, Ms. Slade. You seem bright enough. Thank you for informing us about Margaret." His phone clicked.

Crap.

I flopped back in my chair. Self-reproach rushed in as I recognized that my need to best the Governor outweighed the needs of the rest of the state. Nailing the Governor for such an ancient scandal would do more damage than good in the grand scheme of things. But what would South Carolinians think about a successful cover up kept quiet for a decade? Which was worse?

I called Monroe's desk, but he was out for the afternoon. I started to dial Wayne, but wasn't sure I'd get an I-told-you-so or not . . . so I didn't. Uncertain what to do, I delved into my normal cases, reports, and situations that disrupted our small offices from helping the state's rural communities stay afloat. On days like this, I missed the routine of making loans, keeping farms alive, helping rural schools and businesses take root and grow.

Other than making another call to the hospital and hearing Margaret's condition hadn't changed, I spent the afternoon lost in paper, to avoid thinking about the morning's meeting to nowhere.

Harden poked his head in the doorway. "I assume you kept your appointment today," he said. "Maybe your reassignment to McCormick County will ease the stress out of your life. I hear it's laid back there."

I stared at him without a reply, noticing the button above his belt buckle undone, flaunting an undershirt beneath. Classy.

He hitched his belt, which promptly resumed its original position. "Well, time to clock out," he said, glancing at his watch. "What's on your plate tomorrow?"

"Liaising with the state's agriculture office." I moved a file across my pad of notes. "I'm trying to tie off arteries that may bleed while I'm gone."

He wrinkled his forehead and scoffed, grinning. "Somehow I think we'll survive without you."

"Go enjoy rush hour, Harden."

He turned and left. I heard "Excuse me," as he exited to the hall. I stooped over my desk drawer to extract my purse and leave.

"Hey, CI."

The old nickname from our Charleston case spiked a rush.

"Hey yourself," I said, straightening. "What brings you to the tenth floor?"

Wayne leaned against the doorframe. "Thought you might like to grab dinner."

I avoided looking at him. "What about Pamela?" Then I hated myself for saying it.

"Forget Pamela." He walked over and rested against my desk. "Come on. I'm tired of butting heads, Butterbean."

"She drink my wine?"

"Nope."

With a flare, I ripped off the scribbled interview notes and the two pages behind for safekeeping, folded them in quarters, and tucked them in my purse to shred at home.

As those broad shoulders remained in front of me, mine relaxed. It took me a moment to recognize why—I harbored a fear of how events had turned sour between us in so short a period, yet held the potential of becoming so serious just as fast.

I was too uncertain to make any decision about anything at the moment. Every turn I made in the last week somehow veered off course with nothing to show for my work but misunderstanding and collateral damage. Margaret was a perfect example. Having Wayne back seemed to put one issue back to right, but I worried about jumping back in too easily. I doubted my own judgment. How did somebody fix that?

"I have to call the hospital," I said, lifting the receiver as an excuse to stop my avalanching thoughts. I'd only checked two hours ago, but she could have changed.

Patience settled across his face, his posture at ease as he sat and waited.

No change, still critical. No visitors allowed. I dropped the receiver back in its cradle.

"Well?" Wayne asked.

"She's the same."

His gaze was soft. "Sorry, Babe."

He cared about me, but I felt we should be past this point. I wanted deep commitment with no lies. I'd done lies with Alan. No secret rendezvous with the ex. I massaged my forehead. "This sucks. She's the best boss I ever had."

He stood and came around the desk.

I rolled back. He gently wrapped his hand around mine and helped me from my chair, continuing to draw me to him. "Let's not fuss anymore," he said. "Please."

My arms tucked between us, into my chest, as I folded into him. My fear seeped away, feeling his heart beat in a steady, soothing rhythm. His musky smell came back to me, bringing me home.

And this is where we always stopped progressing. How did I get further than this?

After a few moments, I stepped back and lifted my purse. One step at a time. "Dinner sounds good."

Wayne escorted me toward the elevator, an arm around my shoulder, unusual in the building. Monroe stepped out of the men's room. For a second, a shadow of disappointment appeared in his eyes before he released a wide grin. "Y'all have a good evening," he said, waving as he disappeared through an office door.

My heart tried not to care.

WAYNE AND I sat in a booth away from the noisy bar, toward the back of the Blue Marlin. He ordered fried flounder. I ordered broiled scallops. Chablis washed them down. We tried to speak of weather and the kids, each sentence comprised of careful, benign words.

"Your bruises seem better," he said. "How are the hands?"

"Sore." I held them palm up, studying the bandages, then put them back in my lap to change the subject. "Monroe suggested I confide in you and beg for your help."

Surprised, he smiled. "Good man."

"He most definitely is, Wayne." Realizing the too quick retort, I reached for a sip of wine.

He set his glass down. "Monroe *is* a good man. He's level-headed. You're lucky he watches out for you." His glance fell toward his plate. "God knows I keep failing at it."

My mouth dropped open. Embarrassed, I collected myself and waited, because Wayne Largo, as passionate, protective, and loving as he could be, rarely conceded. Ironically using almost the same words Monroe said about him.

Wayne exhaled long and loud. "If I'm too overbearing, I'm sorry, but the minute I don't worry about you might be the time someone takes advantage. You age me, Babe. You've parked that smart, sassy way of yours in my life, and as irritating as your independent habits can be, I want you around." He stared at the stem of his glass in his hand.

"Wow," I whispered.

He glanced up. "What?"

I slowly swung my head side to side. "I could listen to this kind of sweet talk all night, Cowboy."

The humorous twinkle made me smile wider. His rustic, bearded, tough-guy image melted into one more vulnerable, and my pulse quickened. This was the Wayne who captured my heart a year ago. An intense man who decided I was worth risking his career.

"What happens to us, Butterbean? What do we keep doing wrong?"

"You mean besides keeping Pamela a secret?"

He tensed a bit. "And like you keeping Kay quiet from me?" he said.

"Touché."

The moment lengthened into a silence neither of us seemed to know how to break.

"The whole personal versus professional issue," I finally said. "What do we keep trying to prove? I could've told you about Kay. You could've explained Pamela."

"I'm—"

"A trained professional. Yes, you've reminded me a million and a half times."

He ran a hand over my gauzed one. "Well, I am," he said, grinning. Then the playfulness fell away. "Not that you aren't good at your job. I didn't mean—"

"They dole out truckloads of arrogance with those badges, don't they?" I pinched him. "My job isn't your job. Quit judging me by your standards. Get that through your head, and we'll do a whole lot better. And stop seeing Pamela without telling me."

"What if I told you to stop seeing Monroe without telling me?"

I opened my mouth to say "that's different" and swallowed wrong, coughing. After a swill of water, I wiped my mouth. "We work together."

"Maybe so, but ditto, Butterbean. One day I may have to deal with Pamela again." His face remained serious. "It's not easy, is it?"

"No, it's not. Especially if I'm supposed to be your girlfriend." I stared up at him, searching. "Maybe that's it. You can't separate the two."

"Maybe. Can you? It's who we are."

"So, do you quit your job, or do I quit mine? Unless you want another girlfriend."

His brow creased.

I reached and tried to press the wrinkle away from between his eyes. "Quit frowning so hard. I'm not giving you an ultimatum. I wanted you to hear how it sounds—the black or white way of reading our relationship. Doesn't sound so great, does it?"

The folds around his mouth deepened. "No, it doesn't."

The ground felt more level under my feet now, and I saw his helplessness as cute. "I'm messing with you, Wayne. I don't want your authority to throw somebody in jail. And sometimes we deal with an assortment of people in our jobs. Okay?"

"Heaven help the world if they cut you loose on the criminal element without me, but fine." He finished his wine. "So what's happened with the Governor? Haven't heard anything on the evening news, always a good sign."

"Just because it's not viral on Twitter doesn't mean it's not a train wreck," I said. "There's Margaret, Lucille, the Fants, Wheeler. I'm at a crossroad, maybe with nothing left to pursue."

When I reached the part about my truck and the hotel brick wall, he paled. "Damn. Babe. I don't care if you *hate* me, call me when something like that happens."

"Margaret did nicely." I reiterated what happened in the details I'd denied him in the parking garage. "There's still an SUV running loose," I said. "Monroe suggested you might be able to find info on the car."

He blinked, as if tallying his options. "You tipped your hand when you told Wheeler about the car. If I call about a damaged fleet vehicle after the Governor demanded a briefing on one, they'll see a red flag. Let me think about it."

He paid the check, and we strolled out of the refrigerated restaurant into the sweltering August heat. I glanced up the street, then down.

"Watching for more SUVs?" Wayne asked.

"Maybe."

"See what happens when you stir crap?" he said, his long arms around me on the step. "I feel like punching a wall now because I wasn't with you."

"Well, don't. This place is made of brick."

"I want to lock you in my closet."

I pushed him back gently. "That's sweet and all, Wayne, but I'm not your best boots."

He laughed and walked me toward the car. "Can you come by the apartment?"

I almost said yes. "Whoever tried to run me down remains on the loose. I want to be with the kids . . ."

He recalled their Charleston kidnapping as well as I did. He leaned one stiff arm on the car. "Who's with them?"

"Ally," I said, then rummaged in my purse. "Probably should check on them."

I pulled out my phone. "What about Kay?" I asked him, scrolling to my home number. "She hasn't contacted Ally or me."

He shrugged. "She still won't answer."

Ally answered and reported all in order on the home front, then squealed when I told her Wayne asked me to his place for drinks.

I shielded the phone with my other hand. "So not necessary, Ally."

"Go, go, go," she urged, voice reduced to a whisper. "Spend the night."

"The kids home?"

"Spitting distance."

"Keep them inside." The kids seemed fine, even if their protection was a wayward, scatterbrained aunt. I glanced over my shoulder at Wayne. He gave me a half-grin, as if he read my deliberation. "House locked?" I asked Ally.

"Of course," she said.

"Two hours, then. Maybe three. And set the entry alarm," I counseled, having just coached Ally on how to handle the security system on the house.

Wayne nodded in agreement. Ally squealed again.

"Good gracious, you sound like I'm desperate," I said.

Ally chuckled. "No, you aren't desperate, but it's kind of my fault you fell out with him, so let me babysit. Plant a kiss on that tantalizing mouth for me, Big Sis. Go."

Wayne opened my door, and I eased inside. "Ally, you there?" I asked.

"We love you," came a chorus of kids and aunt in unison.

My heart warmed, and a smile bloomed across my face. "I love you, too, guys."

Wayne started the car, pausing before putting it into reverse. "I have something for you," he said, holding out the key to his place. "Is this yours or not?"

I slid it off his hand and tucked it into my purse.

He grinned. "Let's go open that bottle of wine."

The drive took ten minutes, and we chortled about Harden Harris the entire way, enjoying the lightheartedness of simple chat. Between Wayne's presence and dinner's Chablis, complete ease crept in for the first time in days. As he unlocked the apartment door, I hesitated at the mental moment of my last visit and shoved Pamela's memory aside.

I glanced at my watch. Alone time with Wayne happened all too infrequently. This moment seemed too important to rush, and I wanted each second to count.

Wayne disposed of his pocket contents, badge and Glock, and I inspected the refrigerator for the wine. My sandwich remained intact but hard as a brick, and I tossed it in the trash. The wine, however, was appropriately chilled. I opened a cabinet and reached high for wineglasses.

Arms encircled my waist. A bearded chin nuzzled my neck, and my knees almost gave out. I twisted around to face him. His lips pressed hard, his tongue and mine enjoying each other.

"Not sure I have much time," I whispered.

"Then let's get busy," he whispered back in my ear, nipping it.

I squeezed him hard and released. "Wine and conversation first. Okay?"

He refused to let go. "We did enough of that already."

I gave him another peck. "Then it won't take much time to finish up, will it?"

He planted another kiss, reached over me, and retrieved the glasses. "I can't be held responsible after thirty minutes of more wine," he said. "Talk fast."

Filled glass in my grasp and barefoot, I curled on the sofa, legs tucked, next to Wayne, trying to forget that Pamela had sat one cushion over two nights ago. Wayne propped socked feet on the coffee table. One arm rested on the sofa's back, reaching over to tease the nape of my neck. "So what do I do?" I asked, playing with a button on his shirt.

He stroked the top of my hand on his chest. "About Wheeler, I take it."

"Yes," I replied with a grin. "Focus."

"Probably need to forget him, Slade. You're just in a pissing contest now."

"Damn it, Wayne. I'm frustrated at not having more to be frustrated at."

He tapped my forehead. "Because there's nothing there to go after? Your original case, if you call it that, was determining if Lamar deserved the drug charge. Suddenly you're snooping around about a possible peanut violation that may have happened years ago? You let Margaret distort your focus, Butterbean. You have nothing left to investigate."

"One of the Governor's fleet runs Margaret and me down and that's no case?"

He stroked a thumb back and forth over my jawline. "Hey, I'm not crazy about what happened, but you have no connection to the Governor until the regular police find the car. And I bet DEA drops that case on Lamar."

I followed the wine movement in my glass. "I'll be glad when Margaret's better. She scared the life out of me."

"Thank God that didn't happen." He rubbed my neck again. "But I know. She's a rare breed."

"Especially in Agriculture." I downed a mouthful, tired of sipping, and set my glass on the coffee table. "Ally says she thinks Kay's still at Clay River. They've developed a loose sort of friendship, I think. So there's no skulking around hunting for her anymore, either. We just have to get rid of Pamela somehow."

"I'll take a trip to Pelion tomorrow," he said. "It's time my sister faced reality. If she knows anything, she needs to spill it. If she doesn't, fine. I can't pry Pamela off her back until she comes forward to cooperate." His fingers trailed across my shoulders. One found its way under my collar.

Goose bumps ran down my shoulders and arms. "You plan on doing the nude thing when you go see her? Like I did?"

His mouth fell open then widened in a smile. "You?" He laughed. "How did they talk you into that?"

I snickered, muscles sinking into the sofa. "Ally."

"Well, not this guy."

"Come on, take me or Ally with you. They know us. They're awful skeptical about lone males."

He set his glass down. "My badge works just fine."

"As always."

"Hey," he said and turned to face me. As he eased over, his hands came to rest on the cushions on either side of my hips. "You like the badge, and you know it. Come here."

"Hasn't been thirty minutes."

He nuzzled the valley of my neck. "Close enough," he mumbled.

My head lolled back to give him room. "Your mind is stuck on one channel, Cowboy."

He growled. "Only channel I need."

My cell phone rang from my purse on the kitchen counter.

He fell back with a huge exhale. "Go ahead. Get it."

I scurried into the kitchen. "Give me a minute. Has to be Ally." I found the cell. Caller ID said Baptist Hospital. "Hey, this might be Margaret!" I hit the button. "Hello? Margaret?"

"Carolina Slade?" asked a foreign voice.

"Yes, this is she."

"This is Sarah Hansen, from Baptist Hospital? I'm the nurse you dealt with when you came in with Margaret Dubose. Do you know of a family member we can contact? You seem to be the only person we've spoken to since Ms. Dubose came in."

"Sorry, but she has no family. I work with her, and I was with her when the accident happened. Can I help you? Is she doing better?"

"I hate to notify you like this, Ms. Slade, but Ms. Dubose died a few moments ago."

Chapter 24

I SQUEEZED THE phone white-knuckle tight. The room shifted, and I grasped Wayne's kitchen counter with my free hand. "That can't be right."

"I'm so sorry, Ms. Slade," the nurse added. "Is there anyone I can contact about Margaret's arrangements? We have no one listed."

Of course they didn't. I filled out the papers with what little information I knew. "Arrangements?"

"We need to notify her closest kin."

Margaret had no kin to my knowledge. I'd only recently learned she had a past with the Governor. Lucille would've been on that list. "Um, let me check with her employer and get back to you," I stammered. "Can I call you tomorrow?"

"Sure, here's my direct number."

"Wait a minute . . ." I spun left, and then right, seeking anything to write with. Wayne appeared at my elbow and retrieved a pen from a drawer. "Okay," I said.

He put an arm around me and took the phone as I said goodbye. "What's wrong, Butterbean?"

Blinking, I clutched his shirt, not wanting to speak. Words would make it hurt. Would make it real. Words would start a domino of events I didn't want to happen.

Wayne eased my hands free and walked me to the sofa. "Did Margaret take a bad turn?"

I felt for the cushion beneath me. "She died, Wayne. That was a nurse from the hospital."

"Oh, Babe."

"I never thought she'd die." I stared at the phone as if they'd call back and say there'd been a mistake.

"I know," he said.

Margaret wasn't supposed to die. Lucille had a stroke; she was old. Patsy got cancer. But like CJ, Margaret had years of life ahead. She wasn't ill. She practically laughed off losing her job. She'd become a mentor . . . a friend. I'd just ordered the Governor to give her her job back.

Wayne moved closer. "Slade."

I held up a hand, protecting the moment. Not yet. I groped for logic. I needed to reason this out. I could not accept that someone killed a woman I knew well, in my company, in a parking garage, probably in my place.

Visions filled my head. Margaret and me in her office. Margaret and her long-ribboned straw hat at the Pelion Peanut Festival. Margaret commanding a room from behind a mic.

A tear escaped. Then another.

Wayne reached over and drew me in, crushing me against him.

I cried . . . cried as if I'd lost a dear friend, because that's how I'd come to know her. Margaret had an old soul, and while some saw her as tough, I found her trustworthy, true to form, someone who respected me for who I was. What an impact she'd had on my career, on me as a person. She possessed a commanding art of gently putting me in my place, always for my own good.

She'd become Margaret instead of Dubose.

The pent-up frustration of the last few days gushed atop the sadness, and I couldn't stop weeping. Curled up in the cushions, tucked in Wayne's arms, I rued the day I took my job. Remorse consumed me, as if I'd driven the SUV that crushed Margaret's car. What had I done? What could I have done differently?

Wayne brushed the top of my head. "This is not Beaufort, Slade, and just like you didn't kill those migrants down there on that case, you didn't kill Margaret here."

"I didn't say I did," I said between sobs.

He wrapped arms around me. "Oh, Babe, you forget how well I know you."

Finally, after a half hour of weeping, I lay silent, my cheek wet on Wayne's soaked shirt. The warmth between our bodies enveloped me, as if cuddled in a blanket, lulling me to sleep.

I awoke on his chest, his head lolled back, mouth agape. I tried to slide off without disturbing him, my head so dull, eyes swollen.

He groaned and stirred before I could stand. Rubbing his face, he sat up. "What time is it?"

"Midnight," I said. "Can you take me to my car?"

"Sure." He ran his hand over my hair. "You gonna be okay?"

"Not for a while."

He patted my shoulder. "Yeah, I know." He headed into the bedroom for his keys.

As I waited, the garage accident repeated again and again in my mind. The SUV rammed the BMW, the sound of the car door's crunch as I hid on the other side. Eyes closed, I rocked myself on the sofa's edge and tried to picture Margaret before the tragedy. Tried to recall her alive, not submissive and trapped under a steering wheel. The SUV had acted like a beast as if the machine were alive. Different. What was different? What gnawed at me about that vehicle other than it killed Margaret?

I jumped to my feet. "Wayne!"

He ran out, a boot in his hand. "What?"

"It's murder now. They murdered her."

His face went stoic, revealing he already knew the reality that just smacked me. "Yes, Slade, they did."

Both hands clutched my purse to my stomach. "It could've been—"

"You. I know." He positioned his gun in its holster into his waistband. "Come on. I'll take you to your car and follow you home."

Without traffic noises in the middle of the night, silence in the car magnified. Both of us knew the other thought about close calls and a rogue black SUV. I'd called Harden from Wayne's apartment and left a message. Now I left one with Monroe. They could tell everyone else, and Monroe would start whatever legalities were needed with Human Resources in Washington.

Wayne walked me to my front door, saw me inside, kissing me sweetly before watching me lock up. Satisfied, he strode back and drove away. Ally's brightness dimmed instantly when she read my face. I could barely repeat the evening's event without crumbling again, so I gave her just enough to explain my mood. Then I dropped comatose into bed.

I awoke a few hours later. The nurse's call gushed back to mind, and the weight of a hundred rainy days tried to keep me under my comforter. The dark's softness told me it was about five in the morning.

After a hot shower laced with a few more tears, I tiptoed to the kitchen, shoes in hand. I leaned against the kitchen island and hung my heavy head. God, I didn't want to go to work.

Ally padded in on bare feet, twisting the tie of her robe into a loose knot. "Wayne said to call him before you go in, remember?"

"I can drive myself. He was up late, too," I said, pushing the button on the coffeepot to brew early since the timer wouldn't kick in for another half hour.

She leaned on the bar. "Are you in danger, Sis?"

I shivered. "I don't know, Ally. I always knew before, but now . . . I don't know."

"Stay home," she said. "Please."

I held my car thermos under the dripping coffee. "And do what? Wait until there are no more problems? When is that supposed to be?" A tablespoon of sugar went into the steaming drink, and I stirred, studying the swirl, letting the aromatherapy of the brew soothe me as best it could. "I have to deal with Margaret's death."

"Others can do that."

Not the type of dealing I meant.

I blew over my thermos, desperately needing a sip before I screwed on the lid. "By the way, the interim boss wants to send me to McCormick County for a while. So I have work on my desk to do before I leave."

She frowned. "When?"

"Monday."

She leaned further over the bar. "Do you have to move? Where's McCormick?"

I collected my keys. "Too far for my taste. Hopefully I can convince him to change his mind." The heaviness of all this friggin' reality had convinced me I couldn't outright refuse Harden's orders to work in McCormick without giving him ammunition to fire me. I hoped to convince him otherwise. I hadn't even asked Ally if she'd tend the kids.

"You'll find fresh eggs in the fridge from the Amicks' chickens. Blueberries in the freezer if you want to do pancakes. Otherwise—"

"I got this." Ally followed me to the door. "Keep me informed, okay?"

I flicked her ear like I would Zack. "You sound like Mom."

"Bite me." She closed the door.

I waited until I heard the click and the ding of the alarm setting itself.

I didn't even have to remind her. Whatever happened to me, at least the kids were safe this time.

HARDEN ROCKED his chair from behind Margaret's desk, across from me. "I'll deal with Margaret's business," he said.

His fat butt didn't fit the setting—like someone in dirty sneakers at the opera. He didn't bother wearing a coat, and his wide tie dated back to my high school days. I ground nails into sore palms, wanting to scratch his eyes out for polluting what used to be Margaret's realm. I started to emphasize Margaret was my friend, not his, but my exclamation would only underline what he'd preached for months: that Margaret Dubose was a skirt amidst all the pants, a skirt who favored other skirts. If he only knew.

"I want only good words said about her, Harden."

Harden would be blown away to know Margaret's gay affiliation, and I intended he never find out. A secret she should have been the one to release, not me.

"I don't think she had family," I continued. "She probably had an attorney assigned to handle her affairs." I slid the hospital phone number and name of the nurse across the desk. "Here's who to call. They're expecting information this morning."

No emotion whatsoever showed on the man's saggy face. His head settled into his neck rolls, pushing them over the edge of his frayed button-down collar. "I already called them," he said, irritated. "You don't even recall leaving the number on the phone last night."

In spite of a topic that rated the highest of reverence, he needled.

My anger rose with a white-hot fire as my glare hardened on him. A flash of acknowledgment in his eyes told me he noticed. My breaths intensified. "Her termination was not final yet. She's due all the benefits of any employee."

Springs squeaked under his ass. "Washington will decide the details she's entitled to."

I lowered my hands from the table to my lap, clutching a pen until my knuckles hurt. "Please keep me updated."

"Like everyone else, Slade."

My pen shook. If I stayed longer, I'd say or do something regrettable. Yet I wanted to stay, wanted to get even with this man for sitting in Margaret's chair.

"Anything else?" He dared me to react badly.

"I'll be out of the office today," I said.

"Tick tock." He brushed a thin comb-over lock from his face. "McCormick awaits."

My pen snapped.

I stood, hid the pieces in my fists, and left. Outside I leaned against the wall, a position I found myself repeating every time I exited this office.

Monroe rose from a guest sofa in the outer office. "Heard you were here," he said.

I closed my eyes, tears threatening again if I spoke.

"Take a moment," he said.

"I can't believe she's gone."

He enveloped me in an embrace. I wrapped my arms around him, grateful. But while I relished the opportunity to share my sorrow with someone who legitimately cared, I hated to be so close to the insensitive prick in the next room and felt the urge to escape.

I pushed back. "I have to get out of here, Monroe." I dropped the pen's pieces into the secretary's trash can and snatched open the door.

If Harden became boss, I was as good as fired. Before he had the pleasure, I'd quit. But as long I worked for Agriculture, no doubt he'd come after me.

Monroe followed me to my office. "Why don't you go home? You'll go looney tunes on us if you stick around."

"I'm being shipped out Monday, remember? Work to do."

His expression softened. "At noon, let me take you to Villa Tronco's for a long lunch. If you're not feeling better, I'll take you home. You've had a hell of a lot happen this week." He perched on the edge of my desk. "I'm worried about you."

"I'll be fine."

"Remember, I'm right down the hall," he said before turning to go.

His lecture in the ER came back all too clearly as his back disappeared. "Monroe. I'm sorry," I hollered.

"I know," he called out from the hall.

Ordinarily, I'd relish Monroe soothing me down over eggplant parmigiana with soft mandolin music in the background, but not now. Wayne had said wait for the cops to do their thing, but I sensed that Margaret's murder, or my attempted murder, or both, were indeed malicious, not an accidental hit and run. Not impressed with the Columbia PD thus far, I felt determined to dig on my own. After all, digging is what I did, at least until Monday.

Out of pure respect for Margaret, and for those she believed in, I also hoped to ponder more about the planted drugs at Lamar's apartment. What other connection to our accident could there be? Stopping now left too many lives extinguished for nothing. With Wheeler smiling sweetly from his lofty seat in the state capitol building.

I was the only person left who knew enough to be dangerous.

WAYNE MET ME in the lobby around eleven. With so little research time left before the McCormick reporting date, and with Wayne so attentive to my wishes, I asked him to escort me back to the VA.

Drugs started it all, the connecting vein to every death and fiasco connected to the Wheelers, Margaret, and yes, Pamela. The Governor, as well as Margaret, had sidetracked me, but the goal should have remained the drugs all along. So that's where I would return to try and find answers to who killed whom, who took advantage of whom, and who needed to pay for this domino-effect of life-altering events.

"I was supposed to pick you up this morning," Wayne said, holding the door open for me as we exited the building.

"I like having my own car," I said. "Besides, it was early, and you needed sleep as much as I did."

We walked toward the parking garage where she was killed, and I suddenly stopped, anchored to the spot. Someone's tires whistled around a tight turn on an upper level. Around the corner of this level, a car door slammed. A lady's heels clomped on cement. This was the last place I saw Margaret alive.

Wayne looked back. "Want me to get my car and pick you up here?"

Thank God he read my thoughts. "Yes . . . please."

Once he disappeared, I hugged the edge of a small Kia, then moved near something more substantial, a Lincoln Navigator. A vehicle approached around the bend. I jumped between cars as it eased past. I watched traffic flowing down and out the exit, remembering the day.

I'd have to collect my car sooner or later, but right now it'd be later. The meeting with Harden had stirred memories of Margaret, and this was as far as I dared venture into the garage.

Wayne soon pulled up. He drove us to the exit and glanced both ways before entering traffic. "Steve said he'd meet us behind the VA."

I grasped at straws, but I had to follow any half-assed lead I could drum up. This was the most convenient loose end I could think of at the moment to pick at and try to unravel.

Agent Steve Fulmer met us as planned. I declined the coffee chatter, eager to pry deeper. Time was sparse.

Steve pushed a paper toward me. "I checked the master keys just as you suggested, Ms. Sherlock. All accounted for on the day the pills disappeared." He drummed the table. "You still suspect something nobody else does, or does my report serve your need? I can't believe you came out here about keys."

"I didn't," I said. "Someone died in the interim, and another person had a stroke."

"I see," he replied, his voice softer. "Sorry."

"Every time I turn a stone, five more appear, and I'm tiring of the game. I appreciate you meeting me. Now, what about the cameras?"

He turned to Wayne.

Wayne raised a thumb toward me. "Help her out."

Steve faced me again. "Nothing there, Ms. Slade."

"You're telling me Tom Holcomb left the pharmacy when he said, took his normal route toward the incinerator, and his story checks out?" I asked. "He walked a straight line there and back? At the time specified in the log? All on camera. Yet somehow those pill bottles wound up at Lamar Wheeler's apartment and sparked a DEA investigation?"

"Tom's time was a bit off," he admitted. "He logged the meds out at three p.m., but he didn't take them to the incinerator until he left to go home. To save him a trip. That was four thirty. The incinerator manager's story still jives since he was gone for the afternoon."

I glowered at Steve, disappointed with his inattention to detail. "So he lied."

The agent's discomfort showed in his fidgets. "He didn't follow the regs precisely, and he admitted it and got suspended for two weeks. What else is there?"

"I want to see the tapes from where he left the pharmacy to where he went home," I said.

Steve scowled. "For real?"

"For real," I said.

An hour later, after three phone calls, a couple of arguments, and a hospital-wide announcement for the man in charge of the camera security system, the three of us sat packed into a chilly ten-by-ten office with a beanpole-skinny, red-faced tech kid in his late twenties, viewing video.

"There," Steve said, pointing at the screen. "He's leaving."

We watched the pharmacist lower a roll-up gate in front of the counter. Holcomb exited the lower left hand area of the screen. The top of his head came into view in a hallway, a briefcase in one hand and a gray garbage bag in the other. He strolled from the lower left corner, across the camera view, and exited in the upper right hand corner.

"What's he carrying?" I asked.

"The meds," Steve said. "Same back from when he left the pharmacy."

"How do you know?" Indeed, how could anyone tell what Tom carried, or if he'd passed the pills to someone else sometime between three and when he left. They could've remained in the pharmacy, only to be passed off to someone in the morning. I was dumbfounded that they'd built a case on this.

"He gets in his car without the bag," Steve said. "We have no camera installed at the incinerator. Due to this investigation, though, they're installing one next week."

Three more tapes captured our subject's trek across the facility. The fourth, however, showed the pharmacist exiting the building and tossing the bag in a huge dumpster.

"Aw, damn," Steve said.

Wayne leaned forward to see the film more closely.

The VA agent scratched his head and turned toward the security technician. "I don't recall seeing this tape, do you?"

The young tech shook his head. "Don't blame this on me, man. You asked for footage from the pharmacy to when he left the building. Those DEA types asked for a copy of all my files from that day. I didn't watch any of it, so I have no idea who saw what."

I slowly shook my head. "So much for the incinerator."

Steve's complexion reddened, caught in his mistake. I almost felt sorry for him, but he'd brought it on himself.

"Well, ol' Tom's lied again," Wayne said. "Bet he feels lucky landing only two weeks leave." He nudged the tech.

Pamela wasn't my favorite person, but I saw the DEA diva as anything but sloppy in her police work. She knew more than she let on. She'd seen the tape negating the incinerator disposal and remained quiet. What was she up to? She'd even let the discipline come down on our pharmacist based upon false facts and lies in a signed, sworn statement from the man.

She wasn't done with this case. I could not see her complicit in a cover-up that reached all the way to the Governor's Mansion. On the contrary, I saw her the type to let people lie their butts off, stacking falsehood on falsehood, waiting for the weight of it all to crash down on them. Then she rides in like Ms. DEA Dynamo.

Wayne leaned over in front of me. "What are you thinking about so hard?"

I blinked. "I can't be the first one to notice all this, Wayne."

Chapter 25

IN THE TINY VETERANS Administration computer room, from my metal folding chair crammed between Steve and the technician, I studied the camera's recording of the secluded dumpster and the pharmacist throwing what were proposed to be the missing meds in the trash. Not stolen from an incinerator room, but tossed for any drug dealer or addict to dumpster dive for a fix. No one called his hand on tossing them in the dumpster, so he kept his mouth shut.

I drummed the desk, contemplating who could have retrieved them from the dumpster and then taken them to the Wheeler condo? Who was the real player in this political drug caper? And was Tom dealing, or simply making the stupid mistake of not taking the stuff to the incinerator?

Special Agent Steve blamed DEA for concealing the truth. The VA technician accused Steve of not reviewing every tape before DEA got their hands on them. Wayne listened with arms crossed. I ignored them and continued to watch the recording.

"Any idea when this dumpster's contents were picked up?" I asked over the clamor.

While Steve parlayed insults with the technician, another person limped into view on the computer screen. A guy with dark hair under a ball cap. He gripped the rim of the trash container without hesitation. Most people avoided coming in contact with those receptacles, for obvious reasons. I leaned closer to the monitor.

The man planted a foot on an outcropped metal piece used to lift the dumpster. Belly balanced on the rim, he didn't even sift through the contents, but grabbed the trash bag identical to the one Tom had delivered. The man jumped to the ground and left, bag in hand, not even hiding his effort.

"Okay," I announced over the din. "Did you know people go through your dumpsters?"

"Steve," Wayne said. "Did your pharmacist deliver those pills to someone in particular?"

Steve slumped in his chair. "We don't know now, do we?" he said, annoyance clear.

"Controlled substances disposed in a public dump." I twitched, dying to do a celebratory dance at besting a real agent. But I'd been outsmarted enough times myself to know how bitter humiliation could be.

We studied the recording again, this time to the end. Another person glanced in the dumpster, leaving with something in hand, but it wasn't the gray bag. The ball cap guy definitely left with the same sized gray bag.

Steve sighed. "Can't prove what anybody pulled out. But DEA sure ran with it, didn't they?"

I scoffed at the man's effort at excuses. "Thought this was *your* turf."

Steve addressed me with an edgy tone. "DEA vetted Tom down to his navel, Slade. Everyone's going with bad judgment, not drug dealing."

The room warmed up with the door closed, and all I could smell was men. "Don't get mad at *me*," I replied.

Steve's jaw worked hard under the skin. "I'll talk to DEA again."

"We done?" Wayne asked.

"Sure as hell hope so," Steve grumbled as he swept past the technician to open the door and leave.

We spilled out of the room, the technician probably the happiest that the meeting had ended. Navigating past the cafeteria, we headed back through a short wing toward Steve's office. I studied the plastic nameplates on office doors. Internist, Thoracic Surgeon . . . I stopped. "Do you know any of these guys, Steve?"

"Yeah, some."

I scanned names and titles. "You have a pathologist around here? Could you please introduce me?" Then added, "I'd appreciate it."

"He's in the basement," he said, probably taken aback at my manners. I was trying.

"Take me there?"

"You wanna see the tiles on the roof after that?" he asked.

"Don't give her ideas," Wayne said.

Funny man, that Steve. But he was caught on his back foot and knew it. We retraced our steps the length of one hall and shoved open a heavy metal door with a horizontal push bar. The temperature dropped ten degrees. Steve ushered us to an office located beside a room of tables, glass, and stainless steel.

A lady about my age, only fifty pounds heavier, stared over her glasses. "May I help you?"

"We came to see Dr. Jamison," Steve said.

Her pale complexion screamed for sunshine in contrast to her dyed auburn hair. Silver, dolphin-shaped earrings dangled two inches from her lobes. "Pertaining to what?" she asked, not ugly, but not friendly enough to conjure smiles.

"I have no idea," Steve said under his breath.

Hand held out, I marched up to her desk. "I'm Carolina Slade, from the US Department of Agriculture. I have a possible case of aflatoxin I need to discuss with the doctor."

A nasal twang voice with a Midwestern accent sounded from the room to our left. "Aflatoxin? I seriously doubt that."

Three inches shorter than me, an older gentleman with a dried-prune of a face made his appearance wearing brown twill pants, a short-sleeved Oxford button up shirt and bowtie. Slip-on canvas tennis shoes made me glance twice at his feet.

"Dr. Jamison?" I held out a hand, and he shook it gently. "I happened to be at the hospital and thought you might be able to clarify something for me."

"I can try, dear lady."

"A farmer's wife died of liver cancer a few years back, and we just learned his peanuts didn't pass USDA inspection for mold. After say eight or ten years of living around such peanuts, what are the chances her liver cancer would be associated with a carcinogenic mold such as aflatoxin?"

"Ms. Slade, is it?" Dr. Jamison settled a pair of bifocals on his nose. "I've never experienced a case of aflatoxin. Few people in developed countries have."

"Can you tell me anything about its nature? How deadly it can be?"

He scrunched his mouth. "Hmmm. Let me check." He spoke over his shoulder. "You're lucky you caught me. I was about to head upstairs to a meeting, but this should only take five minutes." He disappeared into the neighboring room, his sneakers noiseless, his steps light.

The three of us stood awkwardly, not having been offered chairs. The secretary returned to her keyboard. Guess they didn't entertain guests in pathology, not such that could sit in chairs, anyway.

"What is your partner doing?" Steve whispered to Wayne.

Wayne leaned toward him. "She's right about there being another case, but go with the flow. She can be like a damn pit bull when she's got something on her mind, but it usually plays out in the end."

"You work with her often?"

"Yep," Wayne replied. "She has her up side, though."

I turned and scowled. "I *am* here, you know. Hush."

Steve pulled back. "Demanding?"

"You have no idea," Wayne said.

The doctor came back. "That's that."

"Pardon?" I asked.

He removed his glasses. "As I thought. No known case of aflatoxin poisoning in this country. *Baselt's Disposition of Toxic Drugs and Chemicals in Man*, the foremost forensic toxicology resource, doesn't even have it listed." His head turned to the side, watching. "Does that answer your question?"

After my amateur online research, I'd only read about a third world presence of this disease, but I had to be sure. For Margaret. "If someone died of liver cancer at a young age, would a pathologist even consider it?"

He shook his head. "It would take years for a related cancer to develop, and that would be after serious exposure and ingestion. If a person developed liver cancer, I doubt very much anyone in the United States would consider an environmental toxin as the etiology." He chuckled. "Sounds like the stuff of thriller movies, don't you think?"

"So it seems," I replied and offered my hand again. "Thanks for your time, Dr. Jamison. I greatly appreciate it."

We retraced our steps through the stale-smelling catacombs until we reached the stairs to Steve's office.

"Coming up?" Steve asked.

"No, but thanks for your help," I replied.

A vein bulged in his neck. "Always a pleasure to be used, Ms. Slade."

Steve and I walked away from each other. I'd embarrassed the man and showed up his investigation, but he hadn't taken me seriously from the moment we met. I considered us even.

Wayne stepped around the car to get in the driver's side, and I dialed the State Director's secretary.

Angela explained Harden had located Margaret's attorney. Personnel in Washington would process her benefits, and in light of the situation, provide her estate the insurance and compensation due a current employee. No date for a funeral yet. I hung up as Wayne steered out of the parking lot and made a left onto Devine Street.

The air-conditioning worked a bit too well, and I moved the vent. "I think I know how the expired pills got from the VA to Lamar's condo."

"Go on," he asked.

"I'd swear on my grandmother's Bible that dumpster diver on the footage was Hugh Fant. The date, the lot number on the pill bottles, the connection between the Fants and the Wheelers. How could he not be the one to remove those pills from VA property? Not saying he put them in the condo, but this coincidence is just too strong to ignore."

Wayne shook his head slowly. "And why continue with this?"

"Pills started all this crap," I said. "I want it closed, for Margaret. Doesn't it bug you that people who get in Wheeler's way die or fall ill?"

"All the more reason to stop, Slade," Wayne said, raising his voice. "Margaret's not here to cover your butt. Nothing stands between you and unemployment other than the good graces of two men who aren't fond of you—Dick Wheeler and Harden Harris."

"There's Lucille, too." I tugged at my seatbelt, searching to grab hold of sound reason.

"She can't help you either."

"Exactly. She's alone now, except for Addie Fant."

At a red light, he twisted toward me. "Who's going to accuse a slow individual like Hugh Fant over a dead boy when it comes to drugs . . . when the situation could be laid to rest, done and over with?"

"Listen to you." I raked my hair back behind an ear. "If it's wrong, it's wrong. Can't believe I'm telling you this, but shouldn't you phone Pamela? Don't you have some sort of obligation as an agent to report new information on a case?"

He gave me a nod as the light turned green. "Steve can do that. Might help his reputation right now. Wouldn't you prefer that to me meeting Pamela again?"

A car braked in front, and he veered left around a driver arguing on his phone. "Regardless who reports what," I said, "this situation is split back open. I feel obligated to talk to the Fants. They might not know what Hugh fell into. What if he just stashed those pills in the condo during some football gathering, for safekeeping? He might not understand, or he has some off-the-wall logic behind what he did. They could be nothing more than treasure to him."

"They might know perfectly well what he did and why," he said, studying traffic hard. This area was noted for fender benders. "You'll piss off Pamela again if you interfere. She still wields some power against you."

"Screw Pamela. You're only trying to cover my ass."

"Which isn't a bad idea, if you think about it. Technically this is Steve's jurisdiction anyway."

"Don't you get it?" I said, biting down on the words. "CJ didn't take those drugs. Neither did Lamar. Somebody set him up and tried to kill me. If I uncover this, I'll be golden in the Governor's eyes. See?"

He stared. "Thought this was about Margaret? And since when do you care about the Wheelers?"

"It's *all* about Margaret. She wanted the truth discovered. She trusted me to do it. If I quit, nothing has been done for her." *Come on, Wayne. Work with me, damn it.* "Wheeler once stated that the Fants could have set up Lamar. That's not so unreasonable now."

Wayne parked near the federal building, on a level below Margaret's accident. In the car, protected from those who might overhear in the office, I picked up my phone to dial Addie Fant.

I waited before hitting the last number. "Will you help me do this? Tell me if I get off track? I have a feeling I only have one shot with her."

"Fine," he offered, "but ease into it." A smirk followed the light tap on my forehead. "With tact, if you can manage it."

I cast him a dour expression. After the fourth ring, as I prepared to leave a phone message, Addie picked up.

"Addie? It's Carolina Slade. I called—"

"Oh, Slade," she said, on the verge of tears. "I just heard about our friend. Someone hit her in a parking garage?"

"Yes, ma'am." The explanation that Margaret died only after I jumped out of the way seemed hollow. "Internal injuries."

"Oh my, my, my. I'm outliving my friends . . . all my lovely friends . . ."

This conversation stung and headed out on a tangent I'd never retrieve if I didn't change it quickly.

"Addie, I just returned from the VA."

Wayne slowly pressed down both hands in the air, a sign to tread softly.

Addie sniffed back tears. "I don't follow."

"You remember those pills found at Lamar Wheeler's condo?"

"Yes."

"The VA found camera footage of what appears to be Hugh going into a dumpster and taking home a bag we believe contained the pill bottles."

She fell quiet. Wayne nodded encouragement.

"CJ had no business bearing blame for an act he didn't commit," I said. "Lucille was crushed. You know that."

"Hugh didn't do *anything*." Addie spit her words, swift and cutting.

I held the phone so Wayne could hear.

"How dare you," Addie continued. "I invite you into my home, and you try to use my poor handicapped son as a scapegoat. Margaret would never go along with this. You heard her. She didn't even want to blame Dick for that deception years ago. She's that kind of person, Ms. Slade, and apparently you fall way short of deserving any affiliation with her."

My eyes scrunched shut. Her words stabbed like knives, over and over.

"Margaret would hate you for this," she added.

"Margaret would want the truth," I said, anguished at her words. "But this isn't about her, Addie. It's about Hugh."

"Rubbish," she said.

"Mrs. Fant, can't we just talk about—"

"How to corner my son? You little bitch. Nobody accuses my son and then expects me to aid their cause against him."

Wayne watched me. He mouthed, "You can do this."

I stared at the floor, regrouping. "Mrs. Fant . . ."

"Don't you *Mrs. Fant* me!"

I reprogrammed my words. "I'm not blaming Hugh. Someone may have set him up, taken advantage, even protected him by disposing of pills on his behalf. Hear me out."

She cut me off with a dial tone.

I studied the phone in my hand.

"You tried, CI," he said. "Give her time to think."

I shook my head and opened the door. "No. I understand her position. I'd tell me to piss off, too." My original fleeting thought that the Fants had sabotaged the Wheelers in perpetuation of a Hatfield-and-McCoy feud, now made the most sense.

We exited the car and headed back to the office. We parted at the elevator, sharing a small peck of a kiss after seeing nobody around. I continued up to the tenth floor and entered the State Director's outer office. Harden's secretary was on the phone, yellow messages piled before her. After thanking the party on the other end, she hung up.

"Calls pouring in?" I guessed.

"Slade, it's a madhouse." She pushed glasses back up her nose. "If I didn't have every other state director, national office dignitary and politician contacting me, I'd be crying." At the mention of crying, her eyes pooled. "She was the best boss, you know?"

I broke our gaze to avoid sharing the misery. "Who's handling the funeral?"

"Jacob Mansfield, an attorney on Main Street. Margaret asked to be cremated. With dozens of people to notify, Mr. Mansfield wants to wait at least five days before a ceremony. It'll take place here in Columbia."

Practical. Sounded like Margaret.

"How are you, Slade?" she asked.

I jerked my head up. "Me? I'm fine."

"You were with her when it happened. You almost—"

"Don't. It's not worth mentioning."

She hushed. I reached over, patted her hand in apology for being short with her.

I returned to my office and fell into my chair. In an hour I could go home. I longed for the peace of my lake.

WHEN I ARRIVED home, Wayne's car waited in my driveway. Inside a quiet house, Ally sliced tomatoes and spread lettuce onto a tray already laden with pickles and onions.

"Where's Wayne?" I asked, dropping my purse on the counter.

"Mr. Handsome is out back, firing up the grill. The kids are with him." She wiped her hands on a dishtowel. "How was your day?"

I lifted a pickle. "It sucked."

She organized the condiments in a neat circular order, moved to the cabinet, and retrieved buns. My deep-fat fryer was already heating on the counter for fries. Ally moved around my kitchen like she owned it, and I was glad.

I intercepted her, removed the tray from her hand, and hugged her, the pickle vinegar and fresh tang of onion catching my nose. "In spite of your craziness, you're keeping me sane."

"Yeah." She shoved me aside to get into the fridge. "Two crazies cancel each other out. It's a formula. Don't you remember something like that from high school?"

I laughed and retrieved a wine cooler from the refrigerator door. "That's negatives. Two negatives make a positive."

"Nope," she said, her hip closing the door. "Two negatives make for a bad evening. Ain't nothing positive about that in any imagination."

Smiling at her logic, I moved to the patio. Wayne instructed Zack on when to turn burgers. Meat sizzled. Both guys held spatulas, using them like batons as they analyzed the finer aspects of outdoor cooking. Ivy sat on the three-foot brick wall surrounding the patio, long thin legs stretched out in front of her, MP3 player buds in her ears, toes wiggling to a tune.

This was so damn perfect. I hoped Margaret was watching.

Wayne moved in my direction and gave me a one-armed hug. "Butterbean."

Zack snickered, a hand over his mouth. "Butterbean. It's so funny when he says that."

I tugged a lock of my son's hair. "We'll have to come up with a nickname for you, whistle pants."

Ivy continued to rock to her music with eyes shut, obliging me with a half-wave. Brown as an Indian, her nudist behavior had indeed coated her from top to bottom with an even tan. God, I didn't want to think about her dating.

Too hot to eat in the sun, we moved to the wrought-iron table on the covered back porch under ceiling fans that knew me well.

"Napkin, please," I instructed as Zack reached over his aunt to stab french fries with a fork. "And ask people to pass food to you. Aunt Ally doesn't need you in her lap."

As the family chowed down, I rocked in my chair and scanned the setting, enjoying the view more than the burgers.

Wayne bit into his sandwich. "Any news?" he asked me after a few chews.

"Margaret knew so many folks they're delaying the funeral for a few days."

Everyone kept eating, some smacking. The question had been asked. Nobody wanted to address it anymore. The evening was too perfect.

"Heard from Kay?" Ally asked Wayne. "She's sticking around. That's a good thing, right?"

"Nope," Wayne said. "Ivy, pass me the salt and pepper, please."

"Wait," I said. "Thought you were going to see her."

"Couldn't get away," he replied from behind his burger, then bit a huge chunk out of it. He chewed it a few times and swallowed. "Someone tied me up. Don't worry about it." In other words, he'd spent the afternoon with me and my issues. I wisely returned to my meal.

Ally didn't. She cast an inquisitive leer at Wayne. "You going out there?"

"That's the nudist colony," Ivy whispered to Zack, who promptly studied Wayne in a new light.

"No way," Zack whispered.

"It's work," Wayne said and turned to Ally. "I might. It's time we had a sit-down discussion. I can't do a thing while she's *on the lam.*"

I appreciated his discrete disguise of the fact Kay evaded the law.

"They have sheep?" Zack asked.

Everyone laughed but Ally. "Kay's not ready," she said.

Wayne lowered his fork. "You don't know that. You just met her."

"I know enough," she said. "She's not ready."

Wayne leaned over his plate. "When exactly will she *be* ready?"

"I don't know, but it ought to be her choice to make, don't you think?"

Wayne's hands went up. "I don't want to argue with you, Ally, but a year's long enough. Between Pamela and me, we ought to be able to deal with Kay's demons."

Ally rested her fork and knife purposely on her plate, as if needing all her attention on Wayne. "Calvin and Prissy are working with her," she said. "Kay's scared shitless, but they're her mentors right now."

Zack covered his mouth. "Uh oh."

"G-rating at the table, if you don't mind," I said.

Wayne hadn't realized the button he'd pushed, but I knew my sister.

"Just enjoy dinner, Ally." I turned to Wayne. "You going alone?"

Wayne glanced over his sandwich. "Absolutely."

"Going out there is stupid," Ally said. "You won't find her."

"I find people for a living," he replied, taking his angst out on a paper napkin as he scrunched it into a tiny ball. "I think I can find my own sister."

Ally smeared a sarcastic grin on her face. "You haven't found her for a year." She aimed her fork at me. "She found Kay for you."

I sighed. "Geez, Ally. Don't do this. Just eat. Everybody, just eat."

Prickly silence blessed the air, thick enough to slice. I hated meals where utensils clinked, voices mute, while thoughts raged like hurricanes in the heads bowed over plates.

After what seemed an eternity of wordless minutes, Ivy saw fit to contribute. "You aren't leaving again, are you, Aunt Ally?"

To that, Ally rose. "Excuse me, but I'm no longer hungry."

"Great," Ivy replied. "Just great. Do I really have to grow up and be like you people?" She left with her plate. "Aunt Ally, wait up."

I dropped my head into my hands.

"She has no idea what's going on with Kay," Wayne said with mild exasperation. "And she doesn't need to get involved."

I started to add to the discussion, then changed my mind. Hand out, I addressed my youngest. "Zack, hand me the fries, please."

He stood and gave me the dish. "We're the smart ones, huh, Momma?"

I stole a glance at Wayne. "Seems that way, sweetheart. Sure seems that way."

Chapter 26

THE NEXT MORNING, I rose to a quiet house, the sun not wholly awake as an orange glow peeked from behind trees across the lake. To be certain Ally hadn't hauled tail in a huff during the night, I peeked in her room. She lay curled in a knot, face under the covers. For good measure, I checked the kids, never tiring of watching them sweetly doze.

Leaning on the kitchen table, a cup of coffee in hand, I enjoyed the bird show of house wrens and chickadees as they played tag on two feeders hung on shepherd's hooks beside the patio. Chickadees gathered seed and darted to the trees while the wrens hung around, social. A male blue jay swooped in, and everyone scattered, my cue to rinse my cup and head to a job where a loud-mouthed jay bullied as well.

Addie Fant ranked prominent on my to-do list after Harden. No joyful anticipation of either task. Especially Harden, a meeting that measured on the level of surgery with a dull, bent spoon.

Without a doubt, Addie loved Margaret and Lucille. Maybe I could use the leverage of that love in drawing out the truth about Hugh. Leaving CJ liable just because he wasn't around to defend himself was a despicable cop out. And disabled or not, Hugh Fant shouldn't deal drugs, nor deliver them to someone who might. If someone took advantage of him, then they ought to be nailed to a wall. Addie would want to know if someone manipulated her son so it didn't continue. I would.

If my questioning uncovered anything, I'd turn it over to Pamela so she'd owe me. No, I'd tell Steve at VA, like Wayne mentioned.

After forging through commuter traffic, parking again in a different parking lot a block away, I failed to locate Harden in the office. My McCormick County transfer, however, loomed. Surely we could attempt civil discourse about the best use of my talents before I reported. Not that I respected the idiot, but he held the reins to my future. We had serious government credit card abuse in the upstate. Nah, he'd ship me up there, further than McCormick. What case sat undone on my desk that I could use to butter him up, convince him that I would make his reputation shine brighter where I was?

Or I could check for job openings. Not exactly my preferred choice, but my family came first.

I called Wayne. He'd gotten roped into a noon conference call to his Atlanta headquarters, but expected to leave for Clay River right after lunch.

"Good luck with Kay," I said. "Hey, if you can talk her into it, invite her over to the house for dinner. Or we can take her out. What's her favorite meal?"

"That's a bit much to ask, Butterbean, but I'll try."

"Well . . . tell her I'm sorry I ticked her off."

"Maybe you can tell her yourself," he said. "Have you cornered that idiot about your transfer yet?"

"Haven't found him," I said.

"Don't get fired." He chuckled. "See you later, Babe. Be careful."

I hung up. Now I could head to the Fants. My last-ditch effort to close the deal for Margaret and give Addie one more chance. I assigned a self-imposed deadline of the funeral to wrap things up. After that, case closed.

It took an hour to reach the farm. The day shined like a new penny, bright and beautiful, and I wished I could appreciate it more. As I stepped out of the car, mockingbirds flew from one crape myrtle to another, then into the pines nearby. Hugh answered the door.

"Hey, Hugh. Remember me?" I held out my hand. "I'm Ms. Slade from the Department of Agriculture. Margaret Dubose's friend. I'm friends with Ms. Lucille, too."

He shook with a firm grip his father had obviously taught him. He wore the same ball cap I'd seen on the tape, his black hair curling out from under the edges.

A happy smile blossomed, then he winked both eyes. "I remember you." He mindlessly blocked the doorway, letting the air-conditioning out.

I seized the opportunity. "I'm so sorry about Ms. Margaret."

He glanced at his sneakers.

I kept the sentences short. "But Ms. Lucille is holding on."

His face brightened. "She kept me out of trouble."

Grinning, I nodded. "I bet she did. She's a sweet lady."

The August heat beat at my neck. I wished he'd ask me inside. Sweat beaded on my forehead. "That must have made you feel safe."

His head bobbed. "Yep. She kept me out of trouble," he repeated.

"How's the peanut business?"

"Everybody likes peanuts," he replied with a wide, mule-eating-briars grin.

"I saw you at the VA hospital the other day."

"They like peanuts, too."

The simple man seemed harmless, but his pill pilfering at the dumpster, regardless how innocent, had started a humongous ball rolling.

"You ever see people get their medicine from the VA?"

A woman's voice echoed from the back of the house. "Hugh?"

He turned. "I'm at the front door, Momma. Somebody knocked."

Crap.

Catlike, Addie hustled into view in orthopedic shoes. She seemed taller and more ominous than I recalled. She wiped her hands on a dishtowel and shoved the door back with an elbow. "Who is it, baby?" Her expression of interest evaporated at the sight of me. "Oh."

Now what? "Ms. Fant, because we parted on such bad terms yesterday, I wanted to come in person to smooth things over. In memory of Margaret. Let's not be enemies."

Addie's stare from atop that huge frame would give anyone pause. Silence told me she sorted the words she intended to deliver. I stood there like a ninny, politely waiting to receive them. Hugh watched patiently.

"You were with her when it happened," she said, her words accusing.

"I . . . yes . . ."

"Let's not forget you were with Lucille when she had her stroke."

My throat tightened. "Yes, I was, but . . ."

She rubbed Hugh's back. "Go on to the garden, baby. I'll be there in a minute."

"Hugh, wait. Ms. Fant, please, let's talk. What if someone is using your son?" I needed him to stick around, to judge his reactions. "Hugh? Do you recall climbing in a dumpster at the VA?"

Addie whirled on Hugh. He understood and headed smartly toward the kitchen.

Then she turned on me. "Hear me good, young lady," she said, her angry deep voice contained behind a wall of control for the sake of her child. "Hugh has limitations."

She squeezed her dishtowel, shaking it with each word. "People take advantage. You're not going to be one of those people."

My upbringing taught me to endure tongue lashings from elder women, and I almost conceded to accept my punishment. But this wasn't just about Addie and me. She was my last hope, my last connection to unravel this entire mess. "Can't we sit down and discuss this like adults?"

"Why? So you can once again weasel into my home life and fish? Without concern for the impact on an innocent?" She pointed to my vehicle, this time no restraint on her tone. "Get out of here."

"I—"

"Get out!" She slammed the door.

I backed up, staring at the golden knocker. If I understood correctly, Addie had directed Hugh to his secret place, the back garden. I darted around the house. A vision of Addie marching through the house spurred me on.

As I rounded the corner, Hugh rose from over his tomatoes, huge Beefmaster beauties filling each hand.

"Hugh. Do you ever get bags out of the VA dumpster?" I asked breathless.

"Yeah."

"Did you bring any of them home?"

He cocked his head, puzzled. "I always bring stuff home. Momma doesn't like it, though."

God, this was like picking fleas off a dog. "But did you give her the bags from the VA dumpster?"

The screen door slammed. "Your fanny is mine, missy," Addie yelled loud enough to be heard in Charlotte.

I held my hands out. "Wait, Addie. If you'll just hear me out."

She waddled toward me, phone in hand. "What's your boss's name?"

Hugh's head swiveled between his mother and me, his features appearing not so much disturbed but entertained.

Addie nodded toward the back door. "In the house, baby."

"But I wanna pick tomatoes," he said, piling both tomatoes in one hand to swat gnats.

"Child, do what I ask. I'll be inside shortly to make you a sandwich. Pick the best tomato and set it on the counter for me, okay?"

Somehow I knew I wouldn't be invited for lunch.

The woman's face turned as red as any tomato in the garden, and she stepped deep into my personal space. "That DEA woman threatened to put him in jail. He about lost his mind in my living room when she said that. I told her to go to hell and called my attorney. I'm not letting that happen again." She shook the phone. "Your boss's phone number. Now!"

I understood a mother's defensive posture, but this was bigger than the Fants. I straightened to my full height, still a good three inches shorter than her. "Then it's okay to let CJ take the blame? He's dead, so that makes him fair game?" I gritted my teeth. "Lucille can't speak up either, Ms. Fant. Dump everything on the two of them, why don't you? Go ahead. Throw yourself into the same lot as Lamar and Dick Wheeler. Alter the truth to get your way."

Addie's lips stiffened, yet her overbearing presence seemed to shrink a bit. Her shoulders dropped.

I was ashamed at back-talking someone old enough to be my grandmother, but I had her attention. "You're protecting your son. I get that. Patsy wasn't around to protect hers, and he died. Lucille lost her daughter and her grandson and has all but lost the will to live. You still have Hugh, your health, and your family. Guilty or innocent, at least he's alive."

She leaned over and grasped a four-foot tomato stake, as if her massive weight had become too much to bear. I waited for the wood to snap. Her complexion paled. Oh God, this was Lucille all over again. I quickly grabbed Addie's free arm and wondered what I'd do if she went down, other than go down with her. She remained bent over, silent.

"Ms. Fant?"

She rose, moving her hand from the stake to the top of mine. As healthy as she was, at this moment she seemed every one of her seventy plus years. Her gaze followed my arm up to my face. Tears pooled in tired eyes. "Hugh wouldn't wrong anyone."

I led her to a weathered, four-legged, handmade stool of two-by-fours set outside the garden fence in the shade of an ancient pear tree. Fruit weighed some of the branches almost to the ground. A few rotted pears lay on the grass, leaving a sweet fragrance in the air. "What is it, Addie?" I asked.

Her chunky hand rubbed an eye before she stared back. "I really liked you, girl."

Pity roiled up again inside me. "I *still* like you, Addie. We aren't so different."

Her features softened, some color returning to her cheeks. "Margaret was a good judge of people."

A hot breeze rustled leaves in the top of the pear tree, only a scant amount reaching us at the bottom. A wasp buzzed frantically inside a rotted pear near my feet.

"I'm going to tell you something," she said, "but I'll deny it if anyone asks. And you make sure nobody questions Hugh. Understand?"

I nodded, but I hadn't the power to stop anyone else from interrogating him.

"You know Hugh visits the VA once a week," she said.

"Yes. I saw him there." I reached around the pear tree, grabbed a bucket, dumped its collection of yesterday's rain on tomatoes nearby, then turned it over and sat near Addie.

"Hugh's daddy gets prescriptions from that hospital. Simeon's taken him to pick them up a time or two. Hugh hates meds. I have to beg him to take his own. However, he's fanatical about his father taking his pills since Simeon's heart attack a few years ago. Every morning, Hugh asks Simeon the same question like a broken record—*Daddy, take your medicine?*"

The screen door squeaked. "Momma?"

"Give me another minute, baby," Addie said.

Hugh went back inside, the door slamming thoughtlessly behind him.

"And the dumpster?" I asked.

Addie frowned. "I have no idea. What's all this about dumpsters?"

"We found video footage of him taking a bag from the same dumpster where the pharmacist tossed expired pill bottles. The same bottles found at Lamar's place."

"So that's where he got them." She rolled her eyes. "We stay after him for rummaging in dumpsters. One day he's gonna hurt himself on a sharp can or a busted bottle. Every dumpster owner in the county has met Hugh."

Stunned, I put pieces and thoughts together. If Hugh retrieved the pills, had Addie planted them at Lamar's apartment? She also adored Lucille, which meant Patsy, giving her vindictive intent against Lamar as well. Was the feud between the Fants and the Wheelers more than peanut competition and college rivalry?

Addie's back straightened. "You do promise to keep Hugh safe, right? You won't tell anyone what I say?"

I tried to formulate a generic, noncommittal response. I took too long. She noticed.

"Best you leave, girl," she said with a heavy weight to her words.

"*You* planted those drugs at Lamar's place?" I asked.

She flushed. "Absolutely not." Her strength returned as fury fueled her temper. "You will only make matters worse. Go on. Get off my place."

But we were so close to some sort of truth. "So Hugh brought pill bottles home. What did you do once you found out?"

She raised her monstrous self and moved into me, brushing my belly with hers until I stepped back. "You came here without an appointment, against my wishes, trespassing in my garden. I'm calling 9-1-1 on you if you don't leave. After what you did at Lucille's, I imagine they'll haul you in this time."

I blinked hard at her altered state. "What? Wait. You said . . ."

She crushed a piece of my sleeve in her plump hand, tightening the material across my chest. "You upset my poor boy, too. Old women and disabled boys. What kind of person are you?"

"Remember Margaret," I said, pulling away, disappointed at her disregard for the truth.

A flash of regret came and went. She spun and headed to the house, shaking the phone in her hand. "Hugh? I'm coming in, but give me one more minute, boy. Got a call to make."

I returned to the car in no rush. She wouldn't dial the authorities. She'd said enough for me to be able to cast disparaging, embarrassing remarks in a police report.

This case was hamstrung. The Wheelers, though nasty enough as people, were absolved from scrutiny. The Fants remained innocent and invisible to everyone but me.

Did Margaret know what Addie meant?

I slid into my front seat, cranked the engine, and left. By the time I reached the edge of West Columbia, I was certain Margaret had understood all the particulars of the Wheeler drug situation, possibly to include Hugh. That's why she'd assigned me the case, even after the Governor removed me from it. And the truth had possibly died with her.

Chapter 27

ADDIE'S ABRUPT about-face under her pear tree continued to stun me as I sat at a red light outside Columbia. So Hugh probably carried the condo pills out of the VA. What now?

Instinctively, I studied my mirrors. No sign of a black SUV. Thank God.

The Governor hadn't called to confirm if the state's fleet contained a damaged vehicle, but that was no surprise. He didn't strike me as a promise keeper. Wish I'd never voted for him. If one of his SUVs was discovered damaged, Dick Wheeler would hide it until repaired. The vehicle probably traveled the highways right now, with fresh paint and a new bumper. He'd have appeared more credible with some sort of follow-up call, laced with assurances that his fleet had nothing to do with the accident.

But why would someone at that level use government property to pull off a crime?

The light changed and I drove on. My truck had a two-week sentence at the body shop. I missed sitting higher up. In this rental I gave eighteen-wheelers a wider berth on the interstate.

I ventured past the Lincoln Street garage and the scene of Margaret's accident. No way could I bring myself to turn in, so I parked at the steel and sandy brick parking facility across from the federal building, behind the Arsenal Hill Presbyterian Church.

Finding an empty slot on the third level, I nosed into a space and shut off the engine. Sinking into the seat, head back, I shut my eyes and thought of my lake, the patient embrace of Mother Nature. Lucille's impatiens and rose beds. The primmest, neatest flowers I'd ever seen. Who would maintain her flowers now?

So many good people sucked into horrendous arrangements. Or were they suckers? Was I a sucker? I'd fallen for lies in my chasing the truth, going against the grain beyond all hope and a hell of a lot of reason.

The car's interior grew sticky hot. I needed to go inside, but the thought almost curdled my stomach. I hit the seat. Pain ripped across my left hand, and I cradled it, missing Margaret so badly.

"Life's not fair, Slade," she'd say. "You have the moxie to finish what you start. Just don't go off half-cocked."

A quasi-smile crept up inside me. *Half-cocked.* She used that expression more than a few times in our closed-door conversations. But even so, she trusted me with sensitive information and assigned me jobs because I was zealous enough to keep digging. Even as Wayne ranted about the official limitations of my authority, Margaret trusted me to walk the fine line and make it work.

My support system gone in Margaret, a demolition crew took her place in the form of Harden Harris.

I closed my eyes again. I was so screwed.

Sitting here wouldn't change anything, though. I collected my wits and left the car, still needing to face Harden and beg to remain in Columbia.

In my office, I checked messages. Nothing earth-shattering, but the long list of mediocre-sized requests exceeded my abilities to wrap them up by tomorrow. Friday, most likely my swan song as an employee in Columbia. McCormick was a temporary detail, but a signature would make it permanent, assuming Harden's pen hadn't bitten the paper already.

A knock on my doorframe shifted attention from my pitiful attempt to prioritize.

Monroe's furrowed brow gave me pause. "Where have you been?" he whispered.

"In the field," I said. "Why? What's wrong?"

"I don't know what his problem is, but Harden has been slinging your name around like it was—"

"Mud? Has he forgotten how to use a phone? They even come without cords now."

"Yes, they do," said a booming voice.

Monroe snapped up at attention.

Harden lightly slapped his shoulder. "Sorry, my man. Didn't mean to stunt your growth." He pointed toward me. "You, in my office."

My heart lodged in my throat. "Why?"

"One of those newfangled cell phone calls happened to find me a few moments ago with a rather disturbing message."

Monroe sensed enough to say nothing. My gut, on the other hand, wrestled with whether to backtalk or throw up breakfast.

Monroe mumbled, "Behave," as I passed him.

Harden held the door to his office for me. His face reflected the color of undercooked hamburger, blotched and mottled enough to look unhealthy. His girth made it hard for me to get by, but I managed without touching him.

"Sit," Harden said, shutting the door.

I bit back a smart-ass response. Why challenge the man until he showed his cards? So I slid into my usual place, the first chair near the director's desk, to his right.

I laid my notepad on the table and uncapped my pen.

"You don't need to write," he said.

"I always keep a record when I'm invited in here."

"I said no need."

I shoved the pad away. Arms crossed, I realized that action spoke animosity, so I laid them in my lap, then on the table, my bottom perched on the edge of my seat.

He marched behind his desk and planted his fists on the table. "Where have you been?"

"Tying up loose ends," I said.

"Since when do we collaborate with the VA hospital?"

Oh crap. Who the hell got back to him on that, especially so quickly? Surely not Steve. I didn't think I embarrassed him that deeply.

"An old case of Ms. Dubose's," I answered. "Closure before I left town."

"And the Fants' farm today?" he added.

"What?" fell out of my mouth before I could stop it.

Damn, Addie *did* call him.

The corner of his mouth twisted. "A certain DEA agent, who shall remain nameless, complained you've interfered yet again with an ongoing investigation."

"Nameless my ass."

"Pardon?"

I stood. "Her name is Pamela Largo."

"We aren't finished," Harden said. "Sit."

I ignored him and walked toward the window where Margaret always faced Finley Park and the state capitol building. Where she contemplated all that piled on her plate, as if the view helped her make sense of life. Standing in her spot, I shut my eyes, then opened them in hope that I could channel some iota of Margaret's backbone—some of her own half-cocked *moxie.* "I don't care to sit, Harden."

He came over and stopped close enough for me to hear him wheeze, my nerve endings almost swearing they felt his breath.

"What makes you think I was involved in that DEA investigation, Harden?" I said in an even tone, giving new strategy a shot. "I was informed about a bribery attempt with a USDA peanut inspector. I'm coordinating with the IG."

"I knew nothing about it," he grumbled, as onion engulfed me.

I rallied, pulse racing. "Can't tell you about it. You know that about bribe cases. And we don't investigate drugs, Harden. Your DEA snitch doesn't know squat. So what will you talk to Washington about?"

"You're lying," he whispered, close enough to be heard clearly.

"Touch me, and you'll regret it," I said low.

"Clear out and go home," he growled. "I'm checking with Washington to see what I can do about your intransigent behavior."

"You can't fire me," I replied.

"Insubordination."

Turning until we stood toe-to-toe, barely eighteen inches separated us. "Your word against mine in a closed room," I said, dying to rip a button or two off my blouse for effect. "Who knows what else was said or done in here. Invent a scenario, and I guarantee I can create one better."

He pivoted, returning to his desk. "I have a complaint from a law enforcement agency, which confirms you were where you shouldn't have been on government time. That's good for at least a week off."

My heart beat a rumba in my ears. I craved to pant harder, faster, but I refused to show weakness before this pitiful excuse for a man.

He scrunched his nose and sniffled, then wiped it with the back of his hand. "You heard me. Go home. I'll be getting in touch about where and *if* you report on Monday."

I took a sidestep around him and strode out. In my office, I sealed off the world and tried to call Wayne.

Voicemail.

I toyed with calling Pamela to vent my aggravation. What did I have to lose? Her card was in my wallet.

I left the room and took the long way down the hall, away from all the department clerks and technicians who'd probably heard Harden bellow my name all morning.

Monroe stood as I slipped into his office, away from being seen in the doorway. One glance, and he rushed to pull out a chair. "Oh hell, Slade, you okay?"

I smirked at making Monroe curse.

Dear consistent, reliable Monroe. He didn't ask what Harden did. He didn't ask what I did. Right and wrong didn't influence his support for me, and that's why I forever found myself in his office.

Exasperation, fear, regret swirled inside, each trying to consume me, the impotency of my predicament stifling. But those emotions stood no chance against the regret eating at my conscience, regret that I couldn't make Margaret's death more dignified by finding the instigators of this whole affair.

"I think I messed up big this time," I said.

Monroe grinned. "Not like I haven't heard that before. What's the verdict?"

"Harden sent me home. I report to McCormick on Monday, unless he thinks of someplace worse. I'm done here in the state office."

Monroe stood and pushed his door closed. "You'll be fine," he said, at the same time making his office private for me to fall apart if needed.

I appreciated his sympathy and wondered what else I could do for a living.

THIRTY MINUTES later, my clerk hugged me with good-bye teary eyes. Monroe walked me to the car carrying a box of the personal belongings that once graced my desk, credenza, and bookshelf. I toted two plastic bags, each step depressing me. Disappointment weighed heavier than anger. I was leaving a job suited to me, convenient to family, close to friends.

The kids thrived in a settled household now, so happy at the lake. I didn't have the heart to move them again, not after all they'd experienced over the last year or so. Ivy and Zack could remain on Catfish Cove, but I'd face a seventy-five mile one-way commute for goodness knows how long, even if I filed a complaint to Washington. I told myself to take one day at a time. Maybe Harden would get run over by a truck tonight on the way home.

We dumped the stuff in my rental's empty trunk. I left my awards and photos on the office wall. Harden wouldn't put someone in my seat anytime soon. If I received them in the mail, I'd know McCormick was more than a temporary assignment.

I slammed the trunk, moved toward the driver's side, and turned to thank Monroe. He caught me in an unexpected hug. My arms jutted out behind him in amazement, then gave in to his consolation and patted his back. I'd miss his afternoon discussions about agriculture, politics, and the idiocy of the human race.

"Harden won't be around forever," I said. "He'll have a heart attack one day or screw over the wrong politician. His days are—"

Monroe's mouth on mine smothered the rest of my sentence.

He pushed me against the back seat door, molding me against the car. My thoughts scattered like a clean billiard break. When I finally collected them, I still hadn't made a move to break the kiss.

Because at that moment, I needed a hug, a kiss, and sympathy.

He leaned back, and as we finally parted, my breath hitched. I covered my face, not wanting to see his reaction, his possible satisfaction. A job transfer was stressful enough. People spiraled into depression over just that. But the death of a friend, Pamela's threats, and of course the whole Kay dilemma strung me out. Then Harden.

Now Monroe.

Monroe moved my hands and wiped tears I wasn't aware of off my face with the pad of his thumb. "Are these for me or just life in general?"

"I have no idea," I said. "Why'd you do that?"

He smiled.

"Wait a damn minute, Monroe." I sniffled. "We're not starting anything here. I'm leaving. This was a goodbye that strayed."

"Had to chance it," he said without missing a beat. "Needed something more than a handshake to see you off."

He leaned in, and I checked him, pushing him away.

"You so got into that kiss, Slade. Don't say you didn't."

"Please don't do this. You're a friend, Monroe. I can say that without reservation. But I'm not available."

"So you say."

A sense of indignation flew through me. "I'm giving you some latitude as a friend, but don't overdo this."

"I told you—"

"I know you did. I've given you no openings whatsoever, either."

I recalled a time in Beaufort, and several innuendo here and there since, when he reminded me he'd be available until such a time as Wayne moved on. I assured him Wayne was long-term. Monroe always smiled, as if knowing better, but he'd remained properly at arm's length.

But now a tiny hint of panic fleeted across his face. "I feel like I'm losing you, Slade. At least I had you here at work."

I pushed him back again. "You never *had* me, Monroe. We worked on the same floor." Whether he lacked social skills or picked a damn sorry moment to become daring, he had just taken advantage of me when my world crumbled. That was not the Monroe I respected. This was not the safe Monroe I could rely on when life tanked. He was supposed to be the one to pick me up when Wayne wasn't around.

Wait. Wasn't that what he'd just done? No, he'd exceeded his boundary. Or had I muddied the waters, making the definition unclear, responding to the kiss?

He opened my door for me with a friendly expression back on his face. "You drive careful on those two-lane roads to McCormick instead of driving like you're at Daytona. And call if you need anything."

I slid into my seat. "Okay."

He slammed the door, and I rolled down the window. He leaned on the opening. I reached to pat his arm, but he stepped back.

"Keep your doors locked, Slade. Take care." He turned briskly and left, his heels echoing on the way out.

Oh, Monroe. Why do this to yourself?

I wiped my face and cranked up the engine. Why do this to me?

Monroe was my best friend in the world outside of Savvy, my

confidante, but that wasn't enough for him. It had been perfect for me.

Heart heavy, I pulled out of the garage. McCormick was a trash assignment, but I had to admit Monroe needed me to be long distance for a while.

Chapter 28

I STARTED THE car to head home from my last day in Columbia. Four in the afternoon and no place to go. No case, no urgency, not even a need to stop for milk. At least not to my knowledge. A typhoon could hit my house and a tornado take out half the state, and I would be oblivious these days. I never saw Monroe coming, him telling me goodbye with that damn knee-weakening kiss.

My stiff shoulders weighed like lead, and a marching band beat a rhythm in my head. Hands were improved, but sore. I craved bourbon and an adult to spill my guts to, or I'd go home and cry myself raw.

I tried Wayne again. Voicemail. He must be out of range or seriously busy not to take my call. And damned if I'd contact Monroe. Ally would be there, though.

Thank goodness for my sister. I never thought I'd say that. Growing up, growing apart, and growing back together proved wondrous for us. Even her babysitting and cooking skills added flavor to the mix.

Wow, a positive thought. There was a God. I might not get drunk.

With no rush hour to contend with, I reached home in record time. The kitchen door held fast when I turned the handle. Locked. Good. I paused on the top step. Too quiet, though, as I let myself in.

"Ivy? Zack?"

Only after I scurried and hunted through bedrooms back to the kitchen did I see the note on the refrigerator.

> *Kids are at the Amicks. Left at 3:00 to go with Wayne to Clay River. Somebody had to get him inside the place. Back by dinner. Let's do Mexican. We'll order a tower of beer. You need it as much as I do. Your illustrious baby sister, Allegra Jo.*

She signed off with a smiley face with a bow on its head and big kissy lips.

I sighed, distraught not to have the chance to girl talk with Ally, but relieved she and Wayne were on speaking terms. She couldn't be in better hands. He couldn't be better entertained.

I confirmed the kids' locale with a call.

"They're watering Buddy's garden right now," Mrs. Amick said to my query. "And each other. You coming to dinner? Country fried steak and fresh-picked field peas. Blackberry cobbler for dessert."

If only my life's choices were so simple. "Thanks, but my sister's taking me out for Mexican," I said.

"Oh," she said, her tone flattening with disappointment.

I knew what she was after. "But the kids can stay and eat, if you don't mind."

"Why, I don't mind a bit," she replied, the lilt back in her voice. "I'll send them home later, fat and happy."

After thanking her, I excused myself to do a few chores while I had the opportunity.

Like drain the inside of a lowball glass of Jack.

Wearing gym shorts and Clemson T-shirt, I slid my feet into flip-flops. The cat hovered at the back door, so I let her out. Normal stuff for a not-so-normal day.

Using my napkin to wipe a bird dropping off my favorite chair, I dropped into a rocker, Jack and water in one hand, hot spicy chips in the other. By the time I neared the bottom of the glass, my mind no longer chugged and smoked like an old Chevy low on oil. No real buzz yet, but I could picture Harden, Margaret, or Wheeler without spitting, crying, cursing, or pulling my hair. One day not so long ago, all my friends, family, and acquaintances functioned in their rightful places. Then my boss asks for a favor and wham, shit boils over like a shaken two-liter cola. That simple ten days ago seemed ages.

I didn't get it—didn't see how events had taken this course. Throwing back the last of my Jack, savoring the hard burn down my throat, I considered another and contemplated drinking myself into a stupor. But I'd throw up before I passed out; I was never meant to be an alcoholic.

My best efforts had turned into pig slop. But regardless how my own environment deteriorated, those around me weren't supposed to suffer.

My boss wasn't supposed to die.

And it damn sure wasn't right for Monroe to take liberties. I didn't hate him for it, couldn't if I tried, but I wasn't comfortable in what he did. Such confusing signals between us.

Maybe I *needed* to become a recluse and provide simple housing loans in McCormick. With my head back, I rocked. The chair creaked. I shifted until it didn't. It was too early for crickets. The only other sounds came from Amick's bantam rooster three hundred yards away.

I woke with my mouth drooped open, like some fleabag wino. The doorbell rang. Had the doorbell rung before? I leaped up and ran toward the entryway. Figures Ally forgot her key. God, please let them have good news about Kay.

Wait. Wayne had a key.

I glimpsed through the blinds of my dining room window at the backside of a woman who was not Ally. She stood taller, mile-long legs holding up a body with twenty pounds on my sister. Shoulder-length straight hair draped over her collar.

With a glance in the entry hall mirror, I raked through my hair and wiped away a mascara smudge. I undid the three-way lock while trying to make out the person distorted by the oblique beveled glass.

With her side to me, Wayne's sister watched the woods that bordered the eastern side of my three acres. She turned as the door opened.

"Kay?" I asked, surprised. She looked different with clothes on.

"Please, can I come in?" She clutched a small brown leather purse as if it held nuclear launch codes.

I stepped back. "Sure." Before closing the door, I scanned the drive and only saw what had to be her blue Toyota. "Where's Wayne? And Ally?"

Kay scooted over the threshold and into the den, like a mouse seeking a shadow. Her jeans were worn beyond anything fashionable, and her tank top and dark tan Birkenstocks had seen better days. Sunglasses sat atop her dark hair, and a leather bracelet wrapped her wrist. She studied the door again, the house, acting like she didn't hear me, panic just under the surface.

"Kay," I said louder. "How did you find me?"

"Ally gave me your address. There's a GPS in the car."

"Oh," I said, glad to hear she'd caught up with Ally and Wayne. "You want something to drink?" I headed toward the kitchen, anxious how to handle this second chance for an introduction to Wayne's sister. "You can do Mexican with us tonight. Are they far behind you?"

"No," she said. "I came here to *find* Wayne." She took the glass from my hand and downed the root beer, as if parched, her movements edgy, eyes flitting. "Where is he?" she asked, lowering the glass and taking a breath. "He didn't answer his phone."

"What?" Wayne would automatically take her call. She'd ignored so many of his over the last year that he'd pick up without reservation. Hell, he'd answer her call sooner than mine. "How did you miss him?" I glanced at the clock, calculating how they could've passed each other. It was already six. So where could he and Ally be?

Her hands worked the strap of her purse. "Can you find him?"

I ran to the kitchen and snatched Ally's note from the refrigerator and held it out to Kay. "Wayne went to bring you back," I said. "Ally went along to get him into Clay River. They've been gone several hours. Where have *you* been?"

Her eyes widened.

My stomach clenched. "What the crap's going on?"

She flapped her arms once. "I don't know. I need Wayne."

I trotted to the bedroom for my phone. Kay wasn't making sense. She'd probably run from people so long she didn't trust a soul. Upon returning to the living room, I tried to speed dial my cell then stopped. He might ignore my call if he were busy, but take hers. "Give me yours," I said.

She dug it out of her jeans' front pocket. "It went dead on the way over here."

My heartbeat calmed. He probably saw her attempted calls and couldn't get through on her dying phone. A cheap, simple phone. Like Ivy's. I ran to my daughter's room and plugged it into the charger on her nightstand. A signal lit up.

"Kay?"

She ran in. I held up the phone and moved aside. "Put it on speaker and call him."

The hollow ring went on three, four, five times before rolling to voicemail. With the chance to speak to a recording, Kay rocked with one arm around her middle. "It's Kay. Don't go to my cabin, Wayne." She halted, taking a quick breath. "Just come back to Slade's. Please." The message clicked off. She stared at me. "Now what?"

Hands on hips, I attempted to analyze what she wasn't saying. She desperately wanted help but didn't want to trust. That much I could read like a McDonald's sign from the interstate. If this involved just her, I'd make her take a shower, give her a beer, and settle her down. We'd acquaint ourselves with each other. This female version of Wayne intrigued me, but there was an unhinged side of her so foreign to Wayne's structure. Her past had unraveled her to a certain degree, and that uncertainty about her personality kept me guarded.

"Are you high, Kay?" I finally asked.

"No," she replied, indignant.

She was a tangled ball of nerves. "I have the right to ask, hon. Your posture, movements, the scared tone in your voice . . . what aren't you saying?"

Tears appeared, but she disposed of them with an erratic swipe of her hand, as if unable to afford the luxury. Her bottom lip was chapped and split in places, and she drew it into her mouth again, biting.

And I stood there wanting to slap answers out of her, but instead drew deep upon my patience while whispers in my head warned time was critical. What was a smart question to ask? What would send her over the edge like this?

Reaching over, I rubbed her back lightly. "Sorry for asking if you were high. Guess that was out of line. Can you focus, though? So we can figure out how to help you . . . and find Wayne?"

Her muscles eased a hair under my touch. A hint of a smile proved she tried.

"Were you followed?" I asked.

Her voice quivered. "Maybe."

Fear seized me. "Have you seen, what's his name . . .?"

"Barker."

"Barker. Is he anywhere around here? Have you seen him?"

"He came to Clay River. I caught a glimpse as he headed into the office, so I left." She cried for real this time, sliding down onto Ivy's bed, hanging over her lap with despair. "I didn't know Wayne and Ally were coming."

Oh, Jesus. Suddenly their inability to call and inattention to time meant more than bad cell zones. Wayne had skills to judge what to do, where to go, how to get away and call for backup, but he was saddled with Ally.

I ran to the front door window, scouting for the drug dealer. "Try Wayne again," I said loud, moving from the dining room window to the rear sliding glass door.

Just as I returned to the bedroom, Wayne picked up. "Kay? You inside?"

Kay's forehead creased. "Inside where?"

Static spit through the speaker. "I'm standing outside your cabin."

Kay jumped up. "Don't go in."

"I've had enough of this—"

"Shut up and listen to me," Kay screamed. "I'm at Slade's."

I dashed across the room to stand closer to the phone.

"Thank God!" he said. "Stay with Slade. I'll pack—"

I grabbed the phone. "Barker's at Clay River, Wayne. Get the hell out of there."

The phone went dead.

My thoughts ran rampant as I stared at the screen reading *Call Ended*. Fearful of what just happened, I hit redial.

Voicemail.

I dialed Ally's number. Her phone rang in the guestroom down the hall, forgotten, like so many times before. Handing Kay the phone, I spun toward my bedroom for my .38, jeans, and the car keys. "Call 9-1-1."

She met me in the living room, palms rubbing her slacks. "Stop and think about this a minute."

I turned on her. "Seriously? A moment ago you were falling apart, and now you're the voice of reason?" I moved to pass her, to lead us to the garage.

She blocked my way. "You don't know these people. They kill for real, and they don't warn you the bullet's coming."

"So call the friggin' cops!"

Kay paced. "The police are no good. They might even make matters worse." She took a few strides, pacing, mumbling more to herself than me. "They want me. Wayne's leverage. How do we deal with that?"

"Shit," I said, an idea smacking me like a brick.

"What?"

I ran to her purse on the sofa, threw it at her, and shoved her toward the kitchen. "Let's go. Now! We'll call in the car." Gun in my purse, I jammed the button to open the garage door. "We'll use my rental car. They're less likely to recognize it." Plus, I had no clue what shape hers was in.

She stopped. "My phone."

"Fuck the phone, Kay! It's not charged." I gripped her wrist and hurled her down the steps toward my car. I set the alarm and locked the door.

Kay dropped in the passenger side. "You can't handle these guys, you idiot. What's wrong with you?"

"Right before the call cut off, Wayne mentioned you were at my place." I let that sink into her head. "If Barker's in there, he probably heard." I threw the car into reverse, crashed first gear, and sped down the drive. "He knows where you are. And that's assuming he didn't follow you."

From the squint in her eyes, her mind appeared to churn. Bad memories? Plans to escape? My sympathies no longer reserved for her, my thoughts shifted to reaching Clay River, my instincts telling me to get there fast.

I dug out my phone. "I need to call my kids' babysitter."

Mrs. Amick answered. I lied about an emergency at work. "Please, please, don't let the kids go back to the house. I'll collect them when . . ."

"So we can keep them overnight?" she asked.

"That would be great."

Silence. "You sure you're all right, Slade?"

"Life just got hectic today, ma'am."

We hung up.

"My turn," Kay said.

I handed the cell to her blindly, my eyes too busy scanning for a tail. "Who're you calling?" I asked.

"Prissy."

Kay dialed Clay River from memory. She pressed her mouth to the cell. "Prissy? It's Nancy. You okay?"

I'd forgotten about the alias. Kay listened, a shadow covering her face. "No, don't call the police," she said.

"Hell, Kay. Let her call," I yelled.

"Prissy, calm down." Kay muted the phone. Her other hand gripped the dash as I rounded a corner. "They took Calvin."

I snatched the phone and unmuted it, correcting the vehicle as it crossed the center line. "This is Carolina Slade, Ally's sister. We're on our way." Which meant absolutely nothing, but it seemed good to say at the moment. I wasn't sitting home waiting for uniforms to ponder whether to go out there. Look what Columbia PD did with Margaret's death. At how Steve had handled DEA. How easily DEA had charged Lamar. "Call—"

Kay tried to snatch the phone back.

An oncoming BMW swerved to the edge of the grass to avoid my crazy zigzags.

"Stop," I said through clamped teeth, jerking the phone away.

"Don't call the police," Kay pleaded. "Not yet."

Prissy sobbed on the other end, capturing my attention. "They said if I tell any cops, they'll kill Calvin. They're watching." Her weeping continued. "When I saw Mr. Largo's badge, I was afraid to speak up. I tried not to give him the key . . . tried to think of a way to ask for help . . ." Sobs turned into wails.

"Stay in your office," I said. "Lock yourself in."

Her cries eased up. "That's it? Just sit and wait?"

"No, honey. I need you to first tell me how many people you saw and what they looked like." Prissy described, and I repeated for Kay's sake. "Okay, so you saw three. One tall Hispanic wearing a red T-shirt—thirty-ish. The other two white, one medium height in slacks and boots, the other a huge guy in jeans. Ages? Not sure? Okay, fine. Now, what are they driving?"

At a three-way in the Peak community, right before the interstate exit, I stopped, grateful for the excuse to think. "What year was this black SUV, Prissy?"

"One year old. Two at the most."

"Make?"

"Chevy Suburban."

So Kay's drug buddy had probably put men on my tail, too. I had no idea where the Governor's agents stopped and these thugs began. While I'd worried about Pamela following me to Clay River, I may have led Kay's stalkers instead. They traced Pamela to me, knowing who Kay's brother was, who Pamela's ex was, who Wayne dated now. Just like Pamela, they scoured the area for Kay. I almost collapsed from all the wrong turns I'd made, or caused.

Had they tried to run me down in the garage? Oh my God, how misdirected had I been thinking the Governor ordered a hit. I could only blame the Governor, my only clue, my judgment slanted because he was an ass with agents at his disposal.

I remembered now, clarity crystal in the peak of anxiety. The garage SUV didn't have the antennae the SLED vehicle did.

Anxiety swelled, pressing my heart and ribs. "Is Ally with you, Prissy, or did she go with Mr. Largo?"

Sobs started again. "She went with him."

Shit. "We'll be in touch," I said. "Stay where you are."

"I did all this by coming to Columbia," Kay said as I hung up.

"And not asking for help," I said, not the least bit sympathetic. I hit the interstate with my foot on the floor. We were headed blind into a huge unknown, scared and undermanned. Oh yeah, completely inexperienced with drug dealers. Wait, that would be me. Kay's resume was longer than mine. At this moment, unreasonably ashamed at my oversight, I shifted blame from Wheeler to Kay. "I'm ringing the sheriff."

Kay let my words roll off, regaining focus. "We'd be better off calling Pamela. Wish I had her number." She smacked the dashboard. "Damn it!"

I threw her my purse. "Look in my wallet for her card. Then ask her what the hell we're supposed to do." My tires thumped on the reflectors embedded in the middle line of the highway, and I righted the car back.

Kay smoothed a thumb across the phone.

Anger flew all over me at her hesitation. "Do it!"

She rocked slightly then spoke in a hushed tone. "They'll kill Calvin. They'll kill Ally. And the minute they get me, they'll kill Wayne, assuming they haven't already."

Terror seized my entire being. "We don't know that."

"I do," she said.

"Shut up," I ordered, gripping the steering wheel. "Get Pamela on the phone."

Chapter 29

AS WE SPED UP the interstate on our way to Clay River, I shouted at Kay, though she sat two feet away. "Put Pamela on speaker when you get her."

Reading from my bent copy of Pamela's business card, Kay dialed on my cell. It rang twice before someone answered.

"Pamela Largo," said the party. "I assume this is Slade."

"No, this is Kay Largo. Shut up and listen. We need your help."

Okay . . . a complete other side of Kay.

"I'm listening," Pamela said, smart enough not to banter with the prey she'd relentlessly hunted for months.

Kay wasn't addled, either. "I think Barker's at my cabin at the Clay River Resort outside Pelion. We suspect he's taken Wayne, Slade's sister, and the manager of the resort hostage. We can't reach Wayne." Steadier than I expected, she relayed details with purpose. "There are three kidnappers according to the wife of the manager. We're headed there now." She turned to me. "Where are we?"

"Turning off I-26 on Exit 113, the airport turnoff," I said loudly. "What the hell do we do when we get there?"

"Fantastic," the agent said under her breath.

"Dammit, Pamela, there's nothing fantastic about this at all," I said. "Wayne and my sister need help! Help me! Help them! You said to call. Here's the freakin' call. Don't be a bitch!"

"Whatever you do, don't go into Clay River," she ordered. "Meet me at the grocery store parking lot where we ran into each other. At that fair thing, remember? The day the kid wrecked his Jeep. If you get there before I do, wait. Don't go to Clay River. You copy that?"

"Copy, grocery store parking lot," I replied. "We're in a silver Sebring. Only the two of us."

"I'm already en route," she said. "I'm calling in for support. Wait for me." She hung up.

I glanced in my rearview mirror, no longer scanning for black SUVs, instead watching for a government Impala flying like a rocket to catch up. I eagerly welcomed her taking over. She served as the link, from the drug dealers to Wayne and everybody in between. She was knowledgeable, quick on her feet, and our best hope.

Hated the person, respected her skills.

I glanced at Kay to take stock of her mental stability. She'd floated from flaky to crazed at my house. In the car she'd turned from despondent about Barker to centered when dealing with Pamela. Who was this girl?

Highway 6 joined with 302. I picked up speed, nervous about every second Ally and Wayne could possibly be spending with Barker, kicking myself for being so closed-minded about the SUV tails . . . always assuming they were affiliated with Wheeler. Speedometer read eighty-five in a fifty-mile-an-hour zone. My foot instinctively lifted off the pedal, but then I mashed it back down.

"You don't know what I've dealt with, so don't judge," Kay said, catching one of my glances. She had a hard sense to her, like a woman who'd missed family Christmases and never understood the need for a good book or a mall shopping spree. Her hair hadn't seen a trim in ages, most likely cut with kitchen scissors, or a pocketknife, in God knows what bathroom on the road. From the wear of her clothes, she wore them often, if not all the time.

"No, I don't know your situation," I said, teetering on whether to scold or console her. I leaned toward stomping her into the ground for what she did to Wayne and for leading this disaster to my part of the world. But we were both after the same end. "But right now it doesn't matter, does it?"

"Guess not," she said, her composure intact. "But I'm sorry. Wayne is my brother. I didn't want him dragged into my shit. I can look at you and tell you care for him, and I figured you'd appreciate my dilemma. While he wanted to protect me, I had to protect him, by keeping him away. All Pamela would do is use him to get to me, so if he didn't know where I was, she couldn't."

Made some sense, but not sure she realized all the hurt she inflicted on her family. "You've been too long inside your head with no outside feedback. I don't like Pamela, and I treasure your brother, but somehow despite their differences, I believe they'd have found a way to save your behind if you'd only called. Instead, we wind up here, like this."

From her caustic glower, it appeared she hated agreeing with me.

The car seemed to hover over the asphalt. I cast a prayer up that every Lexington County deputy was on break.

"This *is* all about me, Slade." Her voice remained firm and open to my challenge. "Barker's holding three people as bait to get me. I'm done," she said. "I'm sick of running. None of this ends if I don't make it stop."

I caught the sight of a fast running car in my mirror. The vehicle flew like it had jets in the trunk.

Pamela pulled up behind, then around, waving for us to follow as she raced ahead. So I floored the gas pedal, thrusting me back in my seat. Three miles to Pelion, and it was a straight shot all the way.

One hundred. The fastest I'd ever driven in my life.

The IGA lot seemed foreign, only a tenth full, and no lights, rides, or fair food vendors surrounding it like before. Pamela's Impala parked beside an 80s Chevy pickup, I guess not wanting to appear the odd white duck in a pond of mallards. We parked beside her and got out.

"Get in," she snapped as she rolled down her window. "Kay, up here. Quick."

We jumped out like a Chinese fire drill. I slid into Pamela's backseat, Kay in the front passenger.

I started to get back out. "Wait a minute. I left my .38."

"Are you insane? I'd be a lunatic to let you carry," Pamela said. "Don't you dare get out of this car. Discretion mean anything to you?"

Kay interrupted. "What are we going to—"

"Slade, you have your phone?" Pamela ordered. I dug it out and showed it to her.

"Kay," she said, "you'll call Wayne on this and ask for Barker."

Kay frowned hard. "And tell him what?"

"You want to meet him."

"Isn't there another way?" I asked. "You've got unlimited firepower and law enforcement resources at your disposal. Can't you overtake him or something? Isn't this rather unorthodox?"

Pamela threw an elbow over the seat back and put me in her sights. I resisted an urge to back away at the ferocity in her stare. "You don't know what the hell you're talking about, so let me deal with this."

I had to make myself breathe again as she turned back to Kay.

"Call him," she ordered Kay. "FBI HRT's scrambling. We've only a small window of opportunity here."

"But the cabin is small," Kay said, the strength ebbing from her voice, "and there are other people at Clay River. It's secluded, spread out. And you don't know this guy."

Pamela scoffed. "I know him well enough after how long I've chased his sorry ass. The longer we take, the less chance we have. He'll get impatient before too long and just take them out. The time is now." She gestured for me to hand Kay the phone. "Do it!"

I hit speed dial for Wayne. "There," I said, handing it back to Kay. "It's on speaker, but who's to say he'll pick up if he's captive?"

The wait for an answer felt heavy, the seconds dragging and weighted. After four rings, the lawman picked up. My heart pounded just knowing he'd read my name on the screen.

"Wayne Largo."

"Hey, it's me, Bubba," Kay said. "You all right?"

Crackling noises sounded as the phone was shuffled, taken, rubbed against something. "Who is this?" came a voice almost tenor in tone. Not the deep, alarm-inducing, pee-down-your-leg threat I imagined from a drug dealing life snuffer. An acute creepy fear slithered down my back nonetheless. This man controlled the future of Wayne and Ally . . . maybe the rest of us.

"It's Kay," she replied, not as bold as before, but firm enough.

I inched forward.

"That's my girl," he said, rolling the words uphill in satisfaction. "So, come on in, and your brother and this woman might live to see another day. What you say, sugarplum? We're tucked in cozy in ol' cabin twenty-four. When did you go hippy on me, sugar? Thought my eyes were gonna bleed from all the nasty naked prancing around out here."

She held the phone with her eyes closed.

Pamela tapped Kay's head hard once to get her attention. "One hour," she whispered almost too soft for me to hear.

"Can't get there for almost an hour," Kay said to the man.

"Too long," he said.

"But I have to drive—" she replied.

"So drive fast. The longer you take the more likely you'll bring help. Sorry. You got thirty minutes."

She studied Pamela for feedback. The agent shrugged and mouthed *okay*.

"I'll try," Kay answered.

"Come alone. Don't call the cops, or your brother dies. You know . . . like the detective shows. And sugar," he said, trailing off a moment. "I'm always a man of my word."

"Yes," she said. "I know."

He huffed once. "Yeah, I believe you do." He hung up.

Pamela nodded approval and cranked her seat back a couple notches, texting on her phone, mine now lying between her and Kay.

"What now?" I asked, reaching for my cell.

"Leave it," she corrected. "I'm sending my people the details, but we're going in."

"But Barker said she had to come alone," I reminded.

Pamela continued to text. "She'll drive. We'll be fine."

"We?" I asked.

Annoyance wrinkled across her mouth. "You won't do anything, Barney Fife. Kay deals with Barker. I'll handle breaking events. *Your* butt stays here."

"Here? As in this parking lot?"

She glanced over the seat again. "Where else?"

The witch couldn't hold me back that easily. "I go along, or I follow."

She laughed. "Get out. We don't have time for argument."

Guess I was to Pamela like Ally was to Wayne. But while I might not be trained to negotiate hostage situations or handle tactical entries wearing body armor like Pamela and her peers, I couldn't see myself waiting for a long-distance hell to break loose. I could see nobody remembering until the next morning that I waited at the IGA for news. "With you, or behind you," I said.

Pamela took her keys and walked to the back of the car, opening the trunk. Kay and I glanced at each other, worried. Pamela quickly returned, constantly scanning the area, and handed Kay a Kevlar vest. "Put this on. It's mine, so it might be a little small."

Oh holy Jesus, I thought, sinking into my seat.

"Now get out," Pamela ordered me.

"No," I replied, buckling my seatbelt.

"Don't make me yank you out of there."

"You're wasting time."

She didn't fire up a retort or open a debate. Instead she stared, mild humor in her face. "Fine, Miss Special Projects Representative. You can represent your ass in the floor of this backseat. At least there you'll be out of the way."

KAY PULLED UP at the Clay River gate, headlights on since dusk had fallen. Pamela and I sat upright, as if coming home for dinner. The guard waved us through.

I tried to avoid studying this new man as we passed. Once the car was inside the facility, I spoke up. "That's not the guard I saw last time. They're supposed to check each nonresident. They don't let nonmembers in after dark. Do you know him, Kay?"

"No, I don't," she replied.

"Do you think it's one of Barker's men?" I asked. If so, he probably phoned the man now, and we were driving into a trap. "Oh God, Kay was supposed to come alone, wasn't she? They know there're three of us."

"Settle down. He's ours," Pamela said. "Do I have to hold your hand on this? Do you want to get out now? Kay, slow down, Slade wants to—"

"No." For a fleeting second, I did want to escape. Knowing the lay of the resort, I could find my own way, find my own hideout, watch from my own vantage point. But I could also get taken like Wayne, or worse, killed. Plus, as caustic and bitchy as Pamela could be, she was my best defense. "Go on. I'm fine."

"Thought so," Pamela said. "Kay, now take it slow. You know where you're going, and there's no need to hurry. He'll be there even though we're a few minutes late. They knew thirty minutes was unrealistic. Chill and play this natural. Our guys are in the woods and everywhere they need to be. Trust me." She reached up and flicked the dome light switch to off, I assumed so it wouldn't come on when a door opened later.

Kay slightly nodded and allowed the car to coast forward. A slight charcoal aroma hung in the air from earlier barbecues, mingled with pine. A low chorus of cicadas started here and there, but would soon grow into full song.

No one was about. Seemed funny that nudists went inside at dark. Maybe Prissy got word out, implementing some sort of unofficial curfew. I could see her trying to do that. I could picture her frantic in her neat office, afraid to leave the room, pacing all naked and scared.

We reached the string of cabins. We turned right and ventured to the end of the two dozen rentals, where Kay probably felt she was most safe once upon a time. Our headlights passed car after car, until I gasped at the sight of Wayne's.

"Down," Pamela hissed.

I dropped to the floor, but not before I spotted a man seated on the front step of Kay's cabin, unaffected by our presence.

Kay stopped and shifted into park, leaving the headlights on. "That's JoJo. What do we do now?"

I hunkered lower.

"Get out," Pamela told Kay. "I'll ease out behind you and use the door as cover."

This didn't seem like the smartest of moves. But as the rank amateur, my job was to listen and be quiet. I could do that well.

Kay opened her door. My hand moved atop some crinkling wrapper I couldn't identify, and I braced, my heart thumping like a bongo pounding for all to hear. Sweat beaded under my T-shirt with the August humidity captured under these trees.

Down on my knees, my butt wedged between the passenger and backseat. No way to hide more than I was. I tried to stay strong with the vision of poised agents cramming the woods. At the same time, however, I wondered why we weren't greeted by the cavalry and some negotiator with a bullhorn. A mosquito hummed in my ear, and I shrugged a shoulder to chase it away.

Kay stopped behind the driver door, and I heard Pamela crawl across the seat to behind the steering wheel.

"Hey, JoJo," Kay said in a droll acknowledgement. My voice would've been cracking, assuming it worked at all. I silently rooted for her. She would know how to maneuver around these guys. Hopefully.

"Hey yourself," JoJo said, shining a flashlight in her direction. "We been looking for you."

"Yeah," she replied. "I just heard. Been traveling."

"Sure you have." His laughter tittered like a monkey. Creepy.

Then nothing happened. Everybody stayed where they were.

"Where's my brother, JoJo? I want to see him."

I missed what the guy said. Then Kay said low to Pamela, "What now?"

"What?" yelled the guy.

"What now?" she yelled to him.

"Come away from the car. We're going to the beach."

"Not so sure I want to," she answered.

"It's okay," Pamela whispered, texting. "Relaying the change in plans."

Surely JoJo could tell Kay was stalling. And after chasing Kay for so long, why wasn't someone prepared to grab her the minute she stepped out of the car? Why didn't some agent barge out of hiding and nab JoJo?

A small whirr of a motor sounded, a golf cart, and JoJo stretched his neck to see who it was. I prayed it wasn't Prissy coming to save Calvin or some such stupid stunt. But the cart came and went, way too far away to recognize the driver. It disappeared, and I hoped to God we didn't later find Prissy as a hostage, too.

I sneaked a look between the seat and the door, checking Pamela's status and choked on my own spit as Pamela stood and revealed herself to JoJo.

Oh crap.

I tightened into the smallest ball I could, waiting for bullets to fly.

By now it sounded like JoJo wasn't but a few feet from the two women. Once they left, I'd retrieve my phone from the front seat, call 9-1-1, then sneak back to the gate to make sure the FBI understood what went wrong.

Assuming I didn't get shot . . . from either side. What was the damn plan?

"What you doing here?" JoJo asked, coming around the car, not in the least threatened by our agent. He raised his light onto Pamela, first her face, then down to her feet. His size made Pamela a molehill to his mountain, but she didn't flinch, almost eager to meet and greet. Damn, what was this woman made of?

"I come with the package, so don't whine about my being here," Pamela said. "What's this about the beach?"

He inspected the front, then the back. "Who the hell is this?" His shotgun tapped the glass above my head. "You too, lady. Out!"

I balled up smaller, stupidly thinking he couldn't see me.

He opened the door. "Get out of there." His hand gripped the neck of my shirt, and I unfolded myself with great effort, wedged as I was, and staggered off balance outside, the door holding me up as I tripped. Words choked in my throat . . . like *Please let us go*, or *Are you going to kill us?* The kids flashed through my mind.

Every muscle in my torso hardened, waiting for the shotgun to do its job. I wasn't part of anybody's plan, Barker's or Pamela's, so taking me out made more sense than anything else we'd seen tonight.

Chapter 30

DRAGGED OUT OF Pamela's G-car by my collar, Barker's hired hand frisked me and left me standing beside the door, shivering. The sun had set, but night fell with a three-quarter moon. Soft gas outdoor lights on poles cast cones of incandescence along the road every six cabins or so. However, at the end of the row, against the woods, cabin twenty-four benefitted from only a diluted hint of the glow.

"Leave her alone, JoJo," Kay complained. "She has no idea what's going on."

"Sure she does," JoJo replied, leaning to gawk in my face. He smelled of beer and Irish Spring soap. "She's the one we tried to nail in the garage. She knows."

Sure I knew. *This man killed Margaret.*

I forced bile down where it belonged. I should've stayed at the IGA parking lot. I should've gotten out at the gate. But no. I had to refuse to get out of the freakin' car. Now my children might become orphans.

Pamela rested hands on her waist and threw him attitude. Geez, she was going to get us killed. "We need the hostages, fella. You've got Largo and the girl. We brought our package for the exchange. Get going to the river."

Okay, maybe she knew what to do. FBI was waiting. That's it. FBI and DEA. Damn, this girl was cool.

Mosquitoes hummed a symphony in my ears. Our captor nudged Kay. "She leads," he said. Then he touched my ribs with his gun's muzzle, sending currents of terror through my nerves. My hand reached for the side of the car as my knees wobbled. "This Slade lady goes in the middle. Now move."

Kay struck out, as if leading a hike. We walked in a single line between cabins and then made our way left behind the rentals. We couldn't see squat below the dense stand of pines, oaks, and gum, away from the road lamps. I tripped several times before reaching the path barely golf cart wide. Once we stepped into the inky tunnel, my eyes took a while to barely make out a hand in front of me, the tree trunks black, shadows blacker. Bugs buzzed my head, bit my arms and neck, but I could see nothing to smack.

We were en route to the nudist beach. God, I couldn't wait to lay eyes on Wayne. Despite everything, seeing him would make me feel safer. Poor Ally was no doubt petrified with fear. I hoped to land a chance to calm her, assure her the cavalry hid in the woods, waiting for the right moment.

Just don't let them be dead.

Pamela told JoJo this was a hostage swap, and I hoped that was just dialogue in our ruse. Didn't we want to go home with everyone? Wayne, Ally, *and* Kay?

My Charleston kidnapper had designed a plan. It went awry over and over during that long, dark October night . . . to include his own death. I recall being held against my will, told I wouldn't come out alive. The uncertainty, the not knowing, the reality I had to think for myself with no help in sight.

But this time was different. So many players. I marveled we were three to JoJo's one and too afraid to do anything about it. Though a shotgun sort of evened the odds. Pamela, however, went along without the least trepidation, willing to indulge until she got her way. Limitless gall and completely unruffled. Probably cursing the fact Kay and I cramped her ability to take this guy down.

I shoved away thoughts of Ivy and Zack, not needing the emotional distraction, keeping my wits about me. Then I shut down my conscience over Ally being drawn into this mess. Another trip over a suspected root warned me to focus. No time for feelings. If I didn't pay attention to movements and sounds, watching for a chance to get away while eyeing Pamela for a clue on how to proceed, I was liable to get shot and not see it coming.

I wasn't sure I wanted to see it coming.

Kay trudged onward, feet shuffling to avoid the obstacles I kept finding.

JoJo loped a couple yards behind us, unconcerned, confident as a varsity player escorting freshmen to the locker room. Were we that unthreatening?

I glanced behind me every few steps, unable to stop myself with JoJo following us with a firearm. Barker's lieutenant was lackadaisical, and I hoped to capitalize on it. That's when I recalled a sharp turn ahead, only twenty or so feet from the open, man-made sandy area that fronted Clay River, where Prissy tried to sell me on a membership.

And as Kay turned left, I did too, only more severely. I stepped into the woods, behind a huge oak before JoJo came around the bend. I stooped and prayed.

At the end of the path, the scenery brightened as moonlight hit white sand. Kay broke into a run. Pamela trotted to keep up. JoJo walked right by me. I retreated further into the trees. He stopped, walked forward several feet, then spun around, hunting for me. "Goddamn it," he muttered.

"You two okay?" I heard Kay gasp. She must have reached the group, but ice water flushed through my veins. Two? Who was missing?

"Where's Calvin?' she asked, her voice not as tremulous as I thought it'd be. I had to contain myself from heaving with guarded relief that the missing hostage wasn't one of my people. I hadn't heard Wayne or Ally speak.

I tiptoed from tree to tree, freezing, then easing closer only when voices spoke and masked my movement. Thank goodness for tree frogs and bullfrogs, cicadas and crickets. This time of evening they sang their loudest. I reached a point six feet from the beach, to the left of the crew, and spotted Wayne about twenty feet away. He stood cuffed to Ally. They'd neutralized his threat by chaining Wayne's right arm to an innocent who might as well be a hundred and twenty pound anchor. Both were gagged, unharmed best I could tell.

However, Ally's eyes were wide with panic. She hugged Wayne, glued to his side.

I willed the reinforcements to attack . . . attack now. Agents and cops probably watched the same scene through scopes and binoculars, wearing black and camo, sweating in the heat and humidity under a layer of bulletproof armor. Moisture ran down my back. So what were they waiting for?

A boat big enough to hold three or four people floated off the end of the dock. The only kind that could navigate the shallow water.

"Thought there was another one," said the tenor voice that had to belong to Barker. Medium and slight in build with jet-black hair that hit his collar, he could sport a taste of gray from the sound of his age. His khakis and buttoned shirt seemed too dressy for the evening's events, and he wore what appeared to be leather boots. A wardrobe that meant he watched and didn't get dirty.

"Where's Slade?" Wayne's ex asked. "Oh, damn."

Kay turned toward Pamela with concern on her face.

Pamela scoured the black forest, hunting in a different direction from where I squatted behind a wax myrtle. I couldn't wave at her without giving myself away to the others. I wished she could tell me what to do. How could I help? What exactly did she have in mind?

"She must've bolted," Pamela said. "She won't get far in the dark."

Love you, too, Pamela. Now be an agent and fix all this.

Barker smiled. "This is the one I wanted anyway," he said, stepping up to Kay, running a knuckle under her chin. "Sugarplum, where have you been?"

At his touch, Kay's shoulder raised in a flinch, and she moved half a step. Wayne lurched forward only to be restrained by a third guy in jeans—a plain, brown-haired white guy except for the three inches he towered over Wayne and the four inches of extra shoulder under a light-colored T-shirt bulging in the arms.

The guard at the gate, and most likely the driver of the golf cart now parked and empty near the woods. A plant. And Pamela called him *one of ours.*

My brain synapses sparked as dots connected.

Nobody cared that Pamela stood there all super-agent pumped. Nobody took her weapon, gagged her, or cuffed her like Wayne and Ally. Kay, previously resolved to turn herself in to save her brother, now fidgeted, casting daunting glances at Pamela. The two guards held their weapons at ease.

This was Pamela's mission, not the ridiculous pill investigation with the Wheelers. A case involving the Governor's kin was a smoke screen to buy her time to deal with Kay. This woman took the term fanatical over the top. Question was whether she was faking out Barker or Kay?

She'd pulled one over on me. My blood began to boil.

"You act like one of them," Kay said, stepping up to Pamela. "Too congenial. Too sure you won't get shot."

The agent stood arms crossed, unimpressed. "Probably kicking yourself for not seeing it coming."

Kay sadly shook her head. "You're right. No regular agent would've persisted like you did."

"What's wrong, sugar?" Barker sure seemed to love hearing himself drag out his pet name for Kay with an air of haughty condescension. Kay's tightening posture screamed disgust.

She studied her deliverer. "I pictured you gung ho patriotic, Pamela. I even had Thanksgiving dinner at your place when you were married to Wayne."

I clamped a hand over my mouth. My stomach roiled again. Resting my forehead against the tree, I all but lost hope for the whole friggin' lot of us. My pulse pounded in my neck at the tiny odds we'd come out of this alive.

Pamela hunted Kay *for* Barker.

All that feminine machismo bottled-necked in a paper bureaucracy needed a more satisfying outlet. Or else Barker just paid well.

I raised my head. Or maybe Pamela put on a great show.

I feared they'd hear my heart hammering as I recognized the possibility this was Pamela's personal undercover affair. Question was, did the woods hold an ample supply of poised agents or not?

Now my fear went frantic. Had Pamela gone rogue, taking on

organized crime alone?

"Where's Calvin?" Kay asked again, though I imagined she knew as well as I did.

Barker raised his hands as if giving up. "Didn't lay a hand on him. Promise. Just collapsed on us. Heart, I guess."

A breath sucked in through my teeth. Poor Prissy.

Knees aching, I moved a few inches.

Barker pointed toward my trees. My body tightened. "JoJo, find that missing bitch. We need to go."

JoJo stepped toward me, but his scanning efforts said to me he had no clue where to start. Easing down, I slid my feet until my knees were in the pine needles and dirt. Then I cowered lower, elbows on the ground, and peered around the tree.

Barker spun on Pamela. "I paid for better logistics than this."

She actually strutted up to him. "If your morons had snatched Slade in the garage as planned, we wouldn't be here now, would we? She'd have led us here. We'd have snagged Kay and been long gone."

Pamela strode over to Wayne, who glared at her as if she'd eaten a dozen babies for breakfast. "I'll take your gag off, then you call your girlfriend."

He gave a muted guttural response along the lines of "Fuck you."

"He won't help you," Kay said, arms wrapped around herself even in the hot night air. "You plan to kill us all anyway. She just might get away."

Barker snapped around. "You gone yet?" he yelled to JoJo.

The hired hand sprang to life, kicking up sand, and returned to the path. He probably assumed I'd made a beeline for the gate, via the path we took to get here. What a fool.

Mosquitoes ravaged my ankles and arms, whining around my ears, biting, and me unable to slap. I had no idea where to go or what to do. Fighting was out of the question, but observing my friends and family die while I hid seemed just as futile.

"I'm tired of this." Barker wheeled and slapped Kay.

Wayne growled and wrangled against his captor, attempting to jump out at Barker, snatching Ally off her feet and onto her knees, her left arm yanked in the process. The big guard snatched Wayne's hair and held him in check amidst a flurry of legs and sand, cursing and grunts.

"Where's the proof you have on me?" Barker continued with a calm snarl aimed at Kay, ignoring Wayne. "I've been warned you have some recording, some video, some *insurance*."

"Safe, just for moments like this," Kay said.

Barker swung for another smack . . . and stopped inches short of Kay's face, her head tucked as tight into her shirt as she could make it.

Barker stroked her cheek instead. "You don't have anything, do you, sugar? Why would you lie to me?"

Time was running out whether the FBI was coming or not. As hard as it was to leave Wayne and Ally, I had to in order to get help. For a moment I watched them, pain climbing in my chest that I might never see them again. Wayne in all his deep-rooted need to protect me. God, I actually loved the man. And Ally, who I learned to adore once she'd landed on my doorstep divorced, homeless, yet full of life.

I rose to full stance, and after one more glance toward the beach, slunk further into the forest, creeping parallel to the path, using trees as cover. I felt my way toward the cabins, hoping the snakes were in for the night, and JoJo wasn't waiting on the other side of a pine, all while imploring to the heavens I wouldn't return to a macabre murder scene that would surely steal my sanity. Wayne beaten to a bloody pulp, his limbs broken, skull cracked. Ally raped, cut, shot to bits.

Someone washed dishes at the kitchen window of cabin three. Scared to involve anyone else, fearful that JoJo would haul more hostages to the beach, I waited until the lady left the sink, then scooted alongside the wall, not willing to draw her into this mess, not knowing where JoJo was. Creeping in the dark, cabin after cabin, I finally reached twenty-three.

Crouched in the shadows of the rental's steps, I listened. Surely JoJo wouldn't expect me to hide in Kay's cabin. He'd head for the gate or the main building. At least that's what I hoped.

Sneaking between the two cabins, I hugged the corner of Kay's, my eyes on Wayne's and Pamela's vehicles. Her driver-side door sat open as we left it. Stooping, I strained to hear for anyone. Then I ran to the Impala. The seat was closer to the steering wheel than fit me, and I barely scrunched in, anything but slick and quiet.

Not certain how to manage the radio, I twisted a knob and clicked a button or two.

"This is Carolina Slade. I'm at Clay River Resort outside Pelion. A man named Barker is holding three hostages along with a federal agent." Damn! What if they didn't take me seriously because of the location? Wait. "Agent needs assistance," I said, whispering distinctly, afraid to speak loud. "Shots fired. Agent down. Repeat, shots fired. Agent down." Then I shut off the radio before someone could pepper me with questions and attract JoJo. I didn't care if I'd lied about the gunplay, because chances were I'd be right before they arrived. Assuming they came.

Eager to return to the beach, I glanced up for signs of anyone. Seeing dim lights along the row of cabins, I popped the trunk lid, slid out, and crept low.

I grabbed the top two items—a 12-gauge 870 shotgun like Daddy had only with a shorter barrel, and a tactical vest with some sort of teargas thingies on it alongside extra shotgun shells.

Now what? Would I shoot these guys? If I had to, but to stalk, set up, take aim and fire without being challenged gave me doubts. I'd decide when the moment came.

I scouted the dark for movement, staying below the level of the trunk lid. This was so out of my league. The most I'd ever shot was my Christmas .38 and Daddy's .45 on rare occasion. I'd only handled a shotgun during the VFW Thanksgiving turkey shoots Daddy and I attended several years ago . . . and when I accidentally killed a hog farmer in Charleston.

Vest on, the shotgun cumbersome, I left the trunk open to avoid making noise, then walked by the open driver's door . . . and had an idea so crazy I worried I'd lost grip of my senses. Looking inside Pamela's Impala, I debated. Then, as I'd heard many times before, I decided a first instinct was usually the right one.

I leaned in the front seat, reached over, jiggled, and touched buttons that did nothing or gave static until I got it right . . . and turned on the police siren.

The wail undulated, up then down, high then low, an ear-splitting shout to the world that an emergency screamed for attention.

Fleeing to the woods, noise no longer an issue, I once again paralleled the line of cabins, then the path, ten feet inside the woods, my rushing now hidden by the racket. People might come boiling out of the cabins, but I didn't have time to ponder that.

The siren echoed throughout the forest, bouncing off this tree, then another, as if it originated from ten directions at once. I dared run, the vest awkward, the shotgun like a heavy log in my hand, both snagging shrubbery along the way.

My chest heaved as I reached the edge of the sand and squatted behind what I thought was the same tree. The moon now hung higher in the starlit sky, my eyes more accustomed to the dark. I panted from exertion and adrenaline, shotgun before me, aimed upward, my back to the tree, primed for my next move.

Which was what?

I evaluated the scene. Kay hung just out of Barker's reach best she could, close to Wayne, her nose bloodied. Ally, bless her heart, hugged up to Wayne, folded in on herself as tight as she could while he clenched his fists, obviously itching for an opening.

"Kill these two," Barker yelled. "Throw Kay in the boat and let's go."

"Kill them, and you get nothing from me," she screamed over the siren's echo.

Barker's slap sent her to the ground.

Wayne connected a left-handed punch upside Barker's head. The drug dealer staggered, then spread his legs, catching his balance.

The siren stopped. Silence fell like snow, an instant confusion as to how much I could hear . . . how readily they could hear me if I moved.

More importantly, who shut it off? And why hadn't Barker and his men scattered when it hushed?

Barker shook Pamela, her tiny frame not jostled as much as I'd have thought. "Go deal with that woman," he yelled.

Pamela jerked loose. "That'll be extra. The half a mil was for bringing you Kay. Slade just happened to be in the mix, and I had no choice but to keep them both."

JoJo crashed up the path, bursting into the open. "Boss, I shut off the siren. Can't find her. I checked inside the house, in the car . . . nothing! People were getting nosy, though. Had to flash my gun to scare 'em all back inside, but someone's surely called the law. I'll keep looking for that woman, though."

"Christ," Barker growled, then waved his arm. "No, take the car and get out of here. Jimmy, do what I ordered you to do." Barker leaned in Pamela's face. "Dispose of that bitch. I'm done here."

What now?

One hand clutched my upper arm. The other wrenched the shotgun from me. "Gotcha, sweet cheeks."

"Don't—" I started, not knowing how to finish the sentence.

"Boss!" JoJo hollered. "I found her."

"Bring her out here," Barker replied.

JoJo jerked me for fun, and my free arm hit two canisters tucked in my vest.

Wayne remained next to Ally, Kay now upright, within his arm's reach, if he could reach.

I yanked one of the canisters out. It was heavier than I thought.

Taking the chance Wayne would think quickly, I screamed, "Wayne, run left!"

Then I elbowed JoJo with as much body weight behind the thrust as I could. Feet planted, I pulled the ring and threw the canister toward the beach.

JoJo dove to the ground. I backed up to the hidden side of the tree, closed my eyes, and for some stupid reason counted. One, two, three . . .

My eyes flew open as the eruptive blast and light burst illuminated the forest.

What the hell had I thrown? I'd expected teargas!

What had I done?

Chapter 31

PETRIFIED AT THE imagined devastation I had just unleashed, I stood fixed, my back to the tree. My heart beat madly.

JoJo tackled me to the ground.

I kicked, but he was too much atop me. So I clawed, feeling skin going under my nails as I dug in to his neck with one hand, his cheek with the other.

He punched me in the ear as I attempted to jerk aside.

Scurrying feet entered the forest off to the side. Terror flooded me as I expected Jimmy or Barker, even Pamela, to come to my captor's aid. I kept expecting a bullet, which made me move frantically all the more.

I renewed a flustered flurry of hits and clawing, kicking then digging in my heels, bucking. Anything to gain freedom, get up and run.

The man's weight left. I snapped over and rolled to the side, seeking my knees to rise up and bolt.

Dragging poor Ally like a rag doll, Wayne laid his bootheel upside JoJo's head, the shotgun barrel in his hand. JoJo let loose of the other end of the gun. Wayne took the weapon and slammed its butt against the guy's head, and the man lay still.

I leaped out, enfolding them from behind.

"Oh my God," my sister cried, busting out in tears.

"Shhh," I said, glancing behind us.

Wayne jumped back. "Quick, Slade. Reach in my back pocket and get my creds. I keep a handcuff key in there."

Retrieving his agent credentials, I fumbled behind his badge and identification and found the key behind his driver's license.

"Hold this," he said, handing me the shotgun.

Wayne uncuffed himself from Ally. Then they smothered me in a three-way hug, Wayne's embrace riding my shirt up my back. "Damn, Slade," he muffled into my collarbone. "Thank God you were here, Babe."

Then Wayne pulled back and shushed us.

That's when I heard Jimmy calling, "Boss? JoJo? Where are you?"

"I thought the can was tear gas," I whispered.

Wayne gave me a tight grin. "Tear gas, hell. That was a stun grenade. You just knocked out their vision and most of their hearing for a few minutes." He inspected me and the vest and eased the shotgun from my grip. "Let me take this. They grabbed Kay, and she's just as incapacitated as they are. Y'all find a hiding place until I call you. I've gotta go get her."

I laid a hand on his forearm. "Pamela—"

"She's on her own," he said. "Not sure what's going on with her." He started to leave.

"Wait," I said low. "I radioed DEA or whoever was on the other end of that radio in Pamela's car. I sort of told them shots fired to get them here."

He touched my cheek. "When this is over, Butterbean, we're getting married."

Thoughts clashed in my head like an interstate pile up. "What?"

"You heard me," he said. "Now hide!"

"Shhh," I said, instinctively tucking my shoulders when I heard Barker cursing. Back on the beach, the drug lord rubbed his eyes. Nobody could hear over the other. Jimmy stood, waving as if it would clear up his head. Kay raised up on her hands and knees in the sand. Pamela walked over and assisted her to her feet.

Without another word, Wayne raised the shotgun and marched into the open, sighting down the weapon. "Let Kay go, Pamela, and move away."

"You don't understand, Wayne," she said overly loud.

Jimmy snapped his shotgun into place on his shoulder. Wayne countered his aim and dropped him in a loud boom. My heart leapt to my throat as he smoothly racked another shell in place. "I'll empty on the next one who moves."

Ally released a sharp, clipped squeal before I slapped a hand over her mouth.

Pamela remained motionless. Kay stood dazed three feet from her.

Wayne said nothing and maintained his aim at the men, his gaze darting back and forth to Pamela.

Even in the dark I could tell Jimmy's light shirt sported a big splash of darkness. Ten feet away, Barker stared from Pamela to Wayne, with glances back toward Jimmy. Pamela walked steadily away, toward the path, Kay in her grip.

I didn't like the unspoken communication between Barker and Pamela. Wayne struggled to maintain an eye on Pamela, at the same time judging Barker. Apparently his threat to shoot the next moving target didn't include his ex-wife, and Pamela widened the gap, no gun drawn.

She broke into a run, dragging Kay. Barker drew a pistol from his back. JoJo staggered out from Wayne's rear left.

Two explosions bounced off the encircling woods and then

reverberated in an echo. This time I covered my own mouth, awestruck at Wayne's ease at pulling the trigger first on Barker, then on JoJo.

JoJo lay on his back, unmoving. Barker fell, legs bloodied, crippled. Wayne ran to the men, picked up the weapons, glanced harder at Barker, and took off in Pamela's direction.

I turned and faced my little sister, my grip embedded in her shoulders. "Stay quiet and come with me. Do exactly what I say. You hear me?"

Ally sniffled and gave me short, choppy nods.

"Good, then come on."

Hands clasped, we ran to the path. We sprinted toward the cabins, fighting not to pant too loud or stomp too hard. "Don't shoot, don't shoot," I whispered under my breath. If gunshots went off again, we'd hide. In a cabin, under stairs, under a car. Wherever we hid, we'd stay there until Wayne came to get us, I told myself. I had to assume only Wayne would be the one left standing.

That siren surely had alerted cabin inhabitants to call authorities. Where were the cops?

We scrambled and reached cabin nine, then ten. A resident came out, robe on, and glared at us stooped beside his backstairs.

I shoved my hand through the air. "Go back in. You might get shot!"

He jumped behind his screen door.

"Wait!" I whispered. "Call 9-1-1. Tell them shots fired."

He gave me a thumbs up and retreated.

"Slade," Ally started, and I hushed her.

We finally reached the cabin neighboring Kay's. Panting, I slipped a look around the corner and saw Pamela standing at her car door, Kay more in the open about three feet away. No weapon drawn. Everyone tense but not at arms. At first I couldn't see Wayne.

"Kay, we're here!" Ally hollered, running ahead of me for her friend before I could stop her. She did not understand on which side Pamela stood. To her, Pamela had just saved Kay.

Pamela raised her weapon and shot.

Ally dropped.

I flattened against cabin twenty-three, gritting my teeth . . . dying to scream "You just shot my sister, you bitch!"

But Pamela could shoot again, and Ally lay in the open, on her belly, not moving. In the half-dark, shadowy alley between the cabins, I strained my eyes to see if she breathed.

"Give it up, Pamela!" Wayne yelled.

"You don't understand," Pamela hollered back, using the same line she used on the beach. "I set Barker up. I had to bring him Kay to draw him out, to capture him. It would've all been fine, Wayne. It can still be fine."

She thought she'd capture Barker alone? There were no agents in the woods, maybe none coming at all. The witch was out of her friggin' mind. How much of the Wheeler situation had she embellished as well to stick around Columbia, just to get to Kay, and ultimately Barker?

Pulse kicking in my head, I darted out, quickly covered the ten feet between us, gripped Ally's shirt at the shoulders with both hands, and dragged her against the cabin wall, back into pure darkness. Thank heaven she was breathing.

"Where are you shot, Ally?" I whispered, fighting for calm for her sake. But she didn't answer. She'd passed out.

Hands frantically feeling, I located a wound in her upper thigh. Blood didn't pulse freely, and she wasn't soaked with blood as I would imagine for a serious wound. I'd have bled out with a pin prick the way my heart pumped now.

I looked back toward the Impala. Pamela held Kay's left arm tight, using half of her as a shield, the Glock in her right hand. Wayne couldn't shoot; he'd hit his sister. Frankly, I wasn't sure he'd shoot his ex.

But Wayne and Pamela were agents. A whole different set of standards, training, and instincts were at play.

"What the hell were you thinking?" Wayne asked.

"I was thinking about taking down Barker," she said, angry. "What the hell else would I be doing?"

"Damn, Pamela," Wayne said, painfully frustrated. "Why didn't you just kill Barker instead of doing all this?"

"Didn't have the chance. It needed to look real, and this would have been perfect. Him grabbing Kay, me coming in and saving her, taking him down." She stood like stone, feet braced and planted. "Never had a clean opportunity. Couldn't risk you dying as fallout. Too many witnesses. Take your pick. Why the hell did you have to come out here?"

Pamela had lost all objectivity ... abandoned her friggin' mind somewhere along the way in making a name for herself with DEA.

"Is he dead, Wayne?" Pamela asked. "Any chance you did it for me?"

"Yes, Barker's dead," he said. "Not my intent, but in the confusion—"

She laughed. "I lived with you, remember? You're lying. You probably winged him."

Wayne lowered the shotgun. "Let Kay go, Pam."

"So he's not dead?"

"No," Wayne replied. "Barker'll live to go to prison."

"Goddamnit!" she yelled, shaking Kay's arm, making Wayne snatch the shotgun back against his shoulder.

I was going crazy wanting to help.

But they continued to face off. Apparently, neither wanted to be the first to shoot.

I rose, made sure Pamela still glared at Wayne, and slid behind Kay's cabin around to the other side. From my vantage, I faced the passenger side of the Impala. The car stood as a barrier between Pamela and me. Wayne held the shotgun on Pamela, still unable to use it. Pamela held her Glock stoically on Kay.

"Please let her go," Wayne said, a weariness in his voice. "You've been in these situations. You know how they play out."

"Ah, but I'm good at my job, Stud," Pamela replied. "Or don't you remember?"

"I remember," he said, sadness lowering his tone.

Even scared, she played him. A woman with a perpetual desire to prove herself.

"You took money, didn't you?" he said. "You knew better than that."

I couldn't see her face, but her altered posture responded in the positive.

"Part of the plan," she said. "I would've given it back. Had to earn his trust."

But Barker was down. Why not let Kay go?

"You don't need Kay any longer," Wayne said. "Don't add kidnapping to the list, Pamela."

"That plane already took off. Gotta go all the way with this now." She cinched up her grasp on Kay's arm. "Just let me go. I won't hurt her. You know that. I'll leave her someplace safe."

"You know I can't do that."

Kay stood loose, not tense, her gaze on Wayne, as if waiting.

Pamela's head shook side to side, her voice unyielding. "Don't make me do this, Wayne."

"Not making you do anything, Pamela. Remember who you're talking to."

The little DEA agent wasn't flinching. She could have argued with federal authorities that she had to go into Clay River without assistance. Say that Barker gave her no choice. Plead that she knew the hostages. Hell, she'd been married to one of them. They'd be dead waiting for the FBI, she could say.

But she was in possession of Barker's money and now held Kay at gunpoint . . . in front of witnesses. If I couldn't see this ending well, how could she?

Crouching, I made my way past the Impala and hid behind a pine, fifteen or so feet beyond the G-car. From this angle, I saw Wayne facing the car and the left side of Pamela near the open door, Kay's right arm in Pamela's grip.

Pamela's plan to play the hero by nailing Barker through her own personal undercover effort had eroded to dust, and failure wasn't registering in her head. Pamela didn't do failure. But she knew better than anyone standing here that DEA would terminate if not prosecute her for the way this mess went down. She was backed in a corner, no longer cool, no longer the super-charged agent who never lost a case.

Hands clamped together, I drew them up under my neck, afraid, anxious. My arms hit the vest. I reached down and pulled out another canister.

Taking advantage of my location, I reached out and waved once, then ducked back. I couldn't tell if Wayne knew I was there, so I waved again.

His head raised and chin jutted out, as if looking down his nose, then he lowered it back to aim down the sights of his gun.

I couldn't tell. Couldn't wait, either. With an underhanded motion, I lobbed the released stun grenade into the open trunk of Pamela's car as Wayne bellowed, "Kay! On the ground!"

I backed around the tree. Even with my ears covered, I heard the explosion, the shockwave traveling through the thick pine. The containment of the trunk gave the grenade an extra *oomph* as the noise boomed, and shockwaves amplified through the night air.

The Glock shot three times in rapid succession, the shotgun discharging somewhere in between with a colossal flash that mirrored off the surrounding forest.

A scream rang out from a cabin.

The world went dark again.

I lowered my arms from my head. Nausea drew clenched hands to my belly, afraid of the silence.

What if they'd shot each other? And Kay?

I eased from behind the old pine.

Wayne ran with a slight stagger toward the car, shaking his head, blinking wide-eyed to see. I ran to Kay sprawled on the pine-needle-covered dirt. I knelt beside her as Wayne stooped over Pamela.

Pamela lay half inside the car, her shoulders on the seat, her position in an awkward backward bending arch. Her right hand still gripped her nine millimeter, only it rested on the floor, midway into the car, her shoulder broken from its awful angle. Regardless, the petite dynamo had held onto her weapon like a pit bull.

Her left shoulder and forearm wedged awkwardly between her and the seat.

Wayne crouched beside his ex-wife as I reached them. "Don't move," he said to her, reaching over to remove the gun from her hand, scanning for the damage he caused.

She scoffed and winced. "I see it in your face, Stud. I'm fucked up."

He didn't deny it. "Don't talk, either." They held a gaze that meant so much more than I cared to understand, a gaze warranted by the grievous nature of the moment.

Maybe she'd been the one unable to aim accurately, knowing Wayne was her target.

"Kay?" Wayne called. "Slade, is she all right?"

I leaned over his sister, brushing hair from her face. "Kay? Hon?"

She opened her eyes.

"Oh, thank God," I said. "Are you shot . . . hurt anywhere? Don't move fast. Take your time."

"Bubba." Her right arm reached out to her brother. "I'm so sorry."

I raised her to a seated position, investigating her for damage.

"I'm fine," she said. "Give me a moment." She glanced at her brother, then down at Pamela's legs motionless on the ground.

Kay tried to move toward Pamela, and I held her back. "Leave them alone," I said, a few tears sliding down my cheeks as I remembered in a sickening coincidence losing Alan to a shotgun blast. As much as I hated the man, we'd had a history. Not all of it had been bad. And that's probably all Wayne could think about at the moment, his and Pamela's past, and how it had led to this.

But I hadn't shot my ex.

"Guess I'm done, Wayne," Pamela said.

"Shut up," he said.

I craved to assure him, *you did nothing wrong,* but now was not the time. After Alan, I fought to control a twisted mess of emotion entangled in the fact I was glad he died instead of me. A process Wayne might have to start as well.

Sirens sounded in the distance.

Ally hopped over and leaned against the front of the Impala. "Is Kay okay?" she asked, visibly shaking from head to toe.

I scurried around to her and made her sit on the ground, away from the sight of anything she didn't need to see. I wasn't a doctor, but her wounded leg seemed to work. "Sit here, Ally. Get off the leg." Then I got down on her level and bear-hugged her. "I was so afraid for you," I whispered.

"Let me see Kay," she whined into my shoulder.

Blood oozed from her leg, irritated by her movement. I drew back and shook my head. "Let us figure this out. Stay here, be patient, and don't get in the way, hardhead. You'll bleed more than you need to."

But she'd passed out again. Scared, I scouted around, hunting for something to add pressure to the wound. Finding nothing, I lifted my T-shirt over my head, bit into the hem, and ripped it enough for me to tie around her leg. God, I prayed she hadn't done something stupid by moving. I didn't like the sight of all that blood that had appeared, that hadn't been there before. Tears streamed down my face. "It'll be all right, Ally. Help's coming."

Lights flashed as two Lexington County patrol cars skidded to a stop in the graveled, pine straw strewn road. Before the four deputies reached us by foot, two unmarked cars pulled up behind the first, those four occupants blatantly federal, who we quickly learned were DEA. Wayne stood. "Senior Special Agent Wayne Largo," he said. "We have an agent down, needing medical assistance. And two civilians, here and over there." He paused. "There are three perps down, back on the beach. One or two should still have a pulse."

A deputy flashed a light on Wayne's credentials, then Pamela. "Ambulance is already on the way, sir. I'll put in a call for two more."

Wayne directed them toward the beach after describing what they could expect. Three of them took off along the front of the string of cabins, toward the path, weapons drawn, one of the deputies familiar with the resort from a previous marital dispute, he said.

A DEA agent waited impatiently for Wayne to explain more, but his flashlight on Pamela caught our attention as we saw blood from her shoulder, down her side, to her lower arm. Red everywhere, glistening in pools in the folds of her shirt. Too much of it.

Prissy came running up, fully clothed. I almost didn't recognize her in jeans and a gauze tunic. Flitting like a moth, she tried to reach Kay, then me, but a deputy kept pushing her back.

"Where's Calvin?" she kept saying, her eyes darting, searching. "It's all over, right? Where's Calvin?"

A tall, curly-haired, dark-headed agent exited the cabin, weapon put away. He approached the agent standing at the car. "Body in there," he said low. "No wounds I could see. Could be a heart attack."

Calvin.

As much as I wanted to console Prissy as someone broke the news to her, I remained with Kay, Ally, and Wayne, unable to spread myself thinner without coming unhinged myself. "Hey," I said to the curly-headed agent. "Could you ask the residents in the other cabins to tend to her? Please?" Observers already spilled out, gaping from their stoops. "That's probably her husband dead in there, and these people know her."

The agent next to Wayne, who apparently ran the show from the way he gave orders, nodded for his guy to follow my suggestion. This place quickly spun into a three-ring circus.

An ambulance pulled up in the parade of emergency vehicles, its LEDs adding to the light show already in place. I backed up as medics ran to Pamela, another to Kay who quickly directed him to Ally.

I rubbed my head at the lights, the smell of gunpowder and pine, the noise of adrenaline-pumped people shouting, phoning, ordering, crying.

Retreating behind the cabin to slow my racing pulse, I eased onto the ground and dropped my head into bandaged hands. I wasn't sure I could do this anymore. My job wasn't supposed to be dangerous. At most, I should feel guarded, leery of insulting someone or watchful of a fired employee taking a swing. I worked for Agriculture, for God's sake!

Covering my face, I tallied the bodies, the injured, the people I'd seen drawn into harm's way in the year I'd held my job. Like a wave in a pond, the ripples spread out, touching so many people. From Margaret dying to Monroe's feelings, and a vast array of characters damaged in between. To tonight, where the carnage could have been much worse for the wrong side.

Who could tell the good guys from the assholes?

Who was good, who was bad? Who deserved jail, and who just deserved forgiveness for what they'd been through? Pamela took good too far, ruining her career, hell, her life. The Governor took bad too far, sabotaging his family in the name of politics. Kay thought she could handle her affair alone and dragged so many people into a firefight. How long would Harden get away with his crap? My innocent sister shot because of me . . .

A deputy rounded the corner. "Ma'am, are you all right?"

Embarrassed and emotionally exhausted, however, I stood and turned away from the young man, my forehead on wood, eyes squeezed shut . . . and cried.

It was over, but it wasn't a happy ending.

Chapter 32

NEVER HAD I known so many patients in one hospital at the same time. My car could drive itself to Lexington Memorial Hospital, an eight-story facility directly on the interstate, twenty miles from home. In the past three days, I'd driven to the complex so many times I had a favorite parking space in the far right corner beneath a young oak, against the curb. The volunteers realized I knew my way around. After all, I knew four people in the place, and two of them had police officers stationed at their door.

Feeding yet another dollar into the vending machine, I punched the button for a diet cola, missing the root beers at home, and sat down on the nearest chair. Barker was on this floor. He hadn't died, much to my disappointment, and I suspected Wayne wanted him alive per some code or something. But, Barker would be a long time walking again, and would do so down the halls of a federal prison infirmary. No doubt he'd disappear from Atlanta's streets for the rest of his days, or at least until he was too old to stir up trouble. I didn't visit him. I'd probably wrap his IV line around his neck and pull too hard.

On another floor, in ICU, Pamela was messed up. Even if she hadn't dirtied her hands with Barker, if she'd been injured in the line of duty, her disabilities would've earned her a premature retirement. Barker would walk before she did, assuming she ever could, assuming she recovered at all. Her injuries proved severe between the shotgun damage and the blast's impact, throwing her against the car door then the frame. Several bones broken, to include her pelvis. She'd taken herself way too seriously, rationalizing she held powers above and beyond standard DEA protocol, and skills to pull off deeds better than the entire agency. If one or two actions had gone differently, she might've succeeded.

Wayne was in a strange place about her situation, visiting her twice a day for the last three days, today being the fourth, talking her through the mental anguish. As I passed her room for the umpteenth time, the door always closed, I reminded myself yet again that I'd had to throw that stun grenade, which made Pamela shoot, which made Wayne shoot. He and I had discussed the sequence of events the previous night in the waiting room, as if saying the words enough times would assuage our guilt . . . as did recalling Kay's safety and Ally's close call.

I saw no need to drop in her room. It wasn't my place. I prayed Wayne would conclude he had no choice but to act as he'd done.

I stood close, though, usually down the hall and around the corner, in Ally's room. He knew where to find me, and every evening he did. We always decompressed someplace quiet, talking through his feelings, once on my dock, another time back at the Blue Marlin. The fact he could go to that restaurant without hesitancy, without the memory of our meeting Pamela there, implied he was on the right track. He just needed time. Having Kay at his apartment gave him good reason to go home and enjoy the reality that he'd saved his long-lost sister. Between Kay and me, I hoped he'd find some sort of peace.

My parents drove up from Ridgeville and boarded in my guestroom. All three of us alternated between taking care of the kids and visiting Ally, who would come home today. Last night I crashed with them in the living room, letting them have an impromptu indoor campout, snacks all over the coffee table. I woke wrapped up with Zack near my head and Ivy at my feet, a kink in my neck.

Thank goodness Ally's wound was a through and through in the fleshy part of her thigh. Blood loss and alarm made her faint. She would make a full recovery . . . except for a small scar, which I was sure she'd flaunt to anyone who'd look.

Mom was none too happy with my sister's participation in the Clay River extravaganza, and her squinted studies of me during conversations with Daddy told me I'd bear blame for some time to come. Daddy remained neutral, bless his heart. What choice did he have among a trio of women? He loved his three girls, and his goal was to be there for each of us.

The fourth person in Lexington Medical was Lucille. More than ever, I felt compelled to visit CJ's grandmother, beyond the promise I made to Margaret to keep in touch with the elderly woman.

As Mom packed Ally's belongings at the hospital and prepared to take her to my lake house, I sat and meditated next to Lucille's bed. The woman stared at the ceiling. Some moments I spoke to her, as if she could speak back. Other times I'd sit and think. I'd thought a lot these last few days. My mind pondered Margaret's mentoring, Addie Fant's loyalty to this frail woman with skin stretched fragile over tiny bones, Hugh Fant's inopportune interference in the lives of so many people, the silly, unfounded fear of aflatoxin and peanuts. My stupid efforts to stir up old gossip about Governor Wheeler and tainted peanut loads. So damn naïve on my part.

I touched lightly her paper-thin skin. "Margaret told me so much about you, Ms. Lucille. She loved you. I wish you and I'd known each other better. I wish Margaret were here for you . . . for both of us."

She blinked. It's all she ever did. When she stabilized better, they would move her to a senior home of some sort. I promised to learn where that was, so I could keep in touch. She'd never recover, but I'd never forget her, or Margaret. As conjoined as they were in their history, I'd never think of one without the other.

What day was this? Monday? No. Tuesday. I missed my reporting date to McCormick and didn't even call Harden. But I had told Whitney, my clerk. Didn't call Monroe back after he left two messages on my phone. Couldn't handle him yet, not on top of everything else.

I stopped rubbing Lucille's hand. There was a task still on my plate. The slow, simple, quiet waiting in hospital rooms gave my memories of the last two weeks time to gel into organized thought . . . to an understanding. No point in delaying my next task any longer.

I patted Lucille's arm, excused myself, and made my way to the room where doctors broke news to families. Nobody there. Good on several levels. I shut the door behind me and dialed the Governor's Mansion from the history in my phone.

"This is Carolina Slade. Is the Governor in?"

"May I ask what it's in reference to?" replied the same svelte blonde.

"The wreck in the Arsenal Hill parking garage," I said, "and Lamar Wheeler's connection to illegal narcotics."

Concise and easy to relay. I waited for ten minutes, imagining people making apologetic interruptions to finally reach Dick Wheeler. Instead, Miss Blondie came back on with a canned reply. "He's not taking appointments today."

I did not want our relationship adversarial again. I didn't have the steam in me. But this task needed a period on it.

"Did you speak to him, or are you just filtering calls?" I asked.

"I can take a message."

"Tell him I have proof who planted the pills in Lamar's condo, and he can hear it from me or read it in tomorrow's paper." I stared at the watercolor landscape on the far wall. Should I paint a darker threat? Mention I'd be forced to take some sort of legal action?

"Here's my number," I finally said. "All I want is ten minutes of his time. I'll await his call. Again, the name is Carolina Slade. He'll know me."

No longer did calling the Governor seem preposterous, and no glamor came with knowing the man. Head down on the table, I played with wording our discussion, part of which would be a humble apology for accusing him of murder. Not something I wanted delivered on some sticky note, or left on an answering machine. He could hear it from me. He owed me. I owed him. Closure. It was just damn closure.

My Clemson University fight song awoke me from a nap I didn't know

I'd taken. "Hello?"

"Like before," he said. "In my office at one p.m. At the mansion, not downtown."

Excellent. Time enough to get Ally home and settled and return to town. Hopefully, nobody would ask too many questions about where I needed to be, or why.

IT TOOK LONGER than expected to get Ally in bed and taken care of, even with three of us doing it . . . especially with three of us doing it. When I tried to excuse myself, Mom cornered me in the kitchen, demanding details as to why I couldn't stick around.

"I have a job, Mom. This appointment can't be rescheduled."

"How well we all know about *the job*," she said. "You aren't in law enforcement, yet you wind up in all these dangerous situations. What have you taken on, Carolina? This new career of yours has endangered you, the children, your father when y'all searched for Ivy and Zack, and now your sister. And it got your husband killed. Look at the bandages on your hands. Where does this damage end?"

"Please don't discuss my cases in the house, Mom," I said, lowering my voice. "I prefer not to bring the details home to Ivy and Zack."

Her dark eyes went flat. "I'd prefer no such details existed that *needed* hiding."

So did I.

I glanced around for signs of little ears and eased closer to her, just in case. "These cases were exceptions. Alan brought his death on himself. That wasn't me. Neither was the kids' abduction."

My own mother glowered at her eldest adult daughter like she was twelve. I recognized the angst about Ally getting shot. Very understandable. But this seemed more over the top than about my sister.

"Well, you need to find another line of work," she said with an aloofness cool enough to chill wine. "Be glad Alan is dead, or he'd be confiscating these children."

Ouch! She'd never reproached me like this. Never—ever.

I didn't have time for a clash, and this was a debate nobody could win. Nodding concession, I started to turn. "Got to go, Mom."

"So go," she said with a saucy air.

"I know you were scared about Ally, and I understand you remember clearly what happened to me last year. But please, don't be like this," I said, then headed toward the door leading to the garage. "Drop the conversation."

Her hand rose to her collarbone. "You've never spoken to me like this before."

I pivoted, slinging my purse on my shoulder. "I could say the same, Mom."

"Just leave, Carolina. We'll probably be here through Friday," she said. "Allegra ought to be getting around by then."

"Stay as long as you like. You and Daddy are always welcome. You know that." And I shut the door between us.

Thank goodness she hadn't mentioned Margaret, or I would've lost it. My self-reproach about my sister would be residual for a long time. And nobody had to remind me about the farmer who'd kidnapped my children last year.

Truth was, Mom didn't say anything I hadn't thought myself.

NODDING PAST the guard at the gate, I entered the Governor's property, my name checked off a list. The young secretary escorted me straight into Wheeler's office where he waited.

"We can't keep meeting like this, Ms. Slade. This is our last time," he said, motioning to the chair I normally sat in. "Now, stun me, Ms. Slade. Let me hear about your threats of tabloid leaks; show me your cheap theatrics."

Taking my seat, I paused, centering my necklace and straightening my blouse. "Mr. Governor, I'd like to begin by apologizing for accusing you of murdering Margaret Dubose. I've since learned that a drug dealer was to blame. I'm sure you heard about Friday night's event—in Pelion."

He nodded. "I'm aware. Sorry you were involved in that."

"No more than I am, sir. But regardless, I regret the accusation toward you."

He hesitated, and then his posture softened. "I appreciate that."

Dry-mouthed, I wished he'd poured me a glass of water like before. "Something else, too."

At the mended fence moment, he eased back in his chair, possibly thinking the worst was over. His original comment about charges being dropped was true. With the case agent gone rogue and Pamela's connections with a drug dealing, murdering kidnapper confirmed, no United States attorney on the planet would prosecute Lamar. They had reputations to maintain, plus juries ranked crooked feds right up there with child molesters.

I eased forward. "Lamar was set up with the pills in his condo, and you need to understand why it happened."

His brow creased all over again. "Damn it, Ms. Slade. You continued to investigate behind my back. Do you ever follow orders?"

I sorely needed to learn, that's for sure. "Yes and no, Mr. Wheeler. Once Margaret died, the facts just came together. I had the pieces for a while, just didn't know how to form the puzzle. Seated in the hospital this past weekend, the answer became all too clear."

"Did CJ plant them?" he asked. "I would be crushed, but not surprised."

Still trying to stick to the public statement, like the savvy politician he was.

The mention of CJ carried my gaze to the credenza where I noted the boy's pictures missing from the Governor's collection. Shame? Or coping?

"Unfortunately, those false allegations regarding Lamar stole CJ's life," I said. "But after his death, you robbed him of his reputation. CJ was innocent, uninvolved, a tragic victim."

He knew I all but shook a fist at him, but whether he was too controlled or realized the truth, I couldn't tell. His composure remained intact.

"Guess your intention is to make me ask, so who was it, Ms. Slade?"

"Ms. Lucille."

He straightened, completely dazed. "Lucille? Are you sure? But why?"

Disappointment seeped into my gut. He had no idea . . . which only saddened me more about her life. "The pills fell into her possession by chance, and no, I do not intend to tell you who and why. Just know the situation was accidental. She carried a deep bitterness about Patsy's death."

His eyes showed legitimate signs of sympathy. "I realize that."

This confrontation was hard. I craved to divert my gaze to his wall of accolades, the signed print behind his desk, but I maintained our visual connection, fidgety hands in my lap. "She'd overheard talk about you bribing a peanut inspector years ago, to get your higher moisture levels approved."

He went rigid.

"Don't worry," I said, so pleased to see his reaction. "No one will dredge up old history. Can't be proven anyway."

He didn't relax. I wouldn't either in his shoes.

"Of course, anyone involved with peanuts knows that moisture means mold which means all sorts of illnesses," I said. "For some reason, aflatoxin stuck in Lucille's head."

Glancing past me to the credenza of family pictures, he appeared stymied, a hand running through his too neat hair. "Aflatoxin doesn't happen in this country."

"I know and you know. But when Patsy died of liver cancer, Lucille acquired just enough knowledge about aflatoxin to convince herself that your peanut handling and her daughter's death were related. Add in the embarrassment of a prenup agreement you made Patsy sign because of hers and Margaret's affair, and Lucille couldn't pass up the chance to lash out at the Wheeler family."

Jitters crept into my legs and arms, my nerves unable to remain subdued. I pushed down emotion, anxious to keep this meeting professional. The minute I caved, I lost all the effect I needed to make on this man. The stress of the last two weeks had weakened my defenses, and sentiment for Lucille sent me here carrying a torch, but the message needed to remain factual and civil to make a difference. "She's been through hell, Mr. Wheeler. Your family and your career took everything from her, and when you blamed CJ for the drugs, you all but spit on her and everything she ever loved."

Why I didn't come to this conclusion sooner, God only knew. Addie all but confessed under the pear tree, before she turned on me, afraid loose talk would backlash on Hugh. Poor Hugh, who'd already told me Lucille saved him from himself. In his typical dumpster-diving fashion, he happened on the pills, taking them home for his daddy, most likely. He already fretted about his father not taking his meds after a previous heart attack. Lucille visited that day, noted Hugh's treasure find, and took them away from the boy-man. But somewhere in the aftermath, when she wondered how to dispose of the pills, her deep-seated hate toward the Wheelers turned into malice and a proactive plan. She planted the pills in the condo, having access to a key and Lamar's social schedule. Then she whistleblew to DEA.

Only Addie and I knew . . . and Lucille.

By now my hands shook, and I clenched them together in my lap. I said all I'd come to say. Wheeler planted elbows on the desk and then rested his forehead on his thumbs. We sat like that, in our respected places, for a long time.

He sucked in some air and came out of his thoughts. "Who knows this?"

"Just me," I replied. "And one other person who has no intention of saying anything for fear of marring Lucille's reputation. I won't tell you who."

He smiled sadly. "No, I imagine you wouldn't."

I rose, a heaviness lifting off me, at the same time a weariness infiltrating me like a cold north wind. "Thank you for meeting me," I said and turned to leave.

Standing, he walked around his desk and stretched out a hand. With hesitancy, I accepted it.

"You're a strong woman, Ms. Slade. No wonder Margaret respected you."

At the mention of Margaret and me in the same sentence, I allowed a grin. Then as I exited, I paused. Reaching over to the credenza, I lifted someone's cross-stitched version of a Harriet Beecher Stowe poem in a gilded frame, tucked amidst handmade paperweights from children and those family pictures so proudly displayed. I studied the quote a moment and then handed it to the illustrious Dick Wheeler.

The bitterest tears shed over graves are for words left unsaid and deeds left undone.

I believed I could venture once again into the parking garage.

Chapter 33

ALMOST AS IF I weren't standing right there in the driveway, Mom begged Ally yet again as my parents packed to leave. "Allegra, please come home with us. You need quiet and rest, and I'll fix you a place in the guestroom. I'll make homemade chicken pot pie. You used to love that. With peach cobbler for dessert."

Ivy linked her arm around Ally. Zack helped Daddy load up the car. Ally stood on crutches smiling, watching Mom be mom, politely waiting for a pause in the conversation. "No, I told you already I want to spend time with Ivy and Zack. They grew a foot since the time I saw them, and I want to get reacquainted. You know, be the good aunt."

"She's a *great* aunt," Ivy said.

Mom smiled at her granddaughter, then turned back to Ally. "Well," she sighed, "so be it. Keep me updated on your recuperation. And call if you change your mind." She shook her head. "I remember when you girls were little and spatted like cats and—"

"We're not kids anymore, Mom," I said.

"You're right, Carolina." Mom walked over to me. Her stiff-armed, light back-patting goodbye spoke loudly. "Let me know if Ally gets to be too much. And think about what I said about changing careers."

Ally rolled her eyes and forced a smile, recognizing as I did Mom's need to win the day.

Daddy loaded the last suitcase into the car and pretended not to notice the tense wall rising between my mother and me. I backed away from her, cringing at her coolness . . . because she made me doubt myself. Made me wonder if my career had overshadowed everything else I held dear.

My parents made the rounds, hugging everyone goodbye. Daddy squeezed me extra tight, and I thanked him with the same. They climbed into Mom's Buick, and as their taillights dimmed down the driveway, I wondered if Mom was right about my profession. If so, what else could I do other than return to making loans to farmers and rural businesses, duties I used to perform so well. Before I learned I could investigate even better.

Back inside, I rushed to shower and dress. I had yet another appointment.

We attended Margaret's funeral at one that afternoon. Monroe,

Wayne, and I sat together, and I wept silently, but hard. My heart hurt so much. I wanted so badly to talk to Margaret, tell her how things had turned out.

Lamar and Dick Wheeler, the Fants, and numerous Washington and South Carolina politicos attended to pay their respects. I didn't speak to any of them, disinterested in conversation about Margaret's attributes or the latest gossip about the attendees. Wayne and Monroe returned to work, but I took the rest of the day off and went home.

My stamina dwindled, beyond drained.

In my mind, Margaret's funeral gave a clear finality to any investigation. DEA would delve into Pamela's past, connections, and collusions, but Wheeler was off the hook, and I wasn't involved. Neither of us could care less about what happened with DEA from here on.

Time to get away from cases and badges and forget about anything government related. I shed the suit and heels for shorts and T-shirt and then returned to the porch with its peaceful lake view and its whispered magic to nurture me.

"You think Wayne meant what he said at Clay River?" Ally asked wistfully as she leaned over the railing, studying the bushes below where wrens guarded a couple of nests. Her crutches rested against a chair.

I shook my head, instantly knowing what she meant, what she'd been dying to discuss but had the sense to avoid in Mom's presence. "Proposing while shouldering a shotgun in the middle of a fight wouldn't be my method of choice, but when you're in a high adrenaline situation, there's no telling what you might say. Life sort of flashes before your eyes. Know what I mean?"

Geez, how that was true. At the packing shed, in the ocean off Beaufort, at a nudist resort. My flashes were turning into reruns.

She hopped around, grabbed her root beer off the wrought iron table, and leaned her behind against the railing. "How well I do, Big Sis. I never understood what you did before now." She toasted me with her glass. "Now, back to the proposal."

"Wait a minute, back to my work," I laughed. "That's not how my job's supposed to function. This mess was not normal, I assure you."

"Still amazing," she said.

"Whatever you do, don't let Mom and Daddy know the nitty-gritty details. They'd go ape-shit crazy."

Ally's brow rose. "Tell it, girl."

"Mom's barely speaking to me now," I said. "She's frustrated, but I can see where she's coming from. I'd be the same if Ivy were grown and in my shoes. Mom and Daddy about lost their minds when Alan—" I caught myself.

I swore never to reveal all the details of my ex's demise to anyone who hadn't been directly involved. Ivy and Zack weren't ready to know about their father's dark side. Or maybe I wasn't strong enough to tell them. However, each person who knew the details only raised the possibility of the kids finding out.

But Ally's experience at Clay River gave her an up-close-and-personal education on the criminal element that lurked around the fringes of my job. Her brushes with pot and traffic tickets paled to all of this. Maybe she could understand how I'd become a widow. And how in the end I thought things had worked out for the best.

My own dark side.

Ally slid into a rocker. "Something upset you big time in Charleston. Enough to put a padlock on Mom and Daddy's mouths. They obviously feel it's your story to tell."

Traumatic memories of those days often returned, especially at night. The scenes when my children disappeared, changing me into an insane woman. The cold, the rain, the fear.

She gripped the arm of my rocker, stopping its movement. "I just learned how strong you are, Carolina. Oh my God, Sis, you blew me away. You're my hero."

I chortled. "Even a blind squirrel finds an acorn once in a while, Ally. Clay River was nothing more than me stumbling, trying to get us out safe. No super powers needed." Then I sighed. "Could just as easily gone the other way, you know. We could all be dead."

The vision of Ally lying on the ground, shot, flew across my mind's eye, and as my grandmother would say, a rabbit ran across my grave as I shivered once. Death had tiptoed all around us the last several days, but Ally had no business experiencing such trauma. She was a little reckless but not that daring. Nothing like the world Kay knew.

My view strayed to Ally's leg, heavily bandaged, then darted back to the lake.

She stared at me from under knowing eyelids. "You've walked this tightrope before. I've been in your house long enough to hear the nightmares from the other side of your bedroom door."

Although the bandages on my palms were smaller, they felt rough as I rubbed my forehead, then my eyes, blocking my sister's plea to be taken seriously and trusted. She waited with her leg propped on the edge of another chair, as if she'd linger as long as it took.

My hand slid over atop hers. "It's not about you, hon. It's about me."

She smiled. "Tell me something I *don't* know."

I blew out long and hard. "You have to keep this to yourself. For the kids' sake."

Her laugh held a soft disciplinary tone behind it. "What do I have to do to prove my love for your brats, Carolina? Take a bullet?"

So, I relived my first case with her, the one that tore my world down, then slowly established a new foundation to build upon. A situation I never would have chosen to be in, but chose to fight my way out of. A time when I learned that being naïve had its shortcomings, and that strength came from a place we cannot see until fate calls upon us to dredge it up as ammunition when we need it most.

Expecting to be the one dissolved to tears, I remained dry-eyed throughout the telling. Instead, Ally Jo skirted from her chair to a seated position before me, and laid her head in my lap.

"I'm happy Alan's dead," she said. "You should've been the one to shoot him."

"Ally!"

She smacked my thigh. "I never liked that bastard. Daddy didn't either."

"Daddy never said anything like that."

"Heck, you *ought* to tell the kids what happened."

I jumped, sending her backward. "No!"

The ultimatum stopped just on the edge of my tongue, something my mother was prone to do. But I wasn't my mother. I saw myself more like Margaret, deciding what was best for me and the kids, regardless of what others thought about my choices.

Damn it, Ally. We'd come so far these last couple of weeks, bridging the gap between us, and here she was about to gut-stab our new relationship.

She rose in an awkward manner, keeping weight off the damaged leg. "Shit, this floor is hard," she said, stooped like she was thirty years older. She fell into her chair, lifted her ice-less drink, and drained the glass.

"Promise me," I said.

"Promise what?" she asked coyly.

I stared her down.

"All right, all right," she replied. "I'll keep quiet. I know how hard it was for you to tell me all that."

Thank God.

"Now," she said, clearing her throat. "What're we going to do about this proposal from Wayne?"

"*We* are doing nothing," I said, marveling at her audacity.

"Hey," she replied, hands on her chest. "I was there. I heard him."

I scrunched my nose and turned, scanning the backyard. "I doubt he meant it. He may not even come around for a couple of days, trying to worm his way out of it. I'm telling you, intense situations draw out all sorts of reactions. The key is to let him off the hook easy so he can save face."

But I hadn't been able to get that moment at Clay River out of my head, either. A tingle ran through me each time I replayed his words delivered in a maelstrom of danger. I'd thought about marrying Wayne. Thought about it hard. Even wanted it. But I saw it happening later down the road, when we had a clearer understanding of each other. Him accepting my job, for starters. I appreciated his work, even understood the fact that as a wife I could get a call one day that some target of his made a target of him. I wasn't one of those women who dwelled on that possibility. Besides, I'd been shot and knifed more than he had.

God, I didn't want to go back to being the old Slade, following only logic, stepping only when rules said to step. But the kids had come close to being orphans three times in a year. They deserved better.

Which brought me back around to whether I was in the right job or not. Damn it, Mom, this was my choice, not yours. Damn you, Harden, for clouding my doubts and forcing me to balk at being removed from investigations instead of making the decision myself. But most of all, damn Margaret. She'd made me want to be an investigator, puffing up with pride at solving cases.

Tears brimmed again. I felt like broken glass since becoming special project representative, though. Pieces glued back together over and over, getting stronger after each breakage, but each time making the reflection a little harder to see. Stronger, intensely driven, as Margaret once told me, but for what purpose? For whom?

Oh my God, was I driven as much as Pamela?

And was that part of Wayne's attraction to me?

Ally nudged me. "What did I tell you on this very spot a week ago?"

No particular thought came to mind. "What?"

She leaned over and smacked my knee.

"Ow," I said. "Don't make me pop you on your shot-up leg."

"I said Wayne's a keeper," she said. "He's like still water that runs deep. You might not be letting him off the hook as much as getting yourself off."

I laughed. "Oh, Ally."

"Slade!" hollered a voice from the corner of the house. "You back here?"

My laughter shut off. Ally's eyes twinkled, humor in the corners of her mouth.

Wayne's boots announced his approach. His steps carried him up the stairs onto the porch, a grin wide as Texas. He reached down and took my wrists, avoiding my bandages, and lifted me from my seat to give me a hug.

Ally slipped over to the sliding glass entrance and eased inside. "Told you so," she said with a wink, then disappeared.

"You're a happy camper on the day of a funeral," I said in his ear, pleased yet puzzled to see his smile.

He rocked me in his grasp. "Not to disrespect Margaret, but I felt it was time we had a decent evening. No more black SUVs. No more . . ."

"Stupid jealousy over Pamela?"

His smile dimmed but remained, conceding. "You had a right to be. I didn't exactly open up to you, Butterbean." He kissed my head. "We were over, Slade. What Pamela did to herself . . . what I did to her . . . stabs me deeply, but there's nothing I can do, could do." He seemed to have reached a mindset I'd hoped to see, accepting the actions as hers instead of his . . . regret without feeling responsible. But there would be relapses. I knew that too well.

"I know," I whispered, respecting his feelings while hating the bitch for what she did to my sister, almost did to Kay and Wayne.

I cinched in my hold around his waist.

"She's out of the woods," he said, "but headed to prison. They'll work a plea to avoid publicity on the agency, the Governor . . . not to mention it all taking place at a nudist resort. She'll get a lighter sentence, but nothing short of a couple decades. Whether she ever walks again is another story."

Who cared to hear any more about Pamela? "How's Kay?"

He pecked me on the forehead. "Fine. She moved to Clay River for a while, to take care of Prissy. Can't seem to get out of the habit of calling her every hour, worried she's taken off again."

The sliding door opened.

"We're headed to the movies," Ivy said. "We flipped a coin and I won, so I get to pick what we see. Zack decides where we eat."

"Who said you were going to the movies?" I asked.

Ally poked her head out the door. "I did. We'll be gone two hours for the movie and another hour for dinner. Add a half hour each way for driving. Later!" She pulled Ivy in and shut the door.

With furrowed brow, I turned to Wayne. "What was that about?"

"This." He drew me to him. His mouth covered mine, his tongue searching, the embrace squeezing the life out of me.

He lightened up on the bear hug and shifted his grip. As he cupped the back of my head, another hand pressed my lower back, trying to close any space between us. I helped him, wanting every piece of me touching every bit of him. No tension, no case, and nobody chasing anyone, made me want this so damn much.

"Too many close calls," he whispered. His lips brushed mine, taking a small, simple taste once, then twice.

"Yeah." I gave him another in return. "We can worry about that later." I ran my hands up his chest to his neck, wove them into his hair, and pulled his face to mine.

"Enough of this sparking on the porch for the neighbors," he said and led me to the door.

"Wait a minute," I said, pulling on his arm.

Grin wide on his face, he pivoted. "What?"

I had to know. After taking a deep cleansing breath, I blew out the air. "Were you serious at Clay River?"

He raised his brows and looked down his nose. "About . . ."

"You know what about." I cleared my throat. "Because if you were, I'm not sure I can marry you. We squabble. You doubt my case-solving abilities. You—"

The joy seeped out of his eyes.

Then again, the fear of losing him scared me. "I'm not saying I don't love you, Wayne. It's just we seem so at odds sometimes. We . . . hell, I don't know what to say here. I'm afraid of what we'll become, but afraid of . . . that doesn't sound right either." I walked to the railing and turned around. "I'm doubting myself a lot since Margaret died." Tears tried to well at the mention of her, and I willed them away. "There're the kids . . ."

He reached into his pocket.

My heart leaped as he moved toward me, nerves twitching. I gripped the railing behind me.

"Slade," he said, the calm back on his face. He pulled out a ring box, held it flat in his palm for me to see, but he didn't open it.

My eyes froze on the small maroon velvet box as if it were about to strike.

"We're a good match, Butterbean. Trust me. You do trust me?"

The memory of those words said a year ago drew a grin. Back when I doubted him, then learned he was the best ally I could ever have. "I do."

He let his gaze drift past me as a smile blossomed. "You're not supposed to say it yet."

"Oh my gosh," I stammered. "That's not what I meant."

His shoulders shook with soft laughter. "Babe, life isn't as hard as you try to make it."

My adversarial side came out of hiding. "Seriously? Want to see my scars? What about my nightmares? What about the string of idiots who tried to send you or me or both to the morgue?" I started counting down. "Then there's—"

The large hand wrapped around mine. "Would you rather weather such storms with me or without me?"

Lips parted to speak, I couldn't answer his direct question so . . . directly. "That's too simplistic."

He shook his head. "Actually, it's not." He placed the box in my hand

and pushed my fingers closed around it. "Take it. Don't decide now. Set it on your dresser, your nightstand, in the bathroom, wherever. Just don't hide it away. Take your time. Answer however you wish, whenever you want. How's that?"

I started to give the box back, then didn't, unable to explain why. He was being so damn sweet and patient about it all. The lid remained shut. Whether it was a quarter carat or two, I didn't want to know.

"Now," he said. "Put it out of your mind. We have . . ." He looked at his watch. "Two hours and fifty minutes left. What do you want to do with all that time?"

This, I could handle.

Inside the house, he kicked off his boots. My pulse picked up speed with the freedom that we owned the house alone.

Bless your heart, Ally Jo.

I drew the drapes, and as I turned, lifted my T-shirt over my head. He followed, grinning that million dollar grin I so adored, the one that lowered his guard and allowed his feelings to ooze from behind that tough exterior. At the bed's edge I pivoted, the backs of my legs brushing against the red and gold quilt.

Ever the protector, he locked the bedroom door and shed his own shirt. He approached and slid his palms down my arms, then up again and down my ribs. He removed one piece of my clothing, then another. I shivered as coolness hit my skin, tightening my abs, tensing my shoulders. Then when I was totally naked, Wayne lifted me and laid me on the bed. I shut my eyes, stretched arms over my head, and enjoyed the nudity, remembering how the sunshine felt perfect on my bareness at Clay River.

My thoughts replayed the incessant dreams I'd had of bringing Wayne to my bed. How many times I had come home from work, stripped and lain on this spot, wishing, missing, craving this man in my house.

His knee made the bed give. I forced myself to wait, to see how he'd greet me, how close he'd come to reenacting my visions.

A kiss began at my navel. I squeezed my eyelids tighter, wanting to remember this time with blind sensory detail.

Lips grazed softly between my breasts, then slid to one, taking it in. I gasped, tilted my head, and arched ever so slightly as beautiful urges pulsed into my belly. He moved to the other side, and I moaned.

"Have I told you how much I love your throat?" he murmured, kissing, nibbling, churning my insides to a state of pure frenzy.

"No, tell me."

He did, up the other side of my neck to my ear.

I couldn't stand it anymore. I threw my arms around his neck and pulled his shoulders down, raising my hips until they connected with his, feeling his desire between us.

Women pined for moments like this. To be loved by a mature man, an intense yet gentle man. To be protected by a man able and willing to kill for her. That was hot as hell in my book.

So why couldn't I tell him yes about the ring?

Forget the ring.

I shifted, wanting him, gyrating enough to let him know. He responded, nudging, easing himself in place.

"Geez, Slade," he groaned in my hair. "I wanted this to last."

My eyes opened, my ego proud to have such effect on him.

His back straightened as he rose up and studied me. "I love you, you know."

"I know," I whispered, staring deep into those gray-blue eyes. "You're not as hard to read as you like to think, Cowboy. You're the sweetest man I've ever known." I placed my palms on both sides of his face. "And I love you, too," I said, my voice husky.

He shut his eyes, a smile beaming through his restraint. He leaned over and kissed along my collarbone.

My mouth found his, and I murmured into it between kisses, "You mean the world to me, Wayne."

As I inhaled, he poised above me. I exhaled, wrapped legs around him, and gave myself to him. Then it was too much to think anymore as we moved in tandem, ecstatic, then shuddering as we created a memory together better than any of the ones I'd dreamed alone.

Moments later, as the fan whirred above us, I dragged a palm across Wayne's chest, drowsy almost to the point of sleep.

Forget Mom. I was a grown woman, making my own decisions, one of which meant what job I worked. If Ivy wanted to live at a nudist resort when she turned eighteen, I'd deal with that on my own, too. If Harden fired me, I'd find something else . . . and remain in Columbia. The box I lived in would be of my choosing.

My gaze strayed to the dresser. The ring box reflected in the mirror. That choice would be mine, too. Just not today.

Acknowledgements

They only allow an author to put her name on the cover, but behind her stands an army of support that make her story into a book.

As always, my family stands by me, willing to Facebook, Tweet, and brag about my latest. Bless you Sweetie, for listening to every page of every chapter of every rewrite, though the bourbon and cigars probably took the edge off the task. Thanks to Nanu for listening and sharing a love of books. Hugs to Tara and Stephen and especially now baby Jack. What other infant has his father reading Carolina Slade to him every night?

My critique family sweats almost as much as I do over these stories, and this one was no exception. Nobody helps me tweak action better than Barrie Kibble, romance better than Sharon Pennington, and plot better than Sidney Blake. I wish I could name everyone who's touched this story in one fashion or another. The smallest suggestion can have such a profound effect, and I am grateful to each and every one of you in the Writing Well and with the SCWW Columbia I group.

Bell Bridge Books has helped my dream come true, and I'd be remiss not to thank Pat Van Wie, Deb Smith, Debra Dixon, Danielle Childers, and all the lovely ladies who breathed life into this book.

My fan base, to include my FundsforWriters followers, provide the joy and momentum I need in this profession. They give me a profound feeling of worth that has no measure. If you write me, I will most assuredly write you back in humble thanks.

Finally, I cherish living in a state that nourishes these stories. *Palmetto Poison* points a playful finger at Pelion, South Carolina, but I truly thank them for being so rich in who they are. It was after a hot August day at the Pelion Peanut Party that I felt compelled to set this story in such a small community, a place where the people enjoy life and each other . . . and celebrate one of my favorite foods on the planet . . . boiled peanuts!

About the Author

C. Hope Clark, the granddaughter of a Mississippi cotton farmer, holds a B.S. in Agriculture from Clemson University, and has 25 years' experience with the US Department of Agriculture. Now a prolific full-time writer, she manages an award-winning publication entitled FundsforWriters that reaches over 45,000 readers. Hope is married to a 30-year veteran of federal law enforcement, now a contract investigator. They live on the banks of Lake Murray and spend their down time at Edisto Beach, both in the South Carolina she loves.

www.chopeclark.com

Made in United States
Troutdale, OR
04/02/2024

18898204R00171